TRUST

EVIDENCE: UNDER FIRE

ME

RACHEL
GRANT

GW01459529

Trust Me

Copyright © 2023 by Rachel Grant

All rights reserved.

ISBN: 978-1-944571-65-8

Cover design by Rachel Grant

This book is a work of fiction. References to real people, events, establishments, organizations, or locations are intended only to provide a sense of authenticity, and are used fictitiously. All other characters, and all incidents and dialogue, are drawn from the author's imagination and are not to be construed as real.

All rights reserved.

No part of this book may be reproduced, scanned or distributed in any printed or electronic form without permission. Please do not participate in encouraging piracy of copyrighted materials in violation of the author's rights. Purchase only authorized editions.

Fiona Carver

Dangerous Ground

Crash Site

Flashpoint

Tinderbox

Catalyst

Firestorm

Inferno

Romantic Mystery

Grave Danger

Paranormal Romance

Midnight Sun

Writing as R.S. Grant

The Buried Hours

This one is for Annika Martin
Thank you for the years of friendship, support, brainstorming, plotting world domination, and belly laughs.

Chapter One

*T*he man stalking her was tall and slender and barely trying to hide his pursuit. Diana took a winding path through the souk, increasing her pace by slow degrees. She didn't want him to guess she'd spotted him until she could tuck into a service corridor and get the drop on him.

Seeing an opening, she ducked into the narrow gap between the colorfully draped stalls and wove between boxes and baskets filled with the overflow of stock.

She should have skipped the weekly visit to the Friday market when her security detail had been unable to meet her this morning, but this was the final market day of the summer season and therefore her last chance to talk to Bibi.

Her last chance to get a line on the Nabataean artifacts that were being stolen from sites in Jordan and Syria.

Diana hurried through the narrow alleyway between the rows of stalls. The aroma from the food court made her belly rumble. She should have eaten breakfast this morning, but she'd been looking forward to shawarma from her favorite food vendor. Knowing this was her last chance to have the best shawarma in Jordan until the market reopened in May left her feeling bereft.

Not that there was any guarantee she would be here next May, but she liked to think she would. Fieldwork had wrapped up ten days ago, and her grad students were ready to delve into analysis and conservation, which meant she had no reason to remain in Jordan much longer. But there was a good chance the university would invite her to return in the spring to prep for another field season—especially if she could deliver more grant money earmarked for excavation.

Plus, there was her work for Friday Morning Valkyries— a group that worked to stop artifact trafficking—that could resume upon her return. Of course, it was probably due to the FMV work that she was being followed, but she couldn't walk away now. Bibi was ready to talk. She knew it.

She needed to get to Bibi's stall before her pursuer caught up with her.

Was she being paranoid? It was a busy marketplace. Was it possible the guy was just another tourist?

She tucked herself behind a stack of boxes and quickly exchanged her red eşarp—a Turkish-style head covering—to a sky-blue Al-Amira two-piece veil. The Al-Amira was a close-fitting cap combined with a tubelike scarf, which changed the shape of her profile, but the cotton fabric was hotter against her skin than the lighter silk eşarp had been, making her wish the change wasn't necessary.

Her white skin marked her as a foreigner, but there were plenty of tourists here, so she didn't have to worry about standing out. She just needed to throw off the man following her.

If there was a man following her.

She always made it a point to vary her route through the market, never going directly to Bibi's stall. She carried more than one kind of headscarf for just this reason. This, however, was the first time she'd had to make the switch in fifteen straight weeks of coming to this market. Naturally, it occurred on the day when she didn't have the usual hired bodyguard following at a safe distance.

Unless the guy following her *was* her new guard?

No. Not possible. She'd had several different guards over the last fifteen weeks, and each time she'd been introduced to them first so she'd recognize them in the crowd and wouldn't do exactly what she was trying to do now—lose the tail.

She squared her shoulders and cut through a gap in the tents, entering the public market again in a different row and far down the aisle from where she'd started.

Music filled the air as the sun shone bright. The aroma of food was stronger this close to the food court and stage where a band was playing. Much as she wanted to get her shawarma, she needed to keep moving. Talk to Bibi. Find out what she could about the antiquities deals that went down in the shadow market, then get back in her car and return to her apartment in the city.

Once home, she'd send Morgan and Freya—the founders

of Friday Morning Valkyries—her final report. FMV had been unofficially dubbed *the Monuments Women* when it was formed two years before the US Army reactivated the famed World War II military unit known as the Monuments Men. But that unit, now called the Cultural Heritage Monitoring Lab, and Friday Morning Valkyries had different missions and objectives, and the initial nickname was fading from use.

CHML was an active military unit that focused on protecting, removing, or restoring artifacts when sites and museums faced imminent danger from weather or war, while FMV was a government contractor doing the covert work of tracing the supply chain once the artifacts disappeared.

The work being covert was key. Almost no one in Jordan knew Diana was a Friday Morning Valkyrie in addition to working with Dr. Fahd Yousef to run the dig on the Nabataean site in the desert.

In this instance, the name Diana's clandestine bosses had chosen was apt, as she always went to the Friday market early in the day. In Norse mythology, Valkyries guided the souls of the dead to Valhalla. Diana's job was only slightly different—she sought to transport the objects of the dead to their rightful owners. In this instance, the people of Jordan or Syria.

In Syria's case, any artifacts recovered would be protected by the United Nations Educational, Scientific and Cultural Organization, better known as UNESCO, until such a time as they could be safely returned to the government.

After nearly four months in Jordan, however, Diana had

only found one solid lead on the antiquities black market, and today was her last chance to get Bibi to talk.

Her cell phone buzzed, and she checked the screen. Morgan. Given that it was nearing noon in Amman, it was before five a.m. in Washington, DC, where Morgan lived. Diana couldn't think of a single happy reason Dr. Morgan Adler would be calling at a time that was ungodly early for her.

Diana tucked herself between stalls again and answered. "What's going on?"

"I was just notified your security detail sent you a cancellation and didn't meet you outside the souk."

"Yeah. I messaged them when no one showed and was told the guard was sick and they were scrambling to find someone to replace him. I guess he was too sick to call in ahead of time."

"You're in the souk now?"

"Yes. And I think someone is following me. But it's not anyone from the security company. I'd recognize them."

"You need to get out of there. Now. The security company had you down as a cancel for the day. No one got sick. Whoever told you that was lying."

Alarm shot through Diana's system. "And they called you, not *me*?"

"They're supposed to send automated texts confirming cancellations to both of us. I'm thinking someone found a way to spoof your phone number, so it looked like it went to you. But they didn't know about the automatic text to me. I called them because I knew you wouldn't cancel. Not when it's the last market day of the season. They're sending someone now, but…"

"I'm leaving," Diana said, stepping back into the central walkway.

"Stay on the phone with me. Tell me what you see," Morgan said. "I'm linking to the security company. They'll be able to hear too."

"The crowd is getting thicker now that the band has started playing," Diana said. "I'm weaving my way toward the central aisle. I'll exit at the main gate where the most people are clustered."

"You said you're being followed. Can you describe him?"

She wanted to close her eyes to aid her memory in picturing the man, but she didn't dare. "Brown male. Maybe six-two or three in height. Thin. Wearing traditional, male, light-colored dishdasha. Head covering is a white gutrah."

Except for the taller-than-average height, those words could describe no fewer than half the men in the market. She supposed that was the point.

As she spoke, she wove through the groups of people milling about, aiming toward the larger groups. Safety in numbers, right?

The route to the exit would go right past Bibi's booth. She considered skirting it and going down a different aisle, but she needed speed now.

Who had intercepted her call to the security company, and how had they managed that?

She reached the stall, which usually stocked with trinkets for tourists—cheap artifact replicas that would fit in a carry-on airline bag—but she saw instead brightly colored fabrics, headscarves of different styles and colors.

Bibi's booth was gone.

What had happened to the woman? Did the black-market suppliers of real artifacts catch on to Diana's interest in Bibi's wares?

She relayed the information to Morgan as she hurried past the stall.

Morgan responded with welcome news. "The security team is just a few minutes out."

She told Morgan where her car was parked, at least a ten-minute walk from the souk. It might be a five-minute run for someone who didn't have metal pins in her right ankle, but Diana was not that person. As it was, the fast walk had triggered her limp, but she didn't let the pain slow her down.

"They're sending two cars—one to the market and one to your car. Stay in the middle of the crowd instead of leaving the market. The streets might be quiet."

"The crowd in front of the stage is growing. Maybe I should go there?"

But if she was in real danger, was she endangering innocent bystanders?

She paused in indecision until the choice was taken from her by a sharp scream, followed by a shout. "Diana!"

She turned to see Bibi in the grip of the tall man in the dishdasha. He held a knife to the woman's throat.

"Run, and Bibi dies," the man said. His English had a Jordanian accent.

Diana met Bibi's gaze. The woman's deep brown eyes were wide with terror.

Bibi's job on market days was to lure tourist buyers into the underground antiquities market with low-end but very real artifacts she had in the back of her stall. She even packaged the goods with the replicas to aid the tourists in getting the items through customs.

A small but not insignificant percentage of those buyers got their first taste of the illicit trade and wanted something more valuable. A true treasure they could only show to certain associates and friends with a whispered *"It's the real deal, but we pretend it's fake because the purchase might not have been entirely legal."*

Bibi identified the big game who hungered for rarer and older artifacts and passed their names on to the dealers, who then worked the clients over and sold pieces of Middle Eastern heritage and history to vain foreigners.

The people who supplied Bibi with her wares got their artifacts by stealing from sites, both known and unknown, across the region. Some were stolen from Petra, a UNESCO World Heritage Site. Westerners knew of Petra from its role in the third Indiana Jones movie, or more recently in the second Transformers movie, in which the filmmakers placed the World Heritage Site in Egypt.

American tourists who purchased artifacts from Bibi were not getting trinkets from a movie set, and it wasn't a harmless crime because there were plenty of artifacts to go around—an argument Diana had heard from more than one dealer. No, these days, the looting of famous sites like Petra and lesser-known sites throughout the Middle East served one primary purpose: funding terrorism.

Bibi was a small but important cog in the system. Diana

had approached her with the ruse of having artifacts to sell in an attempt to infiltrate the supply network. Taking out the suppliers would be far more effective than recovering artifacts one at a time after they'd been sold and illegally imported into the US. Only if they took out the supply line would they be able to stop millions upon millions of dollars from flowing into terrorist pockets and thereby funding attacks throughout the world.

Diana was a hidden soldier in the War on Terror. Her plan had been ambitious, and now…it had failed.

She'd killed Bibi and probably herself.

"I'm sorry, Morgan," she whispered into the phone.

"Diana don't do this. Stall. A security team is on the way."

"He's got a knife to Bibi's throat."

Morgan cursed loud and long. In a different situation, Diana would be impressed with the woman's creativity. "How long ago was your subdermal tracker replaced?"

Diana kept her gaze fixed on Bibi as she did the math. "Three weeks, two days."

"Good. So there's no recent cut to identify where it is under your skin. If they take you, don't trigger it until you *know* you're at your final destination. Once triggered, it only lasts four hours."

Diana had been schooled on this when the tracker was first implanted in her arm, and again when it was replaced in a different spot to keep the battery fresh, but she understood why Morgan needed to say it.

Panic would be so easy right now, and once upon a time, the same kind of subdermal tracker had saved Morgan's life.

"I won't panic." *Not unless they're about to kill me. Then all bets are off.*

"Freya's on the line with the Pentagon now. They can scramble a team from Rota or maybe one of our forward operating bases. Someone will come for you, Diana."

Yes, they would, but the odds these men were going to simply abduct her for ransom were slim. No. They probably wanted to know about her work for FMV and how much Bibi had revealed about their operation.

And then they would kill her.

All at once, Bibi kicked the man with the knife in the knee and dove to the side.

With Bibi no longer in his grip, Diana turned and ran, darting between people who hadn't spotted the drama playing out at the far end of the aisle.

She ignored the pain in her ankle and ran like she'd never been in the accident. Her life depended on her ability to run fast, so she would find a way.

She heard curses and shouts, but didn't dare look back. The man would be chasing her. Her mad dash would give Bibi a chance to escape.

The arched gate was in sight. Maybe the security detail would be on the other side.

She tucked her phone into a hidden pocket in her head covering and ran full out for the gate. She crashed into a man, knocking him to the ground and nearly going down herself, but didn't pause to apologize.

She reached the gate just as a shot rang out.

She prayed her pursuer had shot into the air and there

would be no casualties among the Friday market visitors and vendors.

She cleared the gate.

Was it possible she was free?

She scanned the street. There were pedestrians milling about, and a block away, she spotted Oman from her security team, standing next to a car parked at the side of the road with the passenger door open. He waved toward the open door.

Thank you, sweet Mother Earth.

She reached the vehicle and dove inside. The door slammed behind her, and the car pulled away from the curb, leaving Oman behind.

She grabbed her phone from the pocket and managed to gasp out, "I'm free," to Morgan between heaving breaths. "I made it out of the market and the security team had a car there. We're heading away from the market now."

"Oh thank god!" Morgan said. "But how did security get there so fast? A minute ago, they said they were stuck in traffic. According to my map, they're still several blocks away."

For the first time, Diana looked up at the men in the front seat. She glimpsed the driver's face in the rearview mirror. He didn't look familiar. Nor did the man in the passenger seat.

But it had definitely been Oman who'd waved her into the vehicle.

Oman, who was supposed to pick her up today, but had supposedly been sick.

The security company had claimed her escort had been

canceled. Something Oman could easily have done himself. That wouldn't even require hacking.

The passenger grinned and pulled out his gun, pointing it at her face. "Give me your phone, Dr. Edwards. Where we're going, you won't be needing it."

Chapter Two

USS Dahlgren
Mediterranean Sea

Lieutenant Chris Flyte took his seat at the back of the briefing room, his heart already pumping with energy at the prospect of a mission. The other members of his sixteen-man SEAL platoon took their seats, their faces showing the same curiosity and adrenaline he felt. Even though he'd been a SEAL longer than most in this room, Chris was the newbie here, having transferred from a Coronado-based team to a Little Creek team in July.

His new teammates ranged in age from twenty-one to his own thirty-five. Chris was one of three Black men on the team. One man was Filipino American, another a Native Hawaiian. Four were Hispanic and the remaining seven were white.

He'd had six weeks to train with this team before they'd been deployed to this aircraft carrier for a lengthy rotation as it cruised through the Mediterranean. They'd been on *Dahlgren* for only a few days, running drills, ready to deploy at a moment's notice if needed.

Now it appeared they were needed. His first op with this team.

The leadership of Naval Special Warfare Command entered the room. Everyone stood at attention, then quickly resumed their seats so the briefing could begin. A white male Navy captain directed all eyes to a large monitor mounted to the wall that showed the NSWC logo. The captain clicked the remote to change the slide.

A larger-than-life image of a woman's face and upper torso filled the screen. Lightly tanned white skin, dark hair of indeterminate length as it was pulled back in a tight bun, mottled green-and-brown eyes. Thin nose and pointed chin. Her attractive face wore a serious expression. It was obvious this was a professional portrait of some kind.

The captain began without preamble. "Twenty-five minutes ago, Dr. Diana Edwards was abducted just outside the gate of a public market in Amman, Jordan. Dr. Edwards was working for a local university as a guest professor leading an excavation on a site in the desert with a team of archaeology students from Amman. In her free time—and separate from the dig—she was providing intel for Friday Morning Valkyries, a US Army contractor tasked with gathering information on the theft and sale of Middle Eastern artifacts. FMV coordinates with the Army's Cultural Heritage Monitoring Lab. Together, the teams are working to recover or stop the looting of art and artifacts in the region. The Valkyrie group is made up of a coalition of archaeologists, historians, and art experts intent on disrupting the supply chain of artifacts being sold by the Taliban, ISIL/ISIS, al-Qaeda, and others to fund their terrorist activities."

The senior lieutenant and leader of Chris's new team, Lieutenant Commander Randall Fallon, spoke. "FMV is the group run by Dr. Morgan Adler and ex-CIA SAD operator Freya Lange."

"Yes. It was Adler and Lange who notified us of the abduction," the captain confirmed. "Until recently, Delta Force provided security for FMV's operatives in the field—including Dr. Edwards—but authorization for that detail was cut nine weeks ago, forcing Adler and Lange to hire local contractors. It appears the hired guns had a traitor on their staff."

Curses were muttered around the table, most vehemently by Fallon. Chris assumed he knew one or both women. This mission would be personal for him, which could get him removed from the op if he didn't do better at hiding that fact. Clearly realizing this, Fallon straightened and asked, "What's the current situation for Dr. Edwards?"

Chris focused on the image of the woman again as the captain answered. He'd guess she was in her midthirties. "Lange still has the instincts of an operative and connections with her former CIA colleagues. Weeks ago, she asked one of her former associates to plant an additional tracker on the vehicles used by the new security contractors. A wise move, because as far as we can tell, the company's own tracker was magically disabled. Thanks to the secondary tracker, we know Dr. Edwards is currently on a circuitous route through the city of Amman, generally heading south. Lange believes they will connect with the historic route known as the King's Highway and disappear into the desert."

"What if she's no longer in the initial vehicle?" someone asked.

"We're working on getting a drone in place for more accurate information, but so far, the tracker has indicated the car hasn't stopped long enough for any kind of switch. For now, our ace in the hole is that they don't know we're tracking the vehicle, so there's no reason for them to ditch it."

"So what do we do? Scramble a team to take a position on the King's Highway? We're what—forty-five minutes from Amman by helo?" The question came from a woman high in the ranks of Naval Special Warfare Command.

"We've got two Seahawks on standby. We'll divide the platoon into two Squads, one on each bird. Fallon, you'll lead the first, Flyte the second."

Chris nodded in response.

"We expect she'll be taken to a remote camp. The best-case scenario would then have her abductors making a ransom demand, giving us plenty of time to execute her exfiltration."

"But you don't expect a ransom demand," Fallon said.

"No. We don't believe Dr. Edwards was targeted for a ransom exchange."

"What if Dr. Edwards remains in the city?" This question came from one of the brass.

"We are preparing a statement for the government of Jordan and will hope we don't need it."

Chris laid higher odds on asking for forgiveness, not

permission. The US and Jordan had a decent relationship, but that would change if a team of SEALs was sent into the heart of the capital with a population of over four million people.

Amman's own police or military would want to be part of this rescue. However, given the nature of Dr. Edwards's work—it sounded like she was using her credentials as an archaeologist to act as a spy—that wouldn't be possible.

If Amman's finest was sent in, Dr. Edwards could end up being the one sent to prison.

"Right now, we're gathering intel," the commander continued. "Our first priority is extracting Dr. Edwards. Other objectives may come into play if she is taken to a terrorist stronghold."

Whoa. The commander had just said the quiet part out loud. They were hoping Edwards would lead them to a big fish in the terrorist sea.

Sure, the US military wanted to stop the sale of artifacts to cut the funding to the various groups, but that wasn't the primary reason for this oh-so-fast military response. Was it even a coincidence his SEAL team was on this aircraft carrier just waiting for a mission at the right time?

Ordinarily, he'd blow off that idea. This wasn't his first time hanging out on one of the world's biggest boats with his team on a just-in-case deployment, but the events of last winter had revealed some cracks in Naval Special Warfare Command. Plus, there was that little tidbit about Freya Lange being former CIA.

Had the former SAD operative used her own contractor as bait for a terrorist?

Chris had learned long ago to never trust a spy. Even when they left the business, they remained ready to stab you in the back and claim it was for the greater good.

The commander dismissed the team. They would remain on the carrier, ready to be dispatched within minutes when the order came. On the way out the door, Chris signaled Fallon with a nod. He had questions for his SEAL team leader.

They stepped aside as the others filed out of the room and into the narrow corridor. Between the two of them, Fallon was the senior lieutenant and Officer in Charge (OIC) of their platoon, while Chris was the Assistant Officer in Charge (AOIC). Chris had been in line for a promotion to OIC at Coronado, but when he opted to make the move to Little Creek, all they could give him was a lateral assignment, which was fine with him. More often than not, they split into eight-man Squads or four-man Fire Teams anyway, and he was always senior officer in those situations. Best to get the feel for his Little Creek team after years in Coronado before he took command of his own platoon.

"You know Dr. Edwards?" he asked his OIC.

Fallon—a large white man with blond hair, blue eyes, and a jaw so firm and square, he'd be a casting agent's wet dream for the role of Navy SEAL in an action movie—shook his too-perfect head. "No," he said. "But I know Morgan Adler and Freya Lange. Dr. Adler single-handedly saved a bunch of SEALs from an ambush a few years back when we were in Djibouti."

Chris had heard about that op. It had been whispered about among special forces in all branches of the military and had moved into legendary territory given the number of tangos taken out and young girls rescued. The legendary part was that special forces had barely been involved. Most of the work had been done by one woman with the aid of a captive who was among the rescued. "You're shitting me. Operation Icarus?"

Fallon nodded. "Three Green Berets went in and cleaned up after we were called back. Adler is married to one of them. Lange another."

"But can we really trust Lange?" Chris didn't bother to hide the derision in his voice. The woman might be married to a Green Beret and business partners with the woman who'd been at the center of the Icarus raid, but neither of those things meant they could take the word of a person who'd spent years in the spy game, spinning lies and turning human beings into assets.

"I'd trust her with my life. I *have* trusted her with my life, and she's never let me or any of our teams down. Something went down with her and the CIA when she left Djibouti. I don't know what because, well, CIA. But I *do* know she's still affiliated for the purpose of aiding her consultants, even though there's no love lost there."

Chris was still getting to know Fallon, but he did respect the man and knew he could trust his OIC's judgment. So at least they didn't need to worry they were being sent in to save a woman who'd been set up by her own boss.

He hated cleaning up other people's messes.

"What else do you know about Adler and Lange?"

"I've kept in touch in the years since Icarus. The Friday

Morning Valkyries are well trained, and they take their work seriously."

He wanted to ask what was up with the weird name, but that could wait. "When you say well trained, what do you mean?"

"Physical training—with weapons and hand-to-hand combat. Morgan is a crack shot and has studied martial arts for decades. She teaches those skills to the Valkyries herself. Pretty sure they all do a SERE course too."

Survival, Evasion, Resistance, and Escape, better known as SERE, was a cornerstone training program for military personnel, DoD civilians, and government contractors deployed to hostile environments. "Good to know. We need to brief the team on the off chance Dr. Edwards might take it upon herself to join the fight."

Fallon nodded. "Doubtful, though."

He gave a noncommittal shrug. "Still need to be prepared." Chris, more than anyone, knew how horrifically an op could fall apart when the hostage being rescued behaved in unexpected ways.

§

The skin where the subdermal tracker was implanted itched. Diana knew the feeling was psychosomatic; her brain's way of begging her to signal for rescue. There was no reason for her arm to itch there and only there, yet it did. Beckoning her to rub the spot for ten seconds to trigger it to reach out to the CIA or military or whoever it was programmed to ping.

She wouldn't touch it, though. Triggering it now could be the worst mistake of her life, killing the battery before she reached her final destination. Plus, the tracker was useless if, during the four hours it actively attempted to transmit her location, there was no working cellular or satellite signal to jump on. If there was no phone to provide connectivity, the battery drain would be for nothing. An SOS that went into a void before fading into nothingness.

So she would wait. She wouldn't blow her get-out-of-terrorist-jail-free card by playing it too soon. But then there was the ever-present fear…what if she waited too long?

It would take time to get a team together, even more time for them to travel to wherever it was they were taking her in Jordan. And what if they crossed the border into Iraq, Syria, Saudi Arabia, or Israel?

She kept her gaze fixed out the window, ignoring the throbbing pain in her ankle and the itchy spot on her arm. They were out of the city now, and there was nothing but sand for miles. They'd taken her smartwatch, so she could only guess they'd been driving for about two hours, but her sense of time could be skewed.

Fear did that.

Even in the air-conditioned vehicle, looking out over endless sand made her thirsty. She wasn't to the point of desperation, but it could be worth it to try to engage with her abductors again, who'd said nothing after binding her hands behind her back and securing her bound hands to the built-in child car seat hooks mounted next to the seat belt.

Abductor number one had then climbed back into the

front passenger seat of the moving vehicle and proceeded to fall asleep.

"Water?" she asked in English.

The driver just grunted and ignored her. She considered trying again in Arabic but wasn't sure how much these men knew about her. Did they know she was nearly fluent? It seemed like a good idea to hide her language skills. They might reveal something they wouldn't otherwise.

After winding through the city, they'd gone south on the King's Highway. Historically, it was an important trade route that went from the Sinai Peninsula in Egypt to Damascus and the Euphrates River in Syria, while the modern King's Highway in Jordan was a winding and scenic road that connected Amman on the Mediterranean Sea to Aqaba on the Gulf of Aqaba.

The road cut through desert composed of granitic and metamorphic rocks overlain by sandstone, along with limestone and phosphorite that capped the central plateau. The phosphorite stone was the Hashemite Kingdom of Jordan's principal export. In some places, the drive offered glimpses into slot canyons like the one that gave the first dramatic view of the Treasury in Petra. On any other day, traveling this road would be breathtaking. Something she hadn't tired of, even though she'd driven from Amman to Wadi Rum several times in the last few months.

Today, it took her breath away, but for an entirely different reason.

Now the car left the main road, and she'd lost track of where she was. Another wadi—a gully or stream that was only wet during rainy season—among many. Today, it was two months from the start of the rainy season, and the earth baked in the late afternoon sun as the canyon walls closed in.

Jordan had wadis both big and small, famous like Wadi Rum, and relatively unknown like this one. After some time, the car made another turn, entering a narrower canyon with offshoots on all sides. A maze of rock walls. The road went from paved to packed sand as they wound their way through sandstone and granite pillars.

The car stopped when the canyon narrowed to the point of no longer being passable. Her sleeping abductor sprang awake, making her wonder if his dozing had been an act. Not that it mattered one way or another.

He climbed from the front seat and circled to her side of the car and yanked the door open. He brandished a sharp knife, then pushed her forward and cut the zip tie that bound her to the child car seat anchor.

He then tugged her out of the vehicle without giving her a chance to right herself in the seat. She fell to her knees on the hard ground. Hot wind swirled around her, and she closed her eyes against the sting of the bright, burning sun and fine sand particles that whipped through the air.

The man yanked her to her feet and dragged her away from the car, toward a gap in the slot canyon that was wide enough for a camel but not a car. She stumbled on her weak ankle, but finally managed a few steps that hid her limp.

Don't let them see any weaknesses to exploit.

Behind her, the car door slammed, then she heard the rumble of tires on gravel and sand. The vehicle that had delivered her here was leaving as the man dragged her down the narrow canyon.

After a hundred meters, it opened up, and before her was a line of five Bedouin tents. The Arabic name was *beit ash-sha'ar*, meaning "house of hair." The dark goat hair and sheep's wool curtains would usually be draped over a frame of wooden poles made from fig trees, but these looked like they had aluminum frames.

Was this camp her final destination? If so, all she needed was a working satellite or cell phone and she could send out her SOS.

She turned to see the tight canyon walls behind her. The tents were pressed up against another wall. There were fingers of the canyon that spread in other directions, all too narrow for vehicles. Not even camels could fit through some of the gaps. She looked upward and wondered if the high, narrow canyon walls would prevent a satellite signal from reaching space.

Everything about this moment felt surreal. This couldn't be happening. She was asleep in her bed in Amman, or better yet, asleep in her condo in College Park, Maryland.

But the heat on her skin and the sting of sand in her eyes told her this was all too real.

She again studied the tents. The Bedouin styling had to be a form of camouflage. A way for a terrorist cell to hide in plain sight. Her abductors might be from Jordan, but they weren't Bedouin any more than she could claim to be an Indigenous American just because she was born in a city named for Chief Seattle.

Men holding AK-47s guarded the various canyon openings. She could see three narrow slots and wondered if there were more. Escape would be impossible. She'd easily get lost in the twisted threads of dry gullies. Plus, without water, she wouldn't last long.

Her captors didn't need their automatic rifles or sharp knives to keep her in line. Only a fool would set out alone from here. She was many things, but a fool wasn't one of them.

Her abductor shoved her toward a tent and barked at her to move or he would drag her by her hair.

She took several steps, patting her head to make sure her hair was fully covered before it registered that his words had been in Arabic. So much for keeping her fluency secret.

They'd probably known all along. While the security company didn't know *why* she needed a guard at the Friday market, they did know she was an archaeologist working on a dig for a university.

She'd gotten a research grant to work with a university in Amman from Gardner Holdings, an American company that controlled several businesses, including a large retail chain called Historie, which sold replicas of artifacts and art in addition to licensed cards, mugs, and other trinkets. The company made millions from replicating artifacts and selling them to a high-end market.

Another company in the fold, Gardner Tours, wanted license to sell luxury package tours to Petra and Wadi Rum to American consumers. Included in these packages would be "archaeologist for a day" digs, in which tourists would conduct archaeological fieldwork in areas outside the protected boundaries of Petra and Wadi Rum under the supervision of local archaeologists. To achieve this, the CEO of Gardner Holdings, Dennis Gardner, courted favor with the Hashemite Kingdom of Jordan's government by funding real digs through the university.

While the grant money had gone directly to the university, Gardner had insisted an American archaeologist be included on the dig team. In return, Diana was expected to give him realistic feedback on how best the tourist digs could be run to maximize entertainment and information obtained from digging while limiting the harm that could result from amateurs wielding trowels.

The end result was Diana had spent the last fifteen weeks working with Jordanian archaeologist Dr. Fahd Yousef, overseeing his graduate students excavating and recording a site an hour outside Amman. Yousef hadn't been pleased to be saddled with an American at first, but he appreciated the research dollars she brought to the project, and she'd won him over when he realized she was, in fact, knowledgeable about the Nabataeans and other nomadic cultures that inhabited this region in the thousands of years Before Common Era—BCE—and after in what was now called Common Era, or CE.

If the men who'd abducted her had been watching her or the dig, they would know about her language skills and expertise. Dare she even hope they *didn't* know about her work for FMV?

She stepped inside the tent, thankful for the temporary escape from sun. The thick curtain closed behind her. She stumbled, temporarily blinded by the dark interior after the brightness of the early afternoon sun reflecting off pale pink sand had shrunk her pupils to pinpricks. As her eyes adjusted, she could see the furnishings were neither traditional nor handmade.

In the center of the tent was a long folding table, the same hard gray plastic and metal leg design that could be found the world over. But what lay on top of the table had her complete attention: artifacts.

Prehistoric. Historic. Stone. Metal. Glass. Even bone.

One could describe the entirety of the human history of Jordan with what lay on the table.

"Where did these come from?" she asked in English.

The man ignored her question. "You will go through and tell us the age and culture of each item and how much each one is worth."

Again, the instructions came in Arabic.

She replied in his language. "Archaeologists don't put a value on artifacts. I couldn't say—"

Swift as lightning, an open-handed blow to her cheek had her stumbling backward. Her head rang with the shock of the fierce slap.

For the first time in her life, she understood what it meant to have her bell rung.

She swallowed and faced the table, her vision blurred from both the pain and the tears she'd been holding back from the moment she realized she'd stepped into a trap.

This was real, and it was very much happening to her.

"You will tell us how much to sell each item for."

Her arm itched. She reminded herself she couldn't touch the tracker. Not until she was certain there was a working phone nearby.

She picked up a jar from the table, running her hands over stone that had been smoothed with sand by human hands sometime in or after the eighth millennium BCE. Because she didn't have location or carbon dates to go on, she estimated the age based on the typology of the artifact, guessing they'd want the oldest—and therefore most valuable—age estimation. "Calcite alabaster tripod vase. Pre-Pottery Neolithic B period."

She remembered the slides she'd studied of the artifacts that had been recovered by other Valkyries before she joined the team last year, and the amounts they had reportedly been sold for. "I would guess you could get twenty thousand for this one."

She moved down the line. Twenty-two artifacts. None were fake. She wondered if a few were replicas, but they were handmade, carved from stone, so it was impossible to tell. One oil lamp had been carved, likely recently, adding a symbol to the top that would raise the value from a few hundred dollars to several thousand if it had been original to the piece. "It's poorly done and has depleted the value to worthless because it was altered."

As she examined the artifacts, she wondered if this was some kind of test. Didn't they know where these items came from? What, exactly, did they want from her?

She studied a tablet with Nabataean writing. It was authentic. She searched her memory for a similar one but came up blank.

All the items were standard objects that had survived millennia, but none were familiar, making her think none had been stolen from a museum. They'd been washed, but some still had dirt embedded in grooves. Were she to guess, she'd think these came straight from the ground.

The truth sank in. These were recently looted artifacts, and they needed professional cleaning in addition to some kind of description and assigned value to garner the highest possible price.

These men hadn't abducted her because she was a spy for the US Army. No. They wanted her to prep the haul so they could be sold on the black market.

She'd been brought to the very place she'd been looking for when she asked Bibi about her wares. She was at the center of the hub artifacts passed through before they were lost forever in illicit deals.

Chapter Three

"The car drove deep into this wadi, stopped briefly, then returned to the main road," Captain Dodd said while pointing to a small, narrow valley on the aerial photo. "As near as we can tell, it's a semipermanent camp, but given the limited resources, it might not be her final destination. We need to exfiltrate her tonight before they have a chance to move her again."

In situations like this, when the hostage could be moved again at any time, waiting for zero dark thirty could be too late, but Chris knew they weren't in the air yet because they hoped to gather more intel. Making a move without more information could lead to the wrong casualties, and that valley was narrow at one end.

Would a fully tricked-out SEAL be able to pass through it?

If they tried, they'd be exposed, forced to enter the camp single file.

They needed better aerial images.

Some time ago, an intel breakdown on a hostage rescue had resulted in the deaths of two members of Chris's Fire Team. The fourth team member, Xavier Rivera, had been shot and would have died if Chris hadn't gotten him out when he did.

He'd been with SEALs who'd died on missions before, but the circumstances of that particular night had made it the worst op of his career—until nine months ago, when a training exercise went sideways.

Maybe Chris should have gotten out then. Leave the ops to the younger guys. Rivera had also been part of the night-mare training, and he'd parted ways with the Navy a few months later without hesitation or regret.

But Xavier had a wife waiting for him at the end of the day, while Chris's wife had cheated—with another SEAL. He'd filed for divorce less than two weeks after escaping the training that went FUBAR. If Chris left the SEALs, he'd have nothing after spending most of his adult life in the service.

No purpose. No family.

Instead, he'd moved, changing SEAL teams so he wouldn't have to deal with his ex and her new boyfriend.

And now here he was, on a carrier in the Mediterranean, preparing for yet another hostage rescue. She was an archae-ologist, like Xavier's wife, Audrey, but she hadn't stumbled into this situation in the same way Audrey had last January.

No. Dr. Edwards had chosen to track down artifact traf-fickers to shut down funding for terrorists.

They needed to determine if there were other hostages who could be caught in cross fire and see if they could get a count on how many tangos were in the small camp. He studied the satellite image on the screen. No vehicles in the vicinity of the tents. No camels.

They were stranded.

Fallon stood and circled the table to stand to the right of the monitor, staring at the image. After a long silence, he pointed to the gap between two smaller tents on the north end of the camp. "With Dr. Edwards's location within the camp unknown, we can't go in with a show of force that will alert her captors. We need to move in with just a Squad. Two four-man Fire Teams, one from the east end of the wadi and the other from here." He pointed to a third approach to the west that looked wider than the slot canyon to the north.

Chris studied that route and saw the wisdom of it. It was more twisted, a zigzag through rocks, but it would keep them hidden from the tents longer, and it looked wide enough in places to stand side by side if warranted.

Fallon looked to Chris. "Which route do you want?"

"West approach."

Fallon nodded. "No moon tonight, which is good. We'll need full darkness given the narrow valley."

They all agreed the op wouldn't be a go until after midnight. They'd just have to take the chance Dr. Edwards wouldn't be moved before then.

They spent the next hour going over the layout of the tents and discussing scenarios, developing a plan to invade the temporary terrorist camp on foot in the middle of the night.

◆

*D*iana's shoulders ached after an hour of sitting on the floor with her hands tied above her head to the center post of one of the larger Bedouin tents. She'd been brought here and bound after she claimed they didn't have the necessary supplies for her to clean the artifacts.

Harun—she'd heard another man call him by that name—had backhanded her again before ordering two younger men to tie her up in the bigger tent. This tent was more traditional than the others, having two rooms. The side she occupied didn't have an exit panel that could easily be swept aside. No windows. No doors.

Tied as she was, if she rose onto her knees, lifting her butt from the rug-covered floor, her nose could possibly reach the spot on her left arm where the tracker had been embedded.

It was so tempting, but she still hadn't spotted a working phone, nor was she certain she'd be here for hours or days. She didn't dare initiate the tracker without knowing if she would be here when her rescue arrived. This could be a long game. She had three months and one week before the battery would be naturally depleted without being triggered.

That gave her two months on the safe side.

The idea of being captive for days or even months was chilling, but she couldn't blow it. She had to be patient. Alert. And while she was at it, she could gather intel.

These men were part of the antiquities supply chain. They were probably getting the artifacts from ISIS or al Qaeda. If she could identify the sites where the artifacts were coming from before she was rescued, she could share what she learned with the military. Cut off the supply chain that was putting money in terrorist pockets.

Wasn't that why she'd signed on for this job in the first place?

Now she was here, presumably in the heart of the operation. She could make a difference. That was what she'd wanted when she'd approached Morgan all those months ago—a job that would make her feel again. Give her purpose.

But it was hard to think of noble goals when her shoulders ached and cheek throbbed from two blows.

The tracker itched, begging to be pressed. It was dark now. She didn't think they would move her in the night. Not when they could come and go freely during the day.

Surely these men had satellite phones. How else would they communicate with their overlords? But were the phones turned on?

If so, she could press that spot on her arm, and a team of SEALs would swoop in. At least, that was what Morgan and Freya had said, that SEALs usually performed hostage rescues, sometimes in conjunction with Green Berets. They'd said this with confidence, and both women were married to Green Berets, so Diana had no reason to doubt their veracity.

She'd met their husbands when she'd trained for this with Morgan and Freya. She'd spent months with them in a gym, where she'd learned advanced fighting techniques, and on a firing range, where she learned how to shoot. Private lessons in addition to the paid SERE course she'd completed were something Morgan and Freya offered all their contractors, but few had time like Diana had before she'd headed to Jordan to work on the archaeological dig.

Losing everything she'd ever wanted in a single hour had left a hole in her schedule. She'd had nothing but time and despair to burn.

And now here she was, in an oh-so-different kind of mental void where she felt nothing but pain and fear and had no control over what she'd lost, no clue what the next hours would bring. No idea of how she'd survive.

Her life as she knew it was over. Even if she somehow made it back to her home in Maryland, nothing would be the same after this.

Again.

The sound of male voices speaking Arabic was the only warning that she was about to have visitors. A light shone on her face. She closed her eyes against the bright blow to the pupils after at least an hour of sitting in the dark.

Harun—she recognized his commanding tone—barked an order for her to open her eyes. She complied, squinting.

All she could make out was a tall man looming over her, standing next to Harun. The light remained fixed on her eyes, making it impossible for her to discern more. She couldn't tell if the man was Middle Eastern, but his Arabic words spoken with a Syrian accent quickly answered that question.

"This is the girl who refused to clean the artifacts?"

She tried to get a look at the man's face. She still couldn't see anything distinct. Bearded and wearing a keffiyeh over his head.

"I don't have the proper tools and didn't want to damage them."

Harun slapped her again, but not as hard as before. "You were not spoken to."

The other man spoke. "You have the proper tools to dig, yes?"

There was a long silence as she tried to figure out if he was asking her. Did they want her to dig? Was this slot canyon a…site?

"We have shovels, trowels, brushes, and screens," Harun finally said.

"Then you will dig tomorrow, starting at first light." This time, she was certain the man was addressing her.

Her heart sank as the truth she should have guessed earlier clicked into place. She was to become the *source* of the supply chain.

She opened her mouth to protest, but was at a loss for what exactly to say. Why hadn't she considered this?

The flashlight dropped slightly, giving her eyes a chance to adjust as the men talked about where she would dig and what artifacts they could expect to get from this site.

Her eyes adjusted a bit, and she stared hard at the newcomer's face, then had to work to stifle her gasp.

No.

It couldn't be.

She kept her face blank. She needed to appear broken.

But she wasn't broken, and her mind worked just fine.

During her months of physical training with Morgan and Freya, there had been lessons on the key players in the Middle Eastern antiquities black market. Included in that was what they'd dubbed the Valkyrie cards, much like the deck of cards that had been given to troops to aid in remembering the faces of terrorist leaders at the start of the War in Afghanistan and later the ones that identified antiquities that needed protection in Iraq, Afghanistan, Egypt, and other places.

There were things a person could change about their appearance, but the scar that cut across his nose and cheek was unmistakable. The man standing before her was much more than an artifact trafficker. He was one of the leaders of a terrorist organization. Among other things, he was rumored to have acquired the chemical weapons that had wiped out a village of rebels in a Kurdish-held area in Syria.

She was staring at the Four of Diamonds, Makram Rafiq, a man who had supposedly been killed by a US military strike nearly two years ago.

Chapter Four

*S*atellite images show a vehicle arriving at the entrance to the slot canyon thirty minutes ago," the captain running the briefing began. "Two people got out of the vehicle and were permitted to enter the camp. They were there for thirty minutes. Two people then left the way they came."

"Any clue who they were?" a lieutenant asked.

"No," the captain said. "We haven't been able to get drones in place. The canyons are too narrow for anything other than the smallest short-range drones, limiting us to aerial views."

"Are we sure Dr. Edwards is still there?"

"As sure as we can be. There's no vehicle access other than the route by which she arrived. It's possible she was one of the two people who left, but the images we have show no sign either person who left was a prisoner."

"But it's possible she's been taken deeper into the gullies on foot," Chris said.

"It is possible, yes, but as far as we can tell, there is no other encampment nearby."

"There could be caves," Fallon said. "Those are nomad tents. Any chance her abductors are Bedouin?"

The captain turned to the intelligence officer with a raised brow. The woman stood and said, "With information provided by Freya Lange, we were able to track down the antiquities stall owner that Diana had identified as Bibi. She was…reluctant to answer our questions, but has admitted she told her Syrian associates about Dr. Edwards's interest in her wares. She knew the men intended to abduct the archae-ologist, but didn't expect to be part of the abduction and to have a knife held to her throat. She described the men as belonging to an offshoot of the Islamic State. They could be ISIS, ISIL, or a group we don't know, but it is extremely unlikely Dr. Edwards's abductors are Bedouin."

Again, Dr. Edwards's face filled the screen. This time, she was wearing a headscarf, drawing focus to the distinguishing marks on her face. A freckle on her left cheek. The uneven line of her thick, dark brows. A prominent scar that bisected her bottom lip. The scar was clearly on the newer side and surgery hadn't been able to do much to neaten the appear-ance of what had been a jagged, deep cut.

He wondered at its origin and if she had feeling on the right side of her bottom lip, or if the nerve endings had been irrevocably severed.

"Edwards is nearly fluent in Arabic. According to Lange, she has an exceptional memory. The report from her SERE instructor said she possessed a controlled calm that was quite unusual. She showed fear, but at no point did she come close to panic." The woman smiled. "Of course, SERE isn't real and we have no way of knowing how Dr. Edwards is holding up now, nor do we know what she's been subjected to since she was taken."

"Do we have intel on whether there are other hostages in the camp?" Albrecht, a young petty officer who'd been on this team only a few months longer than Chris, asked.

"At this time we have no reason to believe there are other hostages. Satellite images indicate there are seven guards armed with assault rifles. We believe this is a militarized camp, not a family or nomadic community."

"No other hostages, and no known civilians in the camp," Fallon said, underscoring the message.

The captain nodded. "Anyone who stands between the team and exfiltration of Dr. Edwards is to be considered an enemy combatant and complicit in the abduction of Dr. Edwards."

In other words, the rules of engagement allowed for killing everyone in the camp. But it wasn't a mission objective.

Which made Chris wonder if they hoped Dr. Edwards had gathered intel that would be even more beneficial if some of her captors could be followed back to their cells. It wasn't lost on him—or probably anyone in this room—that Edwards's fluency and brains had been underscored for the team just as Fallon had underscored who the enemy was.

But how much intel could an archaeologist gather in less than twelve hours of captivity?

4

The Seahawk lifted from the flight deck. The mission to extract Dr. Edwards from the terrorist camp was a go. Chris felt the usual thrum of adrenaline. This team might be new to him, but the job was not.

Still, he knew better than to feel any kind of complacency when it came to an op. A rescue mission that should have been a chip shot field goal had been the worst op of his life, and a weeklong training on American soil had turned into a nightmare with a higher body count than any real op since he'd made the teams.

Seven tangos. One hostage.

Don't expect easy.

The only easy day was yesterday.

The helo dropped them six klicks from the camp. Given the tight wadi, they had no choice but to approach on foot from a distance. Chris's Fire Team going in from the west, Fallon's had the easier, but more visible route from the east.

The desert had cooled with the setting sun, but the weight of the pack and body armor as they hurried through the slot canyon in the dark generated plenty of heat.

A short distance from the camp, his Fire Team took cover in every alcove they could find, and Albrecht launched a drone the size of a quarter to scout the camp. Over the radio, Fallon informed everyone his team had done the same.

Chris toggled the controls on his night vision goggles so he could see what the drone saw as it entered the camp.

Intel had identified seven tangos. Two guarded the perimeter; the others were inside the tents. They hadn't been able to identify which tent held Dr. Edwards. Hopefully the drone could do that.

The drone flew high over the head of the sentry who dozed at the west end of the camp.

Fallon radioed that the guard at the east end was awake and patrolling the perimeter.

Chris watched as the drone slipped through a gap in the curtain that covered the first tent in the row. A man slept on a cot, his AK-47 on the ground next to his bed. This appeared to be the kitchen tent, as the drone flew over a table with a camp stove, water jug, and empty basin on top. He guessed the two plastic containers contained nonperishable food. Only one cooler.

It was unlikely these guys planned to stay here long, unless more food was going to be delivered.

Which brought to mind the question of what was the purpose of this temporary camp? Why not take Dr. Edwards to their stronghold?

Was this bait for a rescue attempt?

Over the radio, Fallon shared that the tent on the other end of the camp was empty but for a plastic table and a few boxes. It was unoccupied, which could indicate there were two guards with Edwards.

Neither drone could find a gap through which to enter the other three tents, not without alerting someone, so they'd move in without knowing which tent housed Dr. Edwards.

They set out again, wraiths in the night. There was zero light pollution here and no moon. Stars lit the night sky, but in tight canyons as they were, very little of that light reached the valley floor. It would be impossibly dark without night vision goggles.

They paused a few feet from where the gully intersected with the bowl where tents were lined up like silver bells and cockleshells.

With a hand signal, Chris sent Albrecht and Meyers to the left, while he and Kramer would go right. They'd take out the guard at their end, and then enter two of the three tents with unknown occupants.

Just as Albrecht reached the slumbering guard, they heard the distinctive sound of a burst of fire from an M4 carbine rifle.

4

*S*leep wasn't possible, tied to the center post of the tent as she was, but Diana had managed to slip into some kind of pained daze. The rustling of the curtain between the two rooms roused her. She turned to see who had entered the room, but it was too dark to see anything.

A light flared, and she closed her eyes against the sudden flash of white. She felt hot breath on her face as someone knelt before her. A hand covered her mouth.

Her eyes shot open, and in the dim lantern light, she saw Jamal, the younger of the two brothers Harun had ordered to guard her when he left with Rafiq. Both brothers were young. Still teenagers.

His eyes were cold as he made a shushing sound, his hand clamping tighter on her mouth. He raised a sharp knife, and she twisted her head to escape his hand. Before she could scream, he covered her mouth again and pinched her nose.

The knife bit through the binding that attached her wrists to the post above her head. Her arms dropped, but they were still bound together. She swung them down, hitting his arm and dislodging his hand from her mouth and nose.

Jamal dropped the knife, and his hand returned to her face. With his other hand, he shoved her down so she was flat on her back, making his intent clear when his hand groped at her skirt.

He was going to rape her and didn't want others in the camp to hear.

While he struggled to pull up the long skirt of the abaya she wore, his grip on her mouth loosened. She bit his hand.

He reared back and slapped her.

She shoved at him, hoping to land a knee in his groin. She debated screaming, but would that just bring on the other guards to have their turn?

In the end, it was Jamal who alerted his older brother, Bassam, sleeping on the other side of the curtain, when Diana's knee found the target and he rolled off her, groaning in agony. Bassam came stumbling into the room. He cursed at what he saw, and she was surprised to realize his words were directed at his younger brother. "I told you to leave her alone! They will kill us if she's unable to work."

Jamal paid no attention to his brother and lunged for her. His fingers found her throat and squeezed.

Bassam yanked him off her, wrapping his arm around his brother's neck.

There was a burst of machine gun fire, and Diana's gaze

shot to the panel that separated the two rooms. Was this an attempt by another guard to stop the fight, or did he plan to join in on the raping?

Both brothers froze.

Jamal broke the sudden silence. "That wasn't an AK," he whispered in Arabic.

Bassam released his brother. "Someone's come for her."

Both brothers turned to her as she tried to make sense of the situation.

Someone was here to get her?

Another burst of gunfire. Outside the tent, a man made a pained yelp that ended with an abrupt finality that didn't bode well for the maker of the sound.

This was a rescue.

She glanced at her arm. She hadn't used the tracker. Not even accidently. She couldn't with her hands bound above her head as they'd been.

In a flash, Bassam yanked her to her feet and pressed a knife to her throat. "No sound." He nodded to his brother and signaled to the back of the tent. Behind her.

"We must go," he whispered in Arabic.

Jamal ran forward and lifted a flap at the back of the tent, revealing a small slit that could be crawled through.

Her hands, while freed from the post, were still bound together. "I can't crawl on bound hands," she whispered. Maybe with free hands, she could grab the knife, or one of the AK-47s.

Bassam removed the knife from her neck and sliced the rope, nicking her wrist in the process. Any thought of taking a weapon faded as the numbness in her hands was quickly followed by excruciating pins and needles.

Jamal crawled through the opening, and Bassam pushed at her from behind. She ignored the pain of putting her weight on her hands as she crawled through the flap. Strangely, she felt the pins surgeons had installed in her ankle. At least, that was what her brain said she felt, but it wasn't really possible. It had to be a phantom pain.

Blood rushed in her ears as she took everything in at once. She couldn't focus or think.

This was nothing like SERE.

She'd expected to leave the tent and come up against a sandstone wall, but Jamal dragged her into what must be a low overhang.

The world was pitch-black again, but cool sandstone was just inches above her head as she crawled along the ground. Jamal kept moving, and she realized it wasn't an overhang, it was a tunnel that had either been dug into the sandstone, Nabataean-style, or she was in a natural crevasse.

The row of tents had been placed in front of a hidden escape route.

With Jamal in front and Bassam behind, she was trapped, but no one had a gun or knife on her now. In moments, she would be lost in this tunnel. Consumed by the desert.

Should she scream? Would her rescuers even know she'd been here if she didn't?

Before she could change her mind, she sucked in a deep breath and let out a shrill wail, hoping the sound would reach the tunnel entrance and beyond.

Chapter Five

*C*hris entered the second room in the tent with Kramer at his back and swore at finding it empty. Cut ropes at the base of the center pole hinted that this was where Dr. Edwards had been held.

He crossed to the back of the tent and probed at the curtain with his rifle. Sure enough, there was a slit in the lower panel that, when pulled back, revealed another curtain with a small slit. A back door that required crawling through.

Not wanting to be unnecessarily vulnerable, he used a sharp knife to extend the slit and ducked through the bigger opening, coming face-to-face with a rock wall less than a yard from the rear of the tent. He looked left and right, seeing nothing, then glanced down, where he spotted impressions in the sand that could be drag marks, disappearing under a natural overhang.

A shrill, piercing wail emitted from the overhang.

He dropped to his knees and peered into the gap beneath the overhang. It wasn't an overhang; it was a dark void. A tunnel. With the aid of his NVGs, he spotted the bottom of a pair of boots crawling away from him.

He radioed his team before entering the tunnel with Kramer literally at his heels.

4

*J*amal yanked her from the end of the tunnel. She'd crawled at least a hundred meters and emerged into what appeared to be another narrow wadi. The night was moonless, and with only the light of Jamal's flashlight, she couldn't see more than a few feet in front of her.

Before she could get her bearings, Jamal backhanded her. "You were told to be silent!"

She swayed on her feet as Bassam rose behind her and shoved her forward. "Run!"

His urgency told her that someone had followed them into the tunnel. She took two steps forward, then made herself stumble. It wasn't hard given the pain in her ankle.

She used that pain, and the memory of it when she'd felt it during her SERE training, to ground her.

Pain she could handle. Pain helped her to forget, but it also helped her to remember.

Pretend to go along while slowing them down.

A cold calm settled on her as she remembered that moment in her training when she'd discovered that focusing on the pain allowed her to ignore the fear.

Pain eclipsed fear, and once fear was masked, she'd been able to *think*.

To plan.

Morgan and Freya had said SEALs would be most likely to be sent in to rescue her if she was taken. These two boys —and they were children, sixteen or seventeen at most— were no match for Navy SEALs.

Slow them down.

She stumbled again, this time allowing herself to fall.

Bassam grabbed her headscarf, his fingers digging in and gripping her hair beneath the cloth. He yanked her up and twisted around to face the sandstone wall they'd just crawled through. She found her back pressed to his front—a human shield—as a dark shadow emerged from the tunnel.

Her heart lurched as Bassam's knife pressed to her throat.

Her ankle burned. She remembered staring down at it in the hospital, when it was puffed up like a cantaloupe and the doctors told her she'd been lucky to keep her foot and all she could think was that she'd trade her foot if she could have her fiancé.

But no. The cards she'd been dealt left her with two hands and two feet and an empty heart.

"Stop! Don't come any closer!" Bassam shouted in English.

Behind them, lights came on, shining in the direction of the tunnel, and now she could see that at this end, the tunnel had become a crevasse in the sandstone wall. Whoever had made the tunnel had dug through to a natural opening. If they had Nabataean ancestors, they'd have done them proud.

But then, the tunnel could have been dug in the last

century BCE. She hadn't exactly been able to examine the passageway while being dragged and pushed through, and from what Rafiq had said, this area was an archaeological site.

The lights—which she guessed from the engine rumble that had preceded the glow, were headlights from a vehicle—illuminated a man in full combat regalia, standing directly in front of the crevasse. Another man crouched behind him, having not quite reached the point of being able to stand fully upright before Bassam had put the knife to her throat and ordered them to halt.

The SEAL—she assumed he was a SEAL—kept his gun pointed just to the left of Diana as he raised his NVGs with one hand. His eyes scanned her face, probably the only thing he could see backlit as she was by bright beams of light.

She shifted so her shadow cast on him. She was the cause of the eclipse, not the moon.

But then, Diana was goddess of the moon, so she could embrace this role.

"Dr. Edwards," the man said. Not a question that needed answering. An acknowledgment to let her know his being here was intentional.

The only parts of his body not covered by clothing or gear were his eyes and the skin of his upper cheeks. Both eyes and skin were brown.

His eyes were neither cold nor warm. All business.

She was his mission.

The arm around her waist tightened and the knife at her neck shifted to a scarier angle. But even as she stood frozen, she wasn't afraid. And not because she was focusing on pain.

No. It was because Bassam couldn't kill her. If he slit her throat, the SEAL would kill him.

If they managed to escape and then he killed her, his terrorist buddies would kill *him*. That was what Bassam had said when he caught his brother attempting to rape her.

Diana was valuable to the organization.

So valuable, the Four of Diamonds, Makram Rafiq himself, had visited this desolate little wadi to question her.

She—not the brothers who guarded her—was important to Rafiq's organization.

But…if she helped them escape with her, she'd raise their status. She could make them important too.

Now that her mind wasn't clouded by fear, she thought of that meeting with Rafiq, and a fire lit inside her.

She could do something real and substantial in the fight against looting and trafficking and funding terrorism.

The US and their allies didn't even know Rafiq was *alive*. But she knew. She'd spoken with him. And if she played her cards right, she could lead a team of special forces operators right to wherever he'd been hiding out since his supposed death.

But to do that, she couldn't be rescued now.

In Arabic, she spoke to her captors. "Remove the knife from my neck, and I'll get us out of here."

"He will shoot me if I move the knife."

"You cut open my throat and you'll be shot."

"What did you tell him?" the SEAL asked.

She met her would-be rescuer's gaze. She suspected both Jamal and Bassam spoke English. They would understand if she spoke of Rafiq and her plans to lead the US military to his door. All she could do was look into the man's eyes and say with utter calm and conviction, "Let us go."

His eyes narrowed. "I can't do that."

She couldn't move her head, but her hands were free. She shifted her position so her left hand was clearly visible, pressed flat to her chest below the knife-wielding hand.

She deliberately tucked her thumb to display four fingers, wiggling them slightly. She slipped her thumb between her middle and ring fingers and used the thumb to tap the place where a ring would be. She couldn't be sure he saw it, so she made the motion again. As she moved her fingers, she mouthed the words, *Trust me*.

Chapter Six

*T*rust me. Had she really mouthed those words? Trust her?

He'd learned the hard way to never, *ever* trust a hostage.

They were terrified and irrational. And sometimes they didn't want to be rescued.

The look in Dr. Edwards's eyes told him she was one of those.

What the hell was wrong with her? And what was it with her flashing four fingers like that repeatedly?

He radioed to his team to stay back, and that was when he realized he was dealing with dead air. Behind him, crouched in the tunnel, Kramer said, "Radio's not working."

Chris cursed. He wouldn't be surprised to learn that on this side of the wadi there was a signal jammer of the kind he'd come across in Washington last January. Were Russians in bed with this terrorist cell?

With signals jammed, he couldn't call in a Seahawk to

swoop down in the nearest clearing and whisk Dr. Edwards to safety.

He and Kramer were on their own in this standoff.

Two against two would be fine, even if one side had a vehicle and hostage, but it appeared the hostage had sided with the terrorists.

Which made it three against two.

How deep was Edwards in this? Was she the type to pull a weapon and start shooting?

Chris watched her hands. He would do what he had to if she went for a gun.

She spoke softly to her captor in Arabic. From her tone and cadence, he guessed she was negotiating with him.

Or was she giving him orders?

He wished he spoke more Arabic, but his focus the last several years had been learning Russian and other languages from Eastern Europe. The ops he was sent on from Coronado had been focused in that region. He'd spent time in the Sandbox, but not as much as he would have if he'd been based out of Little Creek from the start of his tenure.

Was she planning their escape?

He hoped to hell Kramer spoke Arabic, but odds were he wouldn't know what was being said until they debriefed and viewed Chris's bodycam.

The knife at her throat lowered a half an inch, no longer pressing to her skin.

Chris breathed a little easier, but there was still a gun pointed at him, and she was no closer to joining team SEAL over team terrorist.

Voice steady, she said in English, "We're going now. Do not follow."

As if he could without a vehicle and no radio, phone, or satellite communication. They'd have to crawl back through the tunnel or find the signal jammer on this side and destroy it.

"Don't do this Doctor—Diana." Maybe using her first name would trigger something for her. His gaze flicked to the man at her back and the second man in the shadows by the truck with the high beams. "They're no match for SEALs."

She held his gaze.

What had the analyst said? Something about being unusually calm during her SERE training.

He could believe that now.

In the middle of the dry desert, this woman was an ice sculpture.

"We're not leaving without you, Diana."

The knife pressed to her skin again, and the man barked something in Arabic.

The eerie, steely calm faded from her eyes. "Please. It's the only way. Let us go." Again her hand did the frantic four-finger thing, then her thumb slipped between ring and middle finger.

What did the gesture mean?

"*Please*," she said again.

Was this a game to give Chris a better shot?

No. No way. He had no shot and didn't see how this could improve that situation.

Trust me.

He knew that was what she'd said. She wanted to leave with these men.

Why?

Before he'd entered the tunnel, four tangos had been killed. Two were here. He didn't know the status of the last one, but that man wasn't here in this canyon.

He and Kramer could take out these assholes, but Edwards was in the way.

"Don't do this," Chris said again.

"I have to."

"Why?"

Again with the frantic fingers. Again with the mouthed *Trust me*.

Dammit all to motherfucking hell. Couldn't he just once have a normal, fucking, clean hostage rescue?

He glared at the woman. The scar that bisected the right side of her bottom lip and trailed down her chin offered undeniable proof that this was Dr. Diana Edwards, the archaeologist he and his team had been sent to rescue.

She stood before him, coldly beautiful as she stared back, her regal calm returned even as the knife pressed to her throat.

He said nothing as she was slowly dragged backward and pushed into the truck.

He pointed his rifle at the windshield as it backed out of the gully. He had no shot at the driver without endangering the woman he'd been sent to rescue.

The truck rounded a corner and disappeared from sight.

Chapter Seven

4

The SEAL hated her. She could see it in his eyes. She couldn't blame him. He and his team had risked their lives for her, and she hadn't played along. She closed her eyes and leaned against the back seat of the battered old vehicle.

Once they were out of sight of the SEAL and his partner, who'd been trapped in the tunnel, Jamal had made a fast one-eighty turn and they barreled through mazelike formations.

She wondered if the boy at the wheel knew his way through the labyrinth.

All at once, what she'd done hit her. She'd rejected her *rescue*.

Who was to say anyone would swoop in if—when—she eventually triggered the tracker?

The SEAL had been pissed. At her. With good reason.

She could right now be in the company of a team of special forces operators, on her way to being dropped safely at an American embassy, but no, she was going deeper into the quagmire of black markets and terrorism.

She'd *chosen* this.

She had to be batshit demented.

She remembered the morning she woke in the hospital after surgery on her ankle. Eighteen months ago. She'd felt hollow. Lost. Salim was gone.

Now she bit her bottom lip, remembering that first time her tongue had probed at the stitches that had repaired her mouth. She could only partially feel the pressure of teeth on lip. That cut, while the least of her injuries, was the most tangible. Every glance in the mirror or bite of her lip brought back the moment of impact. Salim's agonized wail.

The very structure of her world had been wiped out.

She'd kept her foot, but that hadn't meant she could still pursue the job that had been waiting for her. No. She'd lost that opportunity because she couldn't run. She wouldn't ever be considered fully abled.

She'd accepted the loss of mobility. It was the price of surviving a horrific accident.

What she struggled with was not having Salim and then being denied the job. No part of her future had matched the plans they'd made together.

She'd remained empty and adrift until this work for Morgan and Freya had given her a mission. It wasn't *the* job, but it was close. So very close.

It gave her a reason to breathe. To get out of bed. To shower and brush her teeth.

Her work on the dig had been satisfying, but being a Friday Morning Valkyrie had given her life. A purpose.

The vehicle bounced as Jamal raced across uneven ground. After a hard jolt, she tasted blood but didn't feel the pain of the bite.

Her ankle throbbed. Her arm itched.

She accepted that she was following that purpose straight into hell.

⬥

The flight back to the carrier was silent. Chris was still too stunned to fully process what had happened.

He'd been on failed missions. Even disastrous ones. Nightmare ones. But nothing like that.

She'd taken control of the situation, issuing commands to her captors, but Chris would be the one to pay the price for her actions.

They went straight to the briefing room and settled around the table. The top brass from Navy Special Warfare Command were either in the room or would join remotely. And Chris would have to explain why he'd let Dr. Edwards go.

He'd never even made a move to save her.

He was a damn SEAL. A highly trained special forces operator. She was an archaeologist, and they were two baby tangos who probably didn't even have pubes yet.

He was so fucked.

Fallon was supposed to be promoted out of active ops, and Chris was in line to take the reins.

Zero chance of that now.

Hell, he'd be lucky if he was allowed to retire gracefully.

He'd move to the Pacific Northwest. Maybe get a house near Xavier. His old teammate wouldn't hold this fuckup against him. He would understand why Chris had frozen in the moment.

Because that was what he'd done, wasn't it? Frozen when he realized Edwards didn't want to be saved? He'd braced for her to pull a gun and shoot him and Kramer.

He'd been prepared to take action if she did.

Xavier would get it, but no one else would.

Hell, he couldn't look at the faces of the men around this table. His new team.

Every man here knew he was a washed-up coward who'd blown the op.

They just didn't know why.

♦

*O*rgan Adler sat anxiously at her desk and waited for the link to the secure video meeting to go live. Her business partner, Freya Lange, sat beside her.

The op to rescue Diana had begun hours ago, and she could only assume the SEAL team tasked with the mission was back on the aircraft carrier. That NSWC wanted to talk to Morgan and Freya wasn't a good sign.

If the mission had been successful, Diana would be doing all the talking.

Had she been injured? Or…worse?

Morgan didn't even want to think about what *worse* could mean.

The screen flashed and then the video link window opened, and she could see a conference room filled with men in uniform, including a dozen or so men in dirty combat uniforms—they looked fresh from the desert.

Diana wasn't among the group at the table, nor in one of the windows of people joining the meeting remotely like Morgan and Freya.

"Thank you for joining us, Dr. Adler and Ms. Lange," a Navy captain said. "I'm afraid we aren't authorized to share mission details with you at this time, but we wish for you to review bodycam footage taken during the op and ask if you can offer insight into Dr. Edwards's…*actions*."

"Where is Diana?" Morgan couldn't stop herself from asking.

There was a long pause before the captain said, "We cannot answer that question at this time."

Morgan's stomach twisted. Either Diana's whereabouts were secret, or they truly didn't know where the woman was.

She wanted to grip Freya's hand, but this was very much Freya's world, and she wouldn't permit any show of emotion while dealing with the military.

Sometimes she forgot that Freya had once been a stone-cold Special Activities Division operator for the CIA, but in moments like this, she could see the woman Freya had once been, back when her name was Savannah.

"And why can't you answer the question?" Freya asked in a cold, commanding tone.

"We'll get to that. First we want to know what Dr. Edwards was trying to tell our operator in this recording."

The display changed, and a video playback window was full screen on the large monitor. The captain hit Play and the video began.

Diana, backlit by headlights in a halo around her. A man holding a knife to her throat.

This was the stuff of Morgan's nightmares. She placed a hand on her belly as she watched.

The work FMV's field operatives did was frequently dangerous. They all knew it. But it was quite another thing to see the woman Morgan had spent months with in preparation for this job with a knife at her throat.

And from the words of the captain, she assumed Diana was *still* in danger.

They can't say where she is.

Morgan was no stranger to being abducted. The only reason she was here today was because the men who'd taken her needed her alive to see their plan through, so while she'd been starved, dehydrated, and chained for days, she hadn't been otherwise assaulted until the last hours of her captivity.

Diana was at the start of her horrific ordeal and no one knew what they really wanted from her. It almost certainly had to do with her expertise as an archaeologist, but still, that didn't mean she wouldn't be sexually abused, in addition to being starved and beaten.

There was no sound to go with the video, and Freya asked, "Can you turn on the audio?"

"Not yet. We want to know if the hand signals mean anything separate from the words being said by all parties."

They were viewing video from a SEAL's body camera. Morgan had spotted Lieutenant Commander Randall Fallon at the table—he'd acknowledged her and Freya with a slight nod at the start—and wondered if he was the SEAL who'd faced Diana and her captor.

Diana's mouth moved, and the knife lowered ever so slightly. Morgan guessed she was speaking Arabic to her captor. There was a steely calm about her.

Early that morning, she'd again reviewed the SERE trainer's report on Diana. From the looks of it, he hadn't been wrong about Diana's ability to compartmentalize.

At the end of all Diana's training, Freya made the observation the woman would have made an excellent SAD operative. The CIA had known this as well and had even tried to recruit her. The job opportunity had been withdrawn when her ankle injury meant she couldn't meet the physical requirements.

Diana's left hand moved, and Morgan let out a gasp.

Even always-in-control Freya huffed out a shocked breath and said, "Holy shit."

"So the hand motion means something?" someone on an aircraft carrier half a world away asked.

"It does," Freya said. She turned to Morgan. "Where are the cards?"

Morgan was already on her feet, heading for the cabinet where she pulled out the pack of playing cards she and Freya had printed for all their Valkyries. They'd used them as flash cards more than anything, but there had been some late-night poker games once they'd learned Diana was a shark. Watching Freya and Diana play had been entertaining for

Morgan. She'd been relegated to watching because both women cleaned her out quickly.

The video no longer filled the screen, and Morgan could again see the team of SEALs and military brass, which meant the team could now see her and Freya again.

She popped open the pack and dumped the cards on the table, while Freya gave the explanation. "Diana trained with us in the months before she left for Jordan. In addition to basic self-defense based on martial arts taught by Morgan, we studied all the known players in the antiquities black market in the Middle East, including the leaders of all iden-tified terrorist groups."

She grabbed a card from the deck and held it up to the camera. "For that, we created our own deck of cards and had Diana memorize names and faces. It doesn't surprise me that she remembered their suit and number too. Diana has one of the best noneidetic memories I've encountered. She's gifted when it comes to patterns and numbers. She could probably recite all fifty-two cards like some people say the alphabet."

She paused, and Morgan jumped in. "In the video, we see Diana showing four fingers on her left hand, then she tucks her thumb between her middle and ring finger and taps the proximal end of her ring finger. The ring finger of her left hand, where an engagement ring would be worn. I believe she's signaling four of diamonds, as she looks directly at your operator and mouths the words, *Trust me*. This could indicate Diana met with the Four of Diamonds at some point between her abduction and rescue."

"Who is the Four of Diamonds?" one of the SEALs

asked, making Morgan wonder if the video was from his bodycam.

Morgan raised the card to the camera. "Makram Rafiq."

There was a collective gasp. Coming from a group of special forces operators, that was saying something.

"Impossible. He's dead," one of the commanders said.

"Apparently not," Freya said. "Diana has a *very* good memory for names and faces. If she says she saw Makram Rafiq, then she saw him. Now, are you going to tell us where she is and why she asked a SEAL to trust her?"

4

*C*hris cleared his throat and spoke, not waiting for permission. These women had just changed everything they knew about the botched rescue, leaving it open to an entirely different interpretation. No way would he pass up getting answers while he had the chance. "Explain how this would lead to Dr. Edwards helping her two guards escape with her."

The former SAD operator, Freya Lange, let out a curse. "Jesus, it's like Morgan all over again."

Beside him at the table, Fallon let out a grunt and said, "Morgan allowed herself to be taken because she knew they'd take her to Etefu Desta."

This was Operation Icarus they were discussing, and now he had another puzzle piece. "So it's possible Dr. Edwards wanted to leave with her captors because she believes she can lead us to Makram Rafiq." Chris wanted this theory on the record.

"Yes," Morgan said. "She has a tracker with at least three months of battery life left."

A silence settled in the room as the words sank in. Chris played that *trust me* over and over in his mind.

There were grumbles from around the table. "She's fucking nuts if she thinks the military will send in a team to save her again after what she did."

There was a rumble of agreement, and Kramer added, "She never even gave us a chance to rescue her."

Lange responded, "Of course Diana doesn't expect the military to risk another op for *her*. But she knows you'll do it to get Makram Rafiq. He's evaded your bombs more than once, and now he's back from the dead. I would think you'd be more than eager to get the man who orchestrated a number of bombings, including one that killed more than a dozen SEALs."

Chapter Eight

They drove for hours, twisting through wadis and small towns. Bassam and Jamal took turns driving as they waited for instructions on where to take Diana.

The initial plan to have Diana excavate the site near the fake Bedouin camp had been spoiled by the SEALs. Five terrorists in their cell were dead, and now the government of the Hashemite Kingdom of Jordan knew the Islamic State had intended to loot the site.

The tents and digging tools Rafiq had asked about would be seized and the site would be monitored via satellite by the Kingdom and, Diana hoped, also by the Cultural Heritage Monitoring Lab in Virginia. CHML was tasked with monitoring known sites, while the Friday Morning Valkyries' job was to track the supply chain and recover the artifacts.

With the botched rescue behind them, Rafiq was in need of another site to loot, and Diana feared what that meant for her.

After her conversation with Rafiq last night, she'd braced

herself for the job of running a dig for which there would be no data collected and the sole intention was to use the artifacts to fund mass murder. She'd accepted it as what she'd need to do to survive and eventually allow her to tell the US military that Rafiq was alive and operating out of Jordan, not Syria or Iraq, as he'd been before his supposed death.

Now she'd told the military—at least, she hoped Morgan and Freya had interpreted her hand signal correctly—and there was no reason to do Rafiq's dirty work unless it would lead to learning the location of the terrorist leader's base of operations.

At the time of his faked death, Rafiq had officially been the fourth most wanted man in the US's War on Terror. SEALs would come running to save her if they believed they could get Rafiq.

It was the only way to get out of this nightmare alive.

But she feared she'd have to betray everything she believed in to reach the endgame—assuming she survived that long.

⬥

The debriefing continued for hours after Lange and Adler dropped their bombshell about the Four of Diamonds. It was well after dawn when Chris and the rest of the team were released to catch several hours of sleep. Now Chris was in his berth, eyes closed.

Makram Rafiq.

The name changed everything. Probably saved Chris's ass, because it at least made Edwards's actions make sense.

Still irrational and horrifically dangerous, but there was logic in the mix.

Did Edwards have a death wish? Lange and Adler had hinted that the woman might feel like she had nothing left to lose.

Was that what he'd seen in her eyes? The cold calm of someone with no fucks left to give?

But to sacrifice oneself in the way Edwards was doing, it had to mean she cared about *something*. And that something was protecting Middle Eastern antiquities.

Or stopping terrorists.

Or both.

With his eyes closed, he was back in the wadi, reliving the exchange. He'd watched the video dozens of times. He could recite every moment, every expression. The thing the video didn't show was Chris's face and his own thoughts.

His mouth had been covered by a shield. Dr. Diana Edwards had only been able to see his eyes. She couldn't read his lips like he had hers. She didn't know what or if he'd mouthed back. But she'd seen the anger in his eyes, and her gaze had flicked to his rifle when he adjusted his grip as he braced for her to grab her captor's gun and turn it on Chris.

More than two years ago, he'd been on an op where the hostage didn't want to be rescued. To that end, the young woman had taken out two SEALs and wounded a third. Chris had done the only thing he could to save his Fire Team.

In the desert last night, he'd been prepared to do it again.

It wouldn't have taken much for him to turn his weapon on the beautiful Dr. Edwards.

Then she mouthed the words that pulled him back from Belarus and centered him in the Jordanian desert.

He'd done the counseling. He knew he'd done the right thing in Belarus. But now he had to ask himself if he was fit to serve or if he was a danger to the very people he was supposed to save.

Chapter Nine

Bassam blindfolded Diana hours before they reached a house. For all she knew, they drove in circles during that time. Or they could be on the outskirts of Aqaba or even Amman. They had driven for so long, they could be anywhere.

The only thing Diana was certain of was that this house was *not* where Rafiq was holed up. The structure was tiny and ramshackle, and she didn't think anyone lived there. For starters, there was no electricity or water. Just a pit toilet, and their drinking water came from jugs. Cooking was done on an open fire. It would be called camping if the structure wasn't a three-room house.

It was a waypoint. A stopping place to store her until her captors could plan their next move.

She realized they'd be at the way station for more than a few hours when Jamal left her with her hands free but ankles bound together—just enough length between them so she could hobble to the pit toilet as needed—and returned an hour later with groceries for her to cook. That she would do the cooking explained the unbound hands.

Their larder was basic: lamb, chicken, yogurt, pita bread, rice, and the makings for tabbouleh and falafel. Enough to feed the three of them for a day or two if she was careful with portions. She gathered that they'd burned through most of their funds keeping the car fueled as they drove all over the Kingdom.

Abandoning the camp—which had been expensive to set up—had been quite a blow to the organization's finances. She felt a grim satisfaction at that, but also knew it would mean they'd up the pressure on her to provide them with an abundance of artifacts to sell.

It was late on the day after they'd settled in when they had a visitor. It was Harun, the man who'd initially abducted her and later introduced her to Rafiq.

Harun frowned at her unbound hands and ordered Bassam to correct his error.

Once she was properly tied up, Bassam led her into the other room, where an old metal sign was propped on a stack of old tires to make a desk of sorts. Harun stood before the table, where he'd placed a laptop that was in the process of booting up.

As he waited, he turned and studied her. His eyes were cold. Dead. She wasn't a person to him. She was merely a means to an end. She hoped to hell he wouldn't be permanently joining their merry band of three.

Bassam and Jamal she could handle. This man…he'd relish hurting her.

But she also knew she had to be careful in giving cooperation or acquiescence to Harun. If he realized she had her own agenda, he'd kill her.

He spoke to her in English. "You could have escaped last night, but instead you told the SEAL not to shoot your guards."

"I had a knife to my throat."

"They were US military special forces. Your guards are barely trained children."

"A barely trained child can accidently slit a throat where a well-trained man will not. I like breathing. Cooperating with the boy with the knife was the logical choice."

"I don't believe you."

She shrugged. "I don't give a fuck what you believe."

Quick as a flash, Harun's open palm met her cheek. She rolled with the blow, twirling and bumping the table before dropping to the floor.

She only exaggerated the impact a little. The slap hurt like a bitch and did knock her off balance. She cupped her stinging cheek and glared up at him. Her eyes teared—those were real—and she decided to push again. "Fuck you."

He kicked her in the ribs. Painful, but not what it could have been. He'd checked the blow. A show of power, but not bad enough to break ribs.

This was a strange dance, but still, they were both moving to the same song for different reasons. He needed her, but he needed to show power and control. She needed him to believe he'd cowed her into cooperating. She figured she had the upper hand because she knew his motives, but he had no clue about hers.

"Without the site we'd already located, we need to find a

new source for artifacts. You will tell us where to go." His eyes narrowed. "No tricks. We will send a team to check the site is real before we bring you there."

She shifted her position and placed a hand over her soon-to-be bruised ribs. "There are guards at Petra."

He raised his foot to kick her again. Her flinch wasn't faked.

He placed his boot on the ground. "There is much archaeology in Jordan apart from Petra. You know where many sites are. You will tell me."

"I'm an American. I don't know where Jordan's secret sites are."

"You have worked with Professor Yousef."

"So?"

Harun's smile somehow turned even more malicious. He waved a hand toward the laptop on the table. "Stand," he commanded. "And watch."

She slowly got to her feet. Her side throbbed along with her head. She'd be wise to put the show of resistance behind her.

Harun tapped at the keyboard. After a moment, a video began to play.

On the screen, Dr. Fahd Yousef, the professor she'd worked with for the last four months, faced a camera. His face was battered and bleeding, the skin around his left eye swollen, purple, and open only a slit.

Fahd spoke in Arabic. "I will not tell you."

Blood dribbled from his lip.

A voice off camera said, "Then one of your students will."

"They don't know anything but the location of the site they've excavated with Dr. Edwards."

"Dr. Edwards." Her name was spoken in a flat tone. A statement, not a question.

Yousef said nothing.

A fist shot out, and Yousef's head snapped back. His head lolled as he wheezed in a painful breath and struggled to focus. "She's no one. Visiting professor. Paid for by an American corporation. Free labor. Little brain."

Her heart ached. Not at his words, but at his struggle. Yousef hadn't liked her at first, but one thing he did respect was her brain.

He'd tried to protect her, just as he had his students.

"She has seen the maps. She knows."

"No."

Another blow.

"She knows nothing. Stupid American. She speaks Arabic poorly and isn't the expert on Nabataean history she claimed to be."

Later, Diana would wonder if that obvious lie was the tipping point that told Rafiq and his minions that Diana did indeed know everything.

Chapter Ten

4

Amman, Hashemite Kingdom of Jordan
July

Diana rolled her shoulders as she reread the note.

Diana,
Meet me in my office as soon as you're done
uploading the day's notes into the database. – FY

This was the first time Dr. Fahd Yousef had made such a request, and she wasn't sure if it was a good sign or bad. He'd been reluctant to work with her, but she was the price of the funding he'd accepted from Gardner Holdings, which made her Dr. Yousef's assistant in running the dig in the desert.

She'd spent her first weeks here convincing the professor

that she wasn't Gardner's sycophant and mole. She was here for the work and cared for the resource. Gardner was a means to an end for them both.

Dr. Yousef's request to meet in his office was reminiscent of those first weeks, when he monitored her every move and double-checked her work. Perhaps he wanted to see if she was still coloring within the lines now that he'd relaxed his monitoring.

She replied to his message saying she'd be in his office in ten minutes.

After closing the database, she then sent an email to Morgan confirming the security team would meet her at the usual place and follow her into the Friday market tomorrow morning.

Tomorrow, she'd try again to convince Bibi to show her the real artifacts in the back of the stall.

Email sent, she closed her laptop and tucked it into her satchel, then draped the cross-body strap over her shoulder.

She locked her temporary office and went down the hall to meet with her colleague.

Fahd Yousef was a handsome man in his early fifties. His beard was shot with gray, and he looked the perfect example of the Middle Eastern professor of archaeology. He'd been married for thirty-plus years and had six children, who ranged in age from twenty-eight to twelve years old.

He smiled when she entered his office and the tension she'd felt that he might be suspicious of her again receded. "Have a seat, Diana."

Fahd spoke English, as was his custom with her. He was

more fluent in English than she was in Arabic and was quite comfortable with the language.

She settled in the visitor's chair that faced his desk. "I'm surprised you're here so late this evening."

"I had a Zoom meeting with our American benefactor that kept me here after office hours."

She cocked her head, surprised she hadn't been invited to the meeting given that she'd been back from the field since early afternoon.

"I hope all is well with Gardner Holdings?"

Fahd didn't smile or frown. His expression was carefully blank, reminding her again of those first weeks. "What is your take on Dennis Gardner?"

She weighed her options. The Jordanian archaeologist's trust mattered more to her than Gardner's. On a purely mercenary level, while Gardner's grant was paying the bills now, Fahd could open doors for more research for her in this part of the world even after Gardner's funding dried up.

But would honesty serve her if she expressed distrust of the man who financed her position? Was Fahd now the spy for Gardner?

She cleared her throat and went for it. "He's vain and not the intellectual he wants the world to believe he is. He's no champion for knowledge or history. He's driven by profit and doesn't give a damn about science."

Fahd was Muslim and a scientist. He wasn't a man to let his religious beliefs dictate his interpretation of the sites he excavated, which was particularly important in this part of the world where archaeology and three major world religions were deeply intertwined. But archaeology was never without controversy, starting from the days when it was pioneered by white men with their white supremacist and paternalistic views.

There was a huge push by archaeologists to decolonize the profession, and Diana, a white American woman who specialized in the Middle East, believed in that agenda and always sought to tread carefully. She wouldn't have taken this position if it pushed a Jordanian man or woman out. But Gardner wouldn't have funded the dig without her presence, and the fact that she was teamed with and answered to Fahd was what made this particular job work for her. She had no intention of eclipsing Middle Eastern voices in the field. She was a worker bee, bringing knowledge to the table and, in this instance, funding.

Without Salim by her side, that was all she aspired to in this part of the world.

Fahd gave a short nod. "He and his group of financiers are putting together a funding package for next summer." He said this like it wasn't good news.

"Is he planning to replace you?" she asked. "Or me?"

"We did not discuss your role, but I have no doubt he will again insist on an American field director. I will request your return."

She felt a spark of gratitude along with a flare of pride. She'd worked hard to win this man over. His words meant more than she could say.

"Thank you."

"I am concerned because he wants a list of potential

sites. Not just sites, but pertinent details including location, date range, artifacts that have been recovered to determine it is a site. He wants to choose—or rather dictate—where we excavate. I have a feeling he will submit research questions to be addressed as a condition of funding."

She understood his unease. The donor didn't get to decide the direction of the research. And only the government could issue the permit—which would be evaluated based on Fahd's research questions.

"How do you want to respond?"

"I'm not sure. The funding—it's a lot. Enough to pay for a full crew for the entire summer, instead of filling out the team with student volunteers. At least a year of lab analysis for five people. Money for all the scientific tests. Plus ground penetrating radar, lidar, multispectral and RGB drone imaging, photogrammetry, and 3D modeling. But I don't want to let him cherry-pick my research based on his goals for tourist destinations and a desire for new artifacts to replicate in his stores." He paused and held her gaze. "Given your knowledge of the man, what would you do?"

She frowned. She didn't really know Gardner and didn't particularly like what she did know. He was the money guy, and in research archaeology, money guys were a necessary evil.

She had specialized in Middle Eastern archaeology and learned Arabic because she was in love. Plain and simple. The shift had been gradual. She'd been interested in Egyptology, with its deep history in the same region, but slowly, her focus changed as Salim wooed her with his ancestral culture and history.

And she loved the history and culture she'd studied as much as she loved the man. But now she was here, in Jordan, working on the dig of his—and her—dreams, and Salim was gone.

What would her dead fiancé do?

Of course she knew. He'd laugh at the billionaire and find a way to take his money and use it for the good of Middle Eastern archaeology. She took a slow breath as she imagined Salim's glee. He'd have loved this job, and the students would have loved him.

"Give him a list of two or three sites—no locational data, we don't want him to try to investigate on his own—that you believe the government would give you a permit for."

She then sat down beside him to go over his maps with recorded sites and cross-referenced the known data. Included on his list were sites in Syria that were in jeopardy and had been since the rise of the Islamic State.

Khaled al-Asaad, the head archaeologist at Palmyra—a UNESCO World Heritage Site in Syria—had been beheaded in 2015 by ISIS for refusing to disclose the location of valuable relics. His murder had sent shock waves through the community and world. While working for FMV was dangerous, there was a strict protocol that excluded entering Syria in their efforts to stop trafficking.

It was heartbreaking knowing sites were being lost to looting in Syria. And even more devastating that the Islamic State and its offshoots practiced malicious destruction of features too big to transport and sell. Even knowing all this, Syria's archaeological resources were off-limits for protection by the Valkyries. It was just too dangerous.

"You worked in Syria, before the war?"

Fahd nodded, his eyes taking on the sad look of someone who'd lived a dream only to witness its annihilation. He'd probably known al-Asaad. They might even have been friends.

She didn't ask. Didn't want to open that wound.

Fahd pointed to the map. "I spent six weeks on a dig here, postdoc. The site was incredible. I was just a field grunt, helping out a fellow grad student. It was the kind of site a person could work for a decade and still not know the extent of it. This was before advancements in satellite technology to really see beneath the surface without the destructive process of digging, mind you, but we were careful—we knew the technology was coming and we didn't want to be like Schliemann and dynamite our way through the historic layers we were interested in to get to the goodies, so the site went largely unexcavated."

"It's still intact?" Diana asked.

"As far as I know. My friend—the archaeologist who'd been studying the site for over a decade at that point—disappeared in early 2014."

Disappeared. Probably dead. A casualty of the civil war, or a target because of his work? Too much time had passed for clear answers, and Diana's own heart ached at Fahd's loss of friend and colleague.

"I'm sorry," she murmured.

"Over the years, I've wondered if Rabi died keeping the secret of the location of the dig. I make it a regular practice to monitor satellite images of the area, and it remains intact."

Given that Fahd Yousef's specialty was using satellite imagery to find sites in the desert, this wasn't surprising. The man had special access to satellites, granted by his government, so taking a peek just over the border wasn't much of a stretch.

Fahd's eyes took on that wistful look, and he tapped at his keyboard, and next thing Diana knew, she was looking at the satellite images database, and he was typing in the coordinates. His finger hovered over an area of the screen pointing to the eastern edge of Syria where it bordered Jordan. "There is an underground Roman aqueduct not far from here. Hidden for more than fifteen centuries until it was found by an archaeologist twenty years ago. It's a tunnel that runs under the border. Another similar tunnel was found more than a hundred years ago by T. E. Lawrence, but the discovery was forgotten when World War I broke out. A half dozen years or so ago, it was found again and the Kurds were able to use it as an entry point into Syria from Turkey before the Syrian military caught on and blew up all the known entry and exit points, destroying an aqueduct that had survived nearly two millennia.

"The Jordan-Syrian aqueduct is over a hundred miles long, and some sections have been destroyed, but overall, it remains intact, and the site my friend worked was associated with that complex. A town that benefited from the water supplied by the aqueduct. Not as grand as Petra, but a permanent settlement in the desert with underground aqueducts providing precious water."

His finger traced what she assumed was the route of the aqueduct, then paused. He zoomed in and in and in until they had a pristine view that offered crystal clarity enough to identify vehicles on the few roads that crisscrossed the desert landscape.

"No signs of illicit digging," he said with satisfaction.

"How often do you check?" Diana asked.

He cleared his throat and said, "Once a week since I first learned Rabi was missing. At first…I was hoping to find him. Later…well, it was all I could do for him. For his legacy. Monitor his life's work. A few colleagues and I have shared this task, but I'm afraid they can't continue." He held Diana's gaze. "If something happens to me, I need someone I trust to watch over this site and several others."

And then she knew what this meeting was really about.

"I'm sure you have a grad student in mind for this. Faridah or Hana?"

"Both would be good choices, but neither of them are currently working for Friday Morning Valkyries."

Diana's stomach dropped. "You know?"

"It was the reason I agreed to work with you."

His words sent her mind spinning. Of course Freya hadn't told her. She was former CIA and had no qualms lying or omitting and twisting the truth. But Morgan? Diana didn't think the woman knew how to lie.

How wrong she'd been.

Did it change anything beyond lessening her fondness for her secret employers? Not really.

She was nothing better or worse than a spy and a liar herself. She could hardly judge others, especially those involved with putting her in this situation.

"You trust me with this information?" she asked.

"I do. The first weeks…those were a test. You passed."

Her throat clogged. That might be the highest praise she'd ever received. He'd probably seen her background check—she'd expect nothing less given what he was trusting her with.

It was nothing, and it was everything. A watcher. Remote, but still, at the first sign of trouble, she could alert…*someone.*

The legacy of a dead man being watched over by a friend and colleague, and passed on to her in the event of the worst happening.

She met Fahd's gaze. "Why now? It's been years since your friend disappeared."

He took in a slow, even breath, his chest rising, inflating his frame. His beard was more gray than brown. The lines of his face were deeply etched into his skin. He'd been aged by decades in the field, but he was still young, in his fifties, a decade or more from retirement.

"The winds are shifting. I need to look outside my local circle."

She was about as far out of his local circle as one could get.

"You will do this for me? If I'm unable?"

She nodded. "I hope I never need to take up the mantle."

"My wife and children share your hope." He paused. "I'm trusting that you and the Friday Morning Valkyries will know the right thing to do. This site must be protected at all costs." He turned to his computer. "We'll start with the coordinates of the five most important sites. You must memorize them. Do not write them down."

She nodded. She was particularly skilled at memorizing. It was her secret weapon.

Chapter Eleven

Unknown region in the desert, Hashemite Kingdom of Jordan
September

On the screen, Diana watched in horror as her friend and colleague was tortured and questioned. Tears spilled down her cheeks as he refused to give up the coordinates to vulnerable sites in Syria and Jordan.

They went with tried and true waterboarding, and Diana found herself holding her breath and suffocating along with the brilliant professor.

It wasn't lost on her that if they knew she had the information they were after, she'd be next. She could know the same agony. She couldn't imagine she wouldn't break immediately.

She felt sick at the idea she might find out very soon exactly what it would take for her to break.

In the end, it wasn't Fahd who broke under torture, it was his tormentor who unintentionally brought the scene to a close. His torturer set aside waterboarding in favor of death by a thousand cuts, and in a strange, horrific way, it gave Fahd the upper hand when he was careless with the knife. Seeing an opportunity, Fahd pressed forward, into the blade, then twisted his body. It was over before the torturer knew what had happened. Fahd had opened the artery in his arm. Blood spewed from the wound and into the face of his killer. Drowning him in much the same way he'd worked to drown Fahd.

Diana sobbed as she watched Dr. Fahd Yousef die. He'd been a good man. A powerful force for archaeology in the region. A brilliant scholar.

And, briefly, a friend.

"When did this happen?" she asked Harun.

Her captor smirked. "After your botched rescue by the Americans."

Was this her fault? Or had they planned to go after Fahd from the start?

"Why show me this?" She could guess, but might as well make him spell it out.

"So you know what awaits you if you don't tell us where to dig."

Where to dig.

She'd known this was coming, but hadn't expected it in this way. They wanted *all* the sites. Open season on the entire history and prehistory of Jordan.

Just Jordan? Or did they believe she knew Syrian site locations too?

She kept her features still and was thankful for the awful lesson of learning to hide her pain for the last eighteen months. "Come across as a cold bitch and fly under the radar" had been her motto since leaving the hospital. It hadn't failed her yet.

She'd known since she was twelve that she was blessed with a particularly cold resting bitch face. It had served her well.

Salim hadn't been put off by it. Fahd had respected it.

Would Harun see through it to the terror that shook her very core?

"Fahd Yousef was a crackpot zealot for a dying cause," she said.

"Yet you cried when he died. Held your breath as he was drowning."

"That's because what you showed me was horrible. You'd have to be inhuman not to react." She pierced him with her stare, her meaning clear.

Harun gave her a feral smile. "I will enjoy breaking you."

She shivered at that. Did he intend to rape her? "Violate my body, and I won't help you."

"You speak as if you have a choice."

The spot on her arm where the tracker was implanted began to itch again. She *did* have a choice. But if she called for a rescue now, it would be a failure. She had no new intel except the death of Dr. Yousef. And his body had probably been found already.

The SEAL team who'd risked everything to rescue her would be none too pleased to be called back two days later with nothing more to show for a successful rescue. And if it wasn't successful…her life was forfeit. There would be no more chances.

She had made her choice and had to see it through.

But to do that, she had to violate the first thing Fahd had asked of her. She had to give up a site. She had to become the thing she despised.

She would take on the role of looter who dug up artifacts to support the Islamic State.

Chapter Twelve

*C*hris paced the small observation deck. The noise of activity on the flight deck below helped to wrap him in a feeling of isolation in this place where the vessel itself was vast, but there was no privacy in outdoor spaces or areas with enough room to burn restless energy with pacing.

The gym was full of sailors and airmen of all ranks. Too public.

It had been a while since he'd done a stint on an aircraft carrier, and the last time had been with the SEAL platoon that included guys he'd served with for years. They'd been close. Some of his best friends in the world. Now two of those men were dead and one was fucking his soon-to-be ex-wife.

He was still friends with a few of them, but they were either at Coronado still serving with the wife fucker or retired.

There was no one here who *knew* him. No one who knew what it meant for him to have a hostage turn on him.

Damn, he'd give anything to be able to call Xavier right now.

But if he did that, if he let *anyone* know he was struggling with this now, he'd be pulled from the op. Pulled from the carrier. Possibly pulled from the teams all together.

Unfit to serve.

That was what Pam had said in their final argument. That he was too fucked in the head to be her husband. To serve his country. It didn't matter to her that he'd done the work with the special forces shrink. She viewed him as broken, and nothing he did could change that.

So she'd found a SEAL who wasn't messed up.

She was wrong. He'd known it then. But what did he know now?

Had he shut down in the wadi? Had he single-handedly blown the op?

Had there been anything he could have done to change the outcome?

And knowing that Diana Edwards seemed to think she could give them intel on the supposedly dead Makram Rafiq, did he still regret the failed rescue?

As far as he could tell, about half the team was pissed at Edwards, and the other half were on board for a shot at Rafiq.

All he knew was he couldn't stop thinking about the woman. He was in awe of her bravery and pissed as hell at her recklessness.

Haunted by her cold control and fearless sacrifice.

"What's going on with you, Flyte?"

Chris turned to see Fallon, eyes hidden behind aviators,

his mouth a flat line. Chris didn't know the man well enough to know if this was his normal greeting, but it didn't mesh with the lieutenant commander he'd gotten to know over the last few weeks.

Could he trust this guy?

Chris was nobody here. Sure, he was a seasoned SEAL with years on the teams, but not *this* team. Not *these* guys. He was best known for two failed ops.

Now three.

In comparison, Fallon had been on Operation Icarus, which, while not a SEAL success, hadn't been a failure either. And Dr. Diana Edwards was associated with Dr. Morgan Adler.

"What's your take on Edwards? Based on what Adler said?"

Fallon gave a short nod, as if Chris had said just the right thing.

He hated these games. The uncertainty of new teammates. These guys were supposed to have his back one hundred percent. But he feared he'd lost their trust and respect because he'd hesitated when it mattered most.

Motherfucker.

He should quit now.

But if he did, what would happen when Edwards triggered her tracker? Would Fallon and the others give it their all? She'd screwed them all over, but she'd only asked one SEAL—Chris himself—to trust her.

And by hesitating, Chris had defaulted to that promise.

He had to trust her.

He had to save her.

"Morgan is a friend," Fallon began. "A real friend, not a Christmas-cards-only kind of connection."

Chris couldn't help but smile. "You send Christmas cards?"

Fallon smirked. "No. But Morgan does. She, her husband, their kid, plus a dog. Disgustingly cute. Not at all what I expected of Master Sergeant Pax Blanchard."

"Her husband's a Green Beret. Part of the Icarus op."

Fallon nodded. "He's out of the Army now. Working for the military in the DC area. I hear Morgan is pregnant with their second child."

"It's September. That Christmas card update isn't due for a few months."

"Exactly. I see them when I'm in the DC area to visit my sister. Pax, Morgan, and I go out for drinks and reminisce about the good old days in Djibouti. Freya Lange and her husband usually join us too.

"I know Freya and Morgan vet their recruits to the artifact protection game very carefully, and if they say Diana Edwards called off her rescue because she knows something about Makram Rafiq, I'm on board. I know some on the team don't buy it, but Freya…she's not exactly the trusting type. It's her word, more than anything, that tells me Edwards is on the level. And she was definitely signaling four of diamonds in a way she expected to be noticed. She knew you had a bodycam. She wasn't talking to you. She was talking to Morgan and Freya."

As much as Chris wanted to be absolved of his role in the fiasco, he couldn't simply nod and believe. Maybe that would come later.

"So what's next?"

"We wait for Edwards to trigger her tracker."

"That could be weeks. Months, even."

"Two months at the outside."

"What if we get pulled to another op?"

"Then we follow orders and go. But when that's done, we return to USS *Dahlgren* and wait for her SOS."

Chapter Thirteen

4

a week passed before a new camp was set up near the site Diana had identified. Again, they were supplied with Bedouin-style goat-hair tents, which helped cut the heat of the day with their cool, dark interiors. Diana wondered how they were acquired and hoped the women who'd made the hair curtains had been compensated for their labor.

They were deep in another twisted, dry ravine system. Only this time, Diana knew exactly where she was, having been the one to reveal the site location to Harun, who'd thankfully left the way station and hadn't been seen again.

She, Jamal, and Bassam began digging on their second day back in the desert. Diana choosing where to start, knowing that the site had to produce artifacts relatively quickly or they would suspect deceit.

It was with both relief and horror that they excavated the first broken vessel made by Nabataean hands two thousand years ago.

She reminded herself this was for a greater good. She

would make sure she was the one to deliver these goods to Rafiq's center of operations. They would need to be properly cleaned and packaged, an indispensable role she would insist only she could fulfill. Then she'd trigger the tracker, and he would again be targeted for capture or kill.

The man was personally responsible for so many deaths. Children in Syria. Entire villages in Afghanistan. There were rumors he was aiming for the United States next. A civilian target like a sporting event or the power grid across the Eastern Seaboard.

Her money was on the power grid, but she based that on nothing other than the man was clearly more wily than previous leaders. He'd successfully staged his own presumed death in a military raid after his men shot down a transport plane carrying a platoon of SEALs.

Rafiq had been high on the most wanted list for nearly a decade, and the general consensus was that he'd been taken out of the game. But Diana had seen him with her own eyes. He was alive and his network was well organized. So much so, they'd managed to keep his survival a secret for nearly two years.

Bassam and Jamal were at the lowest level of the organization. They probably knew nothing about the big boss, but in being her main guards, they hoped to get attention from higher-ups.

She would use that to her advantage. Feed them information. She was their golden ticket. In time, they might even come to trust her.

*T*en days passed before the camp was expanded to the point where they had five crew members who could dig with enough precision to extract artifacts without destroying them.

At that point, Diana ceased digging herself. She was the task master, patrolling the site and jumping in the pits at the first sign of something that wasn't a rock or other natural feature. If this were a real dig, she'd be the principal investigator, but she shunned that title, feeling the shame she deserved. There was no *investigation* going on. This wasn't a data recovery protocol. Sure, she took notes, but she was only given one piece of paper per day, so her notes had to be precise and minimal.

In doling out paper like a miser, Bassam prevented her from spending too much time on paperwork, recording every detail of the site she could as all context was destroyed.

Instead, she was constantly on the move, making sure the workers were careful in their digging. It was the only kind of protection she could give the pieces of history that were being unearthed.

Artifacts were removed along with the dirt that encased them. Here in camp, Diana would gently process what she could, but she left much of the cleaning to be finished later, preferably in Rafiq's center of operations. There, she'd have the proper tools. Running water. Electricity.

This made for shoddy fieldwork—chunking out the artifacts with minimal processing. Plus there were no soil samples taken, nor would radiocarbon or other dating methods be employed. No pollen or other organic chemical analysis to identify the contents of the vessels in antiquity. There was no science happening here at all. The dig was a disgrace of technique and an irreversible loss, but it did produce items to sell.

Each day, Diana woke up with the knowledge she'd betrayed Fahd. She was a traitor to her country and her profession. Fahd would spit on her in the afterlife. Except she'd never cross paths with him in hell because he'd betrayed none of his beliefs in his death.

She was all alone with that sin.

She didn't actually believe in hell, except the one she was living in now had proven the concept was all too real and not reserved for the deceased.

At the end of the long, nightmarish days, she collapsed on her sleeping pallet in exhaustion and tried not to hate herself so much that she wouldn't be able to sleep.

On the evening of her twenty-first day of captivity, Bassam settled beside her as she ate her evening meal.

"Excavation in the north area will be completed tomorrow, or the next day at the latest. Where will you direct the men after that?"

She shrugged. She'd been trying not to think about it. In her mind's eye, she could see the ground-penetrating radar images Fahd had shown her. She'd been doing her best to avoid the areas likely to have the deepest deposits.

The oldest parts of the site.

This site was a small crossroads, but it had been an important one. A watering hole for traders used by Nabataeans and others for hundreds of years.

It had been a small village. An oasis in the desert.

She cleared her throat. She knew where the men would *not* dig. Someday, real archaeologists might come back. Something could be salvaged from this atrocity. "I was thinking we should drop some exploratory holes to the southeast. See if we can find that border of the village."

"I think we should dig to the west," Jamal said, dropping down on her other side. "It would make sense if there were dwellings there, closer to the spring."

Jamal had managed to get ahold of archaeology textbooks and had the irritating habit of actually reading them. He fancied himself a budding archaeologist, and in any other circumstance, she'd have enjoyed teaching a young local the science.

Here, he was her prison guard, and while his interest appeared genuine, his motive remained the same: looting to fund terrorism. There was no joy in him learning how to determine the best places to dig. "No. The southeast is the best place to explore next."

Jamal backhanded her before she had a chance to brace herself. She dropped her plate and cupped her cheek, then she squared her shoulders and faced down the young man. *Boy*, she corrected herself. "I'm the expert here."

Jamal raised his hand again, but Bassam caught his arm. "No, brother. She hasn't led us wrong so far."

Jamal glared at her, then shook off his brother's grip and stomped off to enter the "lab" tent.

Bassam frowned at her. "You shouldn't speak like that to him when the workers are watching."

"He shouldn't speak like that to me, then, when your workers are watching." She debated whether or not she should show contrition, but decided against it. She wouldn't win over her captors by pretending to be meek. Even as she quivered inside, she needed to show only anger and strength.

◈

On day twenty-eight of her captivity, the break she'd been waiting for finally came. An envoy of the boss arrived on camels. To her great relief, the man sent to check on the dig was not Harun.

She was forced to give the man a tour as if he were a visiting dignitary. The experience was a distorted reflection of her life before abduction, when scholars and government VIPs would visit the excavation she ran with Fahd, and they'd show the features that had been uncovered and then discuss in detail what it could all mean to the history of the region.

The stockpile of artifacts that had been excavated were photographed, and Diana explained the packing materials that would be needed to transport them. She stressed that only she could pack and unpack the artifacts or they were likely to be damaged and rendered worthless. After all, the items would have to be transported in a small wheelbarrow or sled over a kilometer just to get through the slot canyon to the road.

The words left her dry mouth and scraped her throat as if she'd been drinking sand. But she did it. This was the reason she'd overseen the gutting of this site. She'd see it through and deliver pieces of history to the monster himself.

After she made her plea for careful packing and transport, the man studied her. "Why do you care? You support our cause now?"

She gave a sharp shake of her head. "I find your cause vile. I care for the survival of the artifacts, which are irreplaceable."

The words were true, which made the plea easy to say convincingly. Honestly, it was better the artifacts end up in a corrupt man's personal collection than that they be destroyed. At least in a private collection, they might someday be recovered and returned to the people of Jordan. But once an artifact was destroyed, it, and the information it could yet yield, was gone forever.

4

Five days later, a cargo van arrived with packing materials, which had to be hauled in small batches through the slot canyon to the dig site. Once she had the bubble wrap and other items she needed, Diana set to work packing the dozens of artifacts they'd managed to remove from the earth.

Jamal and Bassam insisted she teach them how to pack the artifacts as well, much as they'd wanted to learn not just how to dig, but where and why each location was selected. The brothers were her constant shadow. They followed her around the field—monitoring her every interaction with the workers—and shared her tent at night.

She knew the other men believed the brothers had sex with her, whether forced or not, but thankfully, that was one line they did not cross, and it was due to the fact that Bassam and Jamal watched over her that the workers didn't attempt to harm her in that way.

She'd told the brothers at the start that she wouldn't assist with the dig at all if she was sexually assaulted. She counted on Bassam to keep his brother in line, and so far, he had.

At this point, both boys were more interested in her lifting their status within the cell by delivering valuable artifacts to Rafiq, and so they acted as both her prison guards and protectors.

In the thirty-three days they'd spent together, an ease had developed between them. It wasn't camaraderie. That would never happen. But there was a twisted kind of trust.

Once upon a time, she'd passed the intensive background check and prepared to join a CIA training class at the Farm. She'd been conflicted—mixing spying and archaeology could put professional archaeologists the world over in danger— but professional archaeologists were already in danger, and artifacts were being used to fund terror. She had the skills and the drive. She'd agreed to join the training class and began a physical training program to prepare.

She was excited for the opportunity and had mixed support from her fiancé, Salim, who agreed with the cause but, as the time drew near for her to go to the Farm, grew increasingly uncomfortable with the idea. His parents were immigrants from Lebanon. The Middle East was his heritage.

But then Salim lost control of their car on a rainy, unfamiliar mountain road, and she'd lost her fiancé and opportunity to work for the CIA all at once.

Now here she was, digging in Jordan without Salim and not working for the CIA, but somehow, she had become both a prisoner and a spy.

She looked at Jamal and Bassam and reminded herself that they were neither enemies nor friends. They were a means to an end. She needed to think of them as assets.

⬥

That night, she slipped from the tent to use the latrine they'd set up. The brothers no longer bothered to tie her up at night. It was ridiculous when an escape attempt would mean certain death by dehydration.

After taking care of business, she sat down in the center of the archaeological site and stared up at the stars. It was a cool sixty-five degrees Fahrenheit, the temperature welcome after it had neared ninety at noon that day. They were still weeks from the start of rainy season, and there wasn't a cloud to be seen. The waning crescent moon hadn't risen yet, and without any light pollution, the sky was packed with stars, the most she'd ever seen at any time or place in her life. Over the last weeks, she'd built up a tolerance to this beauty.

But then, it was hard to find beauty in this situation, in which the things she cared most about were being desecrated.

Now she tried to clear her mind and take in this moment. It might be her last moment of feeling any kind of pleasure in this life. It was hard to believe her rescue would be successful. Rafiq might kill her the moment she delivered the artifacts.

The Milky Way was a bright swath, and she thought about the SEAL she'd faced as she signaled with her hand. Had he understood? Did he deliver her message?

His eyes had flashed with hostility. As if *she* was the threat.

But then, wasn't she? Her refusal to cooperate could have gotten him killed.

He could have taken out Bassam and Jamal if not for her.

She should have let him.

Would Fahd be alive now? Had he been tortured because Diana was still a captive, or would they have gone after him anyway once the site they'd planned to loot had been exposed and their camp taken over?

Or had they lied about the timing of Fahd's murder from the start? Perhaps he'd been killed in the days before she'd been taken?

She told herself to stop with the painful questions and instead take in the beauty of the stars. She might never know a moment of peace again after this.

Again, the SEAL came to mind. What did he think of that night? Did he hate her?

If she survived this somehow, she didn't think she'd ever be able to see a photo or video of a man in combat uniform without feeling a surge of thanks mixed with regret.

She focused on the thanks part now as she stared up at a billion shining stars in the night sky. She didn't let herself think of Salim, not when she was trying to find a moment of happiness in this bleak situation, so instead, she focused on the SEAL, her imposing rescuer.

All she'd seen of him were his eyes and cheekbones. The bridge of his nose. Dark skin. Brown eyes.

A knight in shining body armor.

What would it be like to lie under this starry sky and hold hands with a man like that? Strong, bold, confident.

She remembered how he'd said her name, his voice firm, engaging. As if he knew her.

It was the last time anyone had used her first name. The last time anyone had seen her for the person she was and not just a means to an end. A tool to manipulate.

A woman to control.

She placed her hand flat on the sandy ground, burrowing her fingers into the still-warm grains, and imagined the comfort of a hand to hold. Someone with whom to share this magnificent sky.

If she got a second chance at rescue, a second chance at life, she'd embrace it and do everything she could to aid her rescuers.

She wouldn't make him—or whoever was sent after her next time—regret trying to save her.

Chapter Fourteen

Four days after the packing materials were delivered, a cargo van was sent to the site access point. As she directed the loading of the boxes, Diana feared her plan to personally deliver them to Rafiq would be nixed. She again pointed out she was needed to clean them. Write up her appraisal.

Make sure they got top dollar.

While all this was true, in the end, she figured it was Bassam's and Jamal's eagerness to move up in the organization by making themselves useful in the terrorist leader's lair that made the difference.

The three of them would travel with the artifacts, and when they reached their destination, they would be put to work prepping the artifacts for sale.

Once the van was packed, they abandoned the site and set out, passengers in the back of the cargo van. She guessed Jamal and Bassam planned to return to the site to continue the excavation at some point given that the tents, workers, and equipment remained.

For herself, Diana had no intention of returning.

She was blindfolded for the lengthy drive. They made no stops at gas stations. Instead, they stopped and refueled with gas cans that had been strapped to the roof. She estimated they drove for eight hours, but time was hard to estimate without light cues. They were likely avoiding main roads or even actual roads, which meant they could be anywhere.

They hadn't made an official border crossing, but for all she knew, they could have slipped over the border into Saudi Arabia, Iraq, or Syria with bribes paid in advance or in an unmonitored section of desert.

She was alerted to their arrival when she heard clipped shouts for a gate to be unlocked so the van could enter the compound.

The sound of iron slamming closed behind the vehicle had an ominous ring.

This was it. If this was Rafiq's base, all she needed to do now was initiate the tracker once she was certain there was cellular service or a working satellite phone powered on.

The rear cargo van doors were yanked open, and she was pulled from the vehicle. She'd only been permitted one bathroom break during a refueling stop, but they hadn't allowed her much in the way of water, so her throat was more parched than her bladder full, but she still made a bathroom request. She needed a moment of privacy to collect herself.

The blindfold was removed, and she learned it was deep dark night. Not as dark as when she'd stargazed a few nights ago, because here there was the glow of light pollution, letting her know the house was in a populated area.

Still, having seen the position of the constellations in each of the last several nights, she knew it must be past two in the morning.

She scanned the dark grounds, seeing the shapes of outbuildings in addition to a large house. From what she could see, the compound was somewhere in the middle of the pristine to dilapidated spectrum.

It was a far cry from the way station where they'd kept her as the dig site was prepared. It had gates and a high stone wall. Electric lights. Plumbing too, probably.

Plus there were guards who manned the gate, even in the wee hours of the night.

This had to be Makram Rafiq's lair.

*A*s she was led through a side door and into the main structure, Diana was reminded of Osama bin Laden's compound in Abbottabad, Pakistan. It appeared Makram Rafiq had taken a page from the dead al Qaeda leader's book and had been hiding in a populated town in a country with infrastructure and not in a cave in Afghanistan, or as had been speculated in the months before Rafiq's not quite death, a bombed ruin in Syria.

"I must oversee the artifacts' removal from the van," she said to Jamal.

He turned a sharp glare on her, raising a hand to strike her face. Bassam caught his arm. "Save it. No one but me heard her speak to you that way." To Diana, he said, "Do not show disrespect to my brother or me, or you will get more than a slap."

He was right. She couldn't make them look weak in front of the rest of their group. If anyone witnessed a hint of lax behavior toward her, all three of them would be lost.

The only reason she'd been able to control them in the field was due to their age. She'd learned at one point that Jamal wasn't yet sixteen and Bassam barely seventeen. They'd been eager enough to use Diana to gain status, and in general, they'd let her run the show. But this was different. They were nobodies here.

She should behave as if she feared them.

She was led to a bathroom and given a moment of privacy. There was no mirror in the room for her to check her appearance, not that she cared how she looked, but she knew a wisp of hair peeking out from her headscarf could trigger a rebuke and even a punishment from the men inside this compound.

She patted her hairline and straightened the garment as best she could, then stepped back into the corridor. Bassam berated her for being slow, while Jamal used rope to bind her wrists in front of her body. Another man found them and barked an order for the two boys to unload the van. This man would be the one to take her to see the top dog.

He led her down a corridor and up a flight of stairs, then she found herself in the same room with the Four of Diamonds once again.

She entered the room to find Rafiq sitting with his back

to her. He spoke to her in Arabic. "I am told your dig was successful."

She squared her shoulders and took a deep breath. She needed to play a role here. If he guessed at her motives, she was dead. Literally. "Every item pulled from the ground was a failure to me."

Still with his back to her, he said, "That is not my concern." He turned, and in the full light, she could see a new scar on his face in addition to the one she'd spotted to identify him back when she was in the tent thirty-eight days ago.

She wondered if he'd been wounded in the attack that everyone believed had killed him.

Makram Rafiq was in his late fifties, although he looked older. He'd risen through the ranks of various terrorist groups since the Arab Spring. He was one of the hydra heads that had popped up with the removal of their previous leader several years ago.

Rafiq was a chameleon, and it had taken at least two years for intelligence agents to identify him. He was responsible for the deaths of dozens—possibly hundreds—of civilian children on at least three continents. His favorite method of spreading terror was attacking schools. Girls were abducted, raped, and enslaved. Boys were forced to join his army. Their choice was simple and horrific: become like the men who took them, or die.

She didn't know if Jamal and Bassam had come to this organization via abduction, or if it was a path they chose willingly. Either way, she couldn't let it get in her head. They were her jailers, and even if they'd been pressed into service for the monster who stood before her, they still followed his orders and would rape and/or kill Diana if so instructed.

The reason Makram Rafiq had ended up in Freya and Morgan's deck of cards, though, was because Rafiq had come to power and built his terrorist organization with the blood of archaeologists and by trafficking artifacts.

There were rumors that the man had once worked for a museum or he'd been an historian of some sort in Syria, but no one in the cultural protection community outside the war-torn country had been able to confirm it.

Of course, they'd stopped looking when he'd supposedly died.

What had been confirmed was that his rise to power had followed an influx of antiquities being sold instead of destroyed. He'd already been wanted by the FBI and Interpol and most other major police forces when he'd orchestrated a strike on a military transport flight carrying a platoon of SEALs along with other US Navy personnel. He then became a major target, and there'd been much celebration in the military community when it was announced he'd been killed in a strike.

Freya'd had her doubts about the reports of the man's death, so she kept him in the deck of cards, and now here was Diana, facing Rafiq down across his home office desk.

"You must let me unpack the artifacts and complete the conservation efforts I began in the field. Your men will break them or damage them in the cleaning process and make them worthless."

"Anyone who works for me who breaks an artifact will

lose a hand. Break two and they lose a foot. Break three and…what is the term in American? Three strikes and out."

"Why risk losing men and artifacts when I can do it?"

The man gave her a cold smile. He had to know she was trying to make herself indispensable. He then frowned and reached into his pocket and pulled out a cell phone. She saw the screen light up. A call coming in.

He stared at the screen, then said, "Fine. You have two days to clean them so they can be inspected and photographed then wrapped again for shipment." He dismissed her as he answered the phone.

She had what she needed: Rafiq's location, knowledge she'd be here for days, and confirmation of an active cell signal.

Her hands remained bound, but she was able to twist her wrists so her right hand could reach the spot on her left arm where the tracker had been embedded.

She needed to rub the spot for several seconds. It could be triggered with a hard press that lasted ten seconds or longer too. She did both.

Once activated, there was no turning it off. The SOS would go out with her location, which would be snagged from the cell or satellite phone signal the tracker had jumped on.

As before, her rescue would probably come in the wee hours of the night, but unlike before, this time, she'd know they were coming. She'd be ready.

Chapter Fifteen

The team assembled in the conference room, but this time, Chris could tell something had changed after thirty-eight days of waiting. There was a buzz of excitement as no less than the carrier group's commanding admiral entered the room.

Without preamble, the captain at the head of the table immediately stood and pointed to the large monitor, which showed a satellite image of a cluster of residences on the outskirts of Aqaba.

"Dr. Diana Edwards initiated her subdermal tracker at three forty-one this morning."

Chris's heart pounded in a way it shouldn't. This was just a mission.

Right. Like she hadn't been two millimeters from his conscious thought every minute of every day since she mouthed those words.

Half the time, he wrote her off as dead. The other half,

he just considered she *might* be dead. Now she was resurrected. Alive.

And then his brain nearly exploded with the implication, voiced by someone else at the table who was faster on the uptake. "Do we know if Rafiq is at her location?"

A glance at the digital clock on the monitor's upper right corner showed it had been two and a half hours since Edwards had sent her call for rescue.

"We were only able to get clear satellite images of the dwelling where she's being held in the last forty minutes. Right now, there is no movement on the property, no way to confirm either Dr. Edwards's presence or Makram Rafiq's."

"But we know Edwards *is* there, because the tracker is still transmitting?"

The captain nodded. "We'd like to get a visual on Rafiq before making our move. We will have drones in the area within the hour and a team of intelligence officers on the ground by nightfall."

"We aren't going in tonight?" Fallon asked. "We've got nearly twenty hours to prepare and get into position."

"We'll make a move if we find evidence Edwards is in imminent danger, but we feel waiting gives us the highest chance of a favorable outcome. It would be one thing if the location were remote, as it was last time, but this is a house in a neighborhood on the outskirts of Aqaba. If Rafiq is there, we need to approach with extra caution. This is likely to be our only shot."

Chris understood. It was the right plan. The only plan, really. Rafiq was too big a target. But it also meant more time in captivity for Dr. Edwards. Anything could happen.

Hell, she could be dead before lunchtime if Rafiq was done with her.

Did she have any clue what she'd been signing up for when she sabotaged her rescue nearly six weeks ago?

4

*S*leep was always difficult for Diana, but trying to rest in Rafiq's base of operations was next-level impossible. She should be dead on her feet after a long night of driving and then the tense meeting with Rafiq. She'd then helped unload the truck, carefully placing the boxes of artifacts in an empty room that had been designated her conservation laboratory.

She'd labored all day, unpacking artifacts and cleaning off the remaining layers of dirt once Rafiq had acquired the proper tools for the delicate work. She guessed they were near a city. It had only taken a few hours for the supplies to be purchased after she gave a henchman the shopping list.

After a dinner of rice and mutton, she was finally permitted to stretch out on a pallet and sleep for the first time since she'd dozed on the hot, endless ride that had lasted until the early hours of this morning.

Once she lay down, however, she'd felt like a kid on Christmas Eve, in spite of the fact that she feared the moment bullets and grenades would start flying.

She'd seen the movie *Zero Dark Thirty* several times. The re-creation of the raid on Osama bin Laden's residence in Pakistan was seared in her brain.

But that had been a raid, not a rescue. There were

different rules of engagement. Even knowing they'd be careful, there would be cross fire. And she'd screwed up her rescue once, so they might be leery of what she'd do this time.

Still, this was different. She'd signaled for them. Surely they'd get it that she wanted to be rescued now. Of course, it all depended on them figuring out the Four of Diamonds clue. What if Morgan and Freya hadn't seen the video?

There were so many potential pitfalls. She'd spent the last six weeks focused on what she needed to do and refusing to consider the worst-case scenarios.

Now all those worst cases came crashing down.

So here she was, giddy with excitement and frozen with fear. She was the Diana she'd been the day Salim had proposed, and also the Diana who'd been trapped in a car with a mangled ankle and bleeding-out fiancé.

She closed her eyes and listened to the even breathing of Bassam, who slept in front of the door.

She was not permitted to move unescorted through this house. This was a prison in a way being stranded in the desert was not.

Now her hands were tied and one of her guards blocked the doorway.

Any SEAL attempting a rescue would have to go through Bassam to get to her. This time, she wouldn't let Bassam have the upper hand. His knife wouldn't get near her neck. She'd trained with Morgan. Knowing the fight was coming, she'd stop Bassam's attack at the first sign of commotion in the corridor.

She practiced what she'd do in her mind. Her body

coiled with tension as she waited for even the softest of footsteps.

When dawn lit the sky, she felt warm, silent tears sliding down her cheek.

Had she somehow missed it? Had they come like Santa, stealthy and silent, but then didn't find her and left?

Impossible.

She hadn't slept for even a minute. She hadn't missed a telltale sound. If they'd been here, she'd *know*.

And they'd have searched every room for her.

Was it possible the tracker hadn't worked? Had the battery died?

Or had the US military decided she wasn't worth saving? Why save a woman who rejected their first rescue?

She rubbed the spot on her arm once again. Maybe she'd missed the tracker's location yesterday. Maybe it was just now going off.

But deep down, she knew that there were only two options, both of them bad.

Either the tracker had failed or the SEALs weren't coming. She'd destroyed an archaeological site and given up information a great man had died to protect.

All for nothing.

Her work would fund terrorism, and more children would die.

Chapter Sixteen

The metallic taste of fear sat in the back of Diana's throat as she carefully unpacked the artifacts, cleaned them, then set them on a table to display for a monster's inspection and approval.

She swiped at tears as she worked, her inability to stop them telling her that after six weeks of captivity, six weeks of doing the unthinkable, she'd finally broken.

She could not stop crying.

These weren't the gut-wrenching sobs of grief that had consumed her after waking in the hospital knowing Salim was gone. No. These were the slow trickle of tears of lost hope, of knowing she'd broken Fahd's trust for nothing.

She would die here, possibly—probably—today.

Bassam and Jamal worked alongside her. Jamal gave her curious looks. The unending tears were impossible to miss.

Her thoughts on the brothers had swayed back and forth over the last weeks. Bassam wasn't necessarily kinder than his brother, but he understood the system better. He was willing to play the brute in front of others, but when it was just the three of them, he knew Diana would work better if she didn't live in constant fear.

Jamal was harder and colder when compared to his older brother. While she'd come to believe both brothers had been conscripted by Rafiq's terrorist troops, Jamal was the one who might have chosen to join without being forced.

His shrewd brain likely wondered at her tears, not with sympathy, but because he recognized she'd broken and wanted to identify what had been the tipping point.

Thankfully, he asked no questions. She told him no lies.

The label on the box she was about to open indicated it contained cobalt-blue glass ingots.

This had been a particularly exciting find, as it was extremely rare to find whole glass ingots in the ground. In antiquity, glass ingots were used as a transport method for the glass trade. The glass, once traded, was then used for other purposes, much the same as metal ingots. Some ingots were themselves money, as with gold, but often, it was just a way to move the raw material, a basic trade good. So when a glass ingot reached its destination, it was melted and made into a new glass object.

The oldest intact glass ingots ever found by archaeologists dated to the late 14th century BCE. They were among the cargo of the Late Bronze Age *Uluburun* shipwreck, an underwater archaeological site in the Mediterranean Sea near the Turkish shoreline. The only reason the ingots had been recovered intact from that site was because the ship sank before the trade goods could be delivered.

Finding intact glass ingots in the Jordanian desert was potentially the first find of its kind.

Whenever she held artifacts—be they tools, objects of art, or raw trade materials—she thought of the person in antiquity whose hands had created it. The artistic vision or the skills they brought to the piece. She considered the person who bought it and thought of their hands touching the piece, using the tool, or the plan to turn the raw material into something else. Each item went through a chain of hands like hers until they were lost to time.

These ingots had a short chain, or they'd be something else entirely. A mosaic, perhaps. A window. A glass vessel.

She closed her eyes and practically swayed on her feet, her exhaustion was so great, as she wondered at the last human hands to have touched this ingot. How had it been lost before it could be used?

She held the cold glass, which was roughly the size and shape of an eight-inch round cake pan. This was the largest of the four intact ingots they'd found.

How many guns will Rafiq be able to buy with this artifact?

She held it up to the light, looking for cracks or variations in the color.

How many bombs?

The cortex was grainy and the glass opaque.

How many trucks to haul children away from their schools so he can enslave girls and conscript boys?

She would never know if she did it on purpose or not. The act went against everything she believed, but still, it happened. The ingot slipped from her fingers and shattered on the stone floor.

She gasped as it happened, her shock genuine. Bassam and Jamal both cursed. Their faces reflected her own horror.

They all looked to the open door to the hall, and she knew the men were braced for someone to step in and see the destruction.

She had no doubt Rafiq would deliver on his promise to cut off her hand. Perhaps all three of them would suffer that fate. Bassam and Jamal would certainly be beaten.

From the moment the ingot had been extracted from the site, it had belonged to Rafiq, and one did not destroy his property without consequences.

Diana's tears dried up. Fear, it appeared, had quashed her ability to cry.

Glances passed between the two brothers. Jamal flicked his head toward the door, and Bassam, the closest to it, silently pushed it closed.

Without a word, they all began collecting the broken pieces. The largest remaining piece was a third the original size. They couldn't pass it off as all that had been recovered from the field because the break was fresh. No patina. It looked like a blue obsidian artifact, with its bulb of percussion and smooth waves. That grainy cortex on one side.

"We can't salvage any of it," she whispered. "I'll change the count on the inventory."

Both boys nodded.

They gathered all the small, sharp pieces and placed them in an artifact box until they could figure out how to dispose of them. The boxes were numbered on the inventory sheet, and they didn't have extra. Nor did they have a broom. They would need to figure out how to get the shards out of the room without anyone noticing. It wasn't as if they could just toss them in a garbage can.

She stared at the pile of shards, her breathing shallow as she took in the volume. The garment—a dark abaya—she'd been given to wear had no pockets, and Jamal and Bassam couldn't fit a sharp, shattered eight-inch cake into theirs.

Then she remembered the cell phone pocket in her headscarf.

The glass edges were sharp, just like obsidian blades. Little knives.

Weapons.

Jamal cut himself and cursed. Both their attention was on Jamal's bleeding hand. With their focus elsewhere, Diana took a chance and palmed a larger, sharp piece, then brushed at her forehead to wipe away the very real sweat that had appeared the moment the tears stopped flowing.

Still, she dabbed at her cheeks as if the tears might be a problem and hoped neither Jamal or Bassam were paying attention as she slipped the glass blade into the headscarf's hidden pocket.

Did her two guards even know the pocket was there? The man who'd taken her phone from her on that first day had known, but Jamal and Bassam hadn't been there, and they were young and might not know the ways of modern women's headscarves.

She thought about palming another piece, but decided not to risk it.

They swept the floor with small brushes they'd used to clean the artifacts. The smallest of the debris was whisked under a woven rug.

Diana placed a layer of padding over the shards inside the box. The boys agreed to take turns removing them, one pocketful at a time.

After changing the number of ingots on the inventory sheet, Diana resumed her task of unpacking and cleaning, while the brothers took a series of breaks.

It was a shame they no longer had the pit toilets they'd required in the field camp. Flushing toilets wouldn't work for disposing of chunks of glass, but once they left the room, artifact disposal was their problem, not hers. She would claim to know nothing about the brothers' theft or destruction of the artifact.

Bassam returned after one such trip smelling of cigarettes, and she guessed he'd dropped some of the glass in the garden. He gave Diana a hard look, and she resumed her job of unpacking boxes and checking them off in the field catalog.

❖

*S*heer exhaustion having finally caught up with her, Diana managed to sleep fitfully that night. She woke often. Each time she listened for rescue, but all she heard was the sound of Jamal's even breathing as he blocked the door.

The glass shard remained in the pocket of her headscarf.

It was her new hope.

Her only hope.

Once the tears had stopped flowing, she'd been able to think again. If the SEALs weren't coming, she'd rescue herself. She had valuable intel. She'd find a way out of this house. She'd escape and bring what she knew to the CIA or DIA. If she could get to an embassy or consulate, she'd deliver news of Makram Rafiq's operation directly to the US Department of State.

She would probably die before all this was over, but she wouldn't die *here*.

Chapter Seventeen

The early morning briefing promised to be more of the same. In the two days since Diana Edwards had initiated the tracker, there hadn't been a glimpse of the woman or the terrorist leader. Now the signal was long dead.

Was Diana as dead as the signal? Had they failed her by not moving in immediately?

"As previously noted," the analyst who was giving the morning update said, "this isn't a single or even multifamily residence. We've counted at least a dozen armed men coming and going, with at least eight who appear to be living there."

She tapped the mouse, and another image appeared. "In contrast, we've identified two women—wives, housekeepers, or both, we don't know—but no children or anything else to indicate this is a family and not a militant group using the property." She cleared her throat and added, "Yesterday afternoon, our drone captured this recording."

The high-resolution video showed a man leaving the residence by a side door and crossing to what looked like a dry fountain or other decoration of some sort. He wore a rifle slung over one shoulder. The man glanced around, then pulled something from a pocket and dropped it. He kicked at the ground as he took a drag from a cigarette.

The analyst zoomed in on the fountain. The image pixelated, but it looked like a rock garden of sorts.

"He was hiding something in the rocks?" Chris asked.

"We think so," the analyst said. "It could be nothing, but it was unusual compared to the other outside activity we've been able to capture."

The man appeared to stay in the garden long enough to finish the cigarette, then returned to the main house. The analyst clicked again, and now they had a different angle on the same man.

She zoomed in on his face, and Chris took in a strangled breath. "It's him," he said, the words coming out almost unconsciously.

"Yes, Lieutenant Flyte, we agree," the analyst said.

Now another image appeared side by side with the zoomed-in face, this one taken from Chris's bodycam the night of the raid. There was Edwards, her eyes strangely calm as her fingers were frozen in the position that indicated the word *diamond*. There was a knife at her throat. The face of the man who held the knife was clearly visible to the right of Diana's head.

Side by side, it was unmistakable. The terrorist who had escaped with Edwards that night was alive and well and at the house on the outskirts of Aqaba.

"We don't have confirmation Edwards is still being held

there, but this is enough to make the mission a go if we can confirm Rafiq is present."

"What if we don't have a Rafiq sighting?" Fallon asked. "Surely we won't just leave Edwards there?"

"We are monitoring the house closely. If they try to move her, we'll know, and our drones will be able to follow."

"Not good enough. They could be beating her. She could be sick. Dying. We have no way of knowing what they're doing to her," Chris said.

"We're looking at options for getting someone inside the house. A break in the water line or other utility issue that can be specific to that property."

"That takes too much time," Kramer said.

"We're doing everything we can to ensure Dr. Edwards's safety."

Chris refrained from rolling his eyes. *Everything* would have meant getting the woman out two days ago, instead of leaving her vulnerable and afraid.

✦

*R*afiq entered the artifact room after the morning prayers. The artifacts had all been cleaned and laid out on the tables for inspection. Diana had drawn out the process as long as possible, insisting on organizing the items by age and, in some instances, cultural influence.

All items having come from the same site, she had chosen to split hairs and make an evaluation of what outside cultures had influenced the creator. Anything and everything to delay, delay, delay.

She was shoveling bullshit and hoped to bury the man in it.

She'd written extensive notes that made her work sound ridiculously scholarly. It would give the artifacts a perceived higher value, which should please the monster.

The shard of glass remained hidden in her headscarf, and when the terrorist leader entered the room, Diana could feel the weight of it as it pressed to her skin, similar to how her arm had itched in those first days. Only this time, instead of calling for her rescue, she imagined slicing open the man's neck.

Could she do it? Kill him in that way? She'd have to be directly in his face. Hands on him. Go for the jugular. Literally.

She reminded herself of the lives he'd destroyed. Of Fahd and his children, who were now fatherless.

Yes. Yes, she could.

She was dead anyway at this point. Might as well take him out too.

That would be her redemption in this nightmare. She'd kill this man.

But with Jamal and Bassam in the room, it simply wasn't possible. Not today.

All she could do now was tell him about all the amazing artifacts she'd looted for him and, like Scheherazade, weave a fanciful fiction about each one in an attempt to prolong her life.

Her throat went dry and she had to fight dry heaving, but after the first few descriptions were behind her, her stomach righted and calm settled in.

This was like eating an elephant. The only way to do it was to take one awful bite at a time.

At the end of show-and-tell, Rafiq ordered her to photograph and wrap all the artifacts.

Diana found herself with a camera in her hands. She'd had a brief moment of hope that she'd be given a cell phone, but no, it was a point-and-shoot digital camera. Not the latest and greatest, but still, new enough that it had Wi-Fi for uploading photos.

The blue icon wasn't lit, meaning it wasn't connected, but there was a menu to add email addresses for sending photos. She took a chance when Bassam left for a smoke break and Jamal wasn't paying attention and added an old email address she only used for mailing lists. Once that was set up, she attached all the photos she'd taken. If the camera was connected to a computer with internet or connected to Wi-Fi, maybe it would send the photos before anyone noticed there were items in the outbox.

If someone spotted what she'd done before it connected, they'd come after her, but at this point, she was already in danger of being beaten, raped, and murdered. She might as well take every opportunity that presented itself, no matter how dangerous.

4

Two hours later, Diana got to enjoy her first walk in the garden, a reward for finishing her work, she supposed. A high wall—probably seven feet tall—enclosed the property. Made of smooth cinder blocks, there was no way she'd be able to climb it without a rope or ladder.

To make matters worse, the trees and shrubs that abutted the wall were small and sparse. She wouldn't even be able to tuck down and hide. In addition, the outbuildings were too far from the wall to be of use. Rafiq had chosen his lair well.

Then there was the question of what she'd find on the other side, should she manage to scale the unscalable. She imagined a moat full of crocodiles or a river of lava, thinking of the childhood game of jumping from pillow to pillow in the living room because touching the floor meant maiming or death.

Why did children play such gruesome games?

Of course, Ring Around the Rosie was about the Black Death and that was a game played in preschool and kindergarten without fail.

Surely the other side of the wall was quicksand. At least that would be more plausible in this sand-filled corner of the globe. She should have paid more attention to the perils of quicksand in second grade. She circled the yard, allowed to walk by herself as long as she stayed in Bassam's line of sight.

She was glad for this, as she hadn't been alone except for the bathroom since they got here. During the dig, she'd always been within sight of one of her guards, but the range of area she had to explore had been four times the size of this yard. At least she'd been able to get distance and take deep breaths of air that wasn't tainted by cigarette smoke. And at night, there were those few times she'd been able to lie under the stars all by herself and try to find a moment of joy to hold on to.

She'd thought of the SEAL and rescue and hope. But that was all behind her now. The only hope she still had came from what she might do to save herself.

No handsome, powerful SEAL would ride in on a white horse at this late date.

She'd left joy in the remote Jordanian desert. She'd felt nothing but tension and despair since arriving here. This compound was full of men with guns who eyed her in ways that made her thankful Jamal or Bassam slept in front of the door.

Not that either boy could stop one of the others if they decided she was fair game. She suspected Rafiq had given orders to leave her alone until she no longer had value to add to the organization.

So now she breathed cigarette-smoke-tinged air and leisurely walked around the enclosed compound, feeling the eyes of armed men mark her every step. She focused on the grounds and tried to forget the guards. While there was no doubt the property had once been a fine estate, everything about it now was worn down. Dilapidated. The paint on the enclosing wall and buildings was chipped. Metal hinges showed rust, while wood panels decayed.

She circled around the house, checking over her shoulder for Bassam, noting one of the unnamed guards had joined him for a smoke. Bassam's gaze was on her, but he didn't appear to be paying close attention. She imagined he basked in the attention of the older guard.

Bassam wanted to move up in the ranks. To be important

to this group. From his bearing, she knew he was pleased to be considered one of the men. No longer a boy now that he was doing important work for the leader.

She had helped him attain that status, but she could also take it away.

She forced herself not to alter her stride when she noticed the wrought iron gate that crossed the driveway was open slightly. Just enough for a person to slip through.

The gap was explained by a bicycle that leaned against a post just beyond the metal bars.

From where Bassam stood, could he see the gate was open? She hadn't spotted the gap when she first turned the corner, the angle being such that it wasn't obvious.

Whose bike was it, and why were they here?

Diana didn't have a moment to think or plan. It was an opportunity that no one could have predicted. She stood a mere ten feet from the open gate. Bassam and the other guard were more than ten yards away. They were smoking and laughing. Careless of their prisoner, who'd been mostly meek and pliable for six long weeks.

The person who owned the bike could be at the door, on the path, or inside the house. She didn't dare look.

Instead, she ran.

Chapter Eighteen

The team was on the outskirts of Aqaba, ready to move in on a moment's notice. Still, when the signal came, it was a shock. Even more so when the commander explained why.

"What do you mean she just ran out, grabbed a bicycle, and escaped?"

"Exactly that. It appears Dr. Edwards saw an opening and took it."

From the commander's tone, he sounded annoyed that Edwards had mucked up their plans for a tidy rescue, which, Chris had to admit, would be a problem as now they'd have to find her in the city, or worse, if she was captured again, she'd be harder to get to in the compound. If they even bothered to take her alive.

But still, Chris was impressed the woman had made such a bold move. She must have believed special forces wasn't coming to her rescue.

"We'll break into four Fire Teams to search for Edwards," Fallon said.

"We need to send a Squad to the house. If Rafiq is there, this is our only chance to get him," Chris said.

Kramer agreed. "If Edwards isn't recaptured quickly, Rafiq will bolt knowing his location has been compromised."

Fallon gave a sharp nod. "I'll lead a Squad to raid the house. Without Edwards there, it's a capture-or-kill mission."

They all knew Rafiq was the primary. The rules of engagement—ROE—had been spelled out in the briefing room. Given that daytime raids were far more dangerous than night ops, it was better that they wouldn't be dealing with a hostage situation.

Chris signaled to the seven men on his Squad. "Let's go find Edwards."

⬦

*I*t would help if Diana had a clue where she was. Or maybe it wouldn't matter at all because it wasn't like she had any sense of direction other than to get away from the house. She pedaled so hard, her lungs ached and legs burned. Her injured ankle screamed at her to stop, but she couldn't let up.

She twisted her way through a neighborhood of ramshackle houses, hoping that her pursuers wouldn't know which route she'd taken. The upkeep on the houses improved, and she found herself on the edge of a quiet business district. It was early evening—after hours, certainly—

but she wondered what day of the week it was. Was everything closed because it was a weekend?

She darted into a narrow alley between two short buildings, the opening plenty wide enough for the bicycle, but too narrow for all but the smallest of cars.

After several twists and turns, the buildings got taller and the alleys slightly wider, but more debris filled the space, forcing her to dodge traps as she wove through tight spaces.

Then her luck ran out.

She pitched over the handlebars and slammed into the ground. If not for the full head-to-toe covering she'd been required to wear, she'd have road rash in addition to the usual cuts and bruises.

As it was, her right sleeve was torn and there were cuts on her arm. She imagined she was in a great deal of pain, but adrenaline masked it. She got to her feet and nearly collapsed. She didn't know if her legs were done after the intense pedaling, if they'd been injured in the fall, or if her ankle had simply given up. Perhaps it had shattered again, the pins now rattling with her fractured bones.

But it didn't matter what her legs wanted or if her ankle was toast. All parts of her had to keep working, or no piece of her would survive.

She pushed off a wall and began to run. There was a rickety staircase ahead, and she grabbed the railing and pulled herself upward. Better than exiting the alleyway, where a pursuer in a car might have circled around to wait for her.

She went up three flights before she found a door that opened. She darted inside, finding herself in a corridor that appeared to run the length of the building. Was this an office building?

She tried four doors before finding an unlocked one. Taking a deep breath, she entered the room, hoping to spot a phone or computer or anything she could use to call for help.

But the space was empty. Whatever business had operated from here had cleared out months ago, leaving behind desks and shelves and broken chairs. There were multiple empty rooms, all connected. Should she hide here, or was she cornering herself?

She came upon another door that opened to the main corridor. The door had been locked, and now she looked down the long hall, realizing the entire office suite took up one side of the building.

Was the entire floor empty?

What about the building? Was it abandoned?

Where the hell was she?

Just her luck to have escaped into a desert ghost town without phones or computers.

At last, she found a stairwell at the far end of the long corridor. She stepped inside, and the heavy door closed with a loud clang. She tried the knob and found it had locked. She could be trapped in this stairwell, with the only exits being on the ground floor or the roof.

She made her way down, wishing she'd been able to find a weapon of some sort. All she had was a shard of glass smaller than the palm of her hand. On the first floor landing, there were two doors. Gray early evening light spilled through the window in one door. The other door must lead inside to the first-floor offices.

She hadn't given up on the idea of finding a working phone. She took a deep breath and tried the interior door and felt a flood of relief when the knob turned.

She slowly pulled the door open and came face-to-face with Bassam.

Chapter Nineteen

The drone lost her when she reached the business district full of tight alleys. It picked her up again five minutes later—and she'd gotten farther than Chris would have expected in that time—before losing her again.

They had two square blocks with no less than a half dozen buildings she could be inside or hiding in the maze of alleyways in between. She also had a half dozen terrorists in hot pursuit.

The situation was a fucking nightmare.

With the platoon split, there were only eight men searching for Dr. Edwards, while eight men stormed the compound as night fell over the outskirts of the city.

Chris divided the Squad into two-man teams. Chris was with Albrecht, the youngest man on the SEAL team. Together, they moved through the alleyways, looking for building entrances she might have used.

The drone spotted the abandoned bicycle being pulled out of an alley by one of the cell members. With that intel, they narrowed their search area to two buildings. Their best bet was the one with a fire escape that let out into the alley where she'd abandoned the bicycle.

Instead of climbing the outside fire escape, Chris and Albrecht circled to the front face of the building. From the side, the building had looked old and abandoned, but closer inspection showed it was still in use at least at the ground level, which had street-front shops that were shuttered for the evening. He located a door to the main building between two closed shops and hesitated only a moment before using a charge to blow the lock.

He was more concerned with the noise than with the damage to a civilian structure. There was no hiding this op from government officials at this point, and compensation would be made to the business owners.

It would all be worth it if Rafiq was brought in. Sadly, Rafiq's capture or kill was worth far more to the US and their allies than the rescue of Dr. Edwards. But then, even Edwards knew that.

Directly in front of Chris was a narrow set of stairs. Access to the second-floor businesses. Behind the staircase was a door to the ground floor. If Edwards had entered on one of the higher floors, she'd have been looking for a way out on the ground floor.

Chris instructed the two SEALs who were entering on the other side to take the stairs to the second floor. He and Albrecht would search the ground level.

The interior door was unlocked. Chris and Albrecht flanked the doorway and listened. Hearing nothing, Albrecht pulled the door open and Chris went through, scanning the wide corridor with his M4A1. Albrecht followed, covering Chris's six and scanning the other direction.

The corridor appeared to run the length of the building, a simple, basic design. Businesses on the north face, offices, storage, and utilities across the corridor on the south side.

They'd entered the building on the west end, between a small lunch shop and a larger dental office. He and Albrecht moved slowly down the dark corridor.

A shrill scream sounded at the far end. A woman's scream, most likely.

He ran, pausing to listen at closed doors only briefly in search of the screamer. They reached another stairwell. Through the panel, Chris heard a woman speaking in Arabic. Her tone sounded desperate. Something that carried through no matter the language.

He recognized her voice. He'd memorized it after watching his bodycam footage a thousand times.

4

*D*iana shoved against Bassam's hold, letting loose a primal scream that gave her strength. He fell back, and she turned, but he caught her again, wrenching her arm.

"Please, Bassam. You don't have to do this. Let me go."

He snarled and cursed. The young man who had been at times almost kind was long gone. But then, by making her escape, she'd endangered him and his brother again. Even worse than when she'd broken the artifact. Then they'd been allies in the cover-up, but there was no covering up that she'd escaped on his watch.

She kicked at his knee and would have made for the exit, but he fell in that direction, so her only option was to make a break for the stairs. He caught up with her before she reached the second landing. Grabbing her foot, he yanked.

Pain exploded as he twisted her already-abused limb. She fell, her chin slamming on the metal step. She tasted blood, her teeth biting deep into her tongue.

Bassam tugged at her foot, pulling her down the steps. She twisted and spit blood on him as she kicked at his head.

He wrenched her knee, and she let out a shrill scream as she grabbed an iron baluster to prevent him from pulling her down. With his hands on her ankle, he didn't have a hand free to wield a weapon of any kind.

She kicked at his face again. This time, her boot connected with his jaw, and his head snapped back.

Above her, she heard footsteps. She looked up to see Jamal. She'd been cornered before she even ran up the stairs. Before Bassam had destroyed her ability to walk or run.

A window next to the exterior door offered some light in the darkened stairwell. Bassam pulled her down the stairs as if she was a rag doll. Adrenaline no longer masked the pain, and she felt each step as a blow. She grappled for an iron baluster, but couldn't grip anything. Her neck hit a step, and she felt the sharp edge of the glass shard.

At last, she hit the landing, and Bassam pulled her up, but her abused leg would no longer support her.

She exaggerated her fall, twisting so he couldn't see her hand as she plucked the glass from the hidden pocket.

"Don't do this, Bassam! I won't go back." She didn't have to fake the urgency in her voice, but he didn't know what she was pleading for.

She would do anything to escape, even kill him if she had to.

The door to the first-floor corridor opened, and she turned, expecting to see one of the other guards. Her heart leapt when she spotted the outline of a man in full military gear in the dim light.

A SEAL.

"Let her go," the SEAL said. The commanding voice sounded almost familiar, but she doubted it was the same man.

Bassam let out a primal yell and yanked her to him, so he could use her as a shield.

"Not this time," she said, almost in a whisper and brandished the glass shard.

He slapped at her hand, but she blocked him with her left hand, holding the glass with its sharpest edge ready to strike.

The SEAL pointed his weapon at Bassam. "Release her, and I'll let you walk away."

She wondered if that were true.

Not that it mattered at this point. No way was she leaving here with Bassam. Not this time.

Bassam looked over her shoulder and smiled. She realized the SEAL not only couldn't see Jamal, he wouldn't have a line of sight on him if he did. Her rescuer was slowly moving forward, into Jamal's line of sight. And Jamal had an AK-47.

Diana didn't hesitate, she slashed at Bassam's neck. Blood spurted into her face.

Bassam let out a gurgling scream. Diana rolled to the side as Jamal fired. His wild shot missed Diana, and hit his dying brother in the head.

Chapter Twenty

The aftermath was a blur for Diana. One SEAL was in her face, asking if she was okay, while the other exchanged gunfire with Jamal.

Then the two men whisked her outside and into a vehicle, leaving Bassam's body in the stairwell. More SEALs joined them, and she snapped out of her daze to tell them to get Rafiq.

They must get Rafiq, or it would all be for nothing.

"We've got a Squad at the compound," the first SEAL said. He'd raised his NVGs so she could see his eyes, and she could swear it was the same man from the wadi.

"He's why...why I did what I did. Before."

"I know."

"You have to get Rafiq. The SEALs who are searching for Jamal...he's a kid. Rafiq is more important."

The SEAL nodded. "You and Rafiq are our priority. With you safe, we're sending the rest of the Squad to the compound where you were held."

Diana felt guilty that he and another SEAL were tasked with taking her to safety while the others raided the compound, but at the same time, she wouldn't have been able to stand being left alone, no matter how secure the place they left her would be.

She'd killed Bassam. Jamal might have fired the shot that officially did the deed, but he'd only shaved seconds off the young man's life.

Was it weird that she felt bad for both brothers?

Her emotions were in a muddle as she sat in the back seat of a nondescript SUV. Not a Humvee or anything that screamed US military. She wondered where they got the vehicle as they wound through the streets of what she now realized was the outskirts of Aqaba.

She expected them to cross the city and take her to the Gulf of Aqaba and put her on a military ship of some sort, but they went the other way, eventually ending up back in the remote desert.

She had a brief, irrational fear that these men weren't US military at all and she'd just fallen into another trap.

Like that day at the market. She was caught in a vicious loop.

"Who are you?" Her voice came out low and rough as she forced the words out.

"Navy SEALs, ma'am," the Black sailor said.

She knew that. Of course she did. But still, the fear nagged.

"I mean your names."

"We can't share that information," the white SEAL said.

His face was young. Only a few years older than Bassam, were she to guess.

Her gaze darted to the Black SEAL. "It was you, in the canyon. The one I asked to trust me."

He nodded.

"I'm… I'm sorry. But I did what I had to do. All this…" Her voice trailed off, and she shook her head, finding the thread again. "It was the only way to find the Four of Diamonds."

"I know. And if we get Rafiq, it will be worth it."

She thought of the site she'd played a key role in destroying and the dead boy in the stairwell and hoped to hell his words were true.

Chapter Twenty-One

College Park, Maryland
Six weeks later

The first time Diana saw Jamal, she was in the hospital in Germany, practicing using the rolling cart to get around in preparation for her discharge. He was at the other end of the corridor and wore scrubs and a mask, but she recognized him. She knew his posture. His gait. It was him. She'd screamed, and nurses came running with security in tow.

When a Pakistani orderly was presented to her an hour later and she was told that was the man she'd seen, she didn't believe the story. She insisted she'd seen Jamal. That was when she first learned the Intelligence Community was questioning her account of having spotted Rafiq in Jordan.

Now they questioned her ability to tell one brown-skinned man from another, and the implication that she was racist for signaling out the Pakistani man as a terrorist was delivered loud and clear.

It didn't matter that she'd lived with and been engaged to a Lebanese-American, or that she'd lived in Jordan for nearly half a year by the time she was rescued, nor did it matter that she'd spent six weeks in the desert with Jamal. Her identification of Middle Eastern men was suspect.

So when, one week after she returned to the US, she saw Jamal standing on the subway platform at Gallery Place as her Green Line train departed the station, she didn't tell anyone. Not even Morgan and Freya.

She knew it would shake their trust in her, and if she lost their support, she'd have nothing left.

All she could do at the time was lean back in her seat on the train, clutch the shopping bag to her chest, and hope that when she used the tablet she'd just purchased with cash to log into her throwaway email account, the photos of the artifacts would be in her inbox.

An hour later, when she was finally able to check the account, her inbox held nothing but seven months' worth of spam. She'd known it was a long shot, but after weeks of having everything about her story questioned, she'd hoped to have tangible proof of *something*.

She'd told the CIA about the camera and photos, but she hadn't disclosed that she'd used an old, online-only email address with a domain that was phasing out in a slow death by lack of filters and function. In the moment, it had been the ideal choice because the address was a series of digits and letters that wouldn't reveal Diana's identity if someone spotted the draft emails in the camera's outgoing mailbox.

The intelligence officer in the hospital hadn't asked what email address she'd used because they already had access to all her known accounts, and likely had been monitoring her various inboxes from the moment she was abducted.

Diana didn't trust them not to swipe the photos if they arrived and never tell Diana they'd been received. Those photos could give up an IP address with Rafiq's new location. And so, as soon as she felt up to venturing out after her return home, she took the Metro to Pentagon City and bought a tablet and 5G hotspot with cash so she could finally check that old email address, but on the way home from the store, she'd spotted Jamal on a subway platform.

In the ensuing days, she'd managed to dismiss the idea she'd seen the boy turned terrorist. She'd been tired and her ankle hurt after her first big outing since returning. Plus, she'd been doing something proactive, so naturally, she was braced for danger.

At the time of that second sighting, it had been five weeks since she'd fled the compound in Aqaba, but still, her body was wound tight. Would that ever leave her? Or would she expect the worst everywhere she went?

In the first months after the car accident that had killed Salim, every ride in a vehicle had filled her with dread. It wasn't until she could drive herself around again, be in control of the vehicle instead of the helpless passenger, that the feeling began to fade. Now she was again hampered by a rebuilt ankle. Driving was out for the foreseeable future.

But it wasn't cars and rainy, dark roads that scared her.

It was public places like shopping centers. Hospitals with people who questioned her memory and sanity. Airplanes in which she was trapped for hours, returning to a home that was forever changed. It was public transportation of all kinds, where she might see the face of a boy who wanted to kill her.

She also feared rideshare vehicles that she might climb into with a feeling of safety, but then discover the driver was working for the abductor she'd managed to escape in the market.

In short, she was afraid of leaving her condo even if she knew the destination to be safe, but now, a week after that second Jamal sighting, she needed to take the Metro once again.

She considered calling Morgan and un-RSVPing to her birthday party but told herself she needed to be brave. If she didn't start going out into the world now, it would only be harder later. She didn't relish the idea of becoming a recluse, and while she had enough money to live on for several years, she wasn't rich enough to be considered charmingly eccentric.

Plus, there were enough questions about her sanity given her claims to have spoken with a dead man three times.

Still, she wanted to put off venturing out for one more day. After all, she had a doctor's appointment tomorrow. She'd have to take the Metro. That would be enough bravery for one week.

She turned on the TV and went to the home screen, pondering which app to search for something to binge. But she was sick of TV after nearly two weeks at home, and without the distraction of TV, she would spend the evening reliving the moment when the glass shard dragged across

Bassam's throat, opening the taut skin like a separating zipper.

He hadn't shaved in the weeks she'd known him, and his light beard had thickened, inching ever closer to manhood.

She set down the remote, grabbed her crutches, and crossed the living room to her bedroom, where she flung open the closet door and scanned her clothing for something she could wear to the party. A skirt would be best given the padded brace on her right ankle, but it would be chilly, and she didn't have leggings. She'd ordered some online that she'd be able to cut just below the knee to accommodate the brace, but they hadn't arrived yet.

In the end she chose a calf-length skirt and wore a thick knee-high stocking on her left leg. The walk to the pub from the Metro would be short enough that she shouldn't get too chilled.

As she put on makeup, she tried to psych herself up for a night of peopling. She had a sneaking suspicion Morgan had decided to celebrate her birthday in a public place as a way to draw Diana out. And really, if there was anyone who even had an inkling of understanding of what Diana had just been through, it was Morgan.

She was safe with the Valkyries and their friends. It was time to rebuild her life. *Again.*

She'd been numb in the months after Salim died until she'd signed on with Morgan and Freya, and now she'd returned from Jordan numb once again.

She had her second second chance at life, and she should embrace it. Be a butterfly.

She'd survived the unthinkable. She shouldn't squander

this gift. She just needed to figure out how to get over her fear and live with the guilt.

The guilt was worse than the fear. Fear was tangible. Understandable. External.

Guilt was internal, with no possible outlet. It kept her up at night. Every time she closed her eyes, she was back in the desert, stealing history. Worse was when she did manage to sleep. Then she dreamed of Fahd's murder or slicing open Bassam's throat right before his brother's bullet shattered his face and she was pelted with bone and brain matter.

All the horror, death, and destruction had been for nothing. *Nothing.*

Rafiq hadn't been there when the SEALs stormed the compound. He'd slipped through the net.

In the ensuing weeks, she'd learned there were people in the military and Intelligence Community who believed Makram Rafiq was dead and she'd invented or hallucinated her interactions with him. She suspected their desire to discredit her was because they were the ones who'd declared him dead in the first place.

Her ankle throbbed as she put on lipstick, partially covering the scar that was a constant reminder of the accident that had killed Salim. The scar never gave her phantom pain like her ankle had. Now, she again had real pain in her ankle, which flared every time she thought about the smarmy fake-named liaison or analyst or whatever he was who'd visited her in the hospital in Germany.

She understood why they had to question her story, but the hostility and suspicion had gotten under her skin as intended. She'd been wrung out and devastated after he left and found herself questioning her own sanity.

But she knew who she'd spoken with in the slot canyon. The Four of Diamonds. A man who abducted children and made them terrorists and who funded his attacks by selling artifacts. He'd used that money to buy a weapon that was responsible for the loss of an entire SEAL platoon when it shot down a transport plane.

That knowledge had been her battle cry for the decisions she'd made, and now the words were a mantra for defending herself.

Makeup finished, she took a deep breath and studied her reflection. She looked nothing like the woman who'd looted the site in Jordan. The chapped lips and sunburned nose were long gone after weeks indoors.

Did she resemble the woman she'd been before Jordan? She couldn't tell. That woman had been lost in grief and searching for purpose.

She was no longer searching for purpose. The thing she needed most now was unattainable: redemption.

She pulled out her phone. Rideshare apps were out. She had no doubt all the intelligence agencies were monitoring her phone, and she wouldn't make it easy by giving them every destination ahead of time.

She considered taking a taxi to the pub in southwest DC, because at least with a taxi, she didn't have to give her destination up front. But really, the pub was on the Green Line, and a Green Line Metro station was just a few blocks from her home. She'd take the train to the party.

It would be good for her. Back in the saddle, so to speak.

She could take a taxi home from the bar. She'd never been a fan of riding the Metro late at night alone, particularly when she was on crutches. She tucked away the phone, making a deal with herself: if she challenged herself with a train ride to the pub, she could treat herself to a taxi ride home.

Even better, she could pick up a hot guy and forget about everything for a few hours in an anonymous hotel room and avoid the trip home alone late at night altogether.

The thought surprised her. She hadn't been with anyone since Salim, and before him, she hadn't been one for random hookups. But maybe it was time?

Once again, the SEAL who'd rescued her in Aqaba came to mind. Thoughts of him had filled long hours of recuperation in the hospital in Germany.

Kind of pathetic, actually, that she'd fixated on a fantasy man who'd swooped in and saved her. He was as remote as a celebrity. Just as unreal and impossible as a superhero.

She needed to be attracted to someone attainable. A bar pickup. It didn't have to mean anything.

And it would fit with her goal to start living again.

She stared at her ankle and the crutches she needed to get around. They might be a hindrance.

She shrugged away the thought. It wasn't like she'd go through with the wild idea. But it was fun to imagine, and right now, she desperately needed fun.

*C*hris closed the hotel room door and leaned against it, letting out a heavy sigh. The last four days of debriefings at the Pentagon had been long and boring, and more than once, he'd been on the defensive about the decisions he'd made. Now he wanted nothing more than to order room service and sit outside on his private balcony with a view of the Potomac River and Jefferson Memorial. Steak, a baked potato, and a beer, and he'd be a happy man. But the guys on the team wanted to go out now that their Pentagon ordeal was behind them, and he figured he should participate in the bonding ritual.

They'd only been Stateside again for ten days, the last four of which they'd spent at the Pentagon for meetings with SPEC OPS and DIA and CIA analysts and the FBI as the Intelligence Community tried to make head or tail of what had happened in Jordan. As far as he could tell, the verdict was still out on whether or not Makram Rafiq was to be removed from the Captured or Killed list and placed back on Most Wanted.

Chris had his own questions, but the Pentagon wasn't interested in those. They just wanted the blow-by-blow factual account of what he'd seen and done. And he'd given it to them. Over and over.

He was stripping out of his Navy combat uniform and into civvies for a night on the town, when he received a text from Fallon.

RAND

Skip drinks with the team. Meet me here
asap.

The message included a link to a bar that was just a few
blocks from their hotel.

Fallon hadn't planned to go out with the team tonight,
but Chris couldn't remember why.

CHRIS

What's up?

You'll find out when you get here. See you
soon.

Chris stared at the phone. After three months deployed
together, he figured he knew the lieutenant commander, and
this was odd.

Still, he was curious. He could go out with the rest of the
team when they were back in Little Creek. Might as well
humor his OIC.

He paused at that thought, remembering the Officer in
Charge from his last team. He'd give anything to be able to
go out for a beer with the lieutenant commander one more
time.

He quickly finished changing and was out the door. It
was a chilly December evening. The wind coming off the
river had a cold bite to it.

The team had missed Thanksgiving with family and
friends, and it was now just a few short weeks until Christmas. They all had two weeks of leave, starting tonight, and

most of the guys were flying tomorrow to wherever home was. Chris hadn't decided if he should take a trip or just head back to Little Creek and finish moving into his new house.

A year ago, he'd have made a beeline for Coronado, but a year ago, he hadn't known his wife was sleeping with another man. Now Pam was the last person he wanted to see. He'd come home to a packet of divorce papers he needed to read and sign and the news that she and his old teammate were expecting their first child in April.

Reading the papers and signing was on his to-do list for tomorrow. What a way to start a vacation.

Maybe he should go to Port Angeles, Washington, and meet Xavier and Audrey's baby. Georgina was just over four months old now. The latest pictures Xavier had sent were too adorable for words.

Yeah. That was what he should do. He'd been wanting to talk to Xavier since the op went FUBAR in the slot canyon. He wouldn't be able to give specifics, but what he could share would be enough for Xavier to get the gist. He'd understand Chris's dilemma in a way no one else could.

Of course, he should ask if Xavier and Audrey *wanted* company. He supposed if they didn't, he could go hiking in the Olympics. Maybe *this* time, he'd get to enjoy Olympic National Park.

He paused in his walk and shot off a text to Xavier, then continued the last block to the address Fallon had sent him.

It was a new building—everything on the waterfront here had been built in the last fifteen years—and business was booming on a Thursday night. He paused to check the menu posted in the window and discovered Rand had sent him to a gastropub owned by one of the DC area's top chefs. The menu mostly consisted of small plates that promised culinary excellence.

Chris was hungry after a long day of being grilled like a fillet, and wondered if it would be weird to order three of everything as he pushed open the door and stepped into the noisy pub.

A hostess greeted him and asked if he wanted a table or to sit at the bar. Chris apologized and said he was meeting someone, but wasn't sure if he was part of a larger group.

"You look…big. Like several of the guests I've sent up to the private party in the loft. You one of them?" She pointed to the stairs on the far side of the ornately carved bar that filled the back wall. He scanned the patrons packed in the bar area. Randall Fallon would stand out with his blond hair and six-foot-two height, which could explain the hostess's comment on size.

"I'm not sure. Maybe? Fallon party?"

The hostess checked the screen in front of her. "No. It's Adler. A birthday party."

Adler?

The name suddenly clicked. "Right. Morgan Adler."

The hostess smiled. "Go on up."

At the top of the stairs, he met Fallon's cheeky grin. "Figured it out yet?"

"Asshole. You could just have told me it was Adler's birthday."

"Where's the fun in that?" He nodded toward a blonde woman with a round belly, and he remembered Rand telling him she was pregnant back on *Dahlgren.* Adler sat in a big comfy chair, deep in conversation with a pretty Black woman at her right and Freya Lange on her left.

The birthday girl smiled brightly as they approached. "Rand, is this who I think it is?"

Chris offered his hand. "Lieutenant Chris Flyte. It's nice to meet you in person, Dr. Adler." He turned and met Lange's gaze. "And Ms. Lange."

Morgan shook his hand. "Morgan, please. I'm so glad to meet you."

"Freya," Lange said as she shook his hand.

He was then introduced around the group. The Black woman was Kaylea Espinosa, a diplomat currently home on leave from her assignment in Morocco. Her husband, Carlos Espinosa, was a former Green Beret who now served as his wife's full-time personal security while she was abroad. Espinosa had served on the same team as Morgan's and Freya's husbands, Pax and Cal, who were the last people he was introduced to. As the hostess had said, they were all big men. Former Special Forces, now civilians, who worked for the military or in security.

There were over a dozen other guests in the small party, and instead of waiting for their server to return, Chris decided to visit the bar downstairs to get a drink before continuing with introductions. He'd just reached the bottom step when he glanced toward the hostess stand and his heart stuttered.

Dr. Diana Edwards.

No longer beaten, bloody, and terrified.

Her hair in her professional portrait had been pulled

back in a bun, and in person, she'd worn a headscarf. Now he saw she had long, straight, glossy dark brown hair. Her cheeks and nose no longer bore the reddish hue from days in the desert sun, and her skin was now a luminous pale cream.

The woman before him didn't really resemble her official photo, and she was a far cry from the woman he'd carried from the stairwell in Aqaba. No. This version of Diana Edwards was more breathtakingly beautiful than he'd imagined.

And he'd thought of her a lot in the weeks since he'd placed her on a gurney and watched medics load her into a helicopter for the first stage of her medivac transport to a US military hospital in Germany.

Chapter Twenty-Two

"*C*an I help you up the stairs, Dr. Edwards?"

Diana turned at the sound of a deep male voice and jolted in shock. There he was, the object of all her inappropriate fantasies. In the flesh. More real than a celebrity. "What are..." Her voice trailed off. After her ridiculous thoughts regarding him earlier, she was at a loss for words. She didn't even know his name.

He held out a hand. "I think it's safe for me to formally introduce myself now. Lieutenant Chris Flyte."

She took his hand, which enveloped hers, reminding her of the moment when he'd carried her from the stairwell and out into the night, and she'd felt safe for the first time in six weeks.

"This can't be a coincidence. Do you know Morgan?" If so, Morgan had never mentioned it, which would be an odd omission.

"Just met her a few minutes ago for the first time. She knows one of the men on my team, who invited me to tag along." His gaze ran down her injured leg, and he repeated, "Can I help you with the stairs?"

She gave him a rueful smile. "You're determined to save me from stairs." All at once, she realized what she'd said and slapped a hand over her mouth. "I mean—I—"

His smile was warm and handsome, something she'd wondered about in the weeks since he'd saved her. They'd only had about an hour together before the airlift arrived. And she'd spent weeks going over every minute of the exchange. So much of what had happened had been horrific. Thinking of him had been her mental escape.

"I'm not offended, and you didn't mean it in that way. Don't be hard on yourself."

"If only it were that easy."

Of course, for him, the situation was straightforward. She didn't doubt he'd killed for his country. Probably several times. But she doubted he'd ever spent six weeks with the person he'd later had to kill.

He nodded in the direction of the bar. "C'mon. Let's get you a drink…if you want a drink, that is."

Something about his smile made her belly flutter, and she followed him to the bar, where he ordered a beer and she got a Moscow mule.

He picked up both his tall pint glass and her copper mug and nodded to an empty half-moon-shaped booth near the stairs. "Wanna sit and enjoy this first?"

She hesitated a moment, then gave a nod. "We can join the party later."

They slipped into the booth, Diana taking the right side so she could prop up her leg on the curved seat. Chris slid toward the center so they sat side by side. It was cozy and quiet in the otherwise loud room.

"I should text Morgan, let her know I'm here."

"And I'll text Rand and let him know I didn't skip out."

"Did Morgan know you were coming?"

"I'm pretty sure she told Rand to invite me. But he waited until the last minute and didn't tell me anything but the address. Probably knew I'd ask questions if he mentioned it earlier."

"So this was a setup."

"I think so."

How had Morgan guessed that Diana was attracted to the SEAL who'd saved her life? But then, maybe she hadn't guessed. Maybe she just figured Diana would want a chance to say thank you.

How much did Chris know about the investigation and the suspicions surrounding her?

Probably absolutely everything. Hell, he might be at the center of it. That could even be why he was in DC. Was he among the group who thought Makram Rafiq lived only in her head?

That would certainly put a damper on her infatuation with her rescuer.

"Are you in the city for work?" She knew enough to be aware SEALs didn't like to be identified as such in public places.

He nodded. "I was. I'm on leave as of about an hour ago."

"Nice. So you'll be heading home. Is that Little Creek, or Coronado?"

"Coronado up until last July, when I made the move to Little Creek." His deep voice was soft and low, ensuring it didn't carry beyond their booth. There were plenty of people who could connect the dots and would realize he was special forces.

One thing she'd learned in her time in DC—especially since she'd almost joined the clandestine service—was many people didn't identify their government employer. The town was full of people who couldn't admit to working for the FBI, NSA, or one of the many other agencies that traded in secrets. Generally, locals knew better than to ask.

She was breaking those rules now in asking about his work, but then, she already had firsthand knowledge of exactly the kind of work he did, and he knew about her work for FMV. "Why the switch? Wait. That's probably classified."

"Unfortunately, it's nothing so exciting as that. My ex got Coronado in the divorce."

"That's quite a division of property. How does one get a whole island like that?"

He grimaced. "Sleep with a guy on my former team."

She winced. "Ouch. Sorry."

He shrugged. "It sucked." He took a sip of his beer, then held it out to her in a toast. "To starting over."

She raised her glass and clinked it against his even as she wondered if that was what she was doing.

She wanted a reset, but it felt like what had happened in Jordan wasn't finished yet. Hard to start over when you were still floundering in the middle.

But she'd play along. She took her drink, then held up her glass again. "To having devious friends."

He laughed at that. Good lord, this man was handsome. Thickly muscled. Broad nose, warm brown eyes. Five o'clock shadow on his dark brown skin. He had forearms to die for.

Until now, she'd never seen him without his full gear on, but that hadn't prevented her from fantasizing based only on his face and a muscular build that had to be hiding under all that body armor and weaponry. He lived up to her mental pictures and exceeded them.

It had been easy to fixate on him when she was in the hospital. Both times she'd seen him, he'd been larger than life. A savior. But the feeling she got when she looked at him now wasn't gratitude. Not even a little bit.

With his looks and status as a SEAL, he was probably used to women throwing themselves at him.

Did he ever catch?

❡

C hris could hardly believe he was sitting here with Diana Edwards, the woman who'd never been far from his mind in the last three months. At first because she was a job, but later, after her rescue, because he'd seen first-hand what she was willing to risk for the greater good.

How many people would deny their own rescue in an effort to catch a terrorist?

The woman was fierce. Strong. Resilient.

The fact that she was here now was proof of that.

He had no idea what she'd faced on a daily basis. Six weeks of being held captive. Forced to work long days in the desert. And that didn't even take into consideration the physical and sexual abuse she might have suffered. But still she sat here, sipping her drink in the nation's capital, looking like any other woman out on Thursday night.

She had grit.

He knew the questions that swirled around her and her actions. Hell, he'd just spent the last four days being grilled at the motherfucking Pentagon because military intelligence couldn't decide if she was off her rocker or if she really had been an unwilling guest in Makram Rafiq's compound.

But still, this woman whose integrity and sanity was being scrutinized by no less than top analysts in the Intelligence Community sat with her head high, more beautiful than he'd imagined possible.

Their waiter arrived, and Chris remembered his earlier hunger. There was a spread of food for them at the party in the loft, but ascending stairs on crutches was a pain in the ass, and Chris was happy to buy Diana dinner, especially since it gave him time alone with her.

It was wild to realize he could actually talk to her. There wasn't even any kind of conflict of interest, given that his debriefing was done and she knew he was a SEAL and which op he'd recently been sent on. It might be good for her to be able to speak of her rescue and what went down in the stairwell. Not here, of course. No, any conversation about his—and her—work would have to take place in private.

Maybe he could convince her to go to his hotel room. He shook his head at the thought. She'd probably be horrified at the suggestion. Assume he was coming on to her.

"What's wrong?" she asked. "Don't like the menu?"

"No. Sorry. Just got distracted." He quickly ordered a

half dozen small plates and asked if she wanted to try anything else.

She smiled and shook her head. "That sounds like a good start."

The waiter left, and Diana lifted her cocktail and leaned back against the cushion. "So tell me about yourself, Lieutenant Flyte."

Was that a hint of flirtation he heard in her tone? She wasn't the easiest woman to read, but that was probably due to the fact that their brief shared history was…traumatic.

He had no clue who the real Diana Edwards might be. "What do you want to know?"

"How long since the divorce?"

Well, at least she didn't dance around sensitive subjects. "Technically, the papers haven't been signed, but the relationship was officially over last January, and on the rocks for more than eighteen months before that."

Was he trying to signal his marriage was long over with his detailed answer? Yes. Did he want her to know it wasn't too soon for him to move on? Also yes.

"Why haven't the papers been signed?"

"I spent a long time on a…big-ass boat recently. I came home to find the papers in my mailbox. I've been too slammed to read through them, and I never sign anything without reading."

"Makes sense."

"If you're wondering if I'm the kind of guy to draw it out because I'm having second thoughts, the answer is no."

"Any kids?"

"No. It never felt right to start a family with me being

gone so much of the time, and Pam said she was content to wait." No point in mentioning that she was pregnant now, clearly having reached the end of her contentment, but never having shared that detail with Chris when they were still together. "We married when she was just twenty-four and I was twenty-six."

"How long ago was that?"

"Nine years." He took a sip of his beer and turned the questions on her. "What about you? Ever been married?"

She shook her head. "I was engaged, but my fiancé died in a car accident. It will be two years ago in March."

"I'm so sorry."

She nodded and sipped her drink. She set it down and fussed with her napkin. Her voice was even in a way that reminded him of that first night in the wadi, when she spoke with unfathomable calm. "I was in the car. He was driving. It was rainy, and we were on an unfamiliar mountain road. We were arguing. I'd been accepted into a CIA training class, and once it became real and not theoretical, he was no longer comfortable with the idea. He was dubious about me violating archaeologist ethics and using my credentials to gather intel in the Arab world. He wasn't wrong, mind you. It was something I grappled with myself."

She picked up her drink and finished it in a long gulp.

She set the glass down and resumed the tale. "The car hydroplaned and…he didn't regain control in time to stop us from slamming into a tree. We were both pinned in the vehicle."

She paused and took a deep breath, the first break in her calm façade. "I knew he was dying, and I couldn't do anything to help him. My ankle"—she nodded toward the foot propped on the rounded booth seat—"was crushed. I was rescued about an hour later and was lucky to keep my foot."

Chris wanted to take her hand, but her body language indicated his touch wouldn't be welcome. Her hands cupped the sweating copper mug, squeezing tight.

Her tone shifted. Not upbeat so much as a sign she'd made it through the worst part of her story. "The injury kept me out of that CIA training class, so once I was back on my feet—literally—I approached Morgan and Freya about working for Friday Morning Valkyries. If it wasn't for them and the job, I don't know how I would have gotten up in the morning those months after Salim died."

"Jordan was your first job with FMV?" he asked.

"Yes. I would only be useful to them if I could get legitimate work in the country, so when Gardner Holdings set up a grant with a university in Amman and wanted an American involved in the excavation, I jumped at it. Morgan and Freya had been training me prior to that, but once the job came in, my training went in to overdrive. Obviously, with my ankle, there were things I couldn't do physically, but fieldwork wasn't on that list."

"What's the deal with the name? Friday Morning Valkyries is a bit…odd."

She smiled. Damn. Every time she did that, his heart stuttered a bit. Like he was a teenager trying to woo a pretty girl. Except this was no girl. She was Diana Prince, better known as Wonder Woman.

"Not surprisingly, I asked them the same thing. They told me they wanted something odd that didn't give a hint as to what the organization does. If you change the 'a' to 'e' in Morgan, you get the word 'Morgen' in German, which means morning. Freya is a Norse goddess, and sometimes she's Frigg, the goddess Friday is named for. And Valkyries…well, those are Norse women warriors who escort the dead to Valhalla. It was a nod to both the 'Monuments Women' idea and being protectors of the historical record in the form of art and artifacts." She grinned. "Plus it made me feel badass that I could call myself a Valkyrie."

He laughed at that. Thinking of her actions in the desert when she chose to remain a prisoner, and later when she escaped a terrorist compound all on her own, he said, "You are the most badass woman I've ever met. And I know a lot of incredible women in the military and out."

She smiled. "Yes, but you've admitted you don't know Morgan and Freya. They set the badass standard."

"Don't sell yourself short." This came from Morgan herself, who must have overheard the last bit as she approached their table.

Diana shifted as if to stand. "Morgan! Happy birthday! I'm sorry I didn't go up—"

"Don't stand! I'm sorry, I forgot the stairs would be difficult for you. I'm glad you stayed down here and have good company." The woman winked, and Chris didn't know if the gesture was intended for him or Diana.

"We'll come up after we eat—" Diana said.

"Only if you feel up to it. No need to go to the effort for me. I'm just delighted to see you out." She smiled at Chris.

"Don't let her attempt the stairs out of any kind of obligation."

"Yes, ma'am. I promise I'll take good care of Dr. Edwards."

Now Morgan grinned. "You always do."

It was clear Morgan and Rand had conspired to bring him and Diana together. But why?

Had his entirely inappropriate attraction to the subject of the op been obvious to his OIC?

No. Rand had probably figured Chris would appreciate having a chance to talk to her after the failure of the first rescue attempt had gotten into his head.

The waiter arrived with their food, and Morgan instructed the man to add the tab to the bill for the party upstairs, overriding Chris's protest.

"It's my birthday. You have to do what I say."

"I don't think that's how it works," Diana said.

Morgan waved off the objection. "Now, I came down to use the restroom, so I'll leave you. Let us know if you need anything, and enjoy your dinner." With that, Morgan disappeared down the hall next to the stairs.

Chris ordered a second round of drinks, and he and Diana both dug into sampling the small plates before them. Less than two hours ago, Chris had been getting ready for a night out with his new SEAL team, but now he found himself having an intimate dinner with Diana Edwards in something that felt very much like a date.

Still, he had to wonder if the feeling was merely wishful thinking.

Diana offered him a bite of dried fruit and cheese

wrapped in prosciutto. She fed him the morsel, pausing to wipe at the honey that smeared on his bottom lip with her thumb. Instinctively, he licked the digit, catching sweet glaze and just brushing her skin.

He felt a rush of heat low in his belly as he took in her quickening breath. She smiled and pulled back her hand. Holding his gaze, she proceeded to lick her thumb in the same spot.

Now it was his breathing that quickened.

And he had his answer. Not wishful thinking at all.

Without a word, she shifted closer until her shoulder brushed against his, but she didn't pull back to put space between them. They continued like that, shoulders touching as they ate and drank and set aside heavy talk in favor of the movies and TV shows Diana had binged in her recuperation.

Chris had yet to spend time with a remote control, so she listed new shows he might want to check out. Considering all the topics they were avoiding, she was easy to talk to.

He didn't kid himself that this was anything more than a night out for either of them. She'd been through something traumatic, but she knew she was safe with him and didn't have to make explanations.

And he…well, his life had been jacked since before the Lake Olympus Lodge Exercise last winter. His big excitement tomorrow would be reading the thick stack of divorce papers and finally severing all legal ties to a woman who'd moved on a year ago.

This break was more than welcome.

Pam was already pregnant and engaged, while Chris

hadn't once considered dating or even a one-night hookup in the intervening months. Now he found himself at the start of a two-week leave with a beautiful woman who showed every sign of being into him. He wanted to see where this could go.

One part of him worried that she had some hero worship going on since he'd been the one to get her out of that stairwell in Aqaba, but at the same time, it was Diana herself who'd escaped the house and killed her guard. Chris had merely been there to make sure the rest of her escape went smoothly.

Hell, if anything, he was the one who might have a bit of hero worship for her. He'd meant what he said earlier. She was badass, and he was impressed by what she'd been capable of, as a prisoner, no less.

It was nearly impossible to comprehend or anticipate how one would react in a situation like she'd been in. Most people—especially those not trained for it like special forces —would panic and shut down. And while she'd gone through a SERE training, she didn't have the weeks and months— years really—of special forces training to guide her.

"Why are you looking at me like that?" she asked.

"Because I find you impressive." *And hot.*

She smiled, taking the last sip of her drink as she studied him over the rim of the glass.

Their waiter returned and asked if they wanted another round. Diana declined, saying, "I better not. I'm not driving, but it's still not a good idea to be tipsy on the Metro going home."

Chris eyed the brace that protected her surgically recon-structed ankle. "I guess driving is out for a while."

She nodded.

"Tell you what. My hotel is just a few blocks from here. I've got my car parked there. I can give you a ride home, and you won't be stuck taking the Metro by yourself late at night."

"You sure? It's a pain in the ass to get to my condo from here."

"Of course. I can't imagine the Metro is easy on crutches, what with elevator and escalator breakdowns being so common."

"It's one of the reasons I've been a hermit since returning Stateside nearly two weeks ago."

"All right, then. Consider me your chauffeur for as long as I'm in town."

"How long is that?"

He paused and took her hand. When her palm relaxed against his, he smiled and gently massaged the pad of her palm by her thumb. "I think that might be up to you. I'm officially on leave without set plans."

"That's intriguing. To be totally mercenary about this, I have a doctor's appointment tomorrow, and I'm already dreading changing trains at Gallery Place."

"Is it an ankle check?"

She nodded. "Fingers crossed I'll get a walking boot."

"I'm happy to give you a ride."

"That would be great. I'll take you out to lunch after-ward as a thank-you."

"It's a date. Let me know where and when to pick you up."

"My appointment is at eleven, and it's about a thirty-minute drive from my condo."

"I'll pick you up at ten, then."

She smiled in a way that suggested he might already be in her condo tomorrow morning.

If it made her life easier, he was game. He was magnanimous that way.

She glanced at her watch. "Do you mind if we go upstairs and join the party for a bit?"

He held up his hands. "Totally up to you. I don't want to get in trouble with Morgan."

"Right? She's practically a ninja with her martial arts skills and has won target shooting contests. You really don't want to mess with her."

Chris laughed. "Sounds like the woman who was at the center of the Icarus raid."

"You heard about that?"

"Rand was on the SEAL team that would have been taken out."

Diana's eyes widened. "Okay. Now I understand the connection. Rand is up there?" She nodded toward the stairs.

"Yes."

"Let's go, then. I want to meet him."

She carefully slid from the booth, and Chris left a sizable tip on the table to make sure the waiter got his share in case he was left off the party split. Then he carried one of

Diana's crutches as she used the railing with one hand to ascend the stairs one slow step at a time.

When they reached the top, Diana was warmly welcomed by all the people Chris had met earlier and he was introduced around some more. Rand was in conversation with one of the former Green Berets, the white man who was Morgan's husband, Pax Blanchard, if Chris remembered correctly.

Pax gave Diana a hug, then introduced her to Rand. Chris settled in the back against the wall, content to watch Diana work the room. While most of the people here were coupled off, there were a few men who he suspected were single based on the way their eyes followed Diana in the same way his did.

It was ridiculous to feel a surge of possessiveness knowing he was taking her home tonight. Especially since, as far as he knew, he was merely dropping her off. But still, he felt the pull of her and the need to make it clear she was off the market, even if only for one night.

He reined in the feeling. Even as his brain said there was more to it than a car ride.

He'd seen her in Jordan.

Twice.

She'd asked him to trust her.

Asked?

No. Demanded.

And he did. He wasn't certain he believed she'd really seen Makram Rafiq, but he knew *she* believed it, and that was what mattered.

Her eyes met his over the shoulder of some guy who was

standing way too close. Her mouth quirked in a smile as she caught his frown.

She left the guy and approached Chris, her movement with the crutches easy and smooth. She was well used to them at this point. "You look like you want to break someone's face."

"Do I?" he asked innocently.

"What did that poor man do to earn your ire?"

"You know."

"Do I?" she repeated back to him.

He couldn't help but smile. He leaned forward and whispered in her ear. "He looked at you like he wanted to eat you. And I want that privilege for myself."

Chapter Twenty-Three

*H*eat flooded Diana at Chris's blatant statement. Earlier tonight, when she was getting dressed for this party, she'd told herself to let go of her superhero SEAL daydream and pick up a real guy and enjoy a one-night stand. Now, here she was, about to go home with the impossible fantasy.

Her throat went dry. In a good way.

"I think…" She cleared her throat so her voice would be less raspy. "I think I'm ready to leave now."

Chris gave a sharp nod and crossed the loft to Morgan, who was deep in conversation with Rand and Freya's husband, Cal.

Chris offered Morgan his hand. "I'm going to see that Diana gets home safely. Thank you for inviting me to your party."

Morgan rose to her feet, her protruding belly making the feat appear both difficult and impressive. She gave Diana a quick squeeze. "Thank you so much for coming." Then her voice dropped to a whisper, and she said, "You're welcome."

Diana laughed even as she rolled her eyes. "It's just a ride," she whispered back.

"I should hope so. Enjoy it for all it's worth."

Lord. Diana was so out of practice with girlfriends and innuendo that she hadn't seen that coming. Blushing, she hugged Freya and then Pax and Cal, then shook Rand's hand again. Finally, she'd said enough goodbyes to make her escape and followed Chris to the stairs.

This time, Chris took the stairs in front of her, so if she stumbled, he'd break her fall. Luckily, she managed the steps without embarrassing herself, and they soon found themselves on the streets of the southwest DC waterfront on a chilly, almost-winter night.

The walk to Chris's hotel was necessarily slow, as Diana navigated vents and other tripping hazards on crutches.

At one point, the left crutch slipped on a piece of gravel and Chris was there to steady her.

Before she knew it, they were face-to-face, and Chris's hand was on the small of her back. "You okay?"

She nodded. "Ankle is fine."

Standing as they were with only inches separating them, she felt fluttery and warm even as a chill wind whipped around them.

Damn. He was handsome, and he was looking at her lips like he was wondering how she'd taste.

"Do it," she said, her voice a soft whisper.

One corner of his beautiful mouth kicked up. "Right here? In the middle of the sidewalk?"

"We aren't in the Arab world anymore. You aren't in uniform. Public displays of affection are allowed. Besides, my lips are cold."

He let out a quick, warm laugh, and then his mouth was on hers. Soft at first, but then she opened her mouth to let him in, and heat shot through her at the sensation of lips and tongue meeting.

No. Definitely not cold anymore.

His arm wrapped around her, pulling her flush against him. She leaned on him instead of the crutches as he explored her mouth.

A man walked by and muttered, "Get a room."

Chris raised his head and glanced at the man and said, "Solid advice. I think we will."

Diana recognized the blond man as Rand and tucked her head on Chris's chest as she laughed and flushed a little with embarrassment.

Or maybe it was heat and not embarrassment at all.

Chris whispered in her ear, "Lips warm now?"

"Very."

"Let's keep moving, then, so I can warm the rest of you."

They reached his hotel. "I need to grab my car keys from my room."

She nodded, and he held the door for her as she entered the lobby. His room key card was required to operate the elevator. Alone in the box, she cursed her crutches because she would have enjoyed the anticipatory touching of holding hands.

The doors opened, and she made her three-pronged trek down the endless corridor by his side. She was pretty sure they'd traveled more than a mile by the time they reached his room.

Inside, she went straight to the window. He had a great view of the river. The Jefferson Memorial glowed brightly against the dark hillside of Arlington Cemetery.

Chris stepped up behind her. His arms circled her waist as his lips found her neck.

She tilted her head to give him better access. Heat bloomed at her core, and she placed her hands over his on her abdomen. "I'm in no rush to go home…if you'd rather stay here."

His lips left her neck so he could answer. "I want whatever you want. We can stay here and binge-watch one of those shows you mentioned."

She let out a soft laugh. "I don't think I'm in the mood for television."

"What are you in the mood for?"

Twisting on crutches wasn't possible, so she tilted her head back, offering her lips over her shoulder. His hot mouth met hers, and they kissed like they'd just invented a new art form.

He nibbled on her bottom lip, his tongue tracing the scar.

He raised his head. "Can you feel when I suck on your lip like that? Or are the nerve endings severed?"

"There's a small numb spot. Mostly I can feel it. Do it again."

He chuckled and did as she commanded. "Keep telling me what you want. I love hearing what turns you on."

She stroked his stubbled cheek as her head tilted back. "I

want you to make me forget everything that's happened in the last three months. I want you inside my body. I want to make you feel good while you rock my world."

His eyes were molten hot as he ran his thumb over her bottom lip, pausing on the scar. "I can do all that. But you need to tell me if there's anything I do that doesn't feel right, or if you change your mind."

She nodded and realized what he was trying to say, but struggled with how to word it. "If you're worried that I was raped and might have a triggering memory...thankfully, I wasn't sexually assaulted." At least, the one attack had been stopped before it got beyond grabbing hands that were tangled in her skirt.

"I was hit several times. There was bruising and swelling. But the worst physical damage was to my ankle at the end."

"Thank you. I didn't want to ask something that's none of my business. You said you want me to help you forget... and I was afraid we might do something that would cause you to remember."

She supposed it made sense that a rape survivor might want to have sex to replace the memory with a welcome touch. Every woman handled trauma differently.

Chris Flyte was a good man and understanding in a way she hadn't expected. She leaned forward on her crutches so she could turn to face him. Once she was in place, she rose on her good foot and settled her hands on his shoulders for support. His arms wrapped around her bottom, and the crutches fell to the side. At last, she was fully flush against him as they kissed long and deep.

She was breathless as she spoke against his lips. "I want you to make love to me, Lieutenant Flyte."

He bent his knees and lifted her, draping her over his shoulder as he carried her to the king-sized bed that filled the center of the hotel room.

He placed her on the bed and said, "At your command, Dr. Edwards."

✦

*D*iana's eyes were lit with desire as her fingers found the buttons of her blouse and slowly opened them, revealing a sheer bra that overflowed with rounded breasts.

He reached to help her undress, but she shook her head and gave him a different order. "Strip."

He had no choice but to comply. He moved slowly, taking in her avid gaze as he revealed his upper torso.

She practically purred with delight, and he thoroughly enjoyed her reaction. It had been a long time since he'd shown off his physique to an appreciative audience.

He was honed sharp thanks to the latest deployment. She scooted to the edge of the bed so she could touch his chest.

They were a contrast. Her breasts pale, soft and round with pink nipples, while his chest was firm and dark with a smattering of hair and brown nipples. She traced those flat brown peaks with a fingertip, then pressed her palm to his skin and ran her hands over his pecs and biceps. "Damn, you're beautiful."

He pulled one of her hands to his lips and sucked on the tip of her finger. "So are you. I want to see more."

She smiled. "I'm going to need your help getting the skirt off."

"I was hoping you'd say that."

She rose to her good foot, and he reached around to release the lone button, then pulled down the zipper. He pushed the opened waistband to her knees, then she sat back on the bed, allowing him to ease it over the ankle brace. He tossed the garment aside. Next, he removed the knee-high sock she wore on her left leg and tossed it in the same direction as the skirt.

Naked but for undergarments and ankle brace, she was a feast of soft curves. Fit, not slender. Full and lush. Utterly perfect.

His erection strained against his slacks, reminding him of an important detail. "I've got a condom in my wallet."

She grinned. "So do I."

"If we need more, I can get a box from the lobby store."

"I like your confidence."

He laughed. "I should probably run down to the lobby now."

She grabbed his waistline and tugged him toward her, then unbuttoned and unzipped, performing the same service he'd done for her, but facing him, his abs at her eye level.

She just about killed him by licking her lips before she reached into his briefs and freed his cock. She smiled a wicked smile and stroked the shaft, running her thumb over the precum at the tip, then, lord have mercy, she swirled her tongue around the head and took him into her mouth.

She closed her eyes and gave a slight suck as she licked him, not moving to take him any deeper. As if she was adjusting to and savoring his girth.

She let out a soft mew of pleasure, then stroked the shaft from root to foreskin as she suckled the head.

It was wildly erotic to be savored in such a way.

She opened her eyes and tilted her head back to meet his gaze with his cock still in her mouth, and he had to fight the urge to thrust. Her mouth felt incredible, and seeing his cock with her lips wrapped around him only made him harder.

She smiled, then shifted so he could slide deeper, until he touched the back of her throat and she stroked the rest of him with her palm.

She rocked back and forth on the edge of the bed, taking him as deep as she could, then licking the underside of the shaft as he pulled back, giving her just the tip to suck on.

It wouldn't be long before he'd reach the point of no return, and he forced himself to step back out of reach of her mouth and hands.

Her eyes were glazed with lust as he toed off his shoes, then shucked his pants, briefs, and socks.

He stepped closer to her, and she reached for his cock again.

"No. My turn." He reached around her to unhook the sheer bra. "Lie on your back so I can remove your panties, unless you want me to rip them off you."

Her eyes got a wicked glint, but then she scooted back. "Better keep my panties intact since they're the only pair I have with me."

The idea of her going commando in a skirt was a turn-on. He could pull it up and thrust into her, hot and fast. But they could play that game another time.

Lord. He was already planning another time. But it was hard to imagine one night would be enough.

She lay on her back and lifted her ass from the bed to pull down her underwear. He climbed beside her and again eased her last scrap of clothing over the brace.

She was now naked except for the brace that protected her ankle. "I'll be careful," he promised.

"I know you will."

Her trust in him was something. He ran his hand over her skin, pausing to cup her breasts and lick her nipples before giving them a light suck.

Her hand caressed his head, fingers scraping his scalp through his short curls.

"Watching you suck my nipples reminds me of one of the fantasies that got me through recovery at Landstuhl."

"You thought about me?"

"Oh yeah."

He licked a peaked pink tip. "Doing this?"

Her eyes were smokey hot. "Yes."

"What else did you imagine?"

"Sucking on your cock. It was even better than I imagined."

"I mean, what did you imagine me doing?"

"Licking me everywhere. Making me come."

"Did you masturbate while thinking of me?"

"Not until I was back in the US. I'm sure a nurse would

have walked in at the wrong time or the heart monitor would have given me away."

He laughed. He trailed a tongue down her belly. "I'd kind of like to hook you up to a heart monitor now."

"I might break it."

He reached her belly button, then dipped lower and lower.

Her belly trembled, and he hadn't even found home yet.

He shifted position, spreading her legs so he could settle between her thighs, and he looked down at her.

So fucking beautiful.

He brushed her clit with his thumb and she jerked with pleasure and let out a soft hum. He dipped his head down and licked her, circled her clit with his tongue, then alternated sucking and licking. She groaned this time, her thighs tightening against his head as he explored every part of her center with mouth and fingers.

She was wet, hot, and ready for his cock, but he wanted to make her come with his mouth first.

He paused in his play to grab the condom from his wallet, tore open the packet, then laid it on the bed next to him before settling between her thighs again and sliding his tongue inside her slick, wet heat. Enjoying the tangy flavor of her arousal as she began to thrash on the bed, getting ever closer to orgasm.

He had two fingers stroking inside her and his tongue on her clit when she tipped over the precipice and held his head between her palms. She cried out as her body rocked with the sensations he'd triggered.

He kept his tongue on her clit as he grabbed the packet and extracted the condom. He continued to tease her with his mouth even as he rolled on the condom. Then he rose up and settled his hips between her thighs. He gazed down at her, wiping his mouth with the back of his hand as his penis nudged at her opening.

"Please," she whispered.

He pressed into her, thrusting deep with one smooth stroke. He echoed her gasp of pleasure in his mind. Her tight heat enveloped him, the intensity of the incredible sensation increasing as he pulled back slowly and thrust again.

He kept an even rhythm, wanting this to last and last. Her soft moans made his task difficult as they pushed him close to the breaking point.

He kept his weight off her, hands on either side of her head as he slid deep and back again. He bent his elbows to kiss her and next thing he knew, he was resting on his forearms, his tongue doing to her mouth what his cock was doing to her pussy.

And then he couldn't hold back. Couldn't slow himself. He was lost, thrusting hard and deep and fast as she wrapped her legs around his ass and met him thrust for thrust.

He felt the brace against his butt cheek and hoped his movement wasn't putting any strain on her injury as he moved within her.

She came again before he did, crying out with a loud groan that put him over the edge.

He came, his body rocking like he'd been hit with a wave.

It had been a long, long time since he'd been with a partner, and he feared for the condom's durability.

To that end, he slipped from her body carefully, relieved to see it remained intact. He kissed Diana deeply, then said, "Be right back."

He washed up in a flash, then returned to her side. She lay on top of the bed with an utterly content look on her face.

He gathered her against him and nuzzled her neck. "Give me about fifteen minutes, then we can make use of your condom."

She laughed. "I think I'm going to need at least thirty minutes."

"As long as you remember it was you, not me, who needed the longer recovery time."

"Hey, you made me come twice in just a few minutes. Not my fault."

"I suppose I'm willing to take the fall for that."

She snuggled against him, her cheek on his chest. "This isn't what I expected when Morgan insisted I come to her birthday party."

"Right? The gift was all mine."

"And mine."

Her dark hair was beautifully mussed, and he tucked a strand behind her ear. "You really thought about me when you were in the hospital?"

She nodded. "No point in playing cool and coy now." Still, she blushed. Which was wild considering how free with each other's bodies they'd been just a few moments ago.

"I thought about you too. But I had a lot of guilt around that. You were an op, and it was inappropriate to sexualize you."

"I'm not an op anymore."

"And that's the only reason I could act on this…thing I felt for you, even before tonight."

"And I asked myself if my attraction to you was just because I was grateful you'd saved me."

He traced her lip, his finger automatically going to the scar. He remembered the first time he saw this scar, in the briefing room that first day. Her professional portrait presented a pretty, serious woman. But the real Diana was something else entirely. "You got away. Saved yourself. I was just there for the final piece."

"I don't know if I'd have been able to do it, to kill Bassam, if I didn't know that you were about to walk into Jamal's line of fire. One more step and…"

"So really, you saved me."

"I was the reason everyone was in that stairwell to begin with."

He pressed his lips to her forehead. "Are you sure you want to talk about this? I thought you said you want to forget."

She was quiet for a minute, then said, "I guess I feel safe talking about it with you."

"I'm glad I make you feel safe and am sorry you haven't felt that with others."

"Morgan and Freya have been great, but everyone else— even their husbands—have at one point or another given me the side-eye, like they think maybe the whole Rafiq thing was in my head."

"Have you considered that maybe it was just someone who looked a lot like him?"

She stiffened against him, and he felt the weight of his mistake come crashing down like a wall between them.

Chapter Twenty-Four

a bucket of ice water would have been more pleasant and less shocking. Diana scooted away from Chris as she tried to gather her thoughts. Her gaze darted around. She spotted her crutches on the floor, by the window. "I—I need to clean up. Can you get me my crutches?"

"Diana, I'm sorry I—"

"I really need my crutches."

"I shouldn't have said that. I—"

"Give me my crutches."

"I don't want you to think—"

Being trapped like this, unable to cross the room unless she crawled, squeezed like a vise on her chest. "Now, dammit! I will not be held prisoner by my injury or you."

His eyes widened with shock, and he bolted from the bed and brought them to her without a word.

She scooped up her scattered clothing, using the crutches to pull the items closer so she could reach them, then hobbled into the bathroom.

Once the door was closed and locked, she faced herself in the mirror and took several deep breaths to try to get her emotions under control. Once she figured her voice would be steady, she called for a cab.

Knowing she had several minutes before it would arrive, she took her time cleaning up, trying to compose herself into the calm, cold woman who'd faced down an armed SEAL and chose continued abduction over rescue because the cause was greater than herself.

She'd risked her life, put absolutely everything on the line for the right reason, and no one believed her.

Well, no one except Morgan and Freya. But people would say her FMV bosses had their own reasons for backing her story. If Diana was wrong, she'd likely destroyed their entire operation.

No one would trust a tip from anyone associated with FMV again. No more tracker implants to call for rescues.

Her hands shook as she smoothed her hair and reapplied lipstick so she wouldn't look like she'd just gotten fucked to the cab driver and everyone she passed in the hotel lobby.

Not that it mattered, but she wanted to pretend for just one moment that she hadn't just made a colossal mistake and slept with the SEAL who'd rescued her in Jordan.

What had she been thinking?

It had been better when he was nothing more than an impossible superhero.

She took several deep breaths, centering herself. She remembered those early days of training with Freya, and how she'd learned to shove away her pain and grief and focus on the job. Freya had explained how important it was to never allow her face to reveal what was going on inside her head and had taught her tricks for changing her headspace.

She used it now as she prepared to say goodbye to Lieutenant Chris Flyte one more—and very final—time.

She opened the bathroom door and there he was, dressed again and pacing the room. He turned to face her. "Diana—"

"Thank you for the orgasms. My cab will be here shortly. I will see myself out."

"I'll walk down with you—"

"No. You will not."

"Diana—"

"Goodbye, Lieutenant Flyte." She made a beeline for the door and wondered what she'd do if he attempted to follow her to the lobby. She didn't want to make a scene that would cause trouble for him, but he also needed to respect her boundaries.

Thankfully, that was what he did. The door closed behind her, and she slowly made her way down the endless empty corridors for the elevators. With no one able to see her face, she relaxed her guard, but then had to hold her breath against tears.

If she started crying, she'd never stop.

No. She had to get home first, then she'd fall apart. She'd give herself twenty-four hours to feel the hurt, then she'd cut off that part of her heart like she'd had to do with Salim.

Lieutenant Chris Flyte would be as dead to her as her deceased fiancé.

4

*A*s soon as she arrived in her condo, she wrapped her foot and ankle in a watertight cast cover and filled her deep, jetted tub with hot water and a liberal amount of bath salts and aromatherapy oils.

She'd smelled his scent on her body the entire cab ride home, and while it was a pleasant smell, she didn't want to be reminded of him with every breath.

She'd purchased the condo not long after the accident, and the tub was fitted with extra handholds to facilitate getting in and out with only one good leg. She was thankful she'd made the accommodation then, even though by the time she moved in, she'd been almost to full mobility.

Now, she relaxed in her tub, the only place she really felt safe, which was odd given how utterly vulnerable she was between being naked and the complicated movements it took to get in and out without doing further harm to her much-abused joint.

She tried not to think about Chris. He wasn't allowed in her safe space. No, she needed to focus on what her next steps would be to combat the efforts to brand her as either delusional or a liar when it came to Rafiq.

But really, she was at a loss. She'd spoken with the terrorist leader three times, but there was no proof of it.

The raid on the compound had resulted in the questioning of two women who apparently worked in the house as cooks. Diana had never crossed their paths while she was there, and they hadn't known she was there. The women had denied Rafiq or any terrorist group resided there. But then, that was to be expected.

The men had all left in search of Diana.

The artifacts were gone.

Rafiq was gone.

He must've slipped out, hidden among the men in pursuit of her, a keffiyeh covering his head and face so he looked just like the others.

They got nothing from the raid. No proof that Rafiq was alive or had ever been there.

No one questioned her story of being held captive in that house. After all, they had drone video of her escaping. But there were other, more insidious questions being asked. Some in the Intelligence Community suggested her escape had been staged and she'd never been in real danger.

She closed her eyes as she sat in the hot water with the jets pummeling her shoulders.

She saw the bicycle. Inviting and available. Right there by the open gate. Felt the fear that had coursed through her as she made the rash decision to escape because she'd given up on waiting for the US military to save her.

She'd given up on Chris and his team. But then, she'd been certain they'd given up on her.

It had felt like the most dangerous action she'd taken in six weeks of taking dangerous actions—starting with refusing to be rescued the first time.

Now she had to wonder if it hadn't been dangerous at all. If they'd let her go to give them all a reason to abandon the compound before the raid.

Had they known about the tracker?

The secret of subdermal trackers was known among some terrorist groups, but they'd have to have known she was a Valkyrie to suspect she had one, and that was the one thing she'd never been certain they knew about her.

She studied the faint scar on her arm. The dead tracker had been removed when she was in Germany. She was tracker-free.

If it hadn't been for the small chip, she'd never have made the decisions she'd made. She'd have been rescued by Chris that first night. She'd probably be safe and home and whole.

She supposed she was safe and home. And technically, her body was whole. But her life was shattered. Irreparable.

Missing pieces like the glass ingot she'd broken.

She kept telling herself she'd get through this. Rafiq would be spotted by someone else, and her reputation would be restored. If that never happened, then at least with time, people would recognize that everything she'd done was for the greater good, even if it couldn't be proved that the man was alive.

She hadn't worked for a terrorist cell willingly. She had been under duress, in constant fear for her life.

Dr. Fahd Yousef's body had been found within hours of his death. Her account of what she'd seen on the video matched with the wounds on his body. They knew that part of her story to be true.

Her heart ached every time she thought of Fahd and his wife and children.

Answers weren't to be found in the tub, and so Diana opened the drain and then very carefully extracted herself, using all the handholds available and still nearly slipping twice.

She settled on a cold plastic chair she'd set up next to the tub and carefully removed the protective plastic from her leg, followed by the brace. She inspected the bandages before slowly unwrapping them to reveal the joint in all its mottled, sutured glory. She had a web of old scars and new stitches. These stitches were the slow-to-dissolve kind and even six weeks out she faced a patchwork of skin defined by blue lines that crisscrossed her pale skin. The sutures looked good—the sewn skin showing no redness or extra swelling.

She looked forward to hearing the doctor's opinion of her progress tomorrow.

She used a soft cloth and special soap to wash her foot and ankle and then sat with her limb in front of a small portable heater for a few minutes to ensure it was completely dry before she wrapped it in a new bandage and put the brace back on. Only then did she deal with the rest of her postbathing ritual of combing wet hair and applying lotions.

With each step in the process, she tried not to think about anything but the task at hand. Still, Chris came to mind as she remembered the feel of his hands as she rubbed moisturizer into her skin. His lips on her neck as she stood in the window of his hotel room.

It shouldn't hurt so much so quickly. It was just supposed to be a fun fling, and he'd certainly delivered on the fun.

Still, the idea that he of all people—the one person who'd witnessed both her decision at the start and her killing Bassam—could doubt her, was an unimaginable blow.

She pulled on a thick, soft robe and left her bathroom.

Instead of getting ready for bed, she went to the kitchen and poured herself a glass of wine, grabbed her laptop, then ferried the items to the low table on her balcony. The night was cold and cloudless, but the night sky was muted by light pollution from the city.

She sat on the padded bench and turned on the propane fire bowl and wrapped herself in a thick wool blanket.

She really should get an electric blanket for nights like this. She grabbed her laptop and opened a browser, but before she could begin online shopping, she forced herself to check her inbox, braced for the worst. The university in Amman continued to have questions, but she couldn't give them all the answers they wanted. Couldn't tell them about her work for FMV, nor could she share that Fahd had given her coordinates to endangered sites—after all, not even the university knew about his covert work there.

They didn't know she'd identified Rafiq. All they knew was that she'd given up a protected site's location and looted it. She'd never work for the university again. She'd likely never be permitted to excavate in Jordan again.

Given that there was a terrorist cell gunning for her, she'd never be able to return to that part of the world.

Chapter Twenty-Five

*U*sing a cane to prevent her from putting her full weight on her injured foot, Diana stepped outside onto the busy city sidewalk. Her first outing in the new walking boot. Baby steps at last.

She remembered this part of recovery, although it had taken longer to get to this point the second time around. She was just grateful the repair had been possible. In the first days after her rescue, there was talk again of her foot being amputated. But they'd opted to do the surgery first and see if the wounds would repair a second time. She'd likely need more surgeries in the future and might need some bones fused. She would never have full range of motion again, but she hadn't regained it after the car accident anyway.

She might still lose her foot, but for now, she was glad they'd tried this option first as she'd healed better than expected so far. She'd still need the crutches if she was going to walk a great distance, but boot and cane would see her through light activity.

Stairs would be easier, at least.

Traffic on Wisconsin Avenue was always heavy, and this gray Friday morning was no exception. She looked for a place to sit out of the wind so she could check her messages. She could have done the task inside the medical center, but she couldn't stand hospital waiting rooms and had no desire to add a respiratory illness to her list of ailments.

A low concrete wall enclosed a patch of dirt forming a garden of bare trees and low shrubs. She settled on the cold concrete and pulled out her phone. One thing she'd learned during her first round in this rodeo was walking and checking her phone was impossible. It was dangerous for people with two good ankles, but a distraction for her could be deadly.

Her text messages were minimal. Morgan checked in, thanking her for coming to the party, and she wanted to make sure she'd gotten safely home. There was probably a question about Chris in that, but they hadn't been friends long enough for this to be comfortable territory.

In the months that they'd known each other before Diana went to Jordan, she'd been too deep in grief and never considered dating. Hell, she *still* hadn't really considered dating. She'd gone to the bar with thoughts of indulging in a one-night stand.

Then, the man who picked her up was Chris, and for a brief moment, dating might have looked like a possibility.

He'd been perfect. Her body wanted attention after so much heartache, pain, and fear. And Chris had delivered exactly what she'd craved. She should have left before he had a chance to ruin it.

She'd spent most of her night brooding over his words and asking herself if her response to his question had been reasonable. Still, how did he not get what was at stake for her? He knew what she'd risked, which made his doubt all the more crushing.

It was no idle thing for her to have named Makram Rafiq as the man in charge of the operation. She'd risked everything—her reputation, her career, and most importantly, her life—because Rafiq was a dangerous kingpin in the artifact trafficking and terrorist world.

A chunk was taken from her soul every time someone said Rafiq only existed in her head like a boogeyman. She'd have expected Chris—who'd witnessed part of what she'd gone through—to understand.

She hadn't made Rafiq up. She'd seen him. Spoken with him. Destroyed a site for him.

Thinking of Chris stirred up too many emotions, causing a tear to escape. Dammit, what happened to her cold certainty and calm control?

But she knew. It had been shattered the moment she was told she hadn't seen Jamal in the hospital. The moment they began chipping away at her memories. She'd lost her ability to compartmentalize and feared she'd never get it back.

She sent Morgan a quick thumbs-up emoji to the question of whether she'd gotten home okay, then switched to the email app.

She never accessed the email account she'd typed into the camera's memory in Aqaba on her phone. The moment she realized the Intelligence Community was invested in keeping the lie that Rafiq was dead, she knew that if they got access to her email account and the photos landed in her inbox, they might make them disappear.

She'd checked a half dozen times in the last week, and so far, she'd received no photos from the past. It had been twenty-four hours since her last check. She made a mental reminder to check again when she got home this afternoon.

She now read a message from Salim's mom, inviting her to visit his family's home in Upstate New York. Her heart squeezed.

Diana's abduction had been kept under wraps by the State Department, so as far as Salim's family knew, her work in Jordan had been extended by several weeks following the death of Dr. Fahd Yousef.

She sent a quick reply using her ankle as an excuse to put off visiting for a few more weeks. She didn't have the emotional energy to face Salim's parents and tell them the truth about what had happened to her, but she also knew there was no way she could see them and not tell them.

They were the closest thing she had to parents, and with the loss of their son, she was the closest thing they had to a child.

She wanted to keep that relationship for all their sakes, but she didn't know if she could live with the condemnation she would see on their faces when she revealed she'd looted a site in Jordan.

Also in her inbox was a summons from Dennis Gardner, the man who'd set up the grant with the university in Jordan to fund the dig and her work there. It was a very authoritative summons, saying he was in DC on business until Tuesday, staying at the Mayflower. They needed to discuss her work in Jordan. She was to be at his hotel today at one p.m.

She glanced at her watch. An hour and a half from now.

Gardner didn't inquire about whether or not the timing worked for her. His time was clearly more important, and she needed to accommodate his schedule.

If Chris were here with his car as he'd offered, they'd have time for lunch and she could leave the crutches in his vehicle. As it was, she didn't have time to return to her condo and so would have to strap either cane or crutches to her backpack as she took the Metro to Farragut North.

It irritated her that she didn't have a doctor appointment or any other valid reason to refuse the summons. But the truth was, this was a meeting she'd been dreading, so it would be good to get it over with. It was probably better that she didn't have too much time to mentally prepare. If she tried to reschedule, she'd just stress about it and it would be worse when it finally happened. At least now, she'd have it behind her by the end of the day.

She sent a reply saying she would be there, then texted Morgan informing her of the meeting and location, including Gardner's hotel room number.

No way would she meet with anyone to talk about Jordan without letting Morgan and Freya know where and when. These kinds of meetings could easily be a trap.

*C*hris wasn't exactly sure why he was in the FMV office waiting room, but when Morgan and Freya requested a meeting, he couldn't resist the opportunity. Rand might consider them friends, but given everything that had happened to Diana and the way she was being used by the Intelligence Community, he was feeling less charitable toward them today than he had last night when he first arrived at Morgan's birthday party.

He was the one who'd fucked up in questioning Diana's memory, but they were the ones who'd put her in the situation to begin with, right down to feeding her a deck of cards that included a man who'd been taken off the most wanted list nearly two years ago.

Was it possible FMV had set Diana up somehow?

Of course, he couldn't begin to see what purpose that would serve, but when the CIA was involved, he knew to be wary.

The FMV admin, a man Chris had met at the party last night, apologized for the delay again and let Chris know that they were just waiting for one more team member before their meeting could begin.

Chris hoped the person they were waiting for was Diana, only to be disappointed when a brown-skinned woman with glossy black hair entered the office in a flurry of energy. She took one look at Chris and said, "You must be the lieutenant. Sorry I'm late. My daughter is sick and not at school, and I needed to wait for my sitter to arrive, but the sitter got stuck on the Metro. I just need a minute to catch up with Freya then we'll be ready for you." She nodded to the admin then was off down the hall before Chris could reply.

"That was Amira," the admin said. "She wasn't at the party last night because her youngest got sick yesterday. Her husband is deployed, so she's on her own right now."

Chris knew what that was like. He wondered if she'd be on her own with the kids through the holidays. Still, it was hard to be separated from a spouse for long periods no matter the season, and especially so when one had kids. It had been a major reason he and Pam had decided to hold off on having children.

Now Pam was pregnant with a different SEAL's child, and Chris had just signed the papers an hour ago that dissolved their marriage, leaving her free to marry her baby daddy if she wanted.

He didn't love her anymore, and he certainly didn't miss her, but he wasn't quite to the point of being able to congratulate her and raise a toast to her happiness. He hoped to get there someday—he didn't want to be bitter, and he'd loved her deeply once upon a time—but he had no idea how he'd find that path.

At least now that the divorce was final, he wouldn't have to deal with her anymore. He gave thanks to the god of family planning and birth control that they weren't facing shared custody. Someday, he might want kids again, but not with Pam.

After ten more minutes of waiting, he was led into a comfortably appointed meeting room and officially introduced to Amira Ripley and again shook hands with Freya Lange and Dr. Morgan Adler.

If any of the women knew what had transpired—the good and the bad—between Diana and him last night, it didn't show on their faces, and as far as he could tell, only Freya was trained to hide her thoughts and emotions.

"You know, of course, that I'm not at liberty to share any details of the op to save Dr. Edwards with you, regardless of your involvement and security clearance."

Lange nodded. "We've already extracted what we could from Rand."

He smiled at the word she chose, imagining Rand being grilled by the former SAD operative and slowly doling out what he could like teeth removal.

"When was that?" He didn't see Rand happily going to Morgan's party after being subjected to questioning.

"This morning," Morgan said.

"I'm sorry I missed it," Amira said. "Too bad we couldn't Zoom."

Chris snorted. No way could any of these conversations be conducted online. He wouldn't be surprised if the CIA had the offices under constant surveillance. There was a law that prevented the CIA from operating on American soil to surveil American citizens, but the law stopped at former CIA employees. Those they could investigate. They were required to have probable cause and all the other legalities covered, but they were CIA. Breaking laws—foreign, not domestic—was the backbone of how they gathered intelligence. Illegal surveillance was fundamental to their business model, like teaching first graders to add and subtract so they could move on to multiplication and division.

He wouldn't trust the agency to only use legal means to

monitor Freya Lange any more than he'd expect a lion to be vegetarian. His gaze darted around the room. "I'm guessing you scan this place for bugs regularly?"

The former spy grinned. "Often enough to know exactly when they started trying to hack our systems—four days after Diana was abducted. But don't worry. We have the most secure system possible." She nodded toward Amira. "Amira is our in-house tech wizard, and we have other specialists we trust completely. And this room is completely shielded from any electronic signals in or out."

Chris nodded, not surprised to find he was sitting in a vault. It wasn't a conference room set up with a large monitor at the end of a long table. No, it was a series of comfortable love seats and low tables. Like one might find at a coffee shop or wine bar. This was a room for conversations, not computer demonstrations.

"So why am I here?"

"We believe you can help us identify someone." Freya flipped open a file folder and pulled out a stack of small, thick papers.

"Not another deck of cards?"

She shook her head. "No. We want to know if you can identify Jamal from a lineup."

"Jamal? One of the two brothers who were Diana's guards? Why?"

"You were the only operator to see his face. And you saw him twice."

"The first time, he was backlit. My camera couldn't even get his face. Kramer might have gotten a better look. He was in the slot canyon too."

"He didn't. Rand put us in touch. We interviewed him and Albrecht this morning."

He'd known Albrecht never saw the kid's face in the stairwell. Even Chris only got a glimpse before he turned and ran up the stairs.

"The camera didn't get him either time, but *you* saw him, right?"

He closed his eyes and remembered crawling through the low tunnel that opened up and became a slot canyon. He'd gone from shimmying in a belly crawl, to hands and knees, to a stooped walk—the full March of Progress—before the slot opened wide enough for a vehicle to be hidden among the sandstone walls. He'd seen Diana, lit in green through his NVGs, as the boy she later identified as Bassam held a knife to her throat.

Then headlights had flared on, and he'd flipped up his goggles as she was backlit by the bright beams. The light hit her at a faint oblique angle. She and Bassam were lit slightly from the side, and the wash of light reached him, so Diana could see his face too.

Her position then shifted, and she cast a shadow that shielded his eyes from the bright beam, allowing him to see her better. He remembered glancing toward the light source, trying to determine if there was any way Kramer, who was still in the tunnel, could slip out and to the side, and take out the tango who'd turned on the headlights.

The man—more a boy—stood in the wash of light for a moment, but moved back in the shadows as soon as Chris shifted so his body camera could capture him.

Jamal was thin and wiry. His keffiyeh had slipped off,

probably when he'd crawled through the tunnel, and Chris saw short dark hair, a pointed chin and nose. He guessed the boy sported wisps of facial hair, but it wasn't visible given the distance between them.

He'd been a handsome kid. Thick brows and sharp cheekbones.

Chris opened his eyes and faced the three women. "I might recognize him. Maybe."

Freya nodded and picked up the file folder and opened it, standing it up on the coffee table between them. "I'm going to lay out nine photos. I want you to tell me which ones are of Jamal."

"You have photos of him? How did you manage that?"

Freya gave a faint smile. "It's classified."

He rolled his eyes, but he hadn't really expected an answer.

After the images were arranged, she reached for the folder. He held up a hand, "Wait. How many photos are of Jamal?"

"That's for you to tell me, Lieutenant."

She then lifted the folder, and he studied the images laid out in a three-by-three grid. Nine young men. All Middle Eastern, with skin tones that varied from yellow-brown to a deep dark mahogany. None had skin quite as dark as Chris's own dark brown, but one was close.

"Take your time," Morgan said.

Assuming these photos—some of which appeared to have been taken on city streets with the subject unaware of the camera—didn't show boys attempting to change their appearance, he focused on the faces with the skin tone closest to what he'd seen in the canyon. Medium brown with reddish undertones.

His eyes kept coming back to one image. A slight profile, a similar angle to what he'd glimpsed before the boy shifted into the darkness. He studied it for a long moment, trying to decide if the angle of the shot was influencing his thoughts. This boy was younger, maybe thirteen or fourteen. According to Diana, Jamal had been fifteen.

He closed his eyes to again bring the night back into focus. The tilt of the head. The coldness of the eyes as Chris's weapon aimed in the boy's direction as Bassam shouted that Diana would die if Chris fired.

He hadn't believed the threat. After all, Diana was their prize and still alive for a reason, which was why he'd been confident that if Diana hadn't cooperated with the brothers, he and Kramer would've had no problem completing her rescue.

But she'd taken control of the brothers and the op, and now he needed to decide if Jamal was in any of the photos before him.

He opened his eyes and pointed to the image on the right side of the middle row. "That's Jamal."

His declaration was met with silence, and he reconsidered the idea that only Freya knew how to maintain a poker face.

Finally, Freya said, "Are there any other pictures of him?"

He shook his head, but then pointed to the photo on the bottom left. "That's his brother, Bassam. I'm guessing it was taken when he was younger, closer to the age Jamal is now."

It wasn't a photo taken from the drone footage, which was almost a relief because it would only raise questions if Freya Lange had access to Top Secret military images and video.

"How'd he do?" Amira asked.

Freya scooped up the photos. "Passed with flying colors."

"Where did you get these?" Chris asked again.

"I've been digging into where the brothers came from originally. Diana suggested they might have been taken in one of the attacks on a school. We looked at a number of such attacks across the region. Two years ago—before Rafiq's supposed death—one raid in Beirut led to the disappearance of over a dozen children, including brothers named Bassam and Jamal. Their sister, Farah, was also taken."

"Diana never said anything about a girl."

"No. She would have been enslaved or killed early on. Possibly separated from the brothers once their cooperation with the Islamic State group that took them was established."

"Why are you showing me this now?"

"We needed a positive ID so we can get our friends with facial recognition capability to start searching databases to see if Jamal has entered the US, or to stop him if he tries to do so. We were fairly certain these were the right boys, but needed someone who'd seen them both in person to confirm it."

"Why not ask Diana?"

"The Intelligence Community would suspect her identification in a way that they won't yours," Morgan said. "I'm not sure you realize just how dire Diana's situation is. The

Kingdom is on the cusp of demanding she be extradited back to Jordan. If we can't find a way to prove Rafiq is alive, the State Department will likely comply in keeping with our nations' extradition treaty. Diana could face prosecution and imprisonment in Jordan for looting the archaeological site."

Chapter Twenty-Six

*D*ennis Gardner answered his hotel room door with a scowl on his weathered face. "You're late, Miss Edwards."

She gave him a tight smile. "*Dr.* Edwards." She cocked her head for him to open the door wider, as she could hardly pass through the narrow opening while using crutches, wearing a loaded backpack with her new cane strapped to it.

She was tired and frazzled and it had taken her longer to walk the block and a half from the Metro because she'd opted to use the elevator instead of riding the escalator, but the line had been long on a Friday afternoon. "The time you selected for this meeting wasn't convenient for me, Mr. Gardner, but I did my best to accommodate you. You're welcome."

There was a slight cough from inside the room, and Gardner stepped back, letting her see who else was attending this meeting.

She hobbled into the room on three legs and faced

Dennis Gardner's son, Mason, and another man she'd never met before.

Mason was a chip off the old block, a younger version of the sixty-five-year-old third-generation retail magnate. The Gardners were both white and just under six feet tall. The younger son was tanned and fit, with thick dark hair, while the elder was pale with streaks of gray and thinning hair.

The male genes ran strong in this family, as she'd seen the portrait of Dennis Gardner's grandfather, who'd opened the first Gardner Holdings store in the 1950s in Virginia. Now the ever-growing empire showed all signs of being passed on to Mason to keep the vast array of stores in the same family's stewardship for a fourth generation.

Several months ago, they'd broken ground on a new flagship store for their most prominent chain, Historie. The art replica retail giant was best known for the Gardner family's Signature Line of replicas—artifacts of which the Gardner family themselves owned the originals. Every year, they sold a limited run of one-to-one-sized replicas handmade out of the same material as the original for thousands of dollars. In the new store/museum, the originals would be displayed along with a replica in a setting that was also a replica of the type of site where the item had been found.

Given that Mason Gardner's name was all over the press releases for the new store, she gathered it was his baby, his way to show the world he was ready to take over the family business. Still, he'd faced every meeting with Diana with as much enthusiasm as one faced changing a kitty litter box—a chore that was unpleasant whether one loved the cat or not.

She was fairly certain Mason did not like the cat in this

instance. The new store and museum might be his pet project, but he was not an animal lover.

She turned her focus to the stranger in the room, guessing he was probably another company man who was not thrilled to be here. At least he was easy on the eyes.

Very easy, in fact, with cheekbones that could cut glass and eyes the color of a lake on a cloudy day. With pale skin that contrasted with short dark hair and a half day's growth of stubble that wasn't thick enough to hide his dimpled, square chin, he was damn close to perfection in the looks department.

Not that she was interested. As she'd learned last night, dating—or even hookups—weren't a great idea for her right now. And the ring on his finger meant he was definitely not a prospect for either.

Still, the man had good manners and rose to his feet and offered his hand when no one made a move to introduce them. "Dr. Edwards, I'm Ian Boyd. I'm a consultant for a company that does security work in the Middle East, and Dennis has contracted with my employer to conduct this interview."

She frowned even as she shook his hand. "Why?"

Boyd's gaze flicked to Dennis, who must've nodded his assent. "Please, sit down." He pointed to the chair that sat at an angle to his. "And I'll explain."

She settled on the plush chair. She wanted more than anything to prop her foot up, but didn't see a footrest and wasn't about to prop her boot on the coffee table. Boyd caught on to her dilemma and instructed Mason to call the front desk and request pillows to make a footrest.

The young heir looked affronted at being asked to do what an admin would usually be tasked with, but there was no administrative assistant in the room, so he followed his father's barked order to do it.

"As I said, I'm Ian. Can I call you Diana?" Then he repeated the question in Arabic.

Now he had her attention. She responded in Arabic. "Please do."

In Arabic, Boyd explained that he'd been hired because he had experience in the clandestine service and the ability to question her in both English and Arabic, which might aid her memory.

"What are you telling her?" Dennis asked.

"Why I'm the best person to conduct this interview. I want to get a feel for Diana's comprehension level before we begin." To her, he said in Arabic, "You understand the language better than you speak it, am I correct?"

She nodded and replied in the same language, "My fluency improved a great deal while there."

In English, Ian asked, "Did you speak much English during the last six weeks you were in-country?"

"Not much." She paused. The timing was specific. Obviously, this man knew she'd been abducted. How much did he know?

She wasn't sworn to any kind of secrecy regarding her abduction. She was an American citizen working in Jordan. She'd been abducted. A team of SEALs had saved her. The only thing that would violate government secrets would be revealing Chris and Rand as SEALs, but even there, she'd never taken any kind of oath. She hadn't even known their names until last night.

Her work for FMV, however, was different. Gardner didn't know about that. She *was* sworn to secrecy there, but it was an oath to Morgan and Freya, not national security.

Clearly, Gardner had decided to bring in an expert for this debriefing, and she would have to remain vigilant for the boundaries of what she could tell.

For example, she could mention she'd seen Rafiq, but she couldn't explain why she'd recognized him. Best to just leave out Rafiq's name altogether.

By the time Mason returned with an actual footstool delivered by a bellhop, Ian had explained his role. He worked for Raptor, a private security and training organization. The CEO of Raptor was a former SEAL, as were several of the operatives. Ian himself was former Delta and a former case officer for the CIA. He spoke six languages and had worked in the Middle East out of the Istanbul office for several years. He smiled and added, "I think it's worth noting my wife is an archaeologist. We met in Turkey when she was looking for an old Roman aqueduct, but now she works for the Underwater Archaeology Branch at Naval History and Heritage Command, which is based at the Navy Yard. When things settle down, she'd love to meet you."

Her brain had been tripping over the fact that he'd been a case officer, the role she'd aspired to when she'd been accepted into the training class. But she didn't mention that here. Gardner didn't know about her lost dream of working for the CIA.

"I'd be interested in meeting her too. Were aqueducts her

specialty?"

Dennis let out a grunt. "You can trade dig stories on your own time."

Considering she wasn't being paid to be here, she was on her own time, but that wasn't true for Ian, and so far, he'd been kind, so she wouldn't cause trouble. She nodded at the former case officer. "We'll do that. Okay, so why are you here now?"

"Dennis would like a full report of your work in Jordan, as was outlined in your initial agreement. In addition, he's concerned about the ramifications of your abduction having blowback on his company and wishes to know everything you can tell him so he can be prepared for his talks with the State Department."

Diana jolted at that. She hadn't considered that Dennis would be in talks with the State Department, but she should have. He was looking at selling Americans branded tours of Petra and other sites in Jordan, including setting up "dig for a day" tours that would require the Kingdom's oversight, and he'd funded her work.

He actually did have a reason to be brought into the loop.

"The Board of Directors of Gardner Holdings asked for an outside investigator to work with the Gardners to show the company conducted a thorough investigation delineating your role and Gardner Holdings' role in the looting of the archaeological site. To that end," Ian continued, "I've been hired because I know the players and issues particular to the region well. I still have connections within the agency, and, as I've already explained, I can conduct this interview in the languages in which things happened, which will likely aid your memory for exactly what was said and things you might have overheard."

She needed to give Dennis Gardner more credit. He'd been smart to bring in this man. She wished Freya and Morgan had thought of this, but it was almost better that they hadn't. If she'd been debriefed in this manner before, it would show. She might screw up and repeat something she could only know through her work for FMV.

Ian set a digital recorder on the coffee table. "I'd like to record this interview so I can provide a written translation to Dennis. Do you consent to being recorded?"

She nodded.

"Please give your consent for the recording," he gently nudged.

"Right. Yes. I, Dr. Diana Edwards, give permission for this interview to be recorded by Ian Boyd."

And then they were off, speaking in a mix of English and Arabic as she relayed her early weeks in Jordan. She mentioned the Friday market only because it was where she'd been taken from, so she described it as one of her favorite things to do every weekend. Ian was familiar with that particular market, and at one point in his questioning, she wondered if he guessed her true reason for visiting the market regularly. After all, it was a known entry point for the underground antiquities market.

Mason was as bored as she expected him to be and never made a move to interrupt the discussion. Dennis, on the other hand, jumped in a few times with questions on the dig, his passion for the subject showing.

He was, in fact, a pet lover.

It wasn't long before they reached the moment of her abduction, and she said nothing about the subdermal tracker, nor did she offer a reason the SEALs had learned of her abduction so quickly.

In a mix of Arabic and English, she described being brought to what had looked like a Bedouin camp that first afternoon. She described the tent in English and her first impression of it being a clever disguise. She described entering the tent and seeing a table laden with artifacts and the demand that she identify them and put a price on each.

After being walked through everything, she found her cool reserve and employed it to describe the slap that had rung her bell that first day. She'd received more blows in the following days and weeks, but that one had been the scariest with the great unknown before her.

Ian's questions were probing but gentle. Mason was finally interested, no doubt eager for more salacious details. Dennis's look had changed from cold businessman to paternal, and she didn't mind it so much. At least he seemed to be acknowledging something horrible had happened to her, which had been missing from all their earlier communications.

She went on to describe the artifacts and that she'd initially believed that was what they'd wanted her for—to authenticate and value artifacts.

"What did you tell them?" Dennis asked. "How were you able to determine value?"

She couldn't tell him about having studied what things went for in the black market thanks to Freya's work to track the supply, so she shrugged. "I made it all up. I assigned dates at the oldest end of the range for everything, to increase its perceived value. I made it sound sellable even if it wasn't a particularly unique or interesting piece. I figured they want money so I'd make everything sound precious, with the exception of the lamp that had been altered."

"One was damaged?"

"Not damaged. Changed. Some artifact dealers will take an actual historic piece and add something to it to up the value. Like the James Ossuary, a burial box that supposedly bears the remains of Jesus's brother. The inscription in that instance was unusual. Burial box inscriptions, in general, don't include siblings' names. It doesn't *mean* the inscription is fake, added centuries or even millennia later, but given how unusual that is, it's highly improbable that it is real."

Dennis nodded. She bet he knew all about the famous box that some still believed to be authentic.

From there, she described a man showing up to speak with her and learning that she wasn't there merely to authenticate, but that the camp was in the middle of a site, and she was expected to dig to provide them with more artifacts.

She didn't describe Rafiq. Nor did she describe the attempted rape by Jamal. She had no need to feed Mason's growing interest in the physical traumas she'd faced, and it wasn't pertinent to the narrative she was feeding his father.

When it came to the showdown with the SEAL, she described the knife at her throat and feeling scared and trapped and left it at that.

She described the way station where she'd watched the video of Fahd's murder in the briefest of terms, mentioning

Fahd and her role in choosing the dig location not at all. She would leave it up to FMV, the CIA, and DIA if they wanted to share that information with the State Department. The rest of the story was mundane. She oversaw the looting of the site to stay alive.

She could see that Dennis wanted her to describe the artifacts she found, but he didn't dare press for details given that she was describing her worst nightmare. It wouldn't be seemly to ask about the goodies.

She was drained and exhausted when she got to the fight in the stairwell and eventual rescue. A glance at her watch showed only ninety minutes had passed since her arrival. She'd relived it all in that compressed time.

"And then I spent a month in the hospital in Landstuhl," she added, skipping over all the questions that became interrogation with one simple sentence. She took a sip of her water and tried to think of what she could say to wrap up this interview. She had a headache and wanted to go home, crawl into bed, and forget everything she'd just described.

"I appreciate you sharing all this with us, Diana," Dennis said. "But there is one area I feel like I need a better grip on before I meet with the State Department. You see, I'm certain they're going to mention your false identification of the leader of the terrorist group as being Makram Rafiq, a man who has been dead for two years. That's really going to be the major sticking point, and I find it quite...*odd* that you left that out of your story completely."

Diana studied the other two men's faces. Ian wasn't surprised by Dennis's words, but neither was he pleased by them. Mason, on the other hand, looked positively gleeful.

Chapter Twenty-Seven

*D*iana's stomach roiled, but she held back the nausea with sheer will as she crossed the ornate hotel lobby. She wasn't entirely sure what Dennis Gardner's plans were, but they couldn't be good for her, not if he planned to throw her to the wolves with the State Department.

She didn't think the situation could be any worse, until she spotted Chris on the bench seat outside the Edgar Bar in the hotel lobby. Clearly waiting for her.

"Are you following me?" She gripped the cane. She could beat him with it if she had to, but she figured she was safe enough in the busy lobby. SEALs generally couldn't risk assaulting women in public.

"No. I was at FMV this morning. Morgan mentioned you'd be here and conveniently gave me the time of your meeting with Gardner. I figured I could offer you a ride home, since I didn't give you a ride to your doctor's appointment this morning."

It might be a nice gesture, but she doubted it. "Why were you at FMV? Stalking me through them?"

He shook his head. "Morgan called me."

"Why?"

"Let me drive you home, and I'll tell you."

"You're getting creepier by the minute."

He ran a hand over his face. "That's because I'm doing this all backward." He nodded toward the bar. "Join me for a drink? You won't be trapped in a car with me or be required to give me your address. I can apologize and tell you what I learned from Morgan today."

She wanted to say no. She wanted to walk coolly out the door, serene as sunshine. She could leave and never see him again. But she also wanted to know why he'd been at FMV today, and her ego, which had been greatly battered in the last twenty minutes, could use the boost of an apology.

But really, it was the voice of Mason Gardner—who must've followed her down to the lobby—that pushed her to take a step toward Chris. "We're watching you, Miss Edwards." His voice dropped, giving it a hostile edge. "You do anything more to smear the Historie brand, and we'll expose you for the thief you are."

She stiffened, locking her core as she faced Chris. Her face flushed red. Mortification or anger, she'd never be certain. All she knew was she couldn't turn to face Mason. Like any childish boogeyman, if she ignored him, he would disappear.

She took another step toward the SEAL who'd saved her in Aqaba. She placed her hand on his chest, rose on her good foot, and brushed her lips over his. "Sweetheart, thanks so much for waiting for me. Let's have that drink you promised."

Chris stroked her cheek, then tugged her closer and planted a deeper kiss on her mouth. Either he was an opportunist or he'd seen something on the other man's face that spurred the action. Based on previous statements both public and private, she wouldn't be surprised to learn the retail heir was bothered both by public displays of affection and mixed-race couples.

She kissed Chris back.

Dammit. The kiss made her want to find a reason to forgive him.

He raised his head and smiled, and her heart did a ridiculous flutter. Clearly the organ needed a tune-up, because it was not behaving properly.

Chris turned and led her into the bar. She followed without looking back. With the exception of a man seated at the bar with his back to the lobby, the establishment was empty, giving them their choice of seating. Diana chose a low couch under the lobby window, giving her room to prop up her leg and a view into the hotel if she twisted to the side just a bit.

After they ordered their drinks and were alone, she huffed out a breath and whispered, "Thank you for playing along."

"Sweetheart, if you're talking about the kiss, I wasn't playing."

She shrugged. "I was."

He snorted. "Liar."

She'd take offense at the remark, but she was, in fact, lying.

Diana spotted Ian walking through the lobby. His gaze met hers through the window. He paused for a long moment before he turned and entered the bar.

"Shit," she muttered. She didn't think kissing Chris would act as a ward against this demon.

"Who is that?" Chris asked.

Ian was at their table before she could answer. He stood with his back to the bar as he offered a hand to Chris and introduced himself, and they did that thing where manly men assessed each other. She'd bet anything Chris identified the spy as former military and Ian identified Chris as active duty right away.

It was a secret body language in which she only understood basic nouns.

Ian turned to her. "I wanted to apologize for the way that ended, Dr. Edwards."

She shrugged. "It was to be expected." She studied him for a minute and said, "Do you like working for Dennis Gardner?"

He gave her a half smile. "I could ask you the same thing."

"Ah, but I never really worked for him. My allegiance was to the university and Fahd. Gardner was just a means to an end."

"I think Gardner could say the same about you." He set his business card on the table. "The problem is, we need to figure out what his end is, because it's not to cut a deal to run tourist digs in Jordan. Call me if you want to talk."

4

*C*hris watched the man retreat after dropping his cryptic bomb. There was definitely more to the operator than met the eye. And Chris was certain the man was an operator of some kind. What he wanted to know was, who was the guy's real employer? It certainly wasn't Gardner.

He returned his attention to Diana. She looked tired and beautiful, and he wondered if she'd slept any more than he had last night.

Probably not.

"I'm sorry," he said. Before he could continue, the waiter brought their drinks. Diana had ordered one of the bar's signature cocktails, while Chris opted for a nonalcoholic beer, his drink of choice when he needed to stay focused.

"So what, exactly, are you apologizing for?" she asked before taking a sip of the fancy cocktail.

He cleared his throat, trying to figure out the best way to defend himself without putting himself in a deeper hole. "I didn't know how bad the situation was for you when I asked what was an honest question."

She stiffened, but didn't bolt. "Tread carefully."

He nodded. "Freya explained that you could face extradition and prosecution for looting. I understand why the subject is…" He couldn't think of a word to adequately encompass her situation, so he found a meek stand-in. "Painful."

He took her hand and was glad when she didn't pull away. "Diana, I wasn't questioning your integrity. I was asking the same question I'd ask Rand or Xavier or any man on my team in a debrief after an op. It *was* a legitimate question. My team risked our lives twice to save you. I'd just spent four days being grilled like a kebab by the damn *Pentagon* about everything that went down and why. It's not wrong for me to wonder if you've considered that you were in a damn stressful situation and might have made a mistake."

"I didn't make a mistake. It was Rafiq."

"You said his face was more scarred than in the pictures we got of him five years ago. He looked *different*."

"His eyes haven't changed."

"Yeah? Tell me about his eyes, then."

"They're brown."

He snorted. "Good thing no one else in the Middle East has brown eyes."

She pulled her hand from his. "I recognized your eyes. That was *all* I saw of you that first night. But I recognized you when you came to my rescue the second time."

He sat back and stared at her, remembering that moment in Aqaba. She'd been in shock. Scared. Covered with blood. He'd just watched her kill a man.

Then, without any memory prompt from him, she'd said, *"It was you, in the canyon. The one I asked to trust me."*

She'd recognized him after only seeing his brown eyes.

4

*D*iana closed her eyes and leaned back in the seat. She felt wrung out. First by the Gardners, then by Ian and his puzzling remark. Now Chris, who she shouldn't have kissed and shouldn't want to kiss again.

But underneath it all was the question: should she examine her memory of her meetings with Rafiq?

If she did that...she had to question everything she'd done based on believing she'd spoken with Rafiq.

Harun had told her that Fahd was killed after her botched rescue. The rescue *she'd* botched on purpose because of the belief she'd spoken with Rafiq.

Silence stretched between her and Chris as she considered this new nightmare.

Was it her fault Fahd's children lost their dad?

"I want to help you, Diana, and I'm not talking about being your chauffeur because you can't drive. I'm talking about the questions the State Department is asking. And with the PTSD you must be going through. It was shitty of me to take advantage of you last night."

The last statement irked her. "You didn't take advantage of me."

"It was too soon. And even though we barely know each other, we have a history that's traumatic for you. Having sex with you, without considering the emotional ramifications, was taking advantage."

"Then I was taking advantage of you too."

He smiled at that, then nodded. "Fine. But of the two of us, I'm the one who's spent years on a special forces team. I know how to process an op."

"Have you ever interacted with the subject of an op after it was over?"

"No. Usually when we liberate a hostage, they're whisked away on a separate helicopter and never know who was involved in their exfiltration."

"So perhaps this was different for you too. And you had to rescue me twice."

"Yes. You were in my head."

"And I took advantage of that."

He narrowed his gaze, but gave her a nod. "I'm part of this now, Diana. I know you're angry with me, but don't let that influence your decision to let me help you."

"What, exactly, can you do? Can you find Rafiq? Can you convince the Pentagon I saw him? No. There's nothing you can do to help me that won't blow back on you." She finished her drink, gathered her crutches and cane, then stood. "I appreciate the offer, but I'm afraid I have to decline."

"At least let me drive you home."

She stared for a long time into his eyes. Deep down, she knew she could forgive him. Hell, she probably already had. But she couldn't bring him down with her sinking ship and didn't want to start to rely on him.

She needed to take the scary Metro and do all the things that frightened her on her own. Because if she had to go on the run to avoid extradition, she needed to be able to do it alone.

"Thank you for the drink." She left the bar and hotel and headed toward the Metro.

The wind had kicked up again as the day edged toward

sunset. She entered the station almost in a daze as she pondered the events of the last twenty-four hours.

As she rode the long escalator down, she realized she'd never found out why Chris had been at FMV. Morgan would probably tell her. Freya almost certainly would not.

She needed to tell both women about the interview by Ian Boyd, and Gardner blindsiding her with questions about Rafiq.

The train pulled up within a minute of her arrival. The platform was thick with people at rush hour on Friday. She inched inside with the others, squeezing into a standing-room-only car. She braced herself against the vertical handrail closest to the door. She leaned her head against the metal pole and took a deep breath as she tried to process all the emotions she'd left back in the bar with Chris.

It was better this way. She didn't have room for messy entanglements. Her life was a wreck.

Gaze unfocused, she breathed deeply one more time, as if that could expel Chris from her mind. The doors tried to close multiple times, thwarted by bodies blocking the opening. At last, it was sorted with Diana pressed tight between an Asian woman and the short panel by the door. She gazed through the window to the platform and there, just on the other side of the glass, was Jamal, staring directly at her.

He drew a line across his throat as the train pulled out of the station.

Chapter Twenty-Eight

*C*hris watched her leave the bar, making no move to follow even though he wanted to. It was his nature and training to protect her. But aside from the fact she didn't want his protection, there was the small detail that he couldn't protect her from herself.

Once he was certain she'd be halfway to the Metro station, he rose from his seat and went to the bar to ask for the check because the server was busy now that more patrons had arrived.

"Get dumped?" the lone man sitting at the bar asked as he stared down into his drink.

Chris glanced up into the mirror behind the bar and noticed the angle was such that the man had a view of the couch where he'd sat with Diana.

"Yep," he said with a sigh.

"Too bad. She's a pretty thing."

Chris remembered last night, when he'd explored every

inch of her. Beautiful. Sexy. Strong. Goddess of the moon, even. "You have no idea."

The bartender produced a check, and Chris handed her a credit card. She left to run the card.

Chris turned to stare at the table where he'd sat with Diana, which was now being cleared. Removing all traces she'd been there.

"You should go after her," the guy said. He had a slight accent. British, probably. "Aren't women supposed to love that sort of thing?"

He had zero doubt that Diana would freak out if he tracked her down at home. He could easily get her address, but he wouldn't do that. It was bad enough he'd shown up at the Mayflower. But at least it was a neutral place, and he'd stumbled into the information that she was here. He hadn't asked for it.

He turned back to the bar and briefly met the man's gaze in the mirror before the guy took a long drink from a pint of beer. "No way. She'd freak."

The man shrugged. "If you really want her, do you have anything to lose?"

That was the question, wasn't it? Not the "nothing to lose" bit. The "if you really want her" part.

Did he?

It was a one-night stand. Hell, it hadn't even lasted a whole night. It was better that way, this first foray into dating now that he was single again. It had been fun, but now it was over.

The bartender returned with his card. He added the tip

and signed the slip. He wished the guy at the bar a good evening and left.

Cold air slapped him in the face as he stepped out onto the sidewalk. Cars inched along the busy street. Rush hour on Friday lived up to expectations. The sun would be setting soon, and he'd learned twilight was short here. It would be full dark before he reached his hotel.

He claimed his vehicle from the parking garage across the street and set out, wishing Diana had at least taken him up on his offer for a ride home. He was glad to see her in the walking boot, but her ankle had to be aching after the unaccustomed use.

His mind circled back to another question. The one that had started the drama and ended what had to that point been a spectacular date. Had she seen Rafiq in Jordan?

He was certain she believed it—the suspicion that she'd made it up for some unknown agenda had never rung true for him anyway.

He couldn't dispute her claim of recognizing him after only seeing his eyes. In the moment, he hadn't realized how remarkable it was. But then, he'd been wearing the same gear both times she'd seen him, had the same build. Same voice.

Maybe it wasn't so remarkable?

Had she really and truly seen Rafiq?

He couldn't speak to anything with certainty except that *she* believed it. And she was continuing to risk everything for that belief.

Extradition and prosecution for looting…surely the State Department wouldn't fold to that demand?

But then, the secretary of state had the difficult job of making amends to the Kingdom after the US military ran two unsanctioned ops in their sovereign land. The second op had taken place on the outskirts of a major city and involved damage to privately owned buildings.

Dr. Diana Edwards had not only caused an international incident, she'd chosen that path in working for FMV.

This wasn't victim blaming. Even Diana was aware of the decisions she'd made that put her in that market.

Not that any of it mattered to him at this point. He'd done what he could for her in identifying Jamal and Bassam from the photos Lange had shown him. Diana had made it clear she didn't want his help.

There was no reason for him to stay in the city any longer. He could pick up his bags from the hotel and head south to Little Creek tonight. It was only about a three-and-a-half-hour drive. Tomorrow, he could catch a flight to Seattle.

Two weeks of leave stretched out before him.

The first raindrops hit his windshield as he drove down 7th Street, where it split the National Mall. Tourists scurried to take refuge in the Air and Space Museum. He'd planned to take in museums this weekend, but he could do that another time. Little Creek and DC weren't that far apart. But given the rain, he'd head south in the morning. Catch a flight to Seattle, Sunday or Monday.

Decided, he parked in the underground garage and then walked a block to a restaurant he'd enjoyed earlier in the week and got the surf and turf takeout.

Twenty minutes later, he was on the floor of his hotel,

heading down the long hallway. He came to a stunned stop
when he spotted a drenched Diana sitting on the floor,
leaning against the door to his room.

4

*C*hris loomed over her. His expression wasn't friendly
nor was it cold. Not smiling, not scowling. She could
only see what it wasn't, which gave no clue to his thoughts.
He looked handsome and imposing as he waited for her to
speak.

She nodded toward the brown paper bag in his right
hand. "Smells good."

One side of his mouth lifted in the slightest of smiles. He
offered her his left hand. "If I'd known you wanted dinner,
I'd have gotten enough for two."

She grasped his hand with her left while positioning the
cane with her right and rose to her foot. Her ankle was sore,
and she leaned against the door to keep all her weight on the
left foot.

"Don't worry. I won't ask you to share. I just need to use
your phone, then I'll be on my way."

His brow furrowed. "You took, what, two trains and
walked a few blocks in the rain just to borrow my phone?"

"What, is that weird?"

That got a laugh. "Yeah. I think that qualifies."

"What if I said I'm really here for a booty call?"

"I wouldn't believe you."

"But would you have sex with me?"

His gaze raked her from head to toe, and she knew he was remembering last night. "Well, yeah. Obviously."

Now she smiled. "It's a shame I'm not here for a booty call, then."

"No argument from me." He tilted his head to the side and waved his room key in a signal for her to move so he could unlock the door.

She complied, and he pushed the door open, then stepped back for her to precede him.

Last night, when she'd entered this room, she'd gone straight for the window to take in the view. Tonight, she went to the couch and propped her throbbing foot on the cushion. The battered joint didn't fare well with the cold rain, which had naturally turned into a downpour as she walked the short blocks from the Metro.

Chris set the bag of food on the small dining table and proceeded to pull out the contents, placing the large cardboard clamshell on the coffee table before her, then handing her a plastic fork and knife. "We can take turns."

"I'm not here to steal your dinner."

"No, but you look hungry and I know I am, and I'm not going to eat in front of you. Besides, I got a lot of food." He opened the clamshell, revealing a thick juicy steak, a mound of shrimp, creamy risotto, and sautéed vegetables. It was a massive pile of food. He then pulled out a bag of breadsticks with a garlic butter dipping sauce. He smiled. "I was hungry, so I got the large."

"Can you eat all this by yourself?"

"When we're training, sure." He grabbed a breadstick

and dipped it in the butter and took a bite. When she didn't move to eat, he dipped the bread again and offered it to her.

It would be silly to balk at sharing food and utensils considering all they'd both done with their mouths yesterday, so she opened her mouth.

As her teeth closed on the soft bread, she realized how phallic the food was. Nothing about the moment was intentional, but still, she remembered how good it had felt last night to be wild and free and share her body with this man.

She closed her eyes. The warm bread mixed with garlic butter on her tongue, and she discovered exactly how hungry she was. "Oh my god. That is amazing."

"Wait till you try the risotto."

She opened her eyes and took in his assessing gaze with just the slightest hint of sexy smile. She wanted to eat the risotto from his chest.

But that wasn't why she was here. She used the fork he'd given her to scoop a bite of the rice dish into her mouth, then handed the utensil back to him. Not surprisingly, he was right about it being delicious. If she ever got her life back, she'd have to remember this restaurant.

They were each a few bites in when he held on to the fork and said, "Spill, Diana. Why are you here?"

She dabbed at her mouth with the paper napkin he'd ripped in two for easier sharing. She looked longingly at the steak, which was a perfect medium rare, but he had both the fork and the knife. And he had a right to know why she'd crashed his takeout dinner.

She'd spent most of the Metro ride debating whether or not she should lie. The truth was so implausible, he'd never believe her. He'd already questioned her judgment when it came to seeing Rafiq. This would only seal the deal. But she hadn't known where else to turn. And he'd said he wanted to help her.

She met his gaze. "I was scared to go home alone."

Chapter Twenty-Nine

"Why?" Chris calculated the odds that the next words out of Diana's mouth would be true. Everything about her demeanor said she wanted to lie.

What would he do if she did?

He sincerely hoped neither of them would find out.

A series of emotions played across her face. Finally, she reached for his beer, took a long sip, and said, "I saw Jamal on the Metro platform. He drew a line across his throat as my train left the station."

Chris reared back in shock. Not a lie. And he understood why she hadn't been eager to share this truth.

She held his gaze. "Before you ask, yes, I'm certain. I even tried to convince myself I hadn't seen him. But I know what—who—I saw."

He got up and grabbed a second beer from the fridge and popped the top, then handed the full bottle to her. "Okay, then. Tell me everything."

Dinner was less sexy, but still delicious after that.

"So you saw him more than a week ago and told no one?"

She grabbed the last shrimp from the surf side of the dinner box and dipped it in the garlic butter, then popped it into her mouth. He ignored the look of bliss on her face. "Mmmm. You'll be shocked to know that the food they gave me when I was a prisoner left a lot to be desired."

He gave her a fixed look.

She huffed out a sigh. "I couldn't say anything. Do you know what happened when I was in Landstuhl?"

"You have to admit, it would be hard for a fifteen-year-old terrorist to get into a US military hospital. It's difficult to get on base, let alone inside the medical building. I know. I've been there."

Her eyes hardened. "He was *there*."

"I didn't say he wasn't, I'm just saying there was reason to question your sighting."

"I lived with him for six weeks. I know his posture. His gait. All his mannerisms."

"And that's why I believe you."

She reached for a breadstick and tore off half, then took a bite. "Yeah, right." Her mouth was full, and the words came out slightly mumbled.

He took her hand and directed the remainder of the breadstick into his mouth. His teeth might have nipped her fingers, but that wasn't the point. He swallowed and said, "I do, Diana. I can see how Jamal could use his age to get past security. He'd still need a pass, but it's easier to pose as someone's kid, and he sure as hell has reasons to fuck with you. Same goes for him getting into the US. The right amount of money, the right connections, and his age is an advantage. He's a harmless kid. So, what do you think his goal is?"

"Not harmless. He drew his finger across his throat, which is a mite telling. He wants revenge."

"Does he know where you live?"

"Probably. It's not like my address is a state secret. I've only seen him twice, both times on the Metro. I assume he would have to follow me to time it just right."

He took the last sip of his beer as he considered the situation. He agreed with her take. The kid was following her, or he was tipped off on her schedule.

She'd been stationary in the hospital, in the same place for nearly a month, but the DC Metro system? It was busy as hell with six different lines. "You live on the Green Line?"

She nodded. "College Park."

"And you usually change trains at Gallery Place."

"Almost always. L'Enfant when I need Blue or Orange, but since I've been back, my doctor appointments are on Red."

"So what do you want to do?"

She closed her eyes and took a slow, deep breath. When she opened them again, he was reminded of her calm in the canyon that first night. He'd thought then that the woman didn't rattle easily, but now he saw it was the opposite. She'd been deeply rattled when she got here. It was her ability to settle herself that was impressive. Inherent or training? He suspected a bit of both.

"I can't avoid my condo forever. You said you'd like to

help me. I'd like you to take me home and search the place. Maybe sleep on the couch tonight, until I figure out what to do?"

He nodded. "I can do that. I just need to gather my things. I was going to check out tomorrow morning anyway."

It took him less than ten minutes to pack up. He retrieved his gun from the hotel safe, which he'd been permitted to carry in DC while in uniform. But out of uniform, he couldn't carry, so he'd left it in the safe for the last two days.

They set out for the parking garage. Chris opted to drive through the city to College Park rather than skirting around via 295. Rain pelted his 4Runner in the stop-and-go traffic as they inched down New York Avenue. Finally, they crossed the border into Maryland and headed north.

Diana lived in a small building with just half a dozen units on three floors, hers being on the top floor. He circled the block, looking for any sign her building was being monitored. He found a street parking spot and studied the structure. An elevator was situated between the two units on each floor, while separate staircases zigzagged up the building in front of the left and right sides.

He didn't like the layout from a security standpoint. Two outside entry points and no enclosed staircase behind a locked door. "Do the stairs and elevator lead to the same door?"

"No. There's a front and back door. The front door is by the stairs, back by the elevator."

Entry plan formed, he drove two blocks away, leaving the

complex, and parked in front of a tavern that would be open for several more hours. "Sorry about the extra walking, but we don't want my car in front of your place until after I've scoped it out."

She nodded.

Before exiting the vehicle, he grabbed his pistol and holster from where he'd placed them on the back seat. He donned the holster and tucked the pistol into the leather pocket. He was allowed to open carry in Maryland.

"You really think you'll need that?" Diana asked.

"No idea. But I have it, so I might as well."

He rarely wore a weapon when he wasn't in uniform, so this was different, but wearing a weapon was like putting on shoes at this point. It was a bad idea to go into any potentially dangerous situation barefoot.

Diana left her crutches in the vehicle and used her cane. They strolled hand in hand, looking like a couple walking home from a bar on a Friday night. They weren't the only people on the street, making their cover even more plausible.

When they reached her building, they went straight for the elevator. Chris would rather go up the front stairs, but he wouldn't leave her alone to enter separately. At least the elevator required a prox key or to be buzzed in via intercom.

The elevator opened onto a small vestibule with Unit 3A on the right and 3B, Diana's condo, on the left. Chris took her keys and unlocked the dead bolt. He faced her and said, "Stay here, to the right of the door, while I do a quick walkthrough."

He pushed open the door and slipped in without turning on the light.

Instinct told him the place was empty. He flipped the switch and swore. He changed his assessment to *probably* empty, because he figured whoever had trashed her condo was long gone.

Chapter Thirty

4

*D*iana stared in dismay at her home office. Her computers—both desktop and laptop—were gone. A glance in her desk drawers showed the thief had also taken her backup hard disk, thumb drives, and the new anonymous tablet.

Some files were backed up to a cloud, but she couldn't begin to comprehend what she'd lost. Salim's life's work had been on the desktop and backup disk. The university had his dissertation—both print and digital—but she'd had the bulk of his research, the raw files.

Gone.

But of course, it wasn't Salim and his work that was the target. It was Diana. She left her office and went to the front door security panel. The alarm was off. It hadn't beeped when Chris entered, which meant it had been shut off earlier in the day. She could call the security company and get the time.

Chris had followed her and also studied the panel. "Does

your system send an alert to your phone?"

She shook her head. "It's a basic system. I bought this place a few months after the accident and didn't think I'd need anything fancy. Originally, I'd planned to rent it out while I was in Jordan, but I decided it was too much of a hassle, so I paid the complex manager to do regular inspections to make sure there were no issues."

"Did you change the alarm code after you returned?"

She dropped her gaze to her feet as guilt snaked up her spine. "No. I didn't think of it."

"So your alarm code could be written down in the business office. How many buildings are in this complex?"

"Ten? It's a lot. I don't know anyone in the office well and think there were staff changes while I was gone. I would imagine they have strict protocols around protecting things like master keys and alarm codes, but I also know my condo was searched after I was abducted by one federal agency or another. I can't trust that half of DC doesn't have access."

She pressed her forehead to the wall as she considered how horrifically careless she'd been in not changing the password and locks when she'd finally returned.

Arms encircled her waist, and she felt Chris's chest press to her back as his lips touched the top of her head. She leaned back against him, appreciating the comfort he offered.

She tilted her head up, opened her eyes, and found herself staring into his warm brown gaze. His face showed kindness and concern. His mouth was just inches from hers, and she considered taking a mental break by kissing him.

But now wasn't the time. Probably later wouldn't be

either.

It was one thing to lose her computers, but the damage to the kitchen, living room, and bedroom told her that she was in danger.

Chris pressed his lips to the top of her head again, then released her. "Do you want to call the police?"

"I should, but honestly, I don't know how much good it would do. You know this wasn't a normal B and E, and even if it were, it's unlikely they'd be able to recover my computers. Given that I wasn't targeted for the resale value of my electronics, there is no way in hell I'm getting anything back."

"You'll need the police report for your insurance."

"Yeah. I'm not saying I won't report it. Just saying I don't have the bandwidth for it tonight." She turned to face the room. She studied the abject disarray of open drawers, overturned chairs, and seat cushions that had been sliced open. Her home had been ransacked.

In the kitchen, her jars of flour, rice, and coffee beans had been overturned. Drawers removed from the cabinet and emptied on the floor.

What had they thought they'd find in the rice or underneath a drawer? A burner phone might fit in the jar, but did they think she had papers or SIM or SD cards taped under the drawers? What kind of data could she possibly have?

"Do you think that Raptor guy—Ian Boyd—might have done this?"

Chris frowned and shook his head. "When CIA searches, you wouldn't know they were here."

"True."

"Why not Jamal? This looks…angry."

"I don't know that it's not Jamal, but I don't see what he'd want with my computer."

"He's working for someone," Chris said.

"Rafiq would be my guess." She studied his expression, wondering if he'd balk at her mention of the supposedly dead man.

"Why do I feel like I'm being tested?"

She shrugged.

"Pack a bag. We aren't staying here tonight."

"Are we going back to your hotel?"

He paused. "It should be safe, but I have a better idea. You need to stay in DC for any reason?"

"No. Not really. My next doctor appointment isn't for another two weeks. I don't have a job, and I've now fulfilled my obligation to Gardner."

"What would you say to coming with me to Little Creek? No way would Jamal guess you'd be there, and it would buy us time to figure out what's going on here." He waved his arm around to indicate the chaos that was her kitchen.

"How long would we be gone?"

"I've got two weeks' leave. If we don't have answers before my time's up, we'll reassess then."

"'Kay."

"One thing."

"What's that?"

"I don't think you should tell Freya or Morgan where you're going or that you're with me. I don't think you should tell anyone."

A ripple of unease tickled the back of her neck. "Why

not?" She trusted Morgan and Freya far more than she trusted him.

"Because if an extradition order comes in, and the State Department caves and wants to bring you in, the first place they'll turn is FMV. Morgan and Freya would face arrest if they know where you are but don't reveal your location."

"I could say the same for you. Harboring a fugitive is even worse."

"Yeah, but they'd have to ask me. No one at the State Department knows we know each other."

"People have seen us together, including Mason Gardner and Ian Boyd. Morgan and Freya know I went home with you last night."

"Morgan and Freya don't have to admit to anything to do with that, and Gardner doesn't know my name. I don't see Boyd as the type to volunteer the information. Are you in?"

She considered his offer. If they left within the hour, they'd arrive sometime after midnight.

She'd have to ditch her phone and wouldn't be able to reach out to anyone the State Department might question. The list was small, but it included Salim's parents. They would worry if they knew she'd disappeared, but she didn't see how that could be helped.

She pulled out her phone and set it on the counter. She'd already pulled the battery, but now she removed the SIM card and set it on the cutting board. She took the meat cleaver from the drawer and split it in two with one stroke. Then she dropped the pieces in the garbage disposal and flipped the switch.

Chapter Thirty-One

The rain on the road proved to be hypnotic for Diana, who fell asleep not long after Chris completed a surveillance detection route before heading out of the city. It was well after two in the morning when they reached his neighborhood, and she roused herself as he pulled into the garage of a two-story house.

The door rolled closed behind them, and Chris's voice was soft in the dim garage. "Do I need to carry you in, sleepyhead?"

She smiled. It was *very* tempting to let him carry her, but she needed to get her bearings.

"I think I can handle it."

"I'll get your suitcase, then."

She climbed from the vehicle and waited by the interior door while he grabbed both their bags. "I'll do a quick recon before giving you the tour, but my security is solid, and there've been no pings on my phone."

Inside, he reset the alarm before leaving her in the pass-through utility room to ensure the house was clear.

He returned a minute later and took their bags. "All clear."

She stepped into a large open-floor-plan living space. The kitchen had a long bar-height counter that faced the living room. The space was barely furnished. There was no dining table, just barstools at the counter. On the other side of the room, there was a sofa, recliner, coffee table, and large wall-mounted TV.

Diana smiled at his furnishing priorities. "Nice TV."

He smiled, but showed a hint of being embarrassed. "I uh, only moved in two weeks before we were deployed. I was going to order a dining set, but it was going to be delivered while I was on the carrier, so didn't bother. But they had the TV at Costco, no waiting."

His embarrassment was so sweet, she rose on her left toes and brushed her lips over his. "I wasn't judging."

"Yes, you were." His arm caught her around the waist, holding her against him.

He lowered his head and kissed her, his tongue dipping into her mouth. Her drowsy state fled, and she kissed him back, but he ended it nearly as quickly as he'd moved in.

"C'mon. I'll show you your room. Sorry, but both bedrooms are upstairs. My office down here doesn't have any furniture yet other than a desk, so you'll want to be upstairs."

"No problem. It's a lot easier to do stairs now with the walking boot."

She wasn't sure if she was disappointed he was shunting her off to the guest room, but she did know it was the right thing to do.

🝔

*U*nfortunately, Chris's guest room didn't yet have room-darkening curtains, and hours later, Diana found herself raging against the rising of the light. She'd bet Chris's room had dark blinds.

She toyed with the idea of crawling into bed with him, but instead pulled a pillow over her head and went back to sleep. She emerged sometime around noon, woken by the tantalizing scents of bacon and coffee.

She descended the stairs and found Chris sitting at the bar, a heaping plate of scrambled eggs before him. He smiled when he saw her and jumped up. "Coffee?"

"Please."

He circled the counter and filled a mug from the pot. "Cream or sugar?"

"Cream if you have it." In the field, she always drank her coffee black, but she'd take the treat if she could get it.

He went to the fridge and pulled out a small carton of Half and Half and brought it to her. "How'd you sleep?"

"Fine until the sun came up. I was tempted to crawl into bed with you."

His smile said he wouldn't have minded. "Sorry. I forgot about that. I can run to Target today."

He then filled a plate with food for her, and she sat on the barstool next to him to eat. They spoke of inconsequential things while they ate, and it was nice to take a moment to get to know him more before tackling the complexities of her situation.

Had she been crazy to run off with him in the night?

But damn, one look at him and no one would blame her. All those bulky muscles, smooth skin, beautiful eyes, warm smile.

He'd saved her life in Jordan.

He'd offered her protection last night without hesitation.

She was safe with him. She knew it. Knew it like she knew she'd spoken with Rafiq.

After they'd polished off the bacon and eggs, they took their coffee mugs to the sofa. Chris grabbed his laptop and said, "I called a SEAL friend who's a tech wizard, and he walked me through downloading a VPN app and configuring it to hide search history. It's safe for you to open a browser and start digging for info on Rafiq and the Gardners —although I doubt you'll have much luck finding anything on Rafiq."

He handed her the computer. She wiggled her fingers as she stared at the keyboard. Even with a VPN, she'd been afraid to dig deep on her personal computers.

The feds had unfettered access to both her laptop and desktop while she was in the hospital in Germany. She didn't think it was paranoid to wonder if they'd set up some kind of trap or keystroke reader on all her devices. It was prudent. Hell, they probably had a wiretap warrant.

And now they might have taken those devices for examining.

Of course, if they'd been executing a warrant, they wouldn't have been so messy.

"Do you think it's possible that the feds took my computers and *then* Jamal showed up and trashed the place?"

"Unlikely, but at this point, I don't think we can rule

anything out." He rose to his feet. "I'm going to head to the gym on base. I think it's a good idea for me to establish myself as returned…and alone. Some of my team members might be there."

"Do they know we met?"

"It's possible. We walked by the bar where they were hanging out on the way to the hotel. We kissed on the street for everyone to see. If anyone asks who I was with, I'll have to say something about Morgan's party. If any of the team end up being questioned, it would only look worse if I lie now."

She nodded.

He crouched in front of her, meeting her at eye level. "You'll be safe while I'm gone. No one knows you're here."

She nodded again. "I know how to shoot. If you're willing to leave me a gun. I've trained. With Morgan. She took me to a range at least a dozen times before I left for Jordan."

He frowned, then gave a sharp nod. "I can't give you my service weapon, but I've got a few personal handguns and a rifle."

Ten minutes later, Diana was alone in Chris's living room with a fresh cup of coffee, an open computer, and a handgun on the side table.

First, she searched for articles related to her abduction, and only found stories she'd read weeks ago. Next, she searched for reports about the raid on Rafiq's compound in Aqaba on Arabic-language news sites.

There were stories with a heavily anti-US tone, but she could hardly blame them.

She wasn't named. It didn't appear to be public knowledge in the US or Arabic world that Diana had been the focus of the raid. Nor was Rafiq mentioned, but that was to be expected.

This was a useless exercise, but she appreciated that Chris had given her something to do.

She wondered if Morgan and Freya had figured out that she'd left town. Were they concerned? Had they guessed who she was with?

She rose from the couch and refilled her coffee. Three mugs was one past her limit, but she was going nowhere today and was likely to be up half the night anyway given how late she'd slept and the amount of anxiety that would crush her as day slipped into night.

She settled back on the couch and returned to the National Public Radio home page and refreshed the headlines.

A mass shooting at a synagogue in New Jersey had taken at least a dozen lives. She placed her hand over her mouth as she read the brief story that was still unfolding. Gunman at large. The area in lockdown for the manhunt.

Another hate crime.

She scrolled down to see the international headlines. A fire in a factory in Brazil. An E. coli outbreak in the UK. And there it was at the bottom of the screen. A small article with the headline *Kingdom of Jordan Demands Extradition of American Archaeologist for Looting Ancient Site.*

Chapter Thirty-Two

*C*hris found Diana curled in a ball in the back of his mostly empty walk-in pantry. "Jesus Christ, Diana. You scared the hell out of me."

She raised her head, her eyes puffy and her face tear streaked. "They're going to send me back."

He dropped down before her. "Just because Jordan has requested extradition, doesn't mean the State Department will comply." Chris had seen the headline. Kramer had arrived at the gym just as he was finishing and mentioned it. Chris had forced himself to show only mild interest and ended up working out for another half hour so the SEAL wouldn't wonder why he went running off the moment he heard.

She swiped at her cheek. "They'll give in. You know they will."

He rolled to his backside and settled in the corner under the shelves with her. His head brushed the empty shelf above him, and he scrunched down and pulled her to his side.

"We'll fight this. The State Department never moves fast on these kinds of things."

"They're eager to make amends after the failed raid. They'll give me up sooner rather than later."

"Morgan and Freya have connections."

"Not big enough for this. And we can't tell them where I am. You're the one who decided that."

"We'll find a way to communicate indirectly. Hell, Freya is CIA. She probably has back channels set up already."

"If we do that, you can't be part of it."

"I'm on leave. There's no reason I can't help you."

"There is one big-ass huge reason."

"What's that?"

"Aiding and abetting a fugitive."

"You aren't a fugitive."

"Yet."

He had to acknowledge she was right on that point. How many days did they have until the State Department agreed and demanded she turn herself in?

She shifted and cupped his cheeks, looking straight into his eyes. Long gone was the cool, calm hostage who'd orchestrated her escape with her captors in a slot canyon half a world away. Now her eyes were bloodshot and puffy. Her nose red. She looked defeated. "I can't let you risk your career, your life, your freedom for me. I'll turn myself in first."

Fear jolted him. "You can't do that."

"Why not? What I'm accused of…I did it. I looted the site. I'm *guilty*. All because I thought I saw Rafiq. But maybe…maybe it wasn't even him."

Chapter Thirty-Three

*D*iana barely managed to get the last word out before a sob from the bottom of her soul escaped.

There. She'd said it. The thing she'd denied for weeks. The horror she'd buried in the back of her mind from the moment she'd faced a Pakistani orderly and asked herself if that was the man she'd seen at the far end of the hospital corridor.

No. She'd seen Jamal. She *knew* him.

Was she wrong? Worse, had she been wrong about Rafiq?

It was the last thing she wanted to admit to anyone, let alone herself, but she couldn't fight it anymore.

What if she'd been wrong? What if she'd made a mistake that night in September and was so entrenched in the belief she didn't see anything but what she'd expected in late October?

Confirmation bias. She saw what she expected to see and

discarded anything that didn't fit with that narrative. Hell, she'd even discarded Chris for expressing doubts.

The sobs shook her entire body. Fear and loathing were a powerful emetic when set loose. Not that she was vomiting, but the tears came in torrents and felt like a purge.

Chris scooped her up and pulled her onto his lap, and she didn't understand why he hadn't shoved her away in revulsion. She buried her face in his neck and cried harder, while he stroked her back and whispered words of comfort her brain didn't know how to accept.

Eventually, her sobbing lost steam. She took hiccupping breaths and tried not to use his shirt as a tissue, but it was a lost cause.

She closed her eyes in embarrassment and breathed in his scent. He was musky and warm and comforting. His large palm cupped her cheek, wiping away an ocean of tears.

"Diana, sweetheart, it's okay. Even if you were wrong about Rafiq, it's *okay*. You were victimized by a group of terrorists. Rafiq or not, they've built a strong base in Jordan, and you—and only you—located them. Isn't that what you were doing in Jordan in the first place? It doesn't matter if it was Rafiq. These men are murdering, raping, and pillaging. Using terror to seize power. And they're funding it with arti-facts. And *you* were the only person who could bring them to our attention. It doesn't have to be Rafiq to make them worth stopping."

She caught her breath as he uttered the only words that could cut through her misery.

She'd been so focused on Rafiq, this angle hadn't crossed her mind.

But he was right. Rafiq or not, Jordan's archaeological sites were being used to fund destabilization in the region. Paying for the death and conscription of children.

"It doesn't matter if he was the Four of Diamonds." It was both a statement and a question as she verbalized her interpretation of his words.

"No. It doesn't. Whoever it was—and it could still be Rafiq—is dangerous. And he's well funded. Intelligence agencies should be looking into who and where he is instead of focusing on you. But they aren't. They're playing catch-up and appeasement. We need to get ahead of the narrative and nail his ass."

She twisted in his lap, straddling him. She held his cheeks and stared into his eyes. He was so beautiful. A warrior. A straight arrow. A SEAL who'd twice risked his life to save her.

In contrast, she was an absolute mess. No one would call her pretty when she cried. She wasn't noble or strong. She was a traitor to her profession just by agreeing to be a spy.

Salim's last words before he lost control of the car. His condemnation.

And then she'd doubled down, to prove to herself—or to his memory—that her decision was important. Bigger than her.

Had she seen Rafiq in a stranger's eyes to prove to her dead fiancé that she'd made the right choice?

Maybe.

Did it matter in the long run if it was one terrorist or another?

Probably not.

She let Chris and all his beauty see her ugly-cry face. Stripped of the calm façade she'd presented in the slot canyon. Stripped of all confidence that she knew right from wrong. Stripped of her belief in her own infallibility. She let her rescuer and protector see the miserable, stark, unvarnished version of herself. "You still want to help me, knowing I might have been wrong?"

"Of course. It doesn't matter if it was Rafiq or not. What matters is following the artifacts. Following the money. Because we both know it's being funneled to support one branch of the Islamic State or another. It's being used to destroy lives and communities."

"Helping me could ruin you. You could lose your spot on the SEALs. Dishonorable discharge. Imprisonment."

"That won't happen. Not if we get in front of the narrative. Show the *real* truth."

"How can we do that?"

Chris flashed a resolute smile and said, "Trust me."

Chapter Thirty-Four

*M*organ wasn't the least bit surprised to see a representative from the State Department at her door even though it was late on a Saturday evening. But then, it was Sunday in Jordan already, which was the first day of their work week, as most businesses in the country operated on a Sunday to Thursday week.

"Mr. Colt, what brings you here?"

Before he could answer, Morgan's two-year-old daughter, Valentine, came running to the door. "Is it Gramma?"

Morgan scooped up her half-dressed child, who must've been in the middle of a costume change because she wore a diaper and a cone-shaped princess hat and nothing else. The girl tucked her head into Morgan's neck and popped her two middle fingers into her mouth when she took in the stranger at the door.

"No, baby. This is a man associated with Mommy's job."

Pax stepped into the foyer, carrying a mermaid costume.

"C'mon, princess, let's get you changed while Mommy talks to Mr. Colt."

As Pax took their daughter into his arms, he fixed Colt with a look that put the man on notice. Morgan stifled a laugh at the discomfort that flashed across the bureaucrat's face as he watched her husband retreat down the hall with their toddler in his arms.

"Come in," Morgan said, "I'll call Freya, then we can talk in my study."

"No need to include Ms. Lange in this conversation."

"Oh, but I'm sure there is. I presume you're here about Dr. Edwards."

She waved to the couch in the home office as she hit the speed dial button for Freya on the landline phone. Freya picked up immediately.

"Freya, I've got you on speakerphone with Mr. Colt from the State Department, who just showed up unannounced at my house."

"How interesting, because I was just about to call you. I have an FBI agent who just popped in for a visit."

"Does he have a warrant?"

"Not that he's mentioned."

"Interesting," Morgan said.

"I'm told they just want to speak with Diana. To guide the secretary's decision-making process. My guess is that's why you got Colt and I got the cops."

Morgan directed her words to Colt. "I'm sorry to disappoint you, but Diana's not here."

"But you know where she is."

"Actually, I don't. We lost track of her yesterday."

"Lost track? You were tracking her?"

"Not like that, no. But she checked in regularly. Last night, I tried to reach her, and my calls went to voicemail. She also didn't reply to my texts."

"When did you last communicate with Dr. Edwards?"

"She sent me a text yesterday before noon, telling me she was meeting with Dennis Gardner at his hotel—the Mayflower—at one o'clock. Have you spoken to Gardner?"

"He has been in touch with our office, yes."

"What exactly do you want from us?"

"We want you to tell Diana to turn herself in before we need to resort to getting a warrant."

"So the secretary has already made her decision."

"Nothing is official."

"She's been traumatized enough. You need to leave her alone."

Pax entered the office. To Morgan, he said, "Val is watching *Toy Story*." He turned his attention to Colt. "Morgan's right. Why are you doing this? She's the victim here."

"She looted a site under false pretenses."

Anger jolted through Morgan. "*False pretenses?* You're saying she wasn't held by terrorists? Wasn't threatened with the same fate as Dr. Fahd Yousef?"

The man shrugged. "We can't confirm anything. The only thing we do know is she looted a site. The Kingdom has confirmed the digging and destruction."

"That's bullshit, and you know it!"

"Are you saying she didn't loot the site?"

"I'm saying she did it under duress."

"That may be so, or that might be another delusion."

Morgan was going to be sick. The way the government wanted to twist the story was beyond horrific. "Why is State so desperate to hold on to the story that Rafiq is dead? You're more concerned about saving face than admitting the Intelligence Community and military made a mistake."

"There's no evidence mistakes were made by anyone but Dr. Edwards."

"Get out of my house, Mr. Colt. Go to your office and do your *job* instead of making a scapegoat of a woman who worked on the front lines to cut off the funding for terrorists and was nearly killed doing so."

"Tell Diana to turn herself in."

"You tell her."

"Why are you here?" Pax asked. "Why aren't you at Diana's?"

"She's not home. She left her condo in a shambles."

"You went inside without a warrant?" Freya chimed in through the speakerphone.

"Her next-door neighbor noticed the rear door was ajar and, when she went to check on her, noticed the apartment had been trashed. She called the police."

Freya cursed loud and long. Morgan contained herself, barely. She was trying to clean up her language when her daughter was within hearing distance. Inside, she was spewing the foulest phrases she could think of.

She'd figured Diana was laying low, not that she'd gone on the run.

More chilling was the idea she might not be on the run. "How do you know she hasn't been taken? Jesus, why are you here and not out searching for her?"

"There was no sign of a struggle. She took her computers and packed a bag."

"And trashed her apartment before she left? *Sure, Jan.*" Morgan was completely livid.

Colt shrugged. "She wanted it to look like a break-in."

"A break-in explains why she left," Freya said.

"Convenient excuse."

Morgan's hand fisted. "It's not convenient when you're in actual danger."

Pax put a hand on her shoulder. "Cal and I will go check out her place."

Colt didn't let the conversation end there. "If Dr. Edwards is in danger, that's your fault."

His words weren't wrong, which only pissed her off more.

Friday Morning Valkyries had let Diana down in so many ways, but the situation hadn't been imaginable when Diana had departed for the dig in Jordan.

She studied Colt, who was more than a midlevel diplomat. She wished Carlos's wife, Kaylea, who worked for the State Department and the CIA, could offer insight into Colt, but she probably didn't know him and wouldn't cross those ethical boundaries if she did.

"Why now?" Morgan asked. "What's the rush to deal with the situation now, before we get answers about what really went down in Aqaba?"

"Jordan has made the extradition request, and our investigation was completed yesterday. Dr. Edwards's claim that she saw Rafiq is unsubstantiated."

It probably wasn't a coincidence that the case was closed after Rand and his team spent four days being questioned at the Pentagon. They wrapped on Thursday afternoon. The Pentagon's final report had probably been presented to the State Department yesterday. But still, everything was moving awfully fast, especially for what was usually a slow-moving government agency.

Sure, the military knew how to drag their feet—she'd witnessed that her entire life, having a father who was a three-star Army general and working toward four. But the military also knew how to act fast—they had to be ready to respond to a threat in an instant, so that was built in.

Not so the State Department. They usually drew out investigations for months or years, until the story faded from the headlines and no one without a political agenda cared anymore.

"You've been handed something on Diana, haven't you? Some kind of damning evidence has been planted, and you're using it as an excuse to make her a scapegoat."

Like any good diplomat, the guy had a solid poker face, but still, she thought she caught something simply because he hadn't expected her to make the connection.

He gave her a tight smile. "How is it making her a scapegoat when she herself admits she committed the crime she's accused of? How is she a scapegoat when she's the one who created an international incident?"

And then Morgan knew, without a shadow of a doubt

and couldn't hold back a stream of curses before saying, "The military—and the State Department—*knew* Rafiq was alive. But you screwed up, and now you need to discredit her." She glared at the man who was playing international chess with Diana's life. "That's how she's a scapegoat."

Chapter Thirty-Five

Diana felt slightly better after taking a shower. Because of the need to wrap her injured ankle in a waterproof bag, she'd bathed mostly with sponge or tub baths, making this her first real shower since before her abduction. She was thankful that yesterday the doctor had finally okayed removing her brace and bandages for bathing.

Chris didn't have a shower seat, but he did have a plastic garden chair that fit in the master bathroom shower. She toyed with the idea of asking him to help her bathe, but knew she couldn't handle that emotionally, even if they both kept it clinical. They'd already been intimate, so it wouldn't *feel* clinical, and she was in a raw and vulnerable place.

She had no doubt they'd both regret it afterward one way or the other.

At least she no longer regretted Thursday night. On the contrary, she was now grateful she'd made the wild choice to go home with him. Maybe, when this was all over—if that was even possible—they could try dating. A relationship wasn't entirely unreasonable given that they lived just a few hours apart.

Now she stared at Chris as they ate takeout for dinner and imagined what a future with him might look like. She remembered the feel of his big body sliding against hers, his large palms cupping her breasts as he kissed his way downward.

She closed her eyes as her face and body flushed with heat.

"What?" he asked.

She wondered if he'd believe a thirty-two-year-old woman could have a hot flash?

She shifted her focus to the blank corner next to a gas fireplace. "I was thinking this room needs a Christmas tree. If you celebrate Christmas, that is."

"*Sure* you were." He chuckled, then studied the corner she'd indicated. "But yeah, on the tree thing. My ex probably kept most of the ornaments, but I should have some lights and a few decorations buried in the moving boxes stacked in the garage." He glanced at his watch. "It's not that late. We could go to a lot and get a tree tonight if you want."

"Really?"

"Yeah. I like the idea. We've earned a treat. I can get eggnog and put on Christmas music. Do it right."

"Should I stay here? While you go? I mean, we shouldn't be seen together." The news hadn't mentioned a warrant being issued, but she needed to lie low just in case one was in the works.

"The tree lot should be safe enough. No one knows me here. But I'd need to go to a store for a tree stand. Probably best if you don't go shopping with me. Stores have plenty of cameras. If anyone figures out you're with me, they'll review footage from every camera in the area they can find."

Before they left, Chris found the Christmas boxes. They contained what he'd expected: less than two dozen ornaments, but plenty of strings of multicolored lights. After bringing the boxes into the living room, they set out, heading to a tree lot a good distance from the military base in an abundance of caution. They quickly chose a tree, and Diana waited in the passenger seat while he strapped it to the roof.

She felt a strange little spark of happiness at the randomness of the sudden excursion. The 4Runner was parked facing the busy street, and she watched a line of cars filled with holiday shoppers turn into the busy strip mall across the street.

The idea of buying presents hadn't even crossed her mind, and with Chris's reminder about the numerous cameras in stores, it was off the table for her this holiday season.

Watching the cars file into the mall like ants to their colony, she couldn't say she was disappointed, but she'd have enjoyed picking out something special for Morgan's daughter, who had transformed from a babbling toddler to a sprinting chatterbox in the months Diana was in Jordan.

Diana's gaze landed on the mammoth sign next to the shopping center entrance that listed the stores and restaurants to be found in the complex. One familiar logo jumped out at her, and her mood plummeted.

Historie. Marbled-white letters with the capital H made of two Corinthian columns.

She scanned the line of shops, looking for the gift store. She spotted it at the end of the line. Business was booming on Saturday night a little more than two weeks before Christmas.

Had Dennis Gardner spoken with the State Department yesterday after their meeting? Or had he turned around and spoken directly with his contacts in Jordan? Gardner was likely more concerned about his relationship with the Kingdom than with the US government.

She'd read the US/Hashemite Kingdom of Jordan extradition treaty days ago, when she first realized she could be in jeopardy, and went over it with Chris again today. The crimes she was accused of committing: looting an archaeological site, aiding and abetting terrorism, were both subject to extradition of US nationals based on the fact that both crimes were punishable by more than a year in prison.

Furthermore, Diana had actually committed the crimes and had admitted as much. It wasn't like they had to work hard to gather evidence against her. The arrest of Rafiq would have tempered her actions for both countries, but even then, she'd have faced the same scrutiny.

She stared at the replica store across the busy roadway and felt the prick of tears. Dammit. She was supposed to be all cried out at this point. She took a deep breath and listened to the thumping on the roof of the car as Chris tied on the eight-foot fir tree.

What was Gardner's role in all this? She dug through her purse to find Ian Boyd's business card. She hadn't even glanced at it when she'd tossed it in her purse before leaving the bar yesterday afternoon, and now she was curious. At last, she found it and stared at the sharp-beaked bird logo next to the company name: Raptor.

Ian Boyd didn't have a fancy title. He didn't have any kind of job title or description at all. Just his first and last name and phone number with DC area code. She imagined James Bond's card would be similar, except the company name would be Universal Exports.

She'd wonder if Raptor was real, but she was a Maryland resident, and the company owner, Alec Ravissant, was one of her senators. She remembered the headlines when there was an explosion on his estate and it was related to the company.

The driver's side door opened at the same time as she flipped Ian's card over. She gasped after reading the handwritten note.

"What's that?" Chris asked.

She showed him the back of the card.

Tell Freya to call me

"Ian Boyd knew I was a Valkyrie."

"That's…interesting. Did you tell Freya about the interview?"

"Never had a chance. I saw Jamal on the Metro and forgot about everything related to Boyd and Gardner. I changed trains a few times to be certain he wasn't following me, then went to your hotel."

"I've been trying to figure out how we can contact Freya. Maybe we can use Boyd."

"He might turn me in."

"It's a risk, but I won't be direct. I think I know someone who knows his boss."

"The senator?"

"Yes. Him and Raptor's CEO. I can make a call—it will be totally safe. He's one of my closest friends in the world." He started the engine. "Now, let's get this tree home. I was able to buy a stand, so we can get it set up and put lights on it. Might not need to go to the store tonight at all."

"You promised me eggnog."

He smiled. "We'll stop at a convenience store on the way home."

She dropped a hand on his knee, leaned over, and kissed his cheek. "Okay, then. Let's go home, set up our tree, and see if we can find a way to get in touch with Freya."

Chapter Thirty-Six

This was not how Chris had imagined spending the first Saturday night of his vacation, and yet it was the most vacation-like thing he'd done since…last Christmas.

He also could now see how big the cracks had been in his marriage last year, as he and Pam had bickered over every detail. He'd been unaware Pam had been cheating on him for over a year at that point, but in hindsight, it was obvious.

Diana oohed and aahed over the few ornaments he had —all ones that he'd had since childhood. His mom had gifted him with the box the first Christmas he shared with Pam as a married couple, and they'd always been packed separately, which was the only reason he had them now.

He'd probably made a mistake in letting Pam keep all the ornaments they'd collected together, but right now, he didn't care as he watched Diana carefully place on the tree the popsicle stick ornaments he'd made when he was in kindergarten.

She treated them like they were made of blown glass.

The shadows had left her eyes, and she flushed with pleasure as she asked him to give the detailed origin story of each ornament she unwrapped.

He hadn't realized how personal, even intimate, decorating the tree was. At least, that was how it felt doing it with her.

He absolutely wanted her back in his bed. And he wanted her to stay there when this was behind them, which was an even wilder thought.

She pulled a Lego fire engine ornament from bubble wrap. He remembered gluing the red bricks together after he broke his mom's glass fire engine ornament when he was nine. It wasn't a bad replica. He shared the story.

"That is ridiculously sweet." She held it out to him. "You want to hang it?"

He shook his head. If he remembered correctly, there was a different ornament in the box he wanted to find. He dug through the bubble-wrapped pile and spotted a bundle that was the right size and shape.

He pulled the glass globe the size of a tennis ball from the wrapping and held it up to the light. The fake green leaves and red berries sparkled with glitter. When he was in third grade, he'd spent his allowance on this gift for his mom, not knowing what the plant inside symbolized. He just knew she loved gardening and would think it was the most beautiful ornament ever. This ornament had come his way after his mom had passed three years ago. She always swore it was her favorite.

Now he lifted it over his head and waited for Diana to turn around.

He wasn't disappointed by her smile when she did.

"Mistletoe?"

"You know what to do."

She laughed and took a step toward him. "Do I ever."

She paused before him, and he continued holding the glass ball over his head like a fool. But he didn't feel even a little bit foolish seeing the look on her face.

He moved his arm, so now the ornament hung over her head, and with his free hand, he touched her cheek, then slid his fingers through her hair to cup the back of her head as his mouth found hers.

She kissed him back, all in, mouth open, tongue stroking. He set the ornament on the pile of bubble wrap, freeing his arm to circle her waist and pull her flush against him.

They stood like that for a long interval. Kissing deep. She tasted like eggnog and chocolate, and he was hungry for more.

He'd promised himself he wouldn't seduce her today. Not when her life was in scary upheaval, but as she kissed him with the same hunger, he found it hard to remember his resolve.

In the end, it was the buzz of his cell phone on the coffee table that pushed them apart. The call could be important.

He raised his head, but didn't let her go. He stared into her eyes, seeing a reflection of the same arousal and desire that coursed through him. He was at a loss for words. He didn't want to promise restraint, but he knew he should set a boundary, if only to keep himself in line.

Instead, he dipped his head and kissed her neck. "God, how I want to fuck you."

She let out a choked laugh. "Same."

He released her and picked up his phone, which had stopped buzzing.

Missed call from Xavier.

He hit the callback button, watching Diana as she took the ornament from the top of the box and hung it on the tree.

"Xave," he said into the phone. "Sorry I didn't pick up. My hands were full."

Diana let out a soft laugh.

Xavier got right to the point. "You want to talk to Luke?"

"Yeah. I remember him saying something about him and his wife being friends with the former attorney general and the senator from Maryland who owns Raptor?"

"Yeah. Undine worked for NHHC for Mara Garrett— the former AG's wife. Luke has assisted Raptor a few times."

"Do you know if he's met an operative named Boyd?"

"Ian? Yeah. They're friends. Ian and Cressida came to visit in October to meet Undine and Luke's baby girl. We all got together for dinner one night when they were here."

"So they're close friends." This was better than Chris had dared to hope. "You've met him. What's your take?"

"Good guy. Dangerously good at poker. Speaks a gazillion languages. Doesn't miss the CIA. Why so interested in Ian?"

"He's working for the wrong team on something, and I need to know if we can trust him."

"I don't know him well enough to vouch for him. But Luke trusts him. They had each other's back when there was an incident in Palau several years ago. Who is he working for that's causing you to question?"

"Family named Gardner. They own the Historie chain, among other stores."

Xavier was silent for a long moment. Finally, he said, "What's the issue?"

"Dennis Gardner financed a dig in Jordan, and the archaeologist who worked on it for him ended up being abducted."

"You mean the woman the Kingdom is demanding be extradited?"

"You heard about that?"

"Audrey's an archaeologist, and the archaeologist grapevine exploded a few hours ago. Half the internet wants to make an example of her."

Chris's heart sank. Diana would be gutted when she learned. "And the other half?"

"Two-thirds of them want her to be tried in the US."

That wasn't much better.

"And Audrey?"

"Wants more information before she casts judgment, but assumes there's a lot more to the story, especially considering the woman's boss at the university was murdered the day after the abduction."

Chris watched Diana as he listened to Xavier. She stood stock-still. She couldn't hear Xavier's side of the conversation, but he knew she'd guessed what path it had taken.

"Shit, Chris. This is a loaded situation, but I don't think Ian would do anything untoward in favor of Gardner. He's a former CIA case officer, which means he's no stranger to breaking the law, but that's in foreign countries, not on US soil."

"Gardner might not be breaking any laws either, but he can still throw gas on burning embers."

"I'll call Luke. Want me to have him call you?"

"Not yet. Leave my name out of it. No one can know my involvement. Ask Luke to reach out to Boyd. Tell him a Valkyrie has questions."

"How is he supposed to get in touch with this Valkyrie?"

Chris huffed out a breath. Diana was going to hate it, but they needed to go back. Little Creek was just too far from DC to be useful.

"If he agrees, tomorrow in Fairfax. There'll be a cell phone waiting for him at a place to be determined."

Chapter Thirty-Seven

Before going to sleep on Saturday night, Chris went to a drive-through automatic teller machine and withdrew his daily limit of five hundred dollars. On their way out of town Sunday morning, they visited the same teller machine and he withdrew an additional five hundred. Diana tucked down in the well of the seat before they entered the bank parking lot, hoping to avoid being picked up by any cameras in the lot or on the ATM itself.

Not surprisingly, she hadn't slept well given what Chris had reluctantly told her of the archaeological community's unkind verdict. At least Xavier's wife wanted more information.

She honestly wondered what she'd think if she were on the outside looking in. Would she be so quick to judge?

Before she'd contemplated working for the CIA, maybe.

Her decision to apply to the agency had been fueled by reading reports of the beheading of the archaeologist in Palmyra, followed by her shock and anger when the reports of Hobby Lobby buying looted artifacts came out. Nothing could have been done about Palmyra, but if knowledgeable operatives were in place, maybe they could have broken up the network before so much money was delivered into the coffers of terrorist groups.

She had the skills and credentials. She spoke Arabic. And she cared about the resource in a way that someone who stood to make massive profit from the deal never could. Antiquities dealers, no matter how ethical, were in it for the profit, not to protect the resource.

Salim had equal outrage over artifacts being sold to fund terrorism, and it had felt more personal to him given his heritage. He'd been supportive as she'd applied, and it wasn't until she'd been accepted into a training class—a process that took more than a year—that the reality sank in and he grew increasingly concerned.

Had he lived, there was a reasonable chance she wouldn't have gone through with it. But with him gone and the CIA out of reach, she'd opted for the next best substitution. She'd been grief-stricken and angry and devastated, and the idea of doing something to change the system that was doing so much harm to the Middle East and the world had given her purpose. So she'd gone all in.

She knew there were others like her who wanted to make a difference and end artifact trafficking. She felt bile rise in her throat at knowing that many of those people would think she was the enemy. The villain of the story.

But really, wasn't she?

She pulled her knees to her chest as she started to shake.

"Pull up, Diana."

"Am I that obvious?"

"You're in the same position you were in when I found you in the pantry yesterday."

She unfurled her legs as she saw the truth of his words. How many times had she sat in the tent in Jordan, in this same position?

She'd have slept curled in a ball last night, except she'd shared Chris's bed. He'd held her and stroked her back until she'd drifted to sleep, and this morning, she'd woken up curled against his side.

She'd had sex with this man, and she'd slept with him now too, but it wasn't the same. "You think someday we'll have sex *and* sleep in the same bed?"

He laughed. "Talk about your change in subjects."

"Answer the question, Flyte."

He took her hand and brought it to his lips, even as he kept his eyes on the road. "If I have anything to do with it, yes."

"I'm pretty sure that by definition, you have something to do with it."

"Takes two to tango."

She pulled his hand to her lips. "I do want to tango with you."

He pulled his hand away and tugged at his pants, shifting uncomfortably. "It's gonna be a long-ass drive to DC."

"We could pull over…"

"No. I didn't behave like a fricking saint last night to ruin it with a roadside quickie now."

"Bummer."

She rode in silence for a few minutes, then spotted a blue sign listing several stores to be found at the next exit.

"Take this exit."

"No quickies, Diana. I don't *do* quick."

She snickered, but said, "Sorry, this isn't about your body. There's an electronics store, and I need to get a new tablet."

"You can't log in to any of your accounts. You know that."

"I can't log into the accounts the NSA *knows about*, you mean."

She liked that he signaled for the exit, which was coming up fast, instead of waiting for the full explanation. They were off the interstate before she was halfway through telling him about the old email account and the photos she'd sent to that address from Rafiq's camera.

By the time she'd finished, he was in the store parking lot. "Okay. You stay here. Keep your head down, like you're reading." He reached into the back seat and grabbed a winter hat with an embroidered US Navy patch. He placed it on her head and pulled it down to cover her ears. "Still too damn pretty," he murmured. Then he kissed her hard and fast, his tongue invading quickly but thoroughly. Just long enough to leave her breathless.

She locked the door behind him and watched him walk away, admiring one of the finest asses she'd ever seen, before slumping down into the seat as he'd insisted.

She wanted to grumble that she'd only gotten about an hour of Christmas fun before the decision was made to return to DC, but she knew she was lucky to have had an hour.

She was lucky to have had ten minutes.

A dark-haired man climbed out of a vehicle two rows away. The way he moved caught her attention. His gait was familiar. As were his height and build.

Her breath squeezed from her lungs. She wasn't used to seeing him in winter clothing, which would explain the difference in his shape.

But how would Jamal have caught up with her here?

He headed toward the store, and she felt herself close to panic. Chris wasn't wearing his holster. The pistol was in the glove box.

She hit the button, and the compartment opened. There it was.

She could take him out before he entered the store and threatened Chris and dozens of others.

He was half the distance to the door. She wished she had a phone to call Chris. Warn him.

Her eyes pooled with tears. What the hell should she do?

Almost without thinking, she slammed the button for the horn on the steering wheel. The sound blared across the lot, and the man startled, turning in the direction of the noise.

It's not Jamal.

Not even close, really.

She released the horn and slammed the glove box closed, then yanked open the door and leaned out just in time to vomit in the grass strip that bordered the parking lot.

Chapter Thirty-Eight

Something had shaken Diana to the core. Chris could tell the moment he climbed into the vehicle. "I can't help you if you refuse to talk to me."

"You are helping me. And I'm fine. Just a little panic attack while you were in the store."

Chris didn't believe that for a moment, but was hard pressed to come up with any other reason for her to have been rattled so deeply while sitting alone in a car without a phone.

"You don't...have a phone, do you, babe?"

"No, *babe*. You watched me destroy it."

"You don't like being called 'babe.'"

"I don't mind being called 'babe' at all. What I don't like is the question that came with it."

He placed a finger under her chin and gently tilted her head so she couldn't avoid his gaze. "I'm just trying to figure out what happened to upset you. *Babe.*"

A tear spilled down her cheek as she held his gaze. Finally, she said, "I'm just scared."

He wasn't sure he believed it was that simple, but still, it was hard to argue. She had plenty of reasons to be afraid. "We're going to figure this out." He brushed his lips over hers, then released her and grabbed the bag he'd placed in the back seat and set it in her lap. "I got a few burners in addition to the tablet you wanted. We'll leave one of the burners in a park for Boyd to pick up and deliver to Freya."

"You really think he'll do it?"

He put the 4Runner in Reverse and backed out of the parking space. "By all accounts, he's on the level. Gardner was just a contract. Raptor doesn't turn down clients like Gardner without good reason, and this was the first time Gardner hired them."

It had been a complicated game of "Telephone" for Chris to get that information, but he was thankful Xavier and Luke had been willing to play.

He pulled onto the main road and headed back toward the interstate. "Set up the tablet. Check your email." He was surprised he needed to give her the nudge, but she'd been so rattled when he got back to the car, it was as if she'd forgotten about the reason he'd gone into the electronics store to begin with.

She was a far cry from the calm woman he'd first met in a canyon, but then she'd known she had a tiny bit of control in the situation given that she was the valuable asset everyone wanted alive.

Now she had no control, and he'd bet some players in this round of the game wanted her dead.

4

*D*iana opened the sleek new tablet's box. It came only partially charged, so she plugged it into the SUV's power port as she created a log-in with a fake username.

Next, she plugged in and configured the virtual private network on the portable prepaid 5G hotspot Chris had purchased.

"Okay, it's set up."

"Want me to pull over at the next exit?"

"No. There won't be anything in the inbox, and we wasted a lot of time with the last stop."

Even believing that, she held her breath as she logged into her very old email account she'd only ever used to receive marketing emails to receive coupons and online deals. The usual junk filled her inbox. Penis enlargers, home and car warranty scams, notification of payouts from class action lawsuits she wasn't part of, or exuberant messages about being the grand prize winner of a sweepstakes she'd never entered. All she had to do was give them her bank account number to receive her winnings.

She quickly dropped the obvious spam into the trash, then began clicking through the messages that remained. Nothing in the inbox panned out, so she switched to the junk mail filter, which strangely always let scam emails and penis enlargers through, but usually snared the actual emails she wanted to read.

Her heart fluttered when she saw five emails from the same numerical email address. Each message showed a paper clip attachment icon with a subject line that was all question marks. This, she knew, often happened when she received emails written in Arabic. The text usually came through fine in the message itself, but the right-to-left formatting often caused a problem with the subject line, especially for mail accounts not configured to send and receive messages in Arabic.

It could be the subject line of question marks or the attachments that tripped the spam filter. Probably both.

She let out a soft gasp when she saw the time stamp on the series of emails.

"You found something?" Chris asked.

"I think so. It looks like the camera was plugged in and the emails sent on Thursday night. While we were together."

"You didn't check after that?"

"I was…in a state, when I finally got home on Thursday and didn't check. I didn't remember to look Friday before my appointments. By the time I got home on Friday, my place had been broken into and they took the tablet."

"Was it with your computers?"

"Yes."

"Will they get anything off the tablet?"

"No. The only thing I ever did with it was log into this email account, and I didn't save the log-in or password to the device."

"The history will show you used the browser and visited exactly one site."

"Yes."

She returned her focus to the small full-color screen and the list of emails. Did these photos really help her at this point? Unless Freya got a location from the sender's IP address, all they were was evidence the Jordanian government could use against her when she went on trial.

◈

*M*ost of the artifacts didn't look all that exciting to Chris, but Diana gave him the rundown on their age and the inscriptions on some of the tablets. According to her, the lettering was Nabataean, but the words were Aramaic. She explained that while the Nabataeans had their own language and alphabet, they often wrote in the more common Aramaic of the region.

They sat in a fast-food restaurant parking lot, eating french fries and drinking sodas, a short break to give Chris a chance to view the photos. "How much would these be worth?"

She wrinkled her nose. "Archaeologists don't like to put a price on artifacts, but that's exactly what I had to do, both that first night and the last day. Both times, the valuation was for Rafiq."

"*Both* times?"

"The first day—before you came—they tested me. Made me authenticate artifacts. Give them a price to charge. When Rafiq showed up that night, he took the artifacts I'd authenticated. That's when I learned they planned for me to loot the site where we camped. At first, I thought they'd just grabbed me to authenticate the artifacts, like I'd been doing to get an in with Bibi at the market."

She touched the image of what looked like a jug on the

screen. The photo was low resolution, and she'd explained that the camera only sent the smallest version of the files. "So when it came to these, I made up prices based on nothing but my desire to present them to Rafiq and get his location so your team could swoop in and get him. I inflated everything to make them sound more valuable. To be fair, many of them would be quite valuable. The one I broke—a glass ingot—was among the more valuable because it was incredibly rare and the largest of the ingots we discovered…"

She touched the photo of a cobalt-blue glass puck—which, she'd explained, was really the size of a salad plate—then touched her neck. This must be the type of artifact that she got the glass shard from. That shard had probably saved his life. From what she'd told him, he'd been about to walk into Jamal's line of fire. The boy would have had a clear headshot, before Chris would've had a chance to raise his rifle from where it pointed at Bassam.

Diana cleared her throat, picking up the thread where her voice had trailed off. "As an added benefit, I thought the high value of everything might mean they wouldn't just hack away at the site once I wasn't there to oversee the looting."

He noticed she didn't call it excavation, even though that was what she'd tried to do. "Did you take notes on the dig?"

"I tried, but my supplies were limited. Bassam and Jamal literally gave me only one sheet of paper per day in the field. They didn't want me to leave artifacts in situ while I was taking notes. If I couldn't write stuff down, there was no point in finds remaining in the ground."

She'd spent weeks as a prisoner in the desert, painstakingly removing artifacts for the goal of getting Rafiq's location. He understood now even better than he had before how she'd violated everything she believed in. All to get to Rafiq.

Now, those artifacts had probably been sold. The images on the screen were the only tangible evidence they'd ever existed.

The clock on the dashboard indicated they were nearing the afternoon rush hour. They should get moving, but he had more questions. "These photos, they'd make it impossible for someone to buy these artifacts and put them on public display, right?"

"Yes. These photos would undermine any fake provenance. A museum or individual who displayed them would be admitting they'd purchased the artifacts from terrorists, which isn't a good look for most of the world."

"Didn't that craft store chain—Hobby Lobby—buy a bunch of stolen artifacts for their Bible museum? Were they ever punished?"

"Thousands of the artifacts Hobby Lobby acquired were originally from Iraq—either looted directly from sites or items looted from the Iraq Museum in 2003. There've been multiple rounds of repatriation and fines, including the return of five thousand five hundred artifacts in 2017 along with a three million dollar fine. In the most recent round of repatriation, Iraq reclaimed more than seventeen thousand artifacts that had been previously held by the Museum of the Bible. Thousands more artifacts have been returned to Egypt. It's sickening that no Americans went to jail for what they did. To the best of my knowledge, the only arrests made were of artifact brokers in Israel. The charge was tax evasion."

"No one from the museum was arrested?"

"No one. Their own experts warned them as early as 2010 that the types of artifacts they sought to acquire had a high probability of being looted, but they made the purchases anyway, likely knowing *exactly* what they were buying."

"*Likely* being the keyword."

"Exactly. Without proof, they were only guilty of being on the receiving end of the smuggling, which meant fines and forfeiture, but no arrests." She paused, then added, "The FBI takes a different view of artifacts and art than they do theft of other types. The goal is always preservation and recovery of the object first and foremost. Punishment in the form of prosecution is secondary. Really, it's probably tertiary. Collecting fines or taxes being secondary. And the DOJ did that in this case. I'm sure arrests were never on the table."

"You think there's any connection between your dig and the Bible museum?"

She shook her head. "I'm sure the feds have the museum acquisitions department under a microscope at this point. My guess is these artifacts are bound for a private collection, never to be seen again."

"But if they do show up, you've got proof now that will send the buyer to jail."

"The *seller* to jail if they can be identified. The buyer will play dumb, get a slap on the wrist, and pay a fine. Meanwhile, Fahd died to protect artifacts like these. It's no wonder the archaeological community hates me. I think I'd hate me too."

"You've got Morgan and my friend's wife, Audrey."

She let out a sad laugh. "Two archaeologists on Team Diana. Go me."

He took her hand and brought it to his lips. "You've got me."

"I'm afraid of the situation I've put you in."

"Sweetheart, I'm a SEAL. My job is all about being put in dire situations."

She rolled her eyes. "You know what I mean. I'd take a HALO jump over this any day."

"Have you ever HALOed?"

"No, but it's got to be better than this."

He thought about it for a moment, remembering the jump into the storm last winter and being pelted with balls of ice, then landing in a lake that was only a few degrees above freezing. "Compared to what you're facing? Yeah. Piece of cake."

*B*ack on the road, Diana returned her focus to the photos on the screen. "Do you think Freya will be able to track the IP address the photos were sent from?"

"If she can't, maybe Raptor can."

"You're so certain Raptor is going to help us?"

"Call me an optimist."

She choked on a laugh. "You don't strike me as the optimistic type."

"I'm crushed."

She glanced at the small screen. She had twenty-two photos. Low res, but enough detail to be identifiable. She felt sick at seeing them as much as relieved. It made it all the more real somehow, those weeks in the desert. "I'd give anything to know what's happened to the site."

"Is it being monitored by the Jordanian government now?"

She nodded. "In theory, anyway. I gave them the coordinates and told them everything I could about where we dug and what we found. The site is similar to—but much smaller than—the Nabataean city of Hegra." She shook her head, realizing that would mean nothing to Chris. Strange to realize the boundaries of the bubble she'd lived in since grad school, where everyone knew archaeological sites in the Middle East by name and not just the big ones like Petra and Palmyra. The little guys were important too.

"Has the Kingdom stationed guards at the site?"

"More likely a satellite camera is keeping an eye on it. The US Army reactivated their Monuments Officers group a few years ago. They have a lab in Virginia that monitors sites that could be in danger from looting. I wanted to reach out to them…but we both know they'll see me as the villain."

This made her think of Fahd's instructions, all the site coordinates he'd given her, asking her to monitor sites in Syria if something happened to him. The reminder added weight to the guilt that threatened to crush her half the time. To do what Fahd asked, she'd need a computer with access to the satellite feeds. No one would give her that now.

Chapter Thirty-Nine

4

*A*fter planting a burner phone near the fenced-off area of an off-leash dog park, they checked into a vacation rental that Chris's friend Xavier rented for them in Fairfax. The rental was a tiny one-bedroom house in an unincorporated wooded area. Surrounded by trees, it was private, even though the housing lots were relatively small.

It was cute and cozy, and Diana wanted to curl up in front of the fire and do nothing for a week. Well, maybe watch TV, but probably just sleep while being held by Chris.

"I can sleep on the sofa bed," Chris offered upon seeing that the only bed was a double.

She rolled her eyes. "I think we're way past the shy stage."

He slipped an arm around her waist. "I'm not taking anything for granted with you, but given how we pretty much combust when we kiss, keeping things platonic will be harder if we share a bed, and I don't want to take advantage."

"Who said I want platonic? And I'm perfectly capable of giving informed consent. Plus I know you're perfectly capable of keeping your hands off if I don't give that consent. In the same vein, if you say no, I promise not to seduce you while you're sleeping."

He smiled. "Well, now, I don't have anything to look forward to." His lips brushed over hers, then he pulled back and met her gaze. "I want a relationship with you, Diana, and I don't want to fuck it up by doing the wrong thing now, when you're vulnerable."

She gave him a sad smile. "If we wait until my life is straightened out, we might never have sex again." She cupped his cheek. "Sleep with me tonight, Lieutenant Flyte. Whether we have sex or not, I'd like you in my bed. We'll figure out later…later. Now, let's eat dinner before it gets cold."

Diana paced the tiny cabin. Boyd should have picked up the burner phone from the park an hour ago, and she was going to lose her mind from waiting. They had no plan B. She needed information, and she needed Freya to start looking into the IP address of the emails she'd received.

Finally, the burner phone rang.

She met Chris's gaze. They'd agreed that she would answer any calls. Right now, the fact that Chris was the one harboring her was their one secret that was in her favor.

She hit the speaker button. "Yes."

"Valkyrie. I'm surprised it took this long for you to reach out."

"I had a few things on my plate."

"Is your friend who was with you in the bar listening?"

Without looking to Chris for a signal of what to say, she answered. "No."

"Fine. He's probably back in ONP where he spent last January."

She had no idea what that meant, so she didn't have to fake a reaction. "Sure. Whatever."

She met Chris's gaze. He didn't look fazed, but she guessed whatever Ian had said indicated he knew exactly who Chris was. Had one of his friends squealed, or had Ian known when he saw them together in the bar?

She dove in with her first question. "How well do you know Fr—" Almost too late, she remembered that even on a burner, she shouldn't use names. "Friday?"

"Only by reputation."

Boyd and Freya weren't acquainted.

"Did you tell your client about my extracurricular job?"

Had he told Gardner?

"No, Val."

"And why should I believe you?"

"I don't rat out my own kind. Not when they're working for the home team."

"Do you still work for the home team?"

Are you really out of the CIA?

A soft chuckle filled the line. "I was traded down to the minors. Same team name, different employer."

She snorted. "You don't strike me as the type to give up the big league without complaint."

"On the contrary. I asked to be traded. Free agency."

She rolled her eyes even as she smiled at Chris.

Ian switched languages to Arabic. "Listen, I know the lieutenant is listening. Are you with him willingly?"

She was taken aback by the question. She responded in Arabic. "That's an interesting question considering he's the one who told me to trust you."

"And now you've confirmed his identity. Your tradecraft needs work."

Shit. This wasn't even tradecraft. It was basic interrogation. And she'd failed.

"Answer the question. Are you with him willingly?"

"Naeam." *Yes.* She continued, still speaking Arabic, "Why do you ask?"

"There may be a leak on his team."

She kept her face blank, channeling everything Freya had taught her a lifetime ago about facial response. "How is that possible?"

"It happens. In my line of work, you look for cracks and make them wider. It would've been your line of work too had it not been for the accident."

He knew about her previous CIA dreams and Salim.

"What kind of leak?"

"It's possible there was a tip that the raid was coming, which would explain why the big man and the goods weren't there when the time came."

She looked at Chris, again keeping her face blank.

For his part, his poker face was long gone. She knew he

spoke some Arabic—most SEALs knew basic phrases and other key words. He had to be wondering what it was that Boyd didn't want him to know. She'd have to figure out what to say when the call ended.

"Did you tell your client this?"

"He knows nothing but what you said in our meeting. I had to give him a translated transcript."

That was fair. "How did he know about…who I met in the desert?"

"Not from me."

"But *you* knew."

"Yes. And I know you spotted an old friend in Germany. Someone in the IC is being careless—even reckless—with your intel, some of which found its way to my client, possibly to give them ammunition to force your extradition."

Chapter Forty

4

*N*ow it was Chris's turn to pace. Diana was holding something back, and it didn't sit well with him. His phone pinged. Rand had replied to his text. Chris sent a thumbs-up emoji, then tucked his phone away.

At the same time, the burner pinged, and Diana read the text from Ian. "His contact agreed to pass on a thumb drive to Freya. He sent the drop-site location."

"Perfect." The encrypted thumb drive had copies of the photos, their burner phone number, and Diana's log-in and password for the email account that received the original photos. Everything Freya would need to get in touch and get started searching for the IP address. He reached for his boots and pulled them on.

"You going somewhere?" she asked.

"Going to drop the drive, and then I'm meeting with Rand for a beer. Cover for going out." He finished lacing the left boot and moved to the right.

"Meeting Rand is a risk if he's being watched."

He paused in his task and lifted his head to meet her gaze. Her expression was as blank as a bullet packed with cotton wadding. "You have reason to think someone is watching Rand?"

She shrugged. "I'm just struggling with who to trust."

He rose and crossed the short space to her and placed a knuckle under her chin, lifting her gaze to meet his. Up close, her eyes gave a hint of confusion she was mostly good at hiding.

He leaned down and kissed her. Soft and undemanding. She leaned into him, her body pliant.

Okay. It wasn't him she didn't trust.

He released her and took the thumb drive from the counter and slipped it into his pocket. "Lock up behind me. I'll be out late, making sure cameras get me in town. Don't wait up."

She nodded.

"Don't go online without using the VPN on the tablet, and don't check your email, even with that."

"I know."

Before heading for the door, he turned and kissed her one more time, his tongue dipping into her mouth.

Damn. He wanted to stay. Pretend something hadn't shifted between them when she spoke with Boyd, but there was no putting that genie back in the bottle. He had to trust Boyd wouldn't screw them over.

If the guy hadn't been endorsed by Xavier, he'd already have ditched the burner phone and moved them to a new safe house.

Instead, he was leaving Diana alone.

He took a complicated route to the drop site, watching for a tail. He didn't imagine anyone could have followed them to this point, but stranger things had happened. He wouldn't start getting lazy now.

Ninety minutes after leaving Diana, he planted the thumb drive under a trash bin at the playground, then was back on the road, taking another twisted route into the city. His car had an E-ZPass and even though he'd avoided toll roads, he wouldn't be surprised to know there were RFID sensors on the bridges in and out of DC.

Once he was over a bridge and inside the city, he pulled into a parking lot near the Lincoln Memorial and texted Rand.

CHRIS

> Just got to the city. You still at your sister's?

RAND

> Yeah. Be at the bar in thirty. Ran into Albrecht in the lobby after you texted. Told him to join us.

Even better. Albrecht seemed like a good guy, but Chris didn't know him well. Young, skilled, and eager. Chris would be his commander when Rand moved up and out.

Twenty minutes later, Chris was in the pub and grabbed a large booth by the window. The curved booth he'd shared with Diana was a dozen feet away, and he felt a longing to be back in that moment.

Wild to think that was just three nights ago.

Seeing her then had energized him. Those first touches

that signaled interest. It had been a fucking amazing night, and he wanted more of that.

The server came and took his beer order, just what he needed to break his trance as he looked at the booth that was now home to a Black couple who, from their body language, he assumed had been together for a while. Comfortable, happy.

He scanned the room, and his gaze met that of a Black woman with friends standing by the bar. Their gazes held just long enough to not be casual.

In another situation, he'd break the gaze and, if she approached, brush her off. But he had two SEALs showing up, and he counted three women. It wouldn't hurt for him to show interest, especially given that Rand had seen him kissing Diana on the sidewalk that night.

Petty Officer Third Class Bryce Albrecht was the first to arrive. White, single, and in his early twenties, he was six feet tall, built like a tank, and a promising sniper.

He was also perfect for enticing the group of women to their booth. Chris was too old to play the pickup game, and Rand was nearly as old. He had no doubt the blond pretty boy got all the female attention he wanted, but Rand's looks were also the kind that intimidated, while Bryce had "easy lay" written all over him.

Sure enough, the women were checking them both out as they sipped their beers. "So what brought you back to the city?" Albrecht asked.

"I got antsy in my new place all alone. Fucking holiday season in a new area sucks. Decorated my tree and it brought back memories of my ex. So I decided to come back to DC. Take in some museums. Get laid." He shrugged. "Drink beer." He turned the question back on Bryce. "Why are you still here? I thought you were headed to Pennsylvania."

The young SEAL picked up his beer and drank a long gulp, then set it down with a thud. "Got uninvited to spend the holidays with my girlfriend."

"Ouch. What happened?"

"I might have fucked up."

"Might?"

"Probably." He sighed. "Definitely."

The server returned at the same time Rand showed up.

A glance toward the bar and Chris again met the gaze of the pretty Black woman. He felt like a shit for not shaking his head to warn her off.

This espionage stuff sucked.

Rand slid into the booth next to Bryce, giving Chris his own side. After he was settled in with a beer and their server delivered a selection of small plates, Rand fixed him with a look. "Been an interesting few days as far as our last mission goes."

"Yeah," Bryce said. "Was waiting for you to get here to bring that up. Can you believe that shit? We risk our lives to save some chick, and now Uncle Sam is going to give her back?"

Chris appreciated that Rand didn't mention that the last time they'd seen each other, Chris was making out with Diana on the sidewalk.

"It's fucked up," Chris said.

"You think she did it? Was colluding with the enemy?"

Bryce asked. All at once, he seemed to remember who he was talking to. "You're the only one who was there for both rescues. What was your take on her?"

Chris met Rand's gaze. Did he need to confess he'd been with Diana on Thursday night? Would Rand admit to meeting her?

He decided to let the superior officer field the question, and just responded with a noncommittal shrug.

Rand took a sip of his beer. "Not our job to speculate. We just drop in and save the day."

Bryce let out a laugh and raised his beer. "Amen."

Chris remembered being that young. When the job was simple.

Be the hero.

That was before ops went bad. Before he lost teammates.

Bryce excused himself to use the restroom, and Rand fixed him with a look. "How's Diana?"

"I fucked up."

"You were pretty cozy the last time I saw you."

"We were. I fucked up later." He looked down into his beer like it held answers. "I questioned whether or not she saw Rafiq, and she bolted."

"Wow. You did fuck up. Or maybe dodged a bullet."

He took a sip of his beer. "Both, I think." He met Rand's gaze. "You talk to Morgan since the news broke?"

"No. Figured it would be best if I stay out of it. The brass knows I'm friends with both Morgan and Freya, but I never met Diana until that night. They call you yet?"

"No. Pretty sure no one knows we met Thursday—and I told the Pentagon everything I know last week."

"If they talk to me, I have to tell them you met her."

He nodded. "I wouldn't want you to lie."

"You liked her."

"We back in middle school now, Fallon?"

"You know what I mean."

He nodded. "Yeah. I liked her. I fucked up, and…" He didn't know how he could finish that sentence. For the act he was putting on, or in truth.

He could be crass and say she was an amazing lay. Anything other than that and he feared he'd reveal too much.

He was saved by Bryce's return. Which was quickly followed by the three women who'd been eyeing their table from the start. They were single, young, hot, and looking to score. Chris was rusty in this department, but he remembered it from the days before Pam.

He smiled and flirted and tried not to gag at the overwhelming scent of their collective perfume. The booths were a bit long, so with scrunching in tight, they made room for the women. A Latina woman settled in between Rand and Bryce, while Chris found himself next to the pretty Black woman who'd been eyeing him all night and her friend, who was also Black.

Geneva was twenty-four and worked for the Justice Department, which he assumed meant she worked for the FBI but couldn't be that specific. Annabella was clearly interested in Rand. She worked for the Library of Congress, while Iris, who sat directly across from Bryce, claimed to be with the NSA, which he figured meant she worked retail or in the service industry and didn't want to admit that when her friends had more exciting-sounding careers, so she made a joke about it.

He'd tell her about his hours working fast food before he joined the Navy, but instead, he just felt old.

He met Rand's gaze and saw the tired look in his eyes too. Rand was a year younger than Chris, but he'd been in the Navy and SEALs longer. A SEAL year was like dog years.

These women were *way* too young for the likes of either of them.

Geneva was cute and persistent, though, and Chris felt like he needed to play along. It wouldn't do if word got out that he and Diana had hooked up and then he appeared to be pining for her days later.

He toyed with the idea of getting Geneva alone in the corner, making it look like he was interested, then saying something rotten to make her storm off, but that could back-fire in a thousand different ways. So instead, he resorted to talking about Pam.

He embodied the guy everyone hated at the bar. The bitter ex.

Thankfully, the women called a bathroom break, and he was alone with Bryce and Rand.

"Dude, what the fuck?" Bryce said. "You really suck at this."

"Sorry, man. I guess I was looking for a night out with the team. Not a hookup."

Rand gave him an assessing look. He was dangerously close to blowing it.

"I'm just too old for this shit. She's a nice girl, but that's the problem. I know she's a legal adult, but all I can think of is when I was a senior in high school, she was eight years old."

"Dude, channel your inner Leo DiCaprio. She's fucking hot."

Chris grimaced. "Sorry, man. I'm just in a different place." This was a perfect time to make his escape, so he waved his credit card at the passing server. "This is on me, but I'm gonna bail. Tell Geneva I'm sorry, but I don't do hookups."

He caught Rand's look at the blatant lie, but ignored it.

He managed to pay the bill and get out of the bar before the women left the restroom. Thank god.

He took a deep breath of the cool night air that was perfume-free. He glanced at his watch, surprised to see it was nearing midnight.

His phone buzzed as he settled in the driver's seat. He pulled it out and checked the screen.

SMS message with a six-digit pin to unlock his email address.

Someone was trying to hack his account. Two-factor authentication to the rescue.

Another text came, then another. After five attempts, the hacker would be locked out.

They used up all their tries, and the messages stopped.

He tucked his phone in his pocket and put the SUV in Reverse to back out of the spot. He'd be taking the long, long way home to Diana.

Clearly, someone had figured out they were together.

4

*B*eing alone with her thoughts was never a good thing for Diana these days. She was envious of Chris. He'd gotten to go out. But then, she didn't particularly want to *be* out.

Just days ago, she'd had to mentally pump herself up to gather courage to go to Morgan's birthday party. Now she wondered where she'd be if she hadn't gone.

She changed into her comfiest pajamas and climbed into bed with the new tablet. She considered downloading a book to read, but knew she wouldn't have the attention span necessary. Instead she opened the web browser and searched on her name.

Her body nearly seized with anxiety at the list of headlines, and she immediately deleted the search results. She took a slow breath and typed in "Jordan" and "Nabataean artifacts," not really expecting to see anything new. Archaeology news moved slowly, and she'd done this search regularly since her rescue. She was always looking for news in general, but also, she wanted to see if there were updates on Fahd's murder, which would almost certainly be tagged with those keywords if there was new information.

The headline she was looking for showed up on page two of the results.

Historie Strikes Deal with Gillibrand for New Signature Line

The subheading gave more information.

To coincide with the grand opening of the new flagship store and museum in Newport News, Virginia, this summer, CEO of the retail giant, Dennis Gardner, has come to an agreement with Gillibrand Auction House to purchase twenty artifacts in a preempt.

She clicked on the link, which was really a press release put out by Gardner Holdings. The article explained that the new acquisitions would expand the store's Signature Line to a grand total of two hundred and fifty artifacts.

Historie's Signature Line were artifacts owned by the Gardner family, giving them the exclusive right to create exact, licensed replicas. They usually limited the number of replicas to one thousand with the first run, then the duplicated artifact was priced for retail sale in the five-thousand- to ten-thousand-dollar range, depending on size and complexity, given that all replicas were made utilizing the same technique and material as the original.

Therefore, if the item was made of solid gold, so was the replica.

The Signature Line was big bucks for Historie and the Gardner family. It wasn't surprising that they were looking to expand it at the same time they would do the ribbon cutting for the new flagship location.

Her dig was intended to offer insight into how to structure some of the museum displays. She'd been slated to meet with the designers in early October to talk about how best to replicate a dig site.

She'd missed those meetings. Now she wondered who Dennis had hired in her place, because construction was moving forward on schedule.

She scrolled down the press release, her heart pounding, knowing there would be a sneak peek at a few of the artifacts at the end.

The press release claimed the artifacts had been in the private collection of a Jordanian national who'd died a year ago, and his estate was finally being liquidated. It was hard to prove that kind of provenance was fake unless one of the items was a piece that had previously been documented— like the items stolen from the Iraq museum that Hobby Lobby had acquired.

When she saw the first image, she felt a different kind of shock.

These weren't the artifacts she'd looted in Jordan. Not the ones she had photos of on this tablet.

No.

But she had seen these artifacts before. She'd touched them. Held them. Hell, she'd even smelled them.

She closed her eyes and remembered the text she'd received from Dennis Gardner on Friday. He was in town on business. Gillibrand's main office was in DC. The deal had probably closed that morning, the press release prepared immediately, and posted in the afternoon. It had possibly been posted while she was in Gardner's hotel suite telling him through Ian Boyd's interview that she'd appraised these very artifacts on the day she'd been abducted.

Chapter Forty-One

The lights were out in the rental when Chris returned. He tiptoed in and left the lights off as he slipped into the bathroom to get ready for bed. After brushing his teeth, he stripped down to his boxer briefs and the T-shirt he wore to the bar, because he didn't want to disturb Diana and dig through his bag for a different shirt.

He slid quietly into bed and lay on his back, staring up at the dark ceiling. He was tired but wired, and took comfort in hearing Diana's quiet breathing next to him. She was safe.

He wanted to pull her into his arms and press his face into her neck. He wanted to feel the pulse of her heartbeat.

She shifted in the bed, and he inched toward her. Knowing how difficult it was for her to fall asleep, he didn't want to wake her, so he was surprised when she shifted and curled up against his side.

He pulled her snug against him and buried his nose in her hair, which smelled of a flowery shampoo.

All at once, her hands pushed against his chest, and he

released her, worried she'd been startled out of sleep. "It's me, Diana. Sorry if I scared you."

"Oh, I knew it was you. What I didn't expect was that you'd smell like another woman."

Shit. He'd forgotten about the perfume cloud and had gotten used to the scent to the point he didn't smell it on his shirt. "Sorry. Three women joined Rand, Bryce, and me. I played along with the flirting because I couldn't exactly be seen pining for you. But nothing happened, I swear."

She moved closer, but still left several inches between them.

"It's ridiculous." She gave a harsh laugh. "Logically, I know you don't owe me anything. We aren't a couple. We haven't made any kind of commitment to each other. But I smelled another woman on your skin, and logic went out the window."

Her words stirred something in the region of his body dangerously close to his heart. "I'm not sure I can be logical about the idea of you with another man either." He dared to reach out as he scooted closer. His hand found her waist. He would have stopped there, but she scooted a tiny bit closer instead of moving away, so he cupped her ass and pulled her all the way against him.

They lay chest to chest, her warm breath tickling his neck. His hard-on was instant.

She let out a laugh. "You may be turned on, but I still smell another woman in this bed."

"I just want to be clear, there *is* a promise between us. I promised to help you. Hide you. Protect you. That's my commitment. And I might flirt with a woman, but that's to serve the 'hide' part of my promise. But you're the only one I want, Diana. And no one but you will satisfy me."

She pressed her lips to his collarbone. "Okay."

He stroked her cheek. "My ex-wife cheated on me. I know how shitty that is, and I wouldn't do that to anyone."

"We aren't married."

"But we are *involved*. I don't share, and I wouldn't demand from you what I'm not willing to give."

She tucked against him. "Okay. At least it's a nice perfume."

"I can shower if you want."

"No. I um…have to tell you something. It's important. A shower would just waste time."

"What happened?"

"Remember how I told you that I authenticated artifacts for Rafiq that first day?"

"Yes."

"Gardner Holdings just cut a deal with a DC auction house—Gillibrand—to purchase those artifacts for the Historie store's Signature Line."

He stiffened as the meaning sank in. "They're buying artifacts from Rafiq so they can sell replicas."

"Yes."

"And it's going through an auction house, which will get the blame."

"Yes. And as an added bonus, I told Gardner on Friday during our meeting that I'd appraised a bunch of artifacts for Rafiq that first day. He probably guessed they were the same ones."

"And so he sent henchmen—possibly Jamal—to your condo to grab your computers."

"He probably wondered if I'd written up any kind of description after I returned Stateside."

"Had you?"

"No. I was so focused on everything that happened after that first day. I didn't think about those initial artifacts very much."

"Is there any way to prove the artifacts are the ones you examined? That they're looted goods?"

"No. I mean, I could describe them in detail, but in the end, it would just be my word against the auction house."

"And your word isn't in the highest esteem right now. Is that Gardner's motive to get the US to extradite you? To discredit you?"

"Discredit me. Silence me. I did the math tonight, and the Signature Line is worth big bucks to the family. One thousand replicas of twenty artifacts. If they all sold for the minimum five grand, that's a hundred million dollars. And that's only the first run. Every few years, they'll do a limited run of the most popular items, but the second and third time around, they up the price and reduce the run size. Seven thousand dollars for five hundred replicas. A single artifact could gross an additional three and a half million. And that's the base pricing."

"We need to get someone to look into the provenance, then. Isn't that something Morgan and Freya can do?"

"That's exactly what they *do* do. They have specialists on retainer who check provenance. Look for cracks in the supply chain."

"Gardner won't like that."

"Fortunately, Gardner has no say. These kinds of deals go through an auction house like Gillibrand for a reason. Gillibrand will have to allow examination of the provenance. If they don't, US Customs and Border Protection can come at them with a warrant."

"Is Gillibrand crooked?"

"I have no idea. In general, places like Christie's, Sotheby's, and Gillibrand do their best to stay on the right side of the law, and the law says auction houses are supposed to vet provenance before they move forward with a sale."

"Okay, then. This is a solid line of questions to follow." He stroked her hair. "I bet both Gardners shit a brick when you mentioned those artifacts on Friday."

She yawned and snuggled closer, running her hand over his chest. He wished he wasn't wearing the smelly T-shirt and she was touching bare skin. "I'm so angry that this is all just money for them, but at the same time, I'm a bit gleeful that we finally have a solid connection. Even if we can't prove it."

"We *will* prove it. They've made mistakes. Like the press release going out before they knew you could identify the artifacts. They're scared. Of you."

"I like that idea, even if I don't believe it."

"Babe, I'm pretty sure you terrify them. Now go to sleep, Valkyrie."

Chapter Forty-Two

*D*iana woke up alone in the bed. The sound of the shower told her where Chris was, and she pulled his pillow close and breathed in his scent, perfume and all.

Damn, she had it bad for him. In a good way.

But she couldn't spend the day pining for the man in the shower. Today, they could take action. She would finally talk to Freya. No more moving through an intermediary. She'd be able to tell her about the artifacts and Gillibrand.

Everything about the situation was confusing, but now they had a thread. Diana pulled out the tablet and read the press release again, this time making notes of questions to pass on to Freya. By the time she got on the phone with the former spy, she had written down everything she could remember about that first day including a full description of the artifacts and the phrases she used to describe them.

She'd bet anything her descriptions would be verbatim in the provenance.

4

*K*ira Hanson was slightly terrified of Freya Lange. She knew the woman had been some kind of special ops in the CIA and had a gaze that could cut glass. She'd never directed that gaze at Kira, but that made her no less intimidating.

As a specialist in art history, Kira was an introverted nerd who preferred books and art over people. When engrossed in her studies, she didn't find herself mired in interpersonal conflict. The people in conflict had been dead for hundreds, if not thousands, of years, which really was a bonus.

She should have considered that going into the appraisal business would be rife with conflict. And people would insist on talking to her. Face-to-face. On the phone. Zoom.

No, thank you. She'd be happy to send an email with her report.

But no. People *insisted* on looking her in the eye when she gave the results of her research, and Freya was the absolute worst in that regard.

The woman could read her like a comic book. See all the thought bubbles and the little explosions that happened inside her head.

She never should have accepted the regular consulting gig with Friday Morning Valkyries, but she believed in the cause, and FMV paid on time.

Plus, the work itself was always interesting. Whether it was consulting with a museum or auction house on verifying provenance or researching collection records from a hundred years ago, she often got access to new sources of information, or got paid to spend days in an archive, going painstakingly through a collection.

She'd never wanted to do the job of an archivist—arranging and describing collections wasn't her thing—but she loved having access to the end result.

It was unusual to be called and asked for an in-person meeting at a moment's notice, then to be left waiting after she hurried across town and over the bridge to FMV's office in Virginia. The clock ticked by, twenty minutes passing.

Kira could have enjoyed an actual breakfast instead of grabbing an apple and eating it while driving. Finally, thirty minutes after Kira arrived, the admin popped into the waiting room and led Kira to the conference room that was all couches and comfort and no cellular or WiFi.

Before she took her seat, she shook hands with Morgan and Freya and one of the most handsome men she'd ever seen, who was introduced as Ian Boyd. His handshake was firm and professional, and he freaked her out by saying, "I've been following your work for some time, Dr. Hanson."

She blurted out the first words that came to mind. "Why on earth would you do that?"

"I'm in private security, and occasionally my company is approached by clients seeking protection for items, not people. The first rule of taking on that kind of job is making sure the item is authentic from the start. So far, none of those jobs have come to fruition, but you were on our shortlist as a potential consultant if they did."

"And why did those jobs not come to fruition?"

"I believe the client balked at bringing in an outside expert, but naturally, that wasn't the excuse given at the time." He shrugged. "They went elsewhere, I would imagine."

Kira turned to Freya. "So what have you got for me this time?" Friday Morning Valkyries didn't usually deal in art. The job would probably be antiquities, not a painting by an old master, which was a shame. Not that she didn't appreciate antiquities, it was more that there was a certain thrill to being in the presence of something that she knew had been touched by da Vinci, Michelangelo, or Raphael. Their DNA had mixed with the paint, or their sweat had dripped on the marble. These singular men, the greatest minds of their time, had infused their work with their beings.

Not that people didn't do that with their work every day, and she had nothing against modern art, but like the Renaissance masters, there were only a handful of modern artists whose names would be remembered five hundred years after their deaths.

"We're looking at a collection from the Middle East," Freya said.

"That's not really my specialty. There are a half dozen others who would be better suited for this job."

"But I need someone I can trust, and I don't need specific authentication so much as access."

"Why is that?"

"A shipment of stolen artifacts are in the process of being sold by Gillibrand in a preempt. We need to disrupt the close of the sale to give us time to gather the proof we need."

"And how am I supposed to do that?"

"The provenance is fake. We need you to prove it."

"You make that sound…easy? I promise you, it's not."

"It's harder, though, if you don't *know* it's fake. In this instance, we're certain."

"The provenance is going to be written in Arabic. Which I can't read." She could read and write in Italian, Greek, German, and Latin, but her Arabic was limited to numerals.

"We expect some of it to be in English," Freya said. "We even know the exact phrases you should look for, but it will probably be buried in the Arabic paperwork."

"Which is where I come in," Ian said. "I'm fluent. But… I can't approach Gillibrand directly. If you can get copies, I can translate for you."

"You're working for FMV on this?"

He shook his head. "Consulting with, in a coordinated investigation."

She looked to Freya who gave a sharp nod. Not that she expected the woman to deny his claim. It was just odd. This arrangement was quite different from the work she'd done for FMV in the past.

"There's one more thing. Well, two, actually." This came from Morgan, who'd stayed out of the discussion until now. "You can't tell Gillibrand that you're working for us. It's extremely likely they wouldn't let you in the door if you name us as your client. So we've made arrangements for a man who is unaffiliated with FMV and Raptor—Ian's company—to play the role of client. The delay in bringing you in for this meeting was getting that part lined up. He's on his way to the office now."

"Now? Why now?"

"We need this done today. Within the next hour. The deal can't close until the artifacts clear customs—which could happen at any time. While the artifacts remain on the market, we want your client to make Gillibrand a better offer. He just needs to vet the provenance first, which is where you come in."

"You want me to lie to a major auction house that is my bread and butter and claim I'm bringing them a buyer who can afford to outbid a preempt that has already been announced?"

"When you put it that way, you make it sound like it's a bad thing," Freya said.

Kira would laugh if she didn't want to cry. She huffed out a sigh. "Who's the preempt buyer?"

"Your old bosses at Gardner Holdings."

Chapter Forty-Three

*C*hris sat in the grocery store parking lot, reading the text from Freya on his burner phone. They'd found a loophole in the deal between the Gardners and the auction house and were bringing in an appraiser to go in and look at the documents.

They probably wouldn't be able to stop the sale, but it would rattle the Gardners. He tucked away the phone, feeling a rush of relief.

Diana wasn't alone. The Valkyries would protect her.

He climbed from his SUV and headed into the store, grabbing a cart on his way. He'd spent half the night worrying about what he'd do if this wasn't settled before he had to report for duty in eleven days. But Freya and Morgan would protect her, and he'd just be down in Little Creek. She could return with him and stay at his house while Freya untangled the web the Gardners had woven.

They'd finish decorating for the holidays. Maybe he'd have a chance to impress her with his cooking. He'd seen her

kitchen—from her quality knives to her French cookware—
and guessed meal prep was important to her. Except for the
scrambled eggs he made yesterday, they'd eaten nothing but
takeout.

He considered the knives and cookware in the vacation
rental and pushed the cart to the frozen food section.
Impressing her with his skill on the grill would have to wait
for an actual grill, and his sauté prowess would remain under
wraps until he had pans and knives that weren't vacation-
rental quality. In the meantime, he'd get basics to tide them
over.

⬧

*A*fter giving Kira approximately fifteen seconds to
digest the fact that Freya wanted Kira to wave a red
cape in front of her bull of an old boss, Freya dropped
another bombshell.

"We think that in the time you were employed by
Gardner Holdings, they made several questionable deals for
their Historie stores with your name attached as approving
the acquisition."

Kira jolted in her seat, bile climbing up her esophagus.
As the collections manager for the family, she'd had influence
over the purchasing that was done for the store—high and
low end—but her primary work had been overseeing the
family's personal acquisition of more recent art. The Gardners couldn't legally make replicas of most of the items they
purchased for their enjoyment at their estate. She'd had little
involvement with Historie.

"Do you believe I would sign off on a fraudulent purchase?"

"Of course not." Freya opened a file on the table before her. "But you are listed as acquisitions manager for Gardner Holdings on several recorded sales."

"What? I never had that role."

Freya nodded. "I know, but we found a total of a dozen transactions with your name on them in that capacity during the years you worked for the family. There another commonality in those transactions. The brokers on the foreign end always included a man named Harun Taha."

"I've never heard that name." Kira didn't know if she should be relieved or not.

"That will work in your favor when you sue Gardner, then."

That triggered a bitter laugh. "Right. I can't wait to sue those assholes. Wait. I can't. NDA."

"There are ways around the NDA."

She rose from her seat. "Listen. I've appreciated the work you've thrown my way, but I can't spend the rest of my life in court, unable to do the only job I'm good at. And what you're proposing will place me in that exact position."

"Kira, we can help you." This was said by Morgan, the less scary of the two Valkyries.

"Right. You can outspend a billionaire in court. That's how the system works. The person with the biggest moneybag wins. You're government contractors. You can't compete with Mason Gardner."

"Mason? Not Dennis?"

She shrugged. What did it even matter at this point? "They're two sides of the same coin."

The far-too-handsome Ian Boyd shifted in his seat. "Kira, this is the first I've heard about the NDA and understand that's a problem for you, but before you walk out this door, you should know that Harun Taha is a key player in the terrorist Islamic State. Mason Gardner purchased artifacts from him, showing approval from *you* as the Gardner Holdings acquisitions manager. That's *also* a problem for you."

Well now, wasn't that a pretty pickle. She was caught between the NDA that was her only escape from a nightmare family and…aiding and abetting terrorism.

"If you do this for us," Morgan said, "we'll do everything we can to help you get out of the NDA and clear your name of all association with those transactions."

There was a knock on the door.

"That will be Rand," Morgan said as she rose and crossed to the door.

In walked a tall, muscular blond man. Whew. Kira had thought Ian Boyd was handsome, but this guy was chiseled perfection. Just what she needed. Handsome men made her nervous. They triggered her social anxiety and possibly even PTSD.

The blond man looked like the actor who would be cast to play the too-pretty jerk and rival to the dark-haired awkward hero in every romantic comedy ever made.

His disinterested gaze scanned her from head to toe as they were introduced. "Dr. Kira Hanson, this is Lieutenant Commander Randall Fallon."

"Lieutenant Commander?" He was dressed in civilian clothing. Business casual. Military was the furthest thing from her mind.

"US Navy. Call me Rand. We won't be mentioning I'm active duty at the auction house."

She nodded and looked down. His eyes were too blue. She could feel her cheeks flushing. This was ridiculous. He was just a person.

"Have a seat, Rand," Morgan said, "And we'll bring you up to speed."

Kira resumed her seat, just catching Morgan's gaze as the pregnant woman looked guiltily away. Morgan cleared her throat. "As this is a tricky situation, really, the less you both know of the details, the better."

Why did Kira have a feeling Rand already knew way more than her, and *she* was the only one being left in the dark?

Chapter Forty-Four

arun Taha. Having a last name for the man who'd smacked her and forced her to watch the video of Fahd's murder after all this time was…weirdly unsettling. It was even more unsettling to know the man had been trafficking artifacts for a decade.

She assumed she hadn't come across him in her time in Jordan because she'd focused on the market and Bibi as her best gateway into the artifact underworld. Woman to woman.

As their next step, the research wizards at FMV would go through Taha's background and try to find a link with Rafiq. Maybe the rumor that Rafiq had worked for a museum in some capacity before the Arab Spring was true.

She shuddered at the idea that Harun could be the man to run the "dig for a day" excavations for tourists. The field-workers she'd trained in the desert could work alongside wealthy Americans looking to get dirty.

She wished Chris weren't still at the store. She wanted to

talk to him about Freya's revelation that Harun was a legitimate businessman in Jordan.

It all had to circle back to the grant to the university to fund the excavation. Gardner had insisted on having an American on the dig—her—but what had his real goal been in funding her work?

She went through each step in her mind. Applying for the grant sponsorship. The subsequent vetting. There was nothing about the process that showed undue interest in her. She was just the most qualified applicant.

If anything, she was the one with the agenda, looking for a project in the Middle East so she could begin her work for FMV. That wouldn't look great to the State Department as they evaluated whether or not to extradite her.

She was so screwed.

Worse, she could take Chris and Morgan and Freya down with her.

She continued to pace, hating the fact that even going outside felt unsafe and exposed.

They were in the middle of a damn forest. Sure, there were neighbors, but this was ridiculous. It wasn't like her face was all over the news. She was on a few niche news sites, or buried deep on the mainstream ones.

She grabbed her coat and the knit cap Chris had given her yesterday, right before she thought she saw Jamal again.

Was it possible she'd been wrong about seeing him on the Metro? In the hospital?

No. He'd slid a finger across his throat. No way did her mind make that up.

She tugged the cap down over her ears. It was windy

today. She grabbed a scarf and wrapped it around her face, then slipped out into the yard. She circled the cabin to the woods in the back, leaning heavily on the cane as she traversed uneven ground.

She breathed deeply of the almost-winter air. Cold with a biting wind, and a whiff of fireplace smoke. Probably from the cabin next door. Diana had wanted to build a fire, but figured it would be more fun when Chris was back. She intended to seduce him.

Sure, they'd had sex, but now that they knew each other, their relationship had been borderline chaste. She knew he wouldn't make a real move. She had to be the one to initiate it or he'd worry he was taking advantage. A fire in the hearth on a cold almost-winter day was better than chocolates and flowers.

The smell of the pine boughs gave the air a fresh scent, and she breathed deeply of it as she went into the ever-darker forest. The lot the cabin was on was long and narrow and would eventually meet up with another lot hollowed out in the woods. The boundaries were marked with orange flagging tape, and there were notices in the cabin about not trespassing. The neighbors didn't appreciate having a vacation rental in their forested neighborhood.

She kept an eye out for the markers as she went deeper into the woods, sticking to as straight a line as possible to make sure she didn't veer across the property line.

Behind her, she heard tires on gravel. She turned, expecting to see Chris's blue 4Runner approaching the house. With disappointment, she watched a black pickup truck approach the cabin and stop near one of the outbuildings.

Was it the owner of the house? If that were the case, she was better off here, in the woods, where she didn't have to show her face.

The owner couldn't enter the rental while in use, and Chris had specifically asked if any yard maintenance was scheduled and was told no, so maybe they were there to grab something from the maintenance shed and would leave quickly.

She hoped they would, anyway, because it was chilly in the woods. She hadn't planned to be outside for long.

As she watched, a person got out of the passenger seat and approached the house, which was positioned sideways on the property line, so the front would have the most southern exposure. From her spot in the woods, she could see the back and side, with an angled view of the driveway in the front. She tucked herself in the trees, then shifted until she had a clear line of sight.

The person disappeared from view, and she assumed they went to the front door. After a long interval, she spotted a man circling around to the back. He walked stiffly, carrying a satchel and wearing a bulky coat.

Was he a US Marshal? Had a warrant been issued? Was she now considered a fugitive?

No. Freya would have called her.

Diana pulled her burner phone from her coat pocket. No messages. No missed calls.

She again studied the man. He wore a knit hat and was too far away for her to see his features as he hunched down below the bedroom window of the rental house. She raised the phone and hit the Record button on the camera. He didn't look like he was serving a warrant. For starters, he didn't knock or announce himself. She glanced toward the pickup truck and realized it was parked pretty far down the driveway, where the outbuilding would block the view of the vehicle from the house.

The man approached the frosted bathroom window. The light was on because it was the same switch as the fan and the bathroom had been quite steamy after her shower. She'd forgotten to turn it off before she stepped outside.

Now it looked like the man was trying to figure out if someone was inside the bathroom.

The light and fan noise must have convinced him someone was, because he crouched down and pulled something from the satchel and placed it under the window, then hurried around to the front. He then ran down the driveway and climbed into the truck's passenger seat. The vehicle moved in reverse down the narrow drive, not bothering to pull closer to the rental, where there was a wide spot for turning around.

Diana's heart thudded as she turned the camera back to the house and the exterior bathroom wall. She zoomed in on whatever it was that had been placed beneath the window, but all she could make out was a pixelated blob. She reversed the zoom and panned the wall, then watched in horror as the entire backside of the cabin burst apart. The roar and shock wave shook the trees and knocked her off her feet.

Chapter Forty-Five

*R*and's vacation had taken a sharply unexpected turn today. He'd certainly never expected to find himself in his SUV following a pretty but timid woman to her apartment so she could drop her car before they went to the auction house together. Kira Hanson sure was skittish. Always looking down. Flushing red like a lightbulb every time she looked at him.

She reminded him of the young women at the bar last night. Too young by far, but they hadn't been shy.

He wondered how old Kira was and then reminded himself that was a moot point. This wasn't a fix up. He was helping a friend. Well, several friends, because Chris was a friend now too, and if the SEAL had something going with Diana, she'd fall under team protection too. Hell, they'd been sent on two missions to save her. She was practically a team member.

This was about Diana and Morgan and Freya and not

the shy woman who could pull off the sexy librarian look if only she were about ten years older…

There was no parking in the Adams Morgan neighborhood where Kira lived, so Rand pulled into a spot by a fire hydrant while she circled the block several times. After ten minutes, she finally came walking up to his passenger side and tapped on the window. He popped the lock, and she climbed inside.

"Sorry. Finally found a spot five blocks away."

He shrugged. "Must be tough living here."

"I usually take the Metro. Would have today but the meeting was requested last minute and it was faster to drive."

He pulled out into traffic. "How long have you been working for FMV?"

"A few years. Just random contracts here and there, you?"

He shook his head. "I've never worked for them. I'm not now. Just volunteering."

"How do you know Freya?"

He found it interesting that she'd singled out Freya, not Morgan. Most people who knew him always wondered how Morgan fit in the mix. "You know about Freya's previous career?"

Her gaze remained fixed at her feet. "The CIA thing. Yeah. Our parents were colleagues. I've known Freya since seventh grade."

"Seventh grade for you or for her?"

She laughed. "Both. We graduated together."

He would have slammed on the brakes in surprise if he

hadn't taken all the wild driving courses required of special operators. "No fucking way."

"Yes fucking way."

"So, you were like, a prodigy, and graduated five years early?" There was no way this woman was in her late thirties.

"No, Lieutenant Commander. Not a prodigy. Or at least, no smarter than Freya. We're the same age."

Damn. He'd sure had her pegged wrong. She was close to his age. Maybe older. "I was sure you were about twenty-five."

She laughed. "With a PhD? And more than a decade working in my field?"

Okay. So he hadn't thought that through. "My bad."

"I'm told it will catch up with me someday. At least most people assume I'm late twenties or early thirties. I don't even get carded anymore."

He glanced sideways long enough to see her face wasn't red. She was relaxing around him. At least there was a positive result to him speaking like a fool.

"Now, answer my question," she said. "How do *you* know Freya exactly?"

"We worked together in Djibouti a few years ago."

"I thought you were Navy, not CIA? But I don't really know how the CIA stuff works."

He smiled again. "That's kind of the point with tradecraft. But no. I'm a Navy SEAL."

"Get the fuck out of here!"

He laughed at the full reversal of their surprised roles. "Totally fucking true."

"So Freya needs a guy to act like an antiquities buyer, and she just casually calls a SEAL. That is *so* Freya." She said it like a seventh grader, making him smile.

"Well, I was in town. And her husband is a former Green Beret, so she knows a lot of us special forces types."

"I haven't met Cal. I presume he's a good guy?"

"One of the best. Well, for a Green Beret."

She snickered at that, and he felt a little buzz. Weird.

"Are they going to ask to see my ID at the auction house?"

"Yes. They might even make a copy of it. Is that a problem?"

"No, I'll just use my driver's license. Nothing about military or SEALs while we're there, okay?"

"So what do you do?"

"Accountant?"

She snickered again. "No way could you pass for an accountant."

"Hey, that sounds like anti-accountantism or something."

"Is that a thing?"

"I don't know, but you're stereotyping."

"True. But still, if you're going to be acting, maybe don't make it a stretch. I mean, I'd believe actor or model, but to afford these artifacts, you'd need to be *very* successful."

"So you're saying I couldn't make it as a model?" He put indignation in his voice.

"No." She let out an exasperated huff. "I'm saying people would have to recognize you as a nearly naked underwear model they've seen in an ad."

"So you think I'd be a good underwear model is what you're really saying."

He glanced sideways and caught the slight reddening of her cheeks.

"I don't have a clue what you look like in your underwear, so no. It was just a *type* of model that came to mind. I'm sure you'd do better selling beer or cologne."

Damn, how tempted he was to make an inappropriate suggestion about letting her get a peek at him in his skivvies. But not today, Satan. He had a job to do.

In an hour, maybe two, they'd be done. Say goodbye, and he'd resume his vacation. Another day visiting with his sister's family, then he was catching a plane to go skiing in Colorado.

"Okay, so what's my job, then, if I'm not an underwear model?"

"What was your father's job?"

"Drinking, mostly."

"Okay, then. Probably not that."

"Good call."

He considered his options, then his heart kicked up. Could he pull it off?

Do I have a choice?

He cleared his throat. "I have the perfect cover. I'm a novelist. Like Castle. Super rich."

"What about when they ask you why they haven't heard of you?"

"Pseudonym. I don't tell anyone who I am in real life because I write spy thrillers."

"Ohh. I like that. Kind of implies you know your subject matter, like Ian Fleming."

"Exactly. I picked up a passion for Middle Eastern art and history when I may or may not have worked there."

"It's perfect. And you've been there enough to talk the talk, I presume?"

"If you only knew…" He studied her. "You spend much time in the Middle East?"

Her face flushed, and he wondered what triggered it this time.

"No. I've never actually been anywhere."

"You haven't traveled?"

Now she flushed even brighter. "Only by car."

He wanted to ask if she was afraid to fly, but realized that would be extremely personal. Phobias weren't something people generally wanted to discuss with strangers.

Might be extra intimidating coming from him, given that he regularly jumped out of planes for his job. "Well, if you ever get a chance, there are lots of spectacular sites and museums in that part of the world. Assuming art and history are your thing."

"If my PhD is any indication, it is. Maybe someday I'll get to Florence." Her voice turned wistful. She cleared her throat. "But I'm lucky to live in DC, with an entire complex of incredible museums, and most of them are free."

He pulled into a pay lot two blocks from the auction house, which was in the sea of buildings northwest of the Capitol.

Kira paused for a moment before climbing from the vehicle, and he had the sense that she was centering herself.

Or bracing herself. He said nothing, just waited for her to be ready, afraid that if he opened the door and stepped out, he would be rushing her.

After a long moment, she let out a slow breath and said, "Okay. Let's go lie our asses off to these assholes."

That startled a laugh out of him. "Who even *are* you?"

She met his gaze—really met his gaze for the first time. Her eyes were a pretty hazel, and she had long, thick lashes. "Today, and today only, I'm a Valkyrie."

Damn. She wasn't just a Valkyrie, she was a siren.

Chapter Forty-Six

*C*hris watched the pickup truck back out of the driveway and zoom in the opposite direction from his approach. It wasn't right. Chris had specifically requested privacy from the homeowner and had been assured he'd get it.

He debated whether or not he should follow the truck. Was it possible they'd...taken Diana?

Shit. The license number had been a blur as the vehicle sped away.

He had a split second to decide if he should take off in pursuit or check on the rental house. What if he followed, but Diana was hurt inside the house?

Was he being paranoid? No one but Ian and the Valkyries even knew he was with Diana. And no one, not even Ian or the Valkyries, knew exactly *where* they were.

Only Xavier knew that.

His gut said check out the rental.

He was halfway down the driveway when a massive

boom rent the air, a sound he was all too familiar with. A bomb of some sort had taken out the back of the structure.

He slammed on the brakes, jumped from the vehicle, and ran toward the burning structure, his heart ready to burst with every beat.

He didn't have much hope Diana was still alive.

✤

*D*iana hit her head on a tree trunk as she dropped to the cold ground, but she kept her hold on the phone and even managed to turn the recording camera back toward the burning structure.

She'd gotten video of the bomber and hopefully most of the explosion. But it was the bomber who was most important. Maybe FMV would be able to enhance it enough to get the guy's face.

She reached around in the leaves, searching for her cane. What should she do? Hide deeper in the woods? Run to the road?

Someone was bound to report the blast. The fire needed to be contained. The forest was damp and unlikely to catch fire, but still, they couldn't take that chance. If none of the neighbors had reported it, she'd have to call it in.

The men could be waiting on the road, to see if she came out. They could take her then.

And where was Chris? How would he find her if she was taken?

There would be questions about the bombing. No doubt

the Gardners would try to pin it on her. But she had video to prove otherwise. She squeezed the precious phone.

With the cane in her right hand, she managed to get to her feet, but she wobbled. She wasn't sure if it was caused by the knock on her head or some other new injury. She'd banged against the tree pretty hard.

Her vision blurred and nausea rose. She swallowed and would have filled her lungs with air, but the acrid plume from the blast now filled the pine forest with the scent of destruction and terror.

Her ears rang. She could barely hear. She considered her options, but her leg wobbled again and she nearly toppled over. She couldn't hide in the forest. She had to go to the road. She walked toward what was becoming a wall of smoke. She repositioned her scarf over her mouth and nose, using the soft wool as a filter.

Her eyes burned along with her throat, and she coughed as she skirted the woods closest to the burning house and aimed for the open lawn to the left.

She stepped from the cover of the trees and spotted Chris's blue SUV with the driver's door hanging wide open.

"Chris!" She tried to yell, but was seized by a coughing fit, and her words were a raspy whisper—at least that was how they sounded to her muted ears.

Was he in the house, searching for her?

All at once, the roof collapsed.

She let out a yell, this time forcing the sound through her battered windpipe. "Chris!"

She was grabbed from behind and screamed, fearing the bomber had come back.

Lips pressed to her ear, and she could barely make out the most precious words she would ever hear. "Diana! I'm fine. I'm here."

She stopped struggling and turned to face him. His beautiful face was right there. "Oh thank god. I—I thought you were inside."

"I thought the same of you."

She burst into tears as he held her tight. But the embrace didn't last long.

"We need to get out of here. Now."

She nodded and glanced toward the structure that was now rubble and flames.

Nothing was salvageable. But everything inside was replaceable.

Without warning, Chris scooped her up and ran down the long driveway to his vehicle.

He yanked open the passenger door and placed her on the seat. The vehicle was still running. A second later, Chris was in the driver's seat, and they backed up at speed down the driveway, just as the black pickup truck had done.

They had just backed onto the main road when Diana heard the sirens. Help was coming.

Hopefully, they'd be long gone before anyone remembered the make and model of the vehicle they'd spotted fleeing the destroyed vacation rental.

Chapter Forty-Seven

*C*hris thought his heart was going to stop when he circled around the building just in time for the roof to collapse. He'd been certain Diana was inside. That she wasn't was a damn miracle that they would discuss when they both could hear again without shouting through singed throats.

They were on the interstate heading north when Chris finally spotted a sign for a rest area and pulled off.

There were only a few cars in the lot on the winter weekday, and he parked at the far end, closest to the exit, should they need to leave in a hurry.

"How's your hearing?" he asked.

"Getting better. Still ringing, though."

"I need to call Freya. FMV didn't know where we were staying, but the explosion is probably all over the news at this point. If anyone clocked us as a Black man and white woman staying there, Freya will worry."

"They'll probably take hope from the fact that your car isn't there. But yeah, we need to call."

"Tell me what happened first?"

She reached into her coat pocket and pulled out the burner phone. "You can see for yourself. I got it all on video. I think."

His heart leapt. "Holy shit. Really?"

She nodded. "I started filming when I realized the guy wasn't a US Marshal."

He thumbed open the photo app and found the last recording. "Why were you in the woods?"

"Luck. I was going stir-crazy, so I went for a walk, and they showed up."

"They?"

"I only saw the one guy, but someone else drove the truck."

He watched the recording first in real time. It was four minutes twenty-two seconds from start to finish.

She leaned across the center to watch with him. "There. I think I got his face."

Later, Chris would zoom in. Now, he wanted to take it all in at once, just as it had happened to her.

"You kept filming after he left." On the screen, she zoomed in tight on what had to be a pipe bomb.

"I wanted to see what he'd left under the window, but didn't want to give up my hiding place until I was sure they were gone."

"He thought you were in the bathroom. But my car wasn't there, so he had to guess you were alone."

"You weren't the target. And yeah, I think the noise of the fan and light convinced him I was in that room."

So the guy made sure that would be the first room destroyed.

Chris had killed for his country, but it was always a job. At least, it had been until last January, when he and his team found themselves under attack on American soil. On that op, he'd killed for his country—and for his teammates—but it had also been personal.

Now he watched the bomb go off. The camera wobbled when the bomb exploded, and there was a blur of branches, sky, and leaves. Diana groaned, then the bouncing image settled on the back of the house, now burning rubble. Watching it happen from her point of view triggered something fierce.

The feeling inside him was familiar—he was pumped and ready to do battle—but the anger and fervor for the fight was different. Primal.

Diana had been targeted.

She'd be dead if she hadn't needed fresh air while he was off getting fucking groceries.

He set down the phone and cupped her face, then kissed her. His kiss was hard, but not angry. At least, the anger wasn't directed at her.

She kissed him back equally fiercely.

He ended the kiss, then pressed his forehead to hers, breathing heavily. "I could have lost you."

"I thought I'd lost you." She gripped his shirt in a tight fist. "I want you. Now. Here."

He raised his head and glanced around. If they weren't

parked in a public spot, he'd be figuring out how to bury himself deep inside her without the steering wheel digging into her back. "We can't," he whispered.

"Please? I need you," she rasped.

"I want you too. But we need to get moving. We need a new vehicle."

"Why a new vehicle?"

"My best guess is this one's being tracked."

"But when would the vehicle have been tagged?"

He shrugged. "Last week? In Little Creek? Last night? Who knows."

"They could have been tracking us all this time? But why didn't they come after me until today?"

"Maybe our return to the DC area worried them." He kissed her again, fast and fierce. "I'm going to look for a tracker in the undercarriage." He cursed himself for not doing that immediately after he'd pulled over. He wasn't thinking like a special forces operator, and that was a problem.

He found it within minutes. He considered attaching it to another vehicle, but discarded the idea. These people were killers. He couldn't count on them to confirm they had the right target in their sights.

He should just destroy it, but he also wanted to see if there was a way to use it as bait.

He climbed into the vehicle and set it on the dashboard.

"Is that it?"

"Yeah."

"We can smash it with a rock. Flush it down a toilet."

"Or we can give it to Freya to play with."

"How do we do that?"

He put the car in gear. They needed to keep moving. They might have a little time before the pricks who bombed the house realized Diana was alive, but they'd monitor the tracker until then. Just in case.

"I'll drive. Call Freya and put her on speaker."

*T*hey were only a block away from the auction house when Rand let out a low whistle. "Damn, you don't see one of those every day."

Kira followed his gaze, then let out a low curse.

"You don't like vintage cars?" Rand asked.

She studied the pristine 1965 Shelby Mustang GT350. She actually knew almost nothing about vintage cars, but she knew more than she wanted to about this particular car, right down to the detail that the colors were Wimbledon White with Guardsman Blue LeMans stripes.

"*That* vintage car happens to be Mason Gardner's pride and joy."

"Ah. So it's that car in particular you have a problem with."

She grimaced. "I knew we might run into him at the auction house, but now there's no doubt." At least seeing the car was a warning, giving her a chance to brace herself.

Be a Valkyrie.

She straightened her spine and continued down the sidewalk. "They sell licensed replicas of the '65 Shelby at Historie."

"I didn't know they sold anything that was so…*modern*."

"They sell a handful of vehicle replicas now, but it started with Mason's Mustang."

They reached the entrance to the auction house, and Rand held open the door for her. She gave thanks that Mason was nowhere to be seen. Maybe they'd be lucky and not cross paths with him at all.

Rand introduced himself to the receptionist, who was probably in her midtwenties—although Kira knew better than to make age assumptions based on looks—and her eyes went wide as she took in the tall, blond, handsome SEAL.

Honestly, she handled his sheer beauty better than Kira had, given all her fluster and blushing, which was only slightly aggravating to Kira's general anxiety.

Good lord. She was so smitten with her fake client, she was jealous for no reason.

She'd managed to center herself in the car. It had helped that he'd made the ridiculous assumption about her age even knowing about her degree and work history.

They'd both made incorrect assumptions about the other based on looks. She'd figured he would be smart and suave and perfect. He'd been easier to talk to after his blunder. Less intimidating.

Before climbing from the vehicle, she'd reminded herself —and him—that today she was a Valkyrie. She'd be bold. Strong.

Then she saw Mason's car and felt her winged armor crack.

She straightened her shoulders and gave the young woman a professional smile. She was still a Valkyrie, and this auction house was one place in which she was an undeniable and respected expert. "We're here to meet with Mr. Gillibrand about the collection that was in Friday's press release."

"Kira, what a surprise to see you here." She stiffened at the familiar voice. Dammit. So much for not crossing paths.

She turned and gave a polite nod, not bothering with any kind of fake smile. "Mason."

His gaze scanned her from head to toe. The same kind of assessment from other men might make her nervous in a basic social anxiety sort of way, but with Mason, it made her skin crawl. But then, he'd hit on her more than once, and more than once she'd told him no, even using the excuse she didn't date employers or clients in an attempt to soften the rejection.

Then he'd charmingly threatened to fire her.

When she'd pointed out that sounded dangerously close to sexual harassment, he'd gotten defensive and told her she needed to learn how to take a joke.

But that kind of thing was never really a joke. There was nothing funny about being threatened with being fired because she'd turned down someone's advances.

She forced herself to meet Mason's gaze now. "I'm here on behalf of a client." She moved closer to Rand, invading his space in a way that wasn't businesslike at all. His hand went to the small of her back and she could've kissed him for picking up on her cue.

Mason's gaze flicked over Rand, clearly noting the casual touch. He then addressed the SEAL. "And you are?"

"Her client."

"We have that in common, then. She works for me too."

"Worked. Past tense."

"So why are you here?" he asked Rand.

"We have another interest besides the beautiful Ms. Hanson in common."

Kira suppressed the flutter his words triggered. He was playing a role, nothing more.

Rand continued. "I'm interested in the artifact collection from the Middle East that Gillibrand is brokering."

Mason's eyes narrowed. "My family has already placed an offer that was accepted."

"But it hasn't closed yet. We all know how this works. Until the deal closes, Gillibrand can let potential buyers have a peek. Kick the tires, as it were."

Mason looked to Kira. "You're the tire kicker, I take it."

"I want to see the provenance before I advise my client on making an offer."

The CEO of Gillibrand, Davis Edward Gillibrand Jr., entered the foyer. "And so you shall, Dr. Hanson." He turned his attention to Rand. "I'm always pleased to meet a collector. If this doesn't work out, we have more Nabataean artifacts coming in the new year."

Rand smiled. "I'm new to the collecting world, and Dr. Hanson assures me this is an excellent place to begin." He held out his hand. "Randall Fallon."

The two men shook hands. Gillibrand was clearly delighted Kira had brought a big spender into his orbit. She hoped she'd be able to recover Gillibrand's goodwill when he realized Rand was a fraud.

She'd only dealt with Gillibrand directly a few times. He was an older man in his early seventies, with wisps of white hair on a mostly bald pate. He'd founded the auction house over thirty years before and had a reputation for being honest, but as with every auction house, there had been more than a few scandals over the decades.

"My father won't be pleased to hear you're entertaining other offers, Davis."

The cheery man gave Mason his standard smile. "We're all businessmen, and Mr. Fallon is correct. Until the deal closes, I have no reason not to let other buyers inspect the provenance."

Kira added extra sweetness to her own smile. "If I find an issue, surely you'll wish to know about that as well, Mason."

"Very good." Gillibrand turned to the receptionist. "Please take Dr. Hanson and Mr. Fallon to the main conference room and have the files for Lot 842 made available to them."

"I'll join you," Mason said.

She fixed him with a look. "Are you paying my fee?"

"The provenance has already been established to Gardner Holdings' satisfaction."

Interesting word choice. "Who did you hire to vet the chain of title?"

"A consultant in the Middle East who's much more familiar than you are with collectors in the region, including the man who owned these items for the last four decades."

She couldn't really argue with that. It wasn't her strongest area of expertise. And she was, in fact, curious to know if he'd offer up a name for Freya to search on, presuming he wasn't referring to Harun Taha.

Rand was probably wondering if they could squeeze information out of Mason too, because he said, "Sure. Join us." He winked at Kira and added, "Anything you don't want him to hear, you can whisper in my ear."

The way he said it made her go all fluttery inside.

She'd put up with Mason's repeated attempts to hit on her because the NDA with Gardner Holdings prevented her from taking action. The idea of flirting outrageously with her fake client with his big muscles and wildly good looks in front of the little prick who'd done everything he could to all but own her had a certain delicious appeal.

Chapter Forty-Eight

4

*I*t took more than an hour to get to the rendezvous point near Baltimore. Diana was relieved to see Freya's husband, Cal, sitting on the designated bench that faced Chesapeake Bay.

Diana stayed in the car while Chris approached the bench with the tracker in a paper coffee cup. He took a sip as he dropped on the bench, then set the cup on the seat next to Cal.

He sat there for a few minutes, taking sips and looking at the water.

She imagined they had the kind of conversation two strangers would share, observations on the gulls that swooped in the air above the bay. A person walking a dog passed by. The dog paused before Cal, and he scratched it behind the ears. She guessed the dog walker was another player on Team Diana, and she felt a rush of thanks and affection for these people who were rallying to help her.

The dog walker continued on, and Chris stood, leaving

the cup on the bench. He walked toward the public restroom.

While he was inside, Cal grabbed the coffee cup and sipped. She never saw the motion in which he pocketed the tracker, but next thing she knew, he threw the cup in the trash and headed down the path.

From there, she guessed it would take a journey mapped out by Freya, designed to convince anyone monitoring the device that Chris was still unaware he was being tracked. Cal would drive various places in the area to keep it in motion for at least the rest of the day, but eventually it would end up in a garbage can in the parking garage at Dulles Airport.

How long until news was released that no bodies had been found in the destroyed house?

Had the police been able to track down the homeowner? Had Xavier been questioned? Freya had promised to notify Xavier that Chris and Diana were alive.

Diana was at a loss for what to do about the destroyed vacation rental. Who would pay for that? Did homeowners' insurance pay for terrorist acts?

Chris climbed back into the vehicle, and they set out. They had their own planned route, and it would take them to Baltimore Washington International Airport to pick up a car left there by someone connected to Freya just in case there was another less obvious tracker attached to Chris's SUV.

From BWI, they would head to a place in Virginia that Freya had arranged. They'd have a new safe house, and once there, Diana would be able to upload the video she'd taken of the explosion so it could be analyzed.

They would find out who was behind this. And maybe, just maybe, they'd be able to convince the State Department that Diana shouldn't be extradited.

◈

*K*ira's penchant for keeping her head down meant she didn't see most of the hungry looks Mason Gardner sent her way. Except the looks weren't just hungry, they were something else that triggered all of Rand's protective instincts.

And his possessive ones.

It probably made him just as bad as the prick of an heir.

Still, he didn't mind that Kira leaned toward him every time Mason tried to crowd her, which was constantly as they all stood at the conference table as she reviewed the paperwork Gillibrand provided.

She leaned in close and whispered in his ear when she found the name Freya had flagged—Harun Taha. "Pretend I'm saying something sexual."

He tilted back his head and laughed; her words were so unexpected. And he didn't have to pretend because the statement was sexual all on its own.

"I'll keep that in mind," he said in a whisper loud enough for Gardner to hear.

Gardner glowered.

Rand looked at a photo of a small vase. It was labeled as being a calcite alabaster tripod vase from the Pre-Pottery Neolithic B period. Small and gray with rounded sides and very, very old. "This will look great in my study, don't you think?" He wanted to say *bedroom*, but knew that would be going too far for Kira's professional reputation. She still had to work with Gillibrand in the future.

"You're just kicking the tires, Fallon." Gardner's tone was surly. This was a man who'd never faced the word *no*. Well, except from Kira, he'd guess.

And if the little prick hadn't accepted a no from Kira, he'd have to kill him.

Kira drew everyone's attention to the documents spread out on the table. "Harun Taha. His name has come up in my research recently. He's suspected of dealing in stolen goods, if I remember correctly."

"Bullshit."

Rand waited to see if the man would admit to previous dealings with Taha, but he clammed up. Kira's identification had put him on the alert.

Rand didn't know why Taha was important—Freya had meant it when she'd said everything was need-to-know—but Rand would bet the guy was connected to Diana's abduction by a direct line.

"You've worked with Taha before?" Kira asked.

"All our artifact purchases are a matter of public record, as you well know."

"Have you met him, then? That's not public information."

"How am I to know? We travel a lot for our purchases for the store. He probably has offices in Amman."

Meaning he *did* have offices in Amman and Gardner was covering his bases in case some press release had mentioned a visit or deal struck there.

"It's easy to open a storefront and hang a shingle," Kira said. "Have you reviewed his business documents?"

"We hire people to do that kind of thing."

"I know. You hired *me* to do that kind of thing once upon a time. But you've never asked me to look into this particular antiquities dealer. Why is that?"

"Probably because he was vetted before we hired you."

"How many deals have gone through him?" she persisted.

"I don't know. We buy a lot from the Middle East."

"It would be a shame if I find evidence Taha is a fraud. So many of your company's transactions could be suspect if he acted as broker. The law is clear: if you've purchased stolen goods, even unknowingly, you must return them to the rightful owners. And if you colluded with the thieves to knowingly acquire stolen goods, you'd be facing criminal charges."

Gardner's face transformed into an angry mask as he leaned into her. "You little bitch. This is about the NDA. You're trying to get at us from a different direction. It won't work. You break the NDA, and we own you."

The man towered over Kira, and now he was leaning into her, like a cobra ready to strike.

Rand also coiled and prepared to defend, but he held back, giving Kira a chance to handle him first.

She pushed at Gardner's chest. "Back off, Mason. I'm just telling you the truth. I came here to see the chain of title because my client is interested in buying. But I see a red flag in Harun Taha. I'm doing you a *favor* in telling you he's likely to be under investigation. And if you buy this lot, you can't stop me from reporting what I know. This and every transaction you've completed with Harun Taha will come under scrutiny."

Gardner raised a fist, and Rand wasn't about to wait to find out if it was a gesture or if he intended to strike. He grabbed the fisted hand and twisted Gardner's arm until it was behind his back, then shoved the man away from Kira. "Careful there, Gardner. I don't give a fuck who your daddy is. You threaten Dr. Hanson, and you're dealing with me."

"I didn't touch her."

"Only because I stopped you."

"You lie. I never would have touched her."

"You really think this fancy auction house, that deals with items worth millions, doesn't have cameras in their conference room?"

Gardner's eyes darted to the shiny dome on the ceiling, then cast a glare in Kira's direction. "Don't fuck with us, Kira, or you'll never get another client again." He turned and stalked from the room.

Chapter Forty-Nine

4

*R*and pulled into an empty parking spot not far from Kira's apartment building.

"Thanks for the ride," she said.

"Of course." He paused, then screwed up his courage. He didn't know why this felt awkward or difficult. He usually had no problem asking women out. Hell, it was rare for him to be turned down, so he never sweated the asking. "Would you like to get a bite to eat?"

She glanced at her watch. "At three o'clock?"

He shrugged. "I didn't know there were strict rules about eating times."

She rolled her eyes. "It depends on if you're hungry and just made the offer because you thought I might be hungry too, or if this is a sideways way of asking me out."

"Which answer will get me a yes?"

Her nostrils flared, but she didn't otherwise react. Finally, she said, "I'm not hungry."

"Fine, then, dinner later, when you are?"

Again, she stared at him, and he wished to hell he knew what was going on in her head. Was he coming across like that asshole Mason Gardner? The kind of guy who used negging to tear down confidence to convince her that she couldn't do better?

Or did she assume he was an egotistical prick because he was a SEAL? He'd met plenty of those. Hell, last night he'd been at a bar and ready to play that card, without telling anyone he was a SEAL, of course. That was never a good idea when it came to short-term flings.

But Kira knew, and that would give her preconceived notions. Some of which were true. He just wasn't entirely sure which ones.

"I don't plan to be hungry later, either, Lieutenant Commander."

Was it wrong that he liked the way she used his rank, even when she was trying to put him off?

"That's some control you have over your appetite."

"I've found that when I tell men like Mason Gardner that I'm not interested, they get all wounded. So I tell them I don't date clients, which in turn means they threaten to fire me to take care of that problem."

This was no hypothetical example she'd given. "Prick."

"Yes. But anyway, you see, I'm trying to be kind and let you down gently with my lack of desire to eat."

"Well, I guess that means a movie's out too."

She gave him a small smile. "I hate movies. And sports. And long walks through the monuments."

Now he laughed. He picked up her phone, which rested in the center console, and held it up to her face to unlock it.

"Hey!"

"I'm just giving you my number. I won't text myself. I promise. It's yours should you decide you're hungry. Or want to have hot chocolate by the National Christmas tree and watch the yule log burn."

He entered his number, then handed her the phone.

"Noted," she said as she tucked it in her pocket and opened the passenger door.

As she slid out, he said, "I know of one thing you must like."

She faced him through the open door. "Do tell."

"Museums. DC has a lot of great ones. They're even free."

She smiled. "Have a good afternoon, Lieutenant Commander." She closed the door and turned to walk up the path to her building.

He waited until she was safely inside before pulling away.

She'd text him. If not today or tomorrow, sometime.

He headed back to southwest DC and the hotel he'd been living in for more than a week now. Tonight was his last night. Tomorrow, he'd go out to breakfast with his sister, then drive to Little Creek and prep for his trip to Aspen.

It was just after four when he reached the hotel. He spotted PO3 Bryce Albrecht in the lobby and hoped the guy wouldn't see him. He didn't want to answer questions about his day. Albrecht was a chatterbox, and he didn't have the energy. He wanted to go to his room and analyze where he'd gone wrong with Kira as he waited for his phone to ping with a text from her.

She'd be stubborn. Probably she'd break around the time he was on the top of a double black diamond run.

He'd text her a photo of the view when that happened.

He was almost to the elevator when Bryce called out. He stopped and turned to face the young SEAL. "Hey, man. How's it going?"

"I was just gonna hit the bar." Bryce nodded to the one on the other side of the lobby. "Wanna beer?"

Rand considered it and remembered he really was hungry and they'd at least have happy hour snacks if the full menu wasn't available yet. "Sure."

They grabbed a seat near the door, looking out toward the lobby. The hotel wasn't fancy, but it was nice enough and the food was fine. A young white woman took their drink order and gave Rand a bar menu.

As he was studying the list of food, his phone buzzed. Sucker that he was, he got his hopes up before checking and was disappointed to see a text from Freya thanking him for his help today.

He sent a quick thumbs-up, then set the phone down faceup and returned to the menu. If Kira were to text, would she do it sooner or later? Was she a late-night texter?

"Have you talked to Flyte today?"

He kept his face carefully blank. "No. You?"

"He hasn't answered any of my texts."

"He's not staying here. I think he was planning to return to Little Creek today."

"Weird how he came back for one day like that."

Rand raised a brow. "Didn't you do the same thing?"

"I got dumped on the first day of my vacation. What else was I supposed to do?"

"Go home?"

"Nah. I'm bored with Little Creek."

The guy had only lived there for a few months before they'd been deployed. But he was young and new to the SEALs and was probably longing for the sun and glamour of San Diego. He'd joked about being disappointed with being assigned to a team based out of Little Creek, but Rand figured there was truth behind the fake laugh.

"You going to try to fix things with your girlfriend?"

"Nah. We'd only been seeing each other for a few weeks before the deployment. She's not really it for me. I just liked the idea of having a place to go for Christmas."

Rand snickered. "I bet that made her feel special."

"I didn't *say* that. Well, except I sorta did, I guess. She was all eager and excited and talking like we were really serious. It weirded me out."

"Well, you were going to spend two weeks with her family. Over Christmas. Of course that would mean you're serious."

"I guess. It just sounded more casual when we planned it."

"She's an elementary school teacher in Little Creek, right? She planned to spend her entire winter break with her parents. Let me guess, you were video chatting from an aircraft carrier and mentioned that you'd have two weeks off, couldn't wait to see her, yadda yadda… Next thing you know, you're planning to spend Christmas with her and her parents in her childhood home. She probably had big dreams about what you were going to give her for Christmas and if it would be a full carat."

This kid was really clueless. Rand felt sorry for his ex-girlfriend, who'd probably spent the last three months wrapped in a fantasy that had gone poof the moment Bryce landed on her parents' doorstep.

Rand looked forward to being done with breaking in new SEALs. He was moving up and out and would gladly hand over the reins to Chris, who was long past due for command. Rand had only stuck around as long as he had because he'd been injured twice in the last four years, and each time he was back up to speed, he'd asked himself if he was ready to let the job go.

He'd used his recovery time wisely and had a career plan for his postretirement, but still, something had kept him active with special forces until now. Maybe it was time. He could ride out his last few years before retirement with a Stateside posting. The Navy Yard was right in the heart of DC, but the Pentagon might have more opportunities for a former SEAL.

He could take up artifact collecting. He knew exactly who he'd hire to vet his purchases.

His phone buzzed, and he glanced at the screen. Unknown number.

His heart kicked up a beat and he held the phone to his face to unlock it.

This is LT. New phone. How'd it go?

LT was an abbreviation for lieutenant. The message was

from Chris. He frowned. Ridiculous how much he'd wanted it to be Kira.

"What's wrong?" Bryce asked.

"I was hoping it was someone else. But it's Chris."

"Ask him why he hasn't responded to any of my texts."

"You ask him."

Bryce yanked the phone from his hand and started texting.

Rand cursed and said, "I meant from your own phone."

"This works."

"Be sure to tell him it's you."

"Whatever."

After texting back and forth a few times, Bryce let out a laugh, then handed the phone back. Rand cringed when he saw the screen and added to the text conversation.

RAND

Sorry man. Bryce grabbed my phone.

Chris

I figured it was him when he started complaining the women left last night right after I did.

Served him right. He's an ass. Have fun with him when I'm gone.

He'll grow up eventually.

The server arrived with their beers, and Rand ordered sliders and fries. Bryce ogled the woman's ass as she walked away, but from the way she was swinging it, Rand didn't think she'd mind. He was young and not smart, but he was good-looking and powerfully built. The kid might as well enjoy himself as long as he was single and the women consented to the attention.

"How 'bout we place a bet on who gets her number."

"I don't play those kinds of dumbass games. She's not a commodity, she's a person."

Bryce shrugged. "Yeah, I figured she's more into me than you too."

Rand rolled his eyes and sipped his beer, regretting now that he'd ordered food. He was stuck here for a little while at least.

Oh well. It wasn't like Kira was going to text him. Might as well babysit the baby SEAL.

Chapter Fifty

It was early evening by the time Chris punched the code into the rental house's security panel and the door unlocked with a soft click. He pushed it open and entered first, searching both floors before returning to the garage to give Diana the all clear.

The house was a rental in Dumfries, Virginia, arranged by Freya with the actual rental being handled by a Raptor shell corporation so it couldn't be traced back to Chris or Diana.

Freya had managed to get the State Department to back off on their request to interview Diana again until the bombing could be investigated, which gave everyone some breathing room.

For now, any agreement on extradition had been placed on hold.

It was one thing to be hiding from the government—neither FMV nor Raptor could harbor fugitives—but quite another to protect a woman who'd been targeted in a terrorist bombing, and everyone was onboard with that.

It was hard to imagine either Dennis or Mason Gardner being behind the bombing when the only penalty the billionaire family faced was fines for customs violations. But nothing could be ruled out at this point. They still had the money motivation of Diana knowing the artifacts they wanted to replicate were looted goods.

Still, the focus remained on the other side of the equation: the artifact supply chain. The people who had taken Diana were funneling artifacts to the Gardner family and their Historie store, but they also likely had other US clients. With the Jordanian broker identified as the man who'd forced Diana to reveal the site location, they might be able to use the auction house data to figure out who else was buying from Taha and Rafiq.

Freya and Morgan were diving deep in that area. Chris's one job was to protect Diana.

She looked beautiful and tired as she limped into the house. He wanted nothing more than to carry her upstairs and tuck her into bed. Not because he wanted to have sex—although he definitely wanted that—but he couldn't do that because they had too much to do, between uploading the video of the explosion and Diana going over the provenance Freya had managed to get copies of today.

Earlier today, he'd stopped at an electronics store and picked up a bundle of goodies that had been ordered online by a Raptor subsidiary. They had a computer, a new hotspot with a virtual private network, new cell phones, and a new tablet. Chris grabbed the bags of electronics from the back of the SUV and followed her into the house.

"There's a study next to the kitchen. May as well set up the laptop in there while I figure out dinner." The groceries he'd gotten this morning remained in his SUV which was currently parked in long-term parking at BWI. Good thing he didn't buy shrimp or fish. It would be bad enough when the milk went sour.

He'd been given a credit card to use for food delivery. After the attempt on Diana's life when he'd gone out for groceries, he wasn't leaving this house again. He placed an order with a grocery app for some basics and, after asking Diana her preferences, ordered dinner from an Italian restaurant. He went all in on appetizers, dessert, and wine. They couldn't go out, but he could still make this a date.

He headed into the study, where Diana was seated at the desk with her cell phone plugged in to the computer. He kissed her neck, then dropped into the chair beside her. "Food is ordered. Both will be delivered in an hour. Maybe longer."

She nodded. "The video's almost done uploading to Raptor's network." She turned to face him. "It feels weird, handing this over to Raptor and not Freya."

"They have better tech and a lot more resources."

"It was one thing to trust Ian, but can we really trust everyone? It's a huge company."

"Every company that size is going to have bad apples, but my understanding is they have layers of internal security, and there's a tight lid on our particular situation. Just Ian, the CEO—who's a former SEAL—and one or two others."

She gave him a crooked smile. "You trust all SEALs, former or otherwise?"

"Oh, hell no. One—a guy I considered a friend—fucked my wife. Others have been arrested for all sorts of crimes. No one gets a pass. Not even the guys on my current team, to be honest."

"You're not thinking Rand, are you?"

"No. I wouldn't have texted him from my new number if he wasn't safe. No way would Freya have sent him to the auction house if he wasn't trusted."

"Then who? And why?"

"I didn't mean I'm suspicious of anyone in particular, so much as there's just a handful of people I *do* trust at this point. Morgan, Freya, Ian, Rand, and you."

She smiled and leaned toward him. The look in her eyes caused a stirring in his chest. "I trust you too, Chris. Even more than I do the others."

He stroked her cheek and brushed his lips over hers.

The upload bar on the computer screen flashed, then a dialogue box popped up that indicated the upload was complete. "You done here, or did you download documents to review?"

"I'm done for now." She leaned back against the plush office chair. "Wanna sit with me in front of the fire?" She gave him a saucy grin. "I wanted to do that that with you at the rental last night, but you were off hitting on some other woman."

He'd been moving in to kiss her neck again, but he nipped the soft skin instead. "I'm going to be defending myself for that for the rest of my life, aren't I?"

"Depends on how long we're together, really."

He raised his head and met her gaze, feeling a deep sense of sureness in his gut that didn't entirely make sense, but he trusted it anyway. "Forever, then."

⬧

*D*iana couldn't believe the words that slipped out of her mouth. It was an outrageous thing to toss out, and his response even more stunning.

Before she could say anything, he took her hand and said, "C'mon. Let's sit in front of the fire."

He led her into the living room and flicked the switch for the gas fireplace. The rental that had been destroyed had had a real woodstove, which would have been lovely, but fake logs and gas still offered heat and ambiance.

They sat on the sofa, watching the flickering flames in silence. If she could forget the explosion, this moment would be perfect.

But she would never forget the explosion with the waves of throat-burning smoke, and the feel of the heat wave that had washed over her when the ceiling collapsed.

Her throat clogged. "I thought you were inside the house when it collapsed, and I couldn't breathe. It was so shocking and terrifying. I think it hurt more than even the moment Harun slapped me and made my abduction real. Because when that happened, I had a tiny amount of control in the situation. How I reacted would shape what happened next. But this morning…I had no control. Just…devastation." So much like the car accident that had changed everything.

He pulled her onto his lap, his thick arms encircling her. "I thought you were inside when the bomb went off and felt the same helpless horror." He stroked her cheek, tucking her hair behind an ear. "But now we're here. And I'm not going to waste this chance."

His mouth covered hers. His kiss was soft and exploring, but the moment she opened for him, it changed to fire. Deep and hot, he devoured her mouth, and she closed her eyes and enjoyed the sensation of being consumed.

He'd filled her fantasies in the weeks she'd sought mental escape during her recovery, then she had him for one wild, reckless encounter. All that time, he was a stranger.

Now, she'd had a few intense days to get to know him. While his touch had thrilled her that first night, this was different. This wasn't simply satisfying physical desire.

Chris Flyte was so much more now than the embodiment of rescuer. He was the man who'd bought her a Christmas tree because he knew she needed an emotional break. The man who'd held her when she was scared and who'd protected her and reminded her that it didn't matter if the man who'd orchestrated her abduction was Rafiq or not.

He was risking everything that was important to him by being with her. His reputation. His career. Even his freedom.

She ran her hands over his hard chest and found the buttons on his shirt, popping them open one by one. He wore a tight undershirt beneath, and as much as he looked good in the muscle-hugging garment, she wanted to touch and taste his skin.

He chuckled at her urgent tugging on the hem and

shifted to remove her from his lap so he could slip out of the sleeves of the button-down and then peel the undershirt over his head.

Damn, he was beautiful. Smooth, dark brown skin over hard muscles. His pecs were firm, his biceps thick.

She licked a nipple and ran her mouth upward to his collarbone as her fingers traced all his lovely, lovely muscles. She nipped and licked and touched, and her hand found his belt and worked the buckle.

She wanted to go down on him. To give him selfless pleasure.

She licked her lips as she opened his fly. He let out a soft growl and kissed her hard as she reached into his briefs and stroked his thick cock.

She ended the kiss and slid to the floor in front of him. He spread his legs to accommodate her, and she felt a flush of excitement as she wrapped her hand around him and stroked up and down. She raised her gaze to take in the full picture. Beautiful, shirtless, muscled man. A smattering of hair with a thin line leading downward. His slacks open to allow his heavy cock to jut from a nest of dark curls.

"You are so fucking beautiful."

His reply came out rasped. "I was going to say the same to you. Just missing one thing." He tugged at her shirt hem, pulling it up. "Lose this."

She released him and doffed the long-sleeved top.

He fingered a beige bra strap. "And the bra."

She leaned forward and licked his cock from base to tip as she reached behind with both hands to unhook her bra.

"Jesus, that is so fucking hot."

She smiled and took him in both hands after tossing the bra aside. Now they were both topless. There was something so incredibly arousing about this position and the way he looked down at her as she touched him.

She could live in this moment forever. Aching with want, body suffused with pleasure at knowing what she was about to have.

Him.

He reached for her breasts, and she leaned forward to put her body within his reach. She then held his gaze as she licked him, only breaking contact when she tipped her head to take him into her mouth. He filled her, thick and hot. Slick against her tongue.

She sucked lightly, then opened wide and took him to the back of her throat. He groaned and squeezed her breasts, lightly pinching her nipples as she sucked and stroked and tasted.

He thickened further in her mouth. Pleasure surged through her. She'd fantasized about this more than once since their brief time together. She'd left that night before she could make him come in her mouth. She was going to make up for that now.

His fingers threaded through her hair as he began to lose the edge of his control. "Babe, I'm going to—" He panted while his hips bucked. "God. *Babe*. You're going to make me come. If you don't want me in your mouth, you'd better—"

She released him, but only long enough to say, "This is how I want you. Let me have my fun." Then she took him deep again, one hand wrapped around his cock and the other cupping his balls.

He laughed, then let out a pleasured groan around the words, "Yes, ma'am."

He stopped fighting her then. She felt his body relax as he gave in to the pleasure she was eager to give him.

The feel of him in her mouth as his fingers grazed her scalp was wildly hot. His powerful body coiled with tension, on the brink of release as she sucked and stroked with more vigor.

He let out a sharp groan as his entire body stilled, then bucked, and she felt warm pressure in the back of her throat.

She swallowed and kept stroking with her mouth and tongue until he was fully spent.

She softened the pressure of her mouth and gently took him to the back of her throat one more time, before releasing him, then swirling her tongue around the head as she met his gaze again.

His eyes were hot and his smile was satisfied as he scooped her from the floor and pulled her to his lap. "That was incredible." He kissed her deeply as one hand cupped a breast.

She pulled back from the kiss and said, "That's what happens when I spend days fantasizing."

His mouth explored her neck and followed a trail to her breast as he murmured, "A-plus on fantasy execution. Now let's see how I perform." His mouth closed around one nipple, and he gently sucked as he unbuttoned and unzipped her pants with one hand.

"Strong start," she said as she lifted her hips so he could get his hand inside her pants.

He teased her for just a moment, his mouth moving to

her other breast as his fingers lightly brushed over the top of her underwear.

She bucked to press against his hand, but he chuckled and said, "No, sweetheart. It's my turn to have *my* fun." Then he shifted her off his lap, setting her beside him. He tugged down her pants, which caught on the walking boot.

He raised a brow, and she sat up and turned the knob to deflate the air cast, then removed the boot so her pants could come off. Once she was naked, he asked, "Do you want the boot back on?"

She wore a small ankle stabilizer beneath the air cast. It would protect her well enough for sex. "As long as I don't try to put my weight on my foot, I should be fine."

Even a little weight would probably be okay. She'd avoided weight and walking nearly a month longer than last time mostly out of an abundance of caution, given that it was a new injury to the same joint.

Chris had shucked his pants while she removed the boot, and now they were both fully naked on the large, comfy couch in front of the fire. The only light in the room came from the adjacent kitchen and flickering fire. The room was dark with a soft orange glow. She glanced around the space that was cozy and warm, but impersonal. "I really hope the food doesn't show up in the next few minutes."

He laughed. "We've got time. And if it does, I'll pull on my pants and get it. No need for you to dress. But one thing I promise you, if it does show up now, it's going to get cold, because there's only one thing I'm hungry for right now."

"Works for me."

He smiled and stroked his cock, which wasn't hard, but

also wasn't soft. It thrilled her to know he was already warming up for another round. She turned him on that much.

"Now, where were we?" she asked.

He laughed. "I was just about to grab a condom."

"We have condoms?"

"Hell yeah. I bought two boxes this morning. Only thing I grabbed from the grocery bags other than the potato chips you wanted."

Chris and folded-over kettle-style potato chips, her two favorite treats.

He went to the counter where he'd set the one food bag and pulled out a box of condoms.

She snickered at the idea he'd bought two boxes, remembering telling him she liked his confidence that first night. Tonight, he would prove he was up to the challenge.

He pulled out a strip of condoms and tore off a packet, then set it on the coffee table.

Diana lay along the couch, with her injured right leg along the back and her shoulders slightly propped by a throw pillow against the arm. Chris took her left leg and lifted it, placing her foot on the floor, then settled between her legs. His gaze raked down her body.

He ran his hands along the insides of her thighs, and her nerves coiled with anticipation as he drew closer to her center. His thumbs teased her, parting her lips, slipping his fingers inside then spreading the wetness to her clit.

Then he dipped his head down, and his tongue did all the things his thumb had done, and she wanted to close her eyes, but at the same time wanted to watch as he licked her.

His head between her thighs and his tongue teasing her was as erotic to see as it felt. All her senses were soaring.

She had the taste of him in her mouth. The smell of him infused the air. His touch. The sounds he made in his throat combined with the soft scrape and feel of tongue lapping at her clit. Watching him as he did this to her was a ripe strawberry on a hot fudge sundae. Delicious without the added juicy sweet, but the flavor was intensified with the addition of the berry.

So she watched him go down on her, fighting the need to close her eyes.

Her pleasure built, and she gripped the back side of the couch and cushion to keep her thighs from locking tight around him.

His tongue slid inside her. His thumb worked her clit. The pleasure built and built, but he kept her on the edge, never increasing to a tempo that would push her over. It was glorious and agonizing in the best way.

When she couldn't take it anymore, she cupped his head and thrust her hips to add to the friction.

He chuckled and then sucked on her clit. Her hips bucked at the sensation. His teeth grazed her, then he sucked again before his tongue took over the task of applying friction. She closed her eyes and shuddered as her body took a slow ride over the precipice and she was rocked by wave after wave of orgasm, prolonged by the pressure of his tongue.

His mouth left her, and she kept her eyes closed, enjoying the afterglow. The sound of a wrapper being torn dragged her eyes open, and she smiled at the sight of him rolling on a condom. She spread her legs wider, shifting on the couch to make room for his hips to fit between her thighs, and then he filled her, thrusting deep. The feel of him inside so soon after orgasm revived the pleasure before it had a chance to fade completely.

He thrust in a slow, measured rhythm. No hurry to reach a finish line for a race that they'd each already won. The pleasure in this was more in the slip and slide of bodies and skin-to-skin contact and kisses. She could do this with him for hours.

But then his thumb brushed her clit again, and her wants and needs changed. She clenched tight on him, causing him to groan.

She cupped his butt and rocked her hips, and his tempo increased, and then they were both on the path for a second victory.

She came moments before he did.

They were both drenched in sweat by the time they were done, his body pressed to hers, but he kept his weight on his right arm, which lay along her side on the couch. He kissed her softly, then slid from her body, and she turned to make room for him to lie beside her.

He kissed her nose. "One minute. I need to get rid of the condom."

He left for the bathroom, then was back at her side. She was glad the couch was extra deep, making plenty of room for them both to stretch out.

"I checked my phone. Dinner will be here in about ten minutes. Groceries will arrive a little after that."

She ran a hand over his chest. "Is it wrong that I want a little longer like this? Right now, I'm pretty content."

"Same. But we have a few minutes, at least before I need to pull on pants."

They lay side by side, just holding each other in silence, but it didn't take long for the happy glow to fade as reality sank in. That they were even in this strange unfamiliar house was a reminder of their situation.

Her situation.

Someone had tried to kill her this morning.

The State Department had only paused the decision on whether or not to extradite her. They could hit the Play button at any time.

Chris could pay a huge price for protecting her, and it would only get worse for him the longer this went on. How could she do that to him? All he'd ever done was save her. Protect her. Make love to her.

She was falling in love with this man, but being with her could destroy his life.

Chapter Fifty-One

It was with reluctance that Chris dressed, but even more disappointing when Diana pulled her clothes back on too.

"It's okay with me if you eat naked."

"Right. That's *so* me."

"Is it?" He grinned. "Excellent."

She tossed a throw pillow at him. "No, it is not."

"I can't wait to learn all your quirky details." He meant it too. He wanted to know everything about her and her life before Jordan.

"I'm not sure refusing to eat dinner naked is a quirk, when the opposite would be a kink."

"I think I should go down on you while you eat your tiramisu. In fact, I think we should start with dessert."

Fully dressed and wearing her walking boot again, she rose from the couch to stand before him. She pulled his head down for a deep kiss, then said against his lips, "I've already had my dessert and so have you."

He chuckled. "But I want seconds."

She headed toward the study and computer. "You'll get it. *After* dinner."

He watched her disappear into the other room right as his phone pinged with a text.

RAND

Finally got rid of the kid. Can talk now. How is D?

He closed his eyes and remembered the feel of her inner thigh against his cheek. She was probably going to have razor burn. He'd have to put lotion on it for her.

CHRIS

She's okay. Rough morning.

Text me if you need anything. I was going to head to Aspen on Wednesday, but I might stick around another day.

You should go. Unless the Valkyries have another job for you, we're set.

He thought about Diana's questions about Rand. Chris trusted him, but was that because he was a teammate and his commander, or because Freya trusted him?

He thought it was the former, but truth was, he didn't really know the guy.

Ian had changed to Arabic when talking to Diana yesterday, and while they were driving today, she'd told him Ian was looking into Chris and his team.

He knew why Ian would investigate everyone—even,

perhaps especially, the SEAL team members Freya trusted. Ian wasn't biased for or against anyone.

Albrecht had to top their investigation list. It was curious that he was still in town, but also not surprising that a guy who was only interested in getting laid when he was in port would be dumped by his girlfriend as soon as he got home. There was a reason sailors had a reputation the world over, and guys like PO3 Bryce Albrecht were the poster boys for that.

Yet it was hard to imagine the guy committing treason and betraying an op. Still, he'd been at the bar last night and could easily have planted a tracker on Chris's SUV. He could have done it before he even sat down in the booth.

Chris had already told Freya everything they'd done yesterday, everyone he'd spoken to on the phone or in person. It was a short list, and she'd have given Raptor that information to investigate. If anything, the former SEAL who ran the company would look deep into Chris's team first. Every SEAL knew there were bad apples in the ranks. Same with Army Rangers, Delta Force, and Green Berets. There was no special forces group that had a perfect system for weeding out traitors.

Hell, even the CIA had a few high-level traitors in their ranks, and he gathered Freya's bitterness with her former agency ran along those lines.

Special Activities Division was a dark job. Rumored to be the ones who did the wet work. Create coups. Install dictators.

They were a fun lot.

He finished dressing and joined Diana in the study. She

was on the computer, watching the explosion video again. She'd zoomed in on the face of the bomber.

"Not content to wait for Raptor to enhance it?"

"I remembered a program that we used when I was in school to bump up the resolution on low-res images. Sometimes the only photos we have of artifacts are old and blurry, or taken with a Polaroid, which degrade faster than film. We'd scan them to see if we could identify a piece that had been stolen decades before." She pointed to the screen. "There's a free not-so-great online version, but it's better than nothing. I grabbed a still image and was just about to upload it."

He sat in the chair next to her. "I take it you're using the VPN and not the rental house internet?"

She gave him a look. "Of course."

"Still, I had to ask."

She kissed him. "I know. Not mad. I'd ask you the same question."

He probably wouldn't take the risk of uploading the photo at all, but he understood why Diana couldn't wait.

She hit the Upload button and they waited while a pinwheel circle spun to indicate it was processing the request.

"Kind of like *Blade Runner*, isn't it?"

She snorted. "That scene was a total cheat! No way could they get an image from the mirror."

"Bet you loved it anyway."

"Well, yeah. I mean, Harrison Ford in his prime."

"And Sean Young. Damn. She was hot."

The icon bounced, announcing they had an enhanced image to download.

She clicked on the downward pointing arrow. The door-bell rang as the image loaded. He waited for the photo to sharpen.

He shouldn't be surprised. It was what he'd expected, but still his heart squeezed as she sucked in a breath.

Jamal had tried to blow her up this morning.

Chapter Fifty-Two

*D*iana stared at the image while Chris went to get their food delivery. She could hear a third voice and realized both dinner and groceries had arrived.

She waited for the sound of the door closing and the beep of the alarm being reset, then emerged from the room. "I'll put the groceries away while you lay out dinner?"

He nodded.

It was easy enough to unload groceries when the fridge was empty to start with. Chris had ordered the basics: bread, cheese, milk, chicken. Bags of salad.

More of her favorite potato chips.

Ice cream.

What she would have given for chocolate ice cream when she was in the desert with Jamal and Bassam.

She felt a slight tremor as she put the frozen pint in the freezer.

Jamal had tried to kill her. It should be a relief to know

for certain, but she didn't know if she'd be able to eat. "We need to tell Freya."

"She'll know as soon as she sees the enhanced version Raptor sends."

"How?"

"She has a picture of Jamal."

"What? How?"

He shook his head. "Shit. I can't believe neither of us told you about that, but we…sorta got sidetracked, and when we finally talked to Freya, more important stuff was happening."

"*Tell me.*" She heard the urgency in her voice. But dammit, why had Chris kept this from her?

"It's the reason I was in Morgan's office when you texted about your meeting with Gardner. Freya had a photo array and wanted to know if I could identify Jamal. She had a photo of Bassam too."

Bassam.

She would never be able to hear that name without flinching. Without seeing his open throat and the bullet shattering his face.

"Freya found out who they are?" *Who he was.*

"Yes. I don't remember their last name. But they were from Beirut. Taken in an attack on a school a few years ago. They had a sister too."

She closed her eyes. *That poor girl.*

Warm arms surrounded her. She leaned into his embrace.

She would always feel safe in his arms. The smell of him

was imprinted on her brain. He was comfort, safety, and…so much more.

"I'm sorry I forgot to tell you. After a certain point, I guess I forgot that you never had a chance to talk to Freya. She would have told you that night if you'd been able to call her."

"I get it." In the grand scheme of things, it wasn't that important. Having his picture only mattered more now, when they had another picture to match it with.

He was her bomber. And if the hospital security footage had been saved, maybe it could be proven that she'd been right then too.

It was a long shot to think it had been saved when no one had believed her to begin with, but she wasn't afraid to grasp at straws.

Anything that would eventually connect the dots to Rafiq.

"Were Jamal and Bassam and their sister taken in one of the raids Rafiq took credit for?"

"I don't know, but I'm sure Freya does."

He released her and led her toward the table. "We should eat while it's hot."

"I'm not sure I'll be able to."

"I understand. But you should try. Take it slow."

He grabbed the bottle of red wine he'd opened while she put away the groceries and poured them each a small glass.

She took a sip. It was okay, but it was the smell of garlic bread that got her attention. Carbs were her stress food, and nothing beat garlic bread dipped in whatever sauce was on the main course. Tonight it was creamy pesto chicken, and it was divine enough to wake her appetite.

She sipped water and hogged all the bread while Chris told her stories about Navy life and BUD/S.

She liked that he didn't skip over stories that included his ex-wife. They'd been married for a long time, and she'd been integral to his world. It would be weird to pretend she hadn't existed in the same way Diana would never shy away from talking about Salim.

They had both loved other people. They'd both lost them in very different ways. Those losses made them who they were today.

"Last Thursday…you said you were still legally married. Did you ever sign the papers?"

He smiled. "I signed them first thing Friday morning, before going to Freya's office. I'm a free man."

Did he want to *stay* free?

It was a ridiculous question to consider. They'd only known each other since Thursday. It was now Monday evening.

But in that time, they'd decorated a Christmas tree and survived a bombing. That was a relationship on the fast track.

Plus, really, she'd first met him in September, and again six weeks later.

She'd lived a lifetime in the interval.

Chris refilled his wineglass and was about to refill hers, but paused when he saw it was nearly full. "Don't like the wine?"

"It's fine. I was just thirsty with all the salty garlic bread, so I wanted water more."

He gave her a splash more wine, then set the bottle down and picked up his glass. He smiled ruefully at the unlit candles on the table. "I meant to light those. I wanted to eat by candle and firelight and make this feel like a date."

She smiled. "You want to woo me even after I've put out?"

"Absolutely. I want to give you flowers and chocolate and orgasms."

She laughed. "That's all good, but what you've given me is so much more than that."

"What have I given you?"

She almost blurted out the word she was feeling, but it was too scary to put that between them this early. Was it even real? Her heart said so.

She knew it wasn't hero worship. Chris was so much more than her first vision of him in the dark desert night.

But he needed an answer. She didn't want to say *safety* because she didn't want him to think that was the only thing she wanted him for. So she cleared her throat and said, "You." As if that explained everything. Her throat went dry, so she took a sip of water and added, "And I don't plan to give you back."

His eyes went smoldery. "So I'm yours now?"

"Yes."

"Does that mean you're mine?"

"If you want me."

He smiled slowly. "Babe, I will never stop wanting you."

❧

*C*hris wondered what she'd really intended to say, but he wasn't going to fuss about it given that they'd ended up in the same place.

She made him feel impossible things. Hell, he wanted her *again*, and he'd already come twice tonight. But he wanted so much more than sex. He wanted the same thing she'd declared about him. He wanted her. Today. Tomorrow. Next week. Next year.

He picked up his wineglass and drained it.

Too late, he realized he should have grabbed the water. He'd probably had three glasses, given how low the bottle was. Diana had barely had any.

Not that it mattered. They were safe. He even felt a flush from the alcohol, which was rare for him given his build. Maybe it wasn't the wine so much as the fact that for the second time in his life, he was falling in love.

And she'd just hinted that the same mysterious symptoms were afflicting her.

She was his for the having.

He wanted to do the very thing he'd imagined when they first arrived at the house—toss her over his shoulder and carry her upstairs to the bedroom.

He rose to his feet, swaying a little at the sudden motion.

His vision swam.

He knew his body. He was a finely honed weapon. This wasn't love… Or alcohol. "*Shit*."

He looked at the bottle of wine.

His vision danced.

Two and a half…three glasses tops.

He reached for Diana's glass.

"Chris? What's wrong?"

"The wine."

"You want mine?"

There was a kaleidoscope of Dianas before him. Pretty. Concerned. She held out the glass.

He slapped it from her hand. Red liquid splashed across her chest, like she'd been shot.

The image seared into his brain. He tried to speak. Finally managed one word. "Drugged."

His legs gave out, and the world went black.

Chapter Fifty-Three

a wave of terror shot through Diana as Chris hit the floor. She didn't have the reflexes or strength to catch him, but she tried to buffer his landing.

She rolled him onto his back, checking his breath and pulse.

Both were present.

Drugged. The wine had been drugged.

She felt fine. Or at least, any dizziness could be attributed to panic at seeing Chris collapse. But then, she'd only had a few sips.

She tapped his cheeks. "Chris? *Chris?*"

Nothing. Not even a groan.

Would the drug kill him, or was he just knocked out temporarily?

She tapped his face again, using more force. "Chris. Babe. *Please.* I need you. I can't do this without you."

Tears came with the words.

She placed a hand on his chest. His heartbeat was strong.

His chest rose and fell with even breaths. Was it possible it was just a sleeping drug?

She placed her ear where her hand had been. No rattle in his lungs. Not that she'd know what that would mean.

His cell phone had slipped from his shirt pocket when he fell. She plucked it from the floor and dialed Freya, who answered immediately.

"Chris?"

"No. Diana. He's been drugged. He's out on the floor, and I don't know what to do." Her voice cracked as she stifled a sob.

Freya's voice remained even, and Diana remembered her instructions from a year ago on maintaining control and composure. Diana was failing that class now, but was glad Freya's training was ingrained. "Check his pulse. Is it slow or rapid?"

She placed her fingers on his carotid, where it would be most easily felt. It took her a moment—which caused a surge of panic—before she felt the steady rhythm. "I think it's even. His breathing looks even too."

"Good. Probably just a sleeping drug, then. How was it administered? How did they find you?"

"It was probably the wine. He'd ordered a bottle to go with our dinner that was delivered. I only had a few sips. He had two glasses, maybe a bit more."

"He used a food delivery app?"

"Yes."

"What phone are you calling from, the one that made the order?"

"Yes."

"Diana, hang up. Drop the phone. And leave now."

"I—I can't. I can't carry him to the car, let alone lift him inside. Not with my ankle—"

"You need to leave him. Hang up now."

"No!"

"Diana, they aren't after him. They're after *you*. And they have this cell phone number, so they're listening to us now. They know he's down. Hang up the damn phone and go. I'll do what I can for him from here."

She hung up.

Diana stared at the Call Ended notice. Tears streaked down her cheeks.

She couldn't do what Freya had said. Couldn't leave him.

But if she was taken, he would be in the same situation, and she'd be killed by Jamal.

Freya was right.

Tears dripped from her cheeks to his as she leaned down and kissed him. "I'm sorry. So sorry." Then she whispered, "I think I love you. That's what I wanted to say tonight. I love you."

She pulled out his wallet and took all the cash. He had several hundred dollars. She touched his face one more time, then rolled him onto his side, just in case he got sick while unconscious.

She ran into the study and grabbed the computer, 5G hotspot, and her phone. Back in the main room, she glanced around for his pistol, but remembered there was a gun in the car's glove box, courtesy of Raptor. She grabbed the car keys from the counter and headed out the door.

Once she was in the driver's seat, she quickly removed

the walking boot. She'd have to drive with just the support brace and hope that was enough to protect her healing wounds.

The garage door slowly rose, her heart beating frantically with every slow inch. She was panicked at leaving Chris and terrified of not having left faster.

Finally, the garage door had risen just enough, and she hit the accelerator. The car backed out far too fast, going straight into the road. She hadn't even checked for traffic. Thankfully, the road was clear. She slammed the gear shift into Drive and left the quiet neighborhood with a peel of rubber on pavement.

Christmas lights and inflatable reindeer and Santa Clauses were a blur as she searched for the exit to the neighborhood. Finally, she spotted the main road and pulled into Monday evening traffic.

She didn't know where she was going, she only knew she had to get away. An interstate or other highway would be best, because then she could use cruise control to regulate speed, accelerating and braking with her thumbs instead of her right foot.

She didn't know this area, though, and went in circles before finally spotting a sign that would take her to a highway and then I-95.

It was weird to be driving again. But maybe that was just because she was terrified and slightly lost. Plus she had to remind herself to look for a tail.

She couldn't call Freya on her new burner phone. If they'd gotten Chris's new number, they could have accessed his contacts list and would have her new number too.

Freya's number was also compromised, although the security on her end would be locked tight. She needed to find someplace safe to park for a while so she could cry and panic and figure out what to do.

But she was afraid if she stopped, Jamal would catch up to her.

She was back on the bicycle in Aqaba, her ankle burning with pain as she searched for a place to hide.

Except this time, there was no way Chris could save her.

Chapter Fifty-Four

*R*and was on his feet the moment he saw a text from an unknown number.

> This is Freya. Chris needs your help.
> Drugged and passed out.

He hit the Call button as he grabbed his already-packed bag. It held his sidearm and uniform. He'd need the gun.

Freya picked up immediately.

"What's happening?" he asked.

"Chris's phone was compromised. I don't know how they did it, but once they had the number, they were able to get his location when he placed a dinner order. They must've sent someone to intercept the food and injected something into the bottle of wine. He's passed out. I told Diana to leave him and run. We've got a tracker on the vehicle. She's gone."

"Am I going after Diana or Chris?"

"Chris. Diana should be safe as long as she keeps

moving. We'll figure out a way to intercept her, but Chris is our first priority."

"Got it. Where am I going?"

"I'll give you the address once you're on the road. Head south of DC."

He understood why she was playing it close to the chest, but still, it irked him. "You know you can trust me. Whoever drugged him already has the address."

"Go south on 95. You'll get the address when you need it."

He reached the lobby and spotted Bryce. "Albrecht is here."

"Take him with you."

"You sure?"

She paused, then said, "Do it."

$\mathcal{R}$and didn't bother worrying about speed limits. If cops wanted to chase him, he'd lead them to the house where a SEAL had been drugged.

Freya gave him the address when he was two miles from the exit. He asked for an update on Diana, but she didn't respond. The silence told him the call had ended.

He gripped the steering wheel and floored the accelerator, telling himself this was an op. Not one assigned by his superiors in the Navy, but an op just the same. He knew his job.

Get to Chris. Take him to a hospital if needed. Protect his teammate.

"What the fuck is going on?" Albrecht asked for the seventh time.

He gave the same answer he'd given before. "We'll find out when we get there."

"You know something."

"I only know Chris is in trouble."

"And the Diana person you asked about, that's Diana Edwards, right?"

"What makes you think that?"

"Stop being a dick and answer my questions. If I'm running into something dangerous, I have the right to know."

Rand made an illegal pass on the right, narrowly avoiding a mailbox bank.

"What the fuck, man!" Albrecht shouted.

Rand turned into the neighborhood. Almost there.

Albrecht was right about needing to know what he was getting into. Rand had just been putting off telling him as long as possible.

"This morning, the house Chris was staying in blew up."

"What? Blew up? Are you saying that explosion that's all over the news was him?"

"Yes. He found a new place to stay, but now he's been drugged." He turned onto the street. The house would be at the end of the block. "We don't know what we'll find when we get inside, or even if Chris will still be there."

"Why not call the police?"

"He wasn't alone. He was with Diana. Police would put a BOLO on the vehicle she's driving. They'll probably assume she's the one who did the drugging. They might try to pin the explosion on her too."

"Maybe she did it. Dr. Edwards made up that shit about Rafiq. Now she's using Chris to try to make it look like someone is after her."

"Where the hell would Diana get a pipe bomb from? She's been with Chris since Friday night."

"He was with us at a bar last night. I didn't see Diana there."

"She can't drive. Busted ankle."

Albrecht pointed to the open garage door. The double bay was empty. "Yet presumably, she's driving now."

Shit, the kid wasn't as dim as he seemed.

"Forget the bullshit you heard at the Pentagon. Diana wasn't lying when she said she saw Rafiq." As he said the words, he realized he fully believed her for the first time since the search he led of the compound outside Aqaba came up empty. He'd waffled on the idea, believing she'd *thought* she'd seen Rafiq, but had been wrong.

Now he was a believer.

He'd met Mason Gardner. He'd seen the fear in the man's eyes when Kira told him their artifact purchases would be reexamined. If Diana could somehow connect the Gardners' purchases to Rafiq, the family had hundreds of millions of reasons to want her dead.

*T*he room was spinning. Or maybe Chris was. His head throbbed. If this was a hangover, he'd better have had a helluva good time to earn this misery.

He tried to remember where he was. It would help if he could open his eyes, but they wouldn't cooperate.

He couldn't move.

Sleep paralysis? He hadn't suffered from anything like that since he was a kid.

He tried to remember the booze that had brought on this pain.

Diana. Making love to her on the couch.

Diana.

The wine.

"Wake up, Flyte." A sharp smack to his cheek broke the paralysis. A second, much harder slap snapped his head to the side.

His eyes popped open, and there was Albrecht.

"Flyte. You're awake." The kid grinned.

Everything came back to him. The wine. His phone.

Diana.

His gaze darted around the room. She wasn't here. Had she been taken?

"Diana—" The word came out in a croak. He cleared his throat as his gaze went from Rand to Bryce.

"She's not here," Rand said. "Freya said she escaped before she could be taken."

He was going to be sick. He wasn't sure if it was the drugged wine or the knowledge that Diana was out there alone, but his stomach roiled. He lurched to his feet and staggered to the bathroom.

He opened the lid of the toilet and leaned over the basin. When the vomit didn't come on its own, he jabbed a finger in his throat. He'd absorbed a lot of the drug, but some might still be in his stomach.

He retched, and once he started, it didn't stop until the dinner he'd eaten came up too. Cold sweat dotted his brow as he leaned back against the wall, spent.

Diana was gone.

Is she safe?

How had he fucked up so badly?

Bryce's voice carried from the living room. "Still not convinced Edwards isn't behind this. I know Flyte's into her, but she's sketchy."

"Shut the fuck up, Albrecht. No one asked you to think."

Chris got to his feet and splashed water on his face from the sink, then went to the living room entryway. The younger SEAL was a big man—bigger than Chris in height and shoulder width.

The guy was younger. Fit in the extreme. And he knew how to use his strength.

Before this moment, Chris would have said he wasn't too bright, and that might still be true, but now he was calculating how much was an act. A deflection.

Chris relaxed his body, leaned against the arched entry. "Tell me more of your theories, Petty Officer Albrecht."

He shrugged. "Nah. I'm good."

"How is it you happen to be here, with Fallon?"

"Lucky break. I was in the lobby when the lieutenant

commander was passing through. He asked for backup. I said yes. You're welcome."

Chris took a step forward, and before Albrecht could guess what was coming, he pulled back and punched him in the face.

Albrecht's head snapped back, but his reflexes kicked in, and he lunged for Chris.

Chris was still groggy from the drug, but he'd expected a strike. He dodged and kicked and punched. He held nothing back. He landed a second blow. Then a third.

Albrecht managed to graze Chris's jaw with a fist and kicked him in the knee, but nothing could stop Chris, not even Fallon, who tried to pull him back.

"He's just a dumbfuck, Flyte. Don't blow your career with this."

Chris pushed back against Fallon as his hands closed around Albrecht's throat.

"He's not a simple dumbass. He's a fucking traitor. He tagged my 4Runner with a tracker last night. Today, he got my phone number from your phone and gave it to whoever drugged me."

He squeezed tight on Albrecht's throat. The petty officer's face turned bright red as he bucked against Chris's hold. "When I let you breathe again, the first thing you're going to say is who you're working for."

Rand stopped tugging at Chris's arms. "Shit. That's why he was in the lobby. He was tipped when Freya called me and knew I was on my way down."

Chris let the guy take a breath, but then squeezed again before he could say the lie that would surely come.

"The moment they got my burner phone number, they had everything they needed." Chris let Albrecht have another sip of air, then squeezed again. "Who you working for, Brekkie?" He relaxed his hands.

"No one. I—"

Again, Chris took control of his breathing. He made the game-show buzzer sound that came with a wrong answer. "Try again."

"No—"

Fallon reached around and grabbed Albrecht's phone from his pocket. "He doesn't need to talk. I'm sure we'll find everything we need right here."

Albrecht's eyes, already bugging, widened further, and he struggled against Chris's hands.

"I'm guessing this is why Freya told me to bring him along," Rand said. "Wanted to make sure he didn't get away."

"You got handcuffs in your go bag?"

"No. But I've got paracord and duct tape in my emergency kit in my vehicle." Rand left for the garage. A moment later, he was back, and they tied Albrecht's hands behind his back, then taped over the cord. The trussed SEAL wheezed and coughed and looked terrified.

As he should.

"Let's get out of here before they realize we have their pet and try to spring him." Chris led the way into the living room. Before heading out the door, he spotted the cell phone near red wine streaks on the rug. He crossed the room and stared down at the phone for a moment, then slammed his heel into the glass screen.

It wouldn't change anything, but the crunch of glass was satisfying. He wished it was Albrecht's face, but the man had information they needed.

If Diana had been taken, Albrecht was their only hope of finding her.

Chapter Fifty-Five

*S*he should have put the boot on before pumping gas, but she'd been in a hurry, and now she had regrets. Diana leaned against the side of the car, holding her nearly bare foot off the cold pavement as she filled the tank. At least this station had a kiosk right by the pumps so she'd been able to slip two twenties to the attendant to start the pump without having to cross a parking lot.

It shut off automatically when it hit forty dollars, and again, Diana was on the road. Her foot throbbed with unaccustomed freedom and use.

Before getting back on the interstate, she passed a strip mall, spotting the Historie sign prominent on the marquee.

Without taking a moment to think, she turned into the lot and drove down the packed parking lanes looking for an open spot.

Stores were open until ten on Mondays during the holiday season. Thirty minutes before closing, the lot was packed. She found a parking spot that faced the store and turned off the engine and headlights.

Historie was doing a booming business. The items they sold were artsy and beautiful, and each one came with a story. They were perfect gifts for the impossible-to-buy-for friend. At least, that was how Historie marketed itself, and people ate it up.

From inexpensive mugs decorated with historic quotes to licensed artwork, they had a full range of gifts. Shoppers could find two-dollar stocking stuffers or drop several thousand on Signature Line replicas.

She stared at the storefront, thinking of the artifacts she'd appraised and the ones she'd looted.

When was a replica as precious as the original?

She thought of Chris's Lego fire engine ornament, more precious than the glass one it replaced, but this was different.

She'd done a lot of research on replicas before going to Jordan, and Bibi's booth in the Friday market had particularly interested her because she had some of the highest quality work Diana had seen for the basic tourist market.

For a replica to be of value, it had to be made in the same manner as the original—handmade by artisans—of the same material, and at a one-to-one scale.

A true replica didn't need to be indistinguishable from the original—there would be different coloration in the natural base material, among other things—but it should convey the spirit of the original to the degree of being nearly identical in form and artistry.

The Gardners employed some of the best in the business,

and even their inexpensive, mass-produced replicas were quality.

Once a year, the family held a fundraiser in their mansion in Newport News, Virginia, in the gallery where all the Signature Line originals were displayed in a museum-like setting. Soon, that gallery would be moving to the new flagship store and museum just across town.

As far as she knew, the venue for the fundraiser would move to the museum as well. The money raised from the event went to children who'd been displaced in Syria and elsewhere in the Middle East. Boys like Jamal and Bassam and their unnamed sister.

Diana had attended last year's gala, as it had been held in the spring, several weeks before she'd left for Jordan. She'd sipped wine and chatted with collectors and politicians and even a few famous actors who frequently were cast in historic epics. She wasn't sure if they were looking for an endorsement deal or just loved the artistry and art, and really, it didn't matter. The cause was one she believed in, and she'd felt good at the event and even proud of the work she was about to embark on for the retail chain.

Now she stared at the store with bitterness and regret. The Signature Line was a fraud. Not the artifacts themselves —she knew better than anyone exactly how real they were— but they were tainted just the same.

Acquired with blood and murder to fund terror.

With the news that Harun was the broker who'd handled most—*all?*—of the Signature Line acquisitions, it was easy to assume that each and every artifact in the family's private collection was stolen goods.

She pulled the laptop from the seat next to her and powered on the VPN/hotspot and googled the parent company, Gardner Holdings. The store, Historie, had been around for three decades, but the Signature Line of replicas hadn't launched until 2012. After the start of the Arab Spring.

Artifacts in the line came from all over—every region of Africa was represented, as were North and South Asia, Medieval Europe, and the Holy Roman Empire. But no time or place was better represented in the collection than the Middle East, from first recorded human activity to around AD 1000.

There were no New World artifacts in the Signature Line at all. Once upon a time, she'd thought the reason for that was because New World cultures were better suited to sell themselves to a US audience, but now she realized it had been naïve of her to think a corporation would hold back from that market to make room for Indigenous people to profit from their own history.

No. It made more sense that the Gardners just didn't have a line on New World artifacts like they did the Old World. The line they had went through Harun straight to Rafiq.

Freya probably had numbers that would show the expo-nential growth of the company once the Signature Line was introduced, but anecdotally, Diana knew the leap in company value had been huge.

The Signature Line was Cabbage Patch dolls or Tickle Me Elmo or even the next new gaming system, but for the very wealthy, or even the wanna-be wealthy who were eager to show off their one Signature Line piece as an example of their smart tastes and affluence.

Diana didn't blame them. The replicas were stunning. There were a few she'd eyed over the years, including one she'd considered purchasing for Salim's parents, a replica of an artifact from Lebanon, their home country. It was a small statue—a woman's face with a rounded body—from the Canaanite era.

In her work, she'd experienced something few people got to do: touch something that had been made thousands—in a few cases, even millions—of years ago by intentional hands.

It was incredible to hold a rock that had been shaped into a tool by an australopithecine two or three million years ago. To know a bipedal being had created the tool and used it for their survival was almost transcendent as far as understanding where life began and where humanity was now.

It wasn't about the artifact, it was about what one could learn from it.

And a replica could teach as well as the original. Better, even, because it could be made broadly available to curious minds, while it too had been created by intentional hands. Made by Middle Eastern artisans—who were well paid for their art—with the same technique as the original. It had just one more degree of separation from the past.

Past adjacent. But the spirit was true.

Not actual history, but historie.

So the Gardners made their replicas, and until now, it had been a product line she'd supported. If consumers could be content with replicas, they'd leave looted artifacts alone.

Now it made her physically ill to see the packed store and customers exiting with full shopping bags.

She had questions for Dennis and Mason Gardner about the grant and why they'd chosen her. She presumed the supply line for new artifacts had run low. Had Rafiq and/or Harun asked their best customer to find an archaeologist to locate sites and dig for them? Set up a grant with specific parameters that would put an archaeologist with the knowledge and skills in the right place at the wrong time?

She thought of Fahd, who'd spent nearly a decade monitoring sites in Syria to protect the legacy of his friend. He'd chosen to die before giving up site information.

With that thought, everything clicked into place.

She'd been set up from the start.

Chapter Fifty-Six

4

*C*hris insisted on driving Rand's car. It was either that or he'd have his hands free to pummel Albrecht, and that wasn't a good idea. They were taking the traitor to the Raptor compound in Fairfax, where he could be detained and questioned while a team of company techs scoured the internet for every drop of information on the man and what he revealed during interrogation.

"I'm being illegally detained after you beat the shit out of me," Albrecht said from the back seat.

"Nah, that's not how this went down. See, Brekkie, your face hurt my hand." Chris released the steering wheel and wiggled the fingers on his right hand, making exaggerated sounds of pain. "Besides, seeing as how you're working for a group of terrorists, I'm not too worried. We're going to wrap you and Rafiq up with a nice, big, bright red Christmas ribbon."

Rand sat in the passenger seat, Albrecht's phone in his not-damaged hands. He tapped one screen after another, making sounds like he was watching a fireworks display. "You've got some incriminating shit here, Brekkie. It's a shame you never learned to clear your chat history."

"Crying shame," Chris said. From the corner of his eye, he saw the cell phone screen flash. "Who's that from?"

"Looks like it's a message from his 'girlfriend' wondering why he hasn't checked in."

"So the girlfriend in Pennsylvania, was she a lie or a honey trap?"

Albrecht grunted.

Fine. They'd be inside the compound soon and the real questioning could begin.

Freya and Ian met them at the gate, and they were quickly waved through. Ian and another operative—a former Green Beret named Nate—led them and their prisoner into the compound. Albrecht was locked in an interrogation room with a two-way mirror.

"Have you been in communication with Diana yet?" Chris asked as soon as Albrecht was locked behind a soundproof door.

Freya nodded. "She's safe. She used the laptop to draft an email in the online email account she knew we were monitoring. She didn't send it. It's in the drafts folder."

That was basic tradecraft. Create an online email account and use it to post drafts that anyone who logged in could see. No sending required, meaning NSA couldn't flag it for keywords.

They followed Ian down a maze of corridors to a small conference room with several laptops and tablets placed around the table. They were joined by one of the company's tech wizards, who proceeded to clone Albrecht's phone onto a tablet, which he left for them to browse through while he took the original to his office to mine for every scrap of data it could reveal.

As soon as he was given a log-in, Chris signed in to a computer and opened the browser and typed in the domain for Diana's online address.

He logged in and saw a "1" next to the draft messages folder. He opened the folder. The subject line was *Chris*.

He opened the message.

Leaving you like that was one of the hardest things I've ever done. I'm so sorry. Please be okay. Please don't hate me. Please understand.

His heart squeezed. He hadn't expected the raw emotion the words would bring. She was worried about *him*.

Afraid for him. Concerned he'd be angry.

Pam had treated him as if he was impervious to physical and mental pain. She'd never expressed concern for him, even when he came back from the mission that had injured Xavier and killed two others.

It was around that time she'd taken up with one of his former teammates. She was unwilling to be emotionally available for Chris, and so Chris had reacted in kind and cut himself off from her. He'd spent the last eleven months trying to understand what had happened in his marriage so he wouldn't make the same mistakes again.

And now here was this woman, more worried about him than she was about herself when she was being hunted by terrorists.

His eyes burned.

He moved the cursor below her paragraph and replied.

Oh babe, your safety is the most important thing. I'm glad you did what you had to do. I'm probably still a little woozy—don't tell Rand since I insisted on driving—but otherwise fine. We think we know how they found us. My fault.

He paused as he typed. Everything that had happened was his fault. The minute he read the texts that clearly were not from Rand, he should have ditched the phone. It hadn't crossed his mind that Albrecht was the kind of guy who would memorize a cell phone number so he could provide it to terrorists hunting a SEAL teammate.

I'm so sorry, babe. I should have known. I

The cursor flashed next to the I. He couldn't drop those words here, in a message Freya would probably read.

want to hold you. Tell you how sorry I am.

Tell you how I feel.

He changed the subject line to Diana and closed the message.

"What's the plan for getting Diana here?" he asked Freya.

"We aren't. Not yet. I've got her a hotel room not far from the city. She's going to lie low. Maybe tomorrow, she'll talk to the FBI agent investigating the bombing. It depends on what we learn from Albrecht."

"I'll go to her after we talk to Albrecht."

Freya's eyes flashed with some kind of emotion. It surprised him, because her cold mask never slipped, but he almost thought it was regret. "No."

"No?"

"Diana doesn't want you with her."

He wanted to reach for the laptop, read the draft message again, but he knew what it said. She'd apologized. That was all. "Explain."

"I'm not in the habit of passing notes in English class. If she wants you to know more, she can tell you herself." She opened her own laptop. "Now, let me get you up to speed before you talk to Albrecht. First, you should know, I don't think the Gardners want to kill Diana."

"Right. Blowing up a house she's supposed to be inside is a sure sign they just want to *talk*."

"We have proof that it was Jamal."

"Who was working for the same people Albrecht is. Jamal is a kid. He's not the mastermind."

"I agree. Rafiq is the mastermind, but—"

Rand jumped in. "You've confirmed we're dealing with Rafiq?"

Freya nodded. "We finally got intel on Harun Taha. He and Rafiq worked together for three years before the Syrian Civil War started. Also, we've confirmed Rafiq is alive and in the US."

That triggered a jolt. "Here? How?"

"Why take that risk?" Rand asked at the same time.

"It's hardly a risk when the Intelligence Community doubled down on declaring him dead." She faced Chris. "Rafiq has been on my radar since I was in the Special Activities Division. I'm neither CIA analyst nor SAD operative now, but I know his modus operandi. Rafiq wouldn't be here if he just wanted Diana dead. Easy enough to let the Gardners take care of that. No. He *wants* something from her. I'm sure Jamal's role was to torment her—after she spotted him at the hospital, everything she'd said was questioned. Even better to send him here. Let her get glimpses of him on the Metro. She's too afraid to tell anyone. Even me."

Chris's heart ached at that, remembering the first night they were together, and how she'd reacted to his questioning her story of seeing Rafiq. She must have been so terrified. And he'd been another person picking at her sanity, even though he hadn't meant to.

Of course she hadn't dared tell him about seeing Jamal. "So you're thinking Jamal acted on his own this morning?"

Freya nodded. "I think he was sent there to grab her, but he had his own ideas. If Rafiq wanted her dead, the wine would have been poisoned, not drugged. They weren't trying to spare *you*. They were trying to make her easy to grab. They want her for information. Not to kill her."

"They'll kill her once they have the information."

"Of that I have no doubt. If we could figure out a way to protect her from that, I'd send her in right now."

He glared at Freya. "I was sent in to rescue her twice in Jordan. I'm not about to lose her on American soil."

He wasn't about to lose her at all.

"We don't have any reason to put her in danger right now."

"And if that changes?"

"Then it will be Diana's choice."

"This from the woman who sent her to Jordan to be abducted. Once a manipulative spook, always a manipulative spook."

"Hey, now," Ian said, but his tone lacked heat. Like he was just offering the expected umbrage.

"My husband might agree with you at times, but no. It's up to Diana. It was always up to Diana. *She* approached us in the beginning. And this is all hypothetical. Diana has no intention of showing her face unless we *know* it will draw out Rafiq. He's pulling the Gardners' strings right now. All he has to do is reveal he's been their supplier for the Signature Line and they're fucked. They can't hide behind their billions when the whole world sees they've been funding a terrorist for more than a decade."

Chris nodded. "They knew he was alive, and they got him in the country, probably on one of their private jets."

"Easy-peasy with a fake passport. Especially when in every photo the Intelligence Community has of him, he has a long beard."

"He shaved?"

Freya nodded toward Ian. "Raptor's finest got access to the Mayflower's security recordings and got this from one of the elevator cameras."

Freya slid a printout across the table. It had been enhanced by Raptor techs and was crisp and clear. Much better than the photo Diana had run though the free enhancement program online a few hours ago.

He stared at the face, seeing the known scar and the new one Diana had described.

Blood drained from his face. He'd never looked at the guy straight on. The man had kept his head down, but at one point, Chris got a glimpse of his eyes above a beer mug in the mirror behind the bar.

Older man. British accent.

It was all clear now.

Makram Rafiq was the man who'd given Chris relationship advice Friday night in the bar inside the Mayflower.

Chapter Fifty-Seven

*D*iana hit Refresh at least thirty times before the email subject line changed to her name. Freya had told her Chris was safe, but she wouldn't believe it until she'd confirmed for herself.

The words were his. Only Chris would call her *babe*.

She remembered how he'd said it when they'd made love on the couch. She touched the computer screen. Pixels over cyberspace.

A replica of his words. A representation.

And as meaningful and valuable to her as anything handwritten could be.

She leaned back against the headboard in the hotel room Freya had arranged for her and cuddled the computer.

After Salim died, she'd printed out the early emails between them. The love notes they'd exchanged as the thrill of being together bloomed.

She and Salim had probably exchanged a dozen emails before they had sex.

This thing with Chris had taken a different path. These were their first messages to each other. She wanted desperately to see him. Touch him. Explain to him why she…didn't want to see him.

Not until this was fixed.

He'd risked his life to save her in Jordan. Now he'd barely dodged being blown up and hadn't dodged being drugged. Not to mention that if she were extradited, he would fall under suspicion with the FBI and military.

She would remain in this hotel room alone and wouldn't offer explanation. He'd hit the roof at the idea she was protecting him.

He'd talk her out of it.

She couldn't allow that.

No. She had to focus on the real problem of how to draw out Rafiq now that Freya had confirmed he was in the US. And drawing out Rafiq was something Chris would definitely try to talk her out of.

Rafiq was here. For her.

And she figured she knew why.

As long as Chris stayed far away, he wouldn't get caught in the cross fire again.

She picked up the replica of a glass ingot she'd purchased at Historie right before the store closed. She'd entered the store on impulse, wearing Chris's knit cap and her wool scarf over half her face. She'd wanted to see the shelves and the display cases that held the higher-end goodies. She'd been startled to see they had glass ingots.

It was cheap glass, not a true replica in that it wasn't modeled on any actual artifact. A pretty if somewhat odd paperweight. Smaller than the one she'd broken in Jordan and a lighter shade of blue.

Forty bucks later, she had a glass ingot similar to the one that saved her life, but took another's.

She wasn't sure if she'd bought a talisman or curse, but it would forever be the last item she'd ever purchase from Historie.

The Gardners were rich enough to get away with everything.

Pay import fees and fines.

Return the artifacts.

It didn't even have the sting of a slap on the wrist.

The State Department might have backed off for now, but unless she exposed what the Gardners were doing, it wouldn't take long for them to close the investigation again and extradite her to face trial for a crime she definitely and absolutely had committed.

Extradition didn't scare her so much as the knowledge that she wouldn't remain in Jordanian custody for long. No way would Rafiq *not* come after her on his home turf. She'd end up back in the desert with a trowel. Only this time, there would be no subdermal tracker to signal for rescue.

No Chris to swoop in and save her.

No. She needed to deal with this here, on American soil.

Even if it meant walking directly into the spring-loaded bear trap.

*C*hris and Rand faced Petty Officer Third Class Bryce Albrecht across the interrogation room table. The traitorous pup had regained his confidence in the hour he'd waited to be questioned, but that wouldn't last.

He could scream about being illegally detained all he wanted, but his phone had offered up a wealth of info that meant the young SEAL was looking at so much worse than dishonorable discharge.

Freya and Ian watched from the other side of the glass. Everyone agreed the two SEALs from Albrecht's team would be the most intimidating, given that he'd broken a sacred oath. Both Chris and Rand had earpieces so Freya and Ian could offer guidance when needed.

This worked well for Chris. He wasn't the expert in this sort of thing, and the two people on the other side of the glass had devoted their adult lives to espionage and foreign intelligence.

Rand started the questioning. "So how long have you been in bed with Rafiq?"

Albrecht made a show of looking at his wrist that was sans wristwatch. All electronics had been removed from his body. They'd done everything but a cavity search.

Any trackers hidden there would be useless, given that Raptor had signal blockers throughout the compound, and only their approved electronics could function around them.

He gave them a smug smile. "Zero days, zero hours, and zero minutes."

"You're really going to have to do better than that, kid."

Chris knew being minimized would piss off the egotistical SEAL.

"Fuck off."

"You're not my type."

"Yeah. You like traitors. I don't blame you, man. She's fucking hot, and I bet that mouth sucks like a Dyson."

Rand placed a hand on Chris's shoulder when he tensed, but he wasn't about to lose it with this little fuck. There was too much at stake for that.

"The only traitor I know is in this room. The State Department has retracted the order to bring Diana in. You know that, right? The decision was triggered when your little buddy Jamal tried to blow her up."

"Jamal?"

"You're overacting your part. Jamal was central to the debriefing at the Pentagon. If you're going to play dumb, don't avoid what we *know* you know."

"Oh, yeah. Jamal. Crazy bitch said she saw him in Germany. What makes you think she's not lying again?"

"Funny thing. This time, we have video." Chris opened the folder and pulled out the photo of Jamal that Freya had gotten from a source in Lebanon, along with a photo of him setting the bomb and a close-up of his face.

The transformation from sweet schoolboy to hardened terrorist was both chilling and heartbreaking.

Albrecht's eyes widened when he saw the most recent photo. Kid needed to work on his poker face.

"What did he tell you his name was?" Rand asked.

"Never seen him before."

"Bullshit. Cut the crap. We don't have time for games.

We have your phone. You're going down for treason. I look
forward to testifying at your trial. If you help us now, I might
be kind. Maybe you'll be able to cut a deal. You don't, and
you'll be spending the rest of your days in a military prison."
Chris pulled out a printout of one of Albrecht's text conversations. "We have everything we need right here."

The conversation was short and to the point. Albrecht
sent Chris's burner cell number along with the message.

> I got what you wanted, I'm out now.

The response came two hours later.

> Go to lobby. LCDR on his way down. Insist
> on going with him.

Albrecht had given the command a thumbs-up.

"Pretty damning emoji there," Rand said. "Now, tell us
how it all started."

Albrecht stared at the printout. "Someone must've
hacked my phone."

Chris let out a bark of laughter. "Nice try."

After another long silence, the kid said in a quiet voice,
"They were going to kill me. They *will* kill me."

"Them or me. Your choice." There was no hint of
laughter in Chris's voice now. He dropped it to a menacing
whisper. "I promise you, if Diana is taken again, if she's
harmed in any way, I will kill you in the most painful way
possible. You betrayed your country, your team, and me. I
will get away with killing you."

Rand leaned forward. "And I will help hide your body."

"You're both fucking crazy."

"And you were a fool to think this would go well for you." Chris tapped the paper with the text messages again. "How did they recruit you? Or did you go to them?"

"Look, I put the tracker on your vehicle, but you were harboring a fugitive."

Freya's words were a whisper in his ear. "If that were true, he'd have used the excuse immediately."

Chris leaned in. "She was never a fugitive. They only wanted to interview her. Even so, I might have bought it if you'd led with that. It also doesn't explain the phone number, which you gave them after the State Department backed off."

"How am I supposed to know what the State Department is doing?"

Rand took up this line. "You expect us to believe you were willing to plant a tracker on a teammate's vehicle, but you didn't bother to read the message sent to the entire team by our XO with the update that included the fact that an attempt had been made on Dr. Edwards's life this morning?"

"I must've missed that one."

Chris leaned forward. "I'm done with games. Rand, you might want to leave the room for the next part."

Rand stood. "Sure thing. I'm pretty sure he fell down some stairs in the hotel, so bruises and broken bones won't raise any unwanted questions."

"His neck is already bruised. But then, suicide by hanging always marks the neck." Chris grabbed a leather belt from the bag by his feet. Not just any leather belt, though. It was Albrecht's own, confiscated during the strip search.

He laid the belt on the table, then pulled a cloth and pair of gloves from the same bag. "I just need to put these gloves on and wipe down your belt first."

Rand left the room.

Chris pulled on the gloves and thoroughly wiped down the smooth leather and metal buckle.

Albrecht's hands were cuffed to separate bolts in the floor, giving him minimal range of motion. "I need you to run both hands down the belt before we get started."

Albrecht was sweating now as he eyed the one-and-a-half-inch-wide strip of leather. When he refused to touch it, Chris took his right hand and pressed his fingers to the buckle.

Albrecht tried to twist the piece around and whip it at Chris's head, but he was ready for that. In a flash, Chris had the metal prong pressed to the corner of Albrecht's eye.

"You don't need to see to answer my questions."

A tear spilled down the prick's cheek. He let out a choking sob, then said, "My so-called girlfriend. The bitch was a honey trap."

Chapter Fifty-Eight

*O*nce Albrecht broke, it was easy. But also so much worse than Chris had imagined. Freya and Ian, on the other hand, had known what to expect. They'd separately been following the theory that there was a traitor on the team since Friday—before they'd even had a chance to compare notes.

It was simple. Albrecht had met the young "school teacher" through a dating app just weeks before they deployed. She was the kind of honey trap they were all warned about, but fools like Albrecht were certain they were too smart to fall for. She lived in Norfolk and targeted sailors from all the bases in the area. She must've felt like she'd hit the jackpot when she reeled in a SEAL.

While on the carrier, the young dumbass had used unsecure channels to sext with his new girlfriend. In one of his conversations, he revealed that they'd been sent on an op that failed—the first rescue attempt—and six weeks later said they were to be deployed again in the next day or two and to not be surprised if he couldn't call her for his daily jackoff session.

The real kicker, though, was when they got word they were moving in, he sent her a selfie of himself on the helo.

Not surprisingly, *that* photo was deleted from Albrecht's phone, but Ian whispered in his ear that the Raptor tech would have no trouble recovering it.

Chris nearly lost control and punched the prick at that confession.

It was the most basic operational security. "You ever hear of 'loose lips sink ships,' asshole?" Rand asked.

"I didn't tell her where I was! Or what the mission was."

"She knew you were a fucking SEAL," Rand said. "You realize she sold the information on the dark web within seconds after you sent the photo. Of course, by then, she probably knew Rafiq's group was interested after you spilled details of the first op. Given the urgency of what she had, she'd have gone straight to her contact within Rafiq's cell, bypassing the open market and getting premium money for the intel."

"I hope you enjoyed your sexting," Chris said. "Worth betraying your team and country for?"

In his ear, Freya told him to move on.

She was right, dammit. But he longed to punch the fucker one more time.

"Okay, so they knew we were coming in Aqaba. That's why Rafiq and the artifacts were gone by the time the team got there." He glared at Albrecht again. "When did you find out she was a honey trap?"

He dropped his gaze to the floor. "Saturday, when I went

to Pennsylvania to supposedly meet her parents. There were some guys there."

"Middle Eastern?"

He shook his head. "American. They said they were with the FBI and wanted information on Edwards. The news that Jordan had demanded extradition had just dropped, so I believed them. I told them I saw you kissing Diana on the sidewalk—we all saw you through the bar window—but I think they already knew about you two."

Because Rafiq had seen them together at the Mayflower on Friday, and Chris had left his signed credit card slip on the bar when he left. Rafiq had his name before Chris even knew there was reason to conceal it. But Chris didn't tell Albrecht that.

"You say you thought they were feds," Rand said. "That doesn't make your girl a honey trap."

"I didn't figure that out until Sunday. It was just her and me in this big old house she'd supposedly grown up in, but there were no photos on the walls. It was sterile and bland… and I started to think about how generic everything she'd told me was. I asked about her students and how it went the last week before winter break, and she just brushed aside the question. She just…didn't sound like a second-year kinder-garten teacher at all. And her parents were supposedly called away for a funeral of an old family friend, but she slipped and changed the friend's name. I don't think she even cared if she kept her story straight."

"Because she'd gotten what she wanted from you and was done with the ruse."

Albrecht reddened. His ego had to sting at that. His spy

girlfriend didn't enjoy fucking him enough to keep the game going. Poor baby.

"What happened when you called her on it?" Rand asked.

"I sneaked in on her when she was masturbating for another guy on FaceTime in her 'parents' bedroom. I could see from the background that the guy was on a ship. Before she could close the laptop, I told him she's fucking half the fleet including me, and used that as my excuse to pack my bag."

He closed his eyes. "She guessed I'd figured out the truth. Before I could leave, she gave me some trackers and said everything would be fine if I tagged you or your vehicle once I was in Little Creek."

"And you agreed."

"What else could I do? Shit. The stuff I'd told her…"

Chris kept a lid on his temper and refrained from listing all the other choices the prick could have made.

"I left, and while I was driving, I got a message saying you'd left Little Creek and they thought you were headed back to DC, but they didn't know where you were staying. They told me to head back to the hotel where we'd stayed last week. Fallon was still there, and you and Fallon were tight."

"Who was texting you all this?" Rand asked.

"I don't know. It wasn't Emily's phone number. But I knew it wasn't a fed, even though that's who they still claimed to be. They even said tagging your car was fine because you were harboring a fugitive."

"So you tagged my vehicle, then what?"

"I texted from the bathroom at the bar that I'd done the deed and I wanted to head home to Little Creek. I was told I couldn't do that. They might need me again, so I went back to the hotel." He ran a hand over his face, the manacle around his wrist limiting his movement so he had to dip his head down to perform the action.

He then straightened and said, "This morning, Jamal showed up at my hotel room. Told me he had a gift to deliver. I didn't recognize him. I didn't see his face in Aqaba."

"But surely you suspected," Chris said.

He shook his head. "I didn't know what to think. He said he was Emily's half brother, but I knew that was bullshit."

"Emily being the honey trap?"

Albrecht nodded. "I can give you her name, but now I'm thinking it was fake."

"No shit, Sherlock."

In his ear, Freya snickered. "This one's a real brain trust. But Raptor got her photo and dating app profile from Albrecht's phone. They're scanning other apps for more profiles. Odds are Albrecht is one of dozens of marks."

Rand picked up the line of questioning. "So you drove Jamal to the coordinates that had been transmitted via the tracker and left a pipe bomb as a *gift* for your teammate."

Chris tilted back in his seat, remembering the pickup truck pulling out of the long driveway before he pulled in. Jesus. That had been Albrecht's truck. He didn't know what the guy drove, hadn't recognized it. But damn, if he had, they'd be in a different situation right now.

"I didn't know it was a bomb! I asked to see the so-called

gift. He showed me an artifact. A tablet of some kind. Said it was from Jordan."

Albrecht kept his head down, refusing to meet Chris's gaze.

"I swear, I didn't know he was going to plant a bomb. I didn't even know about the bomb at all until I saw the news two hours later. We got to the rental house, and your 4Runner wasn't there. Jamal hopped out of the car and went to the porch. I'd parked so my truck couldn't be seen from the front door, so I couldn't see him as he approached the house. Next thing I knew, he was circling around from the back. He said, *'They're not here. Let's go before they get back.'* And we left."

"After you learned about the bombing, you had your last chance to come clean," Rand said. "You could have come to me, your superior officer, and spilled your guts. You could have gone to the Pentagon, JAG, or NCIS. Hell, you could have gone to the FBI or State Department, but you didn't."

"I—I—I'd given operational details to my girlfriend while I was on an aircraft carrier. I was with a guy who tried to bomb my teammate and the woman we'd been sent to exfiltrate. I was facing criminal charges…"

Chris held his gaze. "And here you are, in the exact same place, but we're feeling a helluva lot less charitable than we would have earlier today."

The only thing that even slightly tempered his anger was knowing the SEAL must've shit his pants when he saw the news about the explosion. "What happened to Jamal?"

"I dropped him off at a Metro station in Virginia."

"If he's smart, he's on the run now," Freya said in Chris's

ear. "My guess is he was on his own revenge mission, which is why he needed to use Albrecht to get to the house. Jamal was sent here to torment Diana, not kill her. Rafiq needs her alive. He'll kill Jamal for this betrayal."

There was a sureness to Freya's tone that Chris found interesting.

Ian spoke next. "Listen, I think Freya's right, and if we're going to figure out a way to use this dumbass, we need him to check in with his handler. Maybe he can get a hint as to their next move."

Chapter Fifty-Nine

*A*fter hours of searching through every database she had access to, Kira had definitive evidence of the connection between Harun Taha and Makram Rafiq—they worked together in Damascus prior to the Arab Spring uprisings—and also had managed to locate the records for every Signature Line purchase by the Gardners. Taha's name was on ninety percent of them.

Kira bundled the information she'd gathered into a file and uploaded it to the FMV portal, then set her laptop to the side of her bed and stretched her neck. It was midnight, and she was tired, but wired.

She only knew pieces of what was going on at this point, but it had something to do with Dr. Diana Edwards and the extradition request from the Hashemite Kingdom of Jordan. Kira didn't know anything about Dr. Edwards, but anyone who found themselves on the opposite side of Mason Gardner was an ally.

Mason had texted her several hours ago, telling her the

deal with Gillibrand had closed and the artifacts were already en route to Newport News. He was returning home tomorrow, and if she was interested in personally inspecting the artifacts, she was welcome to see them in his bedroom.

She'd forwarded his text to Freya since the news of the deal closing was important. Freya had replied with an apology for placing Kira back in Mason's crosshairs.

But Kira didn't hold it against her. How could she when she'd never told anyone the extent of the harassment?

She rose from the bed, grabbing her phone from the nightstand before heading to the kitchen. She had the munchies. Thankfully, there was a pint of strawberry ice cream in the freezer. She grabbed a spoon from the drawer and was pulling off the top when her phone pinged.

Freya thanking her for uploading the data.

She sent a thumbs-up, then tapped the arrow at the top for the list of conversations. Again, she went to the draft message she'd considered sending Rand after receiving Mason's creepy text.

But she didn't have a clue what to say and hadn't gotten past identifying herself. Now she deleted even that. A text now would be the equivalent of "you up?" and she did *not* want to give him that idea.

She scooped a bite of ice cream as she stared at the blank message box.

She remembered the feel of his hand on the small of her back. It was ridiculous that she remembered that singular touch, especially given that he'd only done it for Mason's benefit.

Damn. Did the SEAL have to be so hot?

Even worse, he was *confident*.

She took another bite of ice cream and imagined licking it off his chest. She hoped he wasn't allergic to strawberries.

She imagined asking that question as her first text message to him and groaned at her own dorkiness.

I can't even have a basic sex fantasy without worrying about allergies.

So charming and sexy. It was a wonder she was alone.

The sound of footsteps outside her apartment caught her attention. The building was an old embassy that had been converted into apartments. There were only two apartments on each floor, and hers was on the fourth and top floor at the end. Her neighbors were on vacation—spending the holidays with their grandkids in Upstate New York. She knew this because she was in charge of watering their plants and collecting their mail.

There was absolutely no reason for anyone to be outside her door at midnight like this.

She remembered the look on Mason's face today when she'd questioned his artifact acquisitions for the store, followed by his gross, harassing text message.

He was a wealthy man who expected to get away with everything he did. He had little reason to fear real trouble for buying looted artifacts as long as all the transactions went through the auction house. The onus was on the house to confirm provenance.

Was Gardner angry enough to come after her?

There was a soft click as the knob to her apartment door turned. The dead bolt was engaged, so the door didn't open, but if they could pick the doorknob lock, they could probably get past the dead bolt.

She grabbed her phone from the counter and typed a message in the empty box.

Help

She hit Send, then yanked up the kitchen window. She climbed out, standing on the roof of the apartment below hers. She was about to close the window, but her apartment door opened.

She moved away from the open window. It was freezing, with a biting wind, and she wore only thin flannel pajamas. No shoes or socks.

She was on the third-floor roof. There was no fire escape on this side of the building. It wouldn't take them but a second to find her with the open window. She rounded the corner and tucked against the wall.

She texted Rand again.

Please. It's Kira. They broke in. I'm on the r

Steps sounded around the corner. She hit Send, then dropped the phone. It slid down the slight incline and caught on something before it could drop into the gutter.

Please, Rand. See my message.

In the end, she never even saw a face. The man wore a ski mask. It was the only thing that registered before she went lights out.

Chapter Sixty

*R*and was on his way out the door before the second message landed. "They're splitting the team monitoring Diana," Ian said.

"I don't give a fuck."

"Neither do I. I was just clarifying the situation."

Chris had gone to Diana's apartment, making a show of the fact they weren't together for anyone watching over her place. Freya would stay in the compound, going over the data Kira had sent just before her urgent texts to Rand.

The Raptor compound was at least thirty minutes from Kira's apartment. "You call the police," he told Ian. "I'll drive."

For the second time in eight hours, Rand drove like a madman through the DC metro area. They arrived at Kira's minutes before the local police arrived. It was a busy night for crime in the city, apparently.

Rand was on the roof and had just spotted her phone when the police finally showed up. He pointed the phone out to the cop and stepped back to let the official investigation begin.

He chafed at having to follow the rules, but doubted they'd get anything from the cell phone anyway. He had the time stamps on the texts he'd received. They knew exactly when she'd been taken.

And he sure as hell bet he knew who was behind her abduction.

4

*D*iana had never even heard of Kira Hanson until Freya had mentioned the woman hours ago, and now she'd been taken hostage.

Because of her.

She knew the game the Gardners and Rafiq were playing. They'd hoped to use fear of extradition to get to her, but the State Department paused on making an extradition decision while the bombing was investigated. It was only a matter of time before the fact that Rafiq was alive would be made public. At this point, Diana could hide indefinitely, which would give the feds all the time in the world to gather intel on the Gardners' dealings with Rafiq.

But they'd taken Kira Hanson, and that changed everything.

She knew they were trying to draw Diana out. Prevent her from hiding and waiting out the investigation.

Anything could happen to Kira while Diana hid in comfort.

Worse than just being bait for Diana, Kira's expertise fit

well with what Rafiq needed. He could drag her to Syria and put her in charge of creating false provenance so he could keep trafficking artifacts all over the world.

Diana had planned to wait a few days. See if FMV could take down the Gardners via legal means. Dig up evidence of their corruption. Let the FBI raid their offices.

But with Kira's abduction, she couldn't hesitate. She had to act now, before they could even begin to suspect she was coming for them. Catch them off guard and red-handed.

There were a limited number of places the Gardners were likely to take Kira, and all three had heavy security. Mason had said the artifacts had been sent to Newport News already, and he was heading south today. She'd bet anything Rafiq was also in Newport News, protected by the same security that would keep Kira prisoner.

Rafiq wanted Diana alive, which meant she could get inside that secured space. And once she was there, she could unleash the tiny drone cameras that Raptor had provided. The drones could search for Kira and capture Rafiq's face for undeniable proof he was alive and working with the Gardners.

Because Rafiq wanted her alive, she'd have time for the FBI to review the live video and move in to save her.

It was a solid, albeit risky, plan.

She'd refused to discuss it with Chris, instead sending him a message via her email drafts folder. She'd spent precious minutes drafting it when she needed to be refreshing her memory on lockpicking, but she'd needed to tell him.

When the Monuments Men formed in WWII under the directive of Dwight D. Eisenhower, they knew that lives are worth more than objects. Two Monuments officers died in the performance of their duties. The head archaeologist at Palmyra was beheaded by ISIS because he refused to divulge the location of artifacts. My friend and colleague Fahd chose death over revealing site locations. These men didn't die in vain because they died for an object. They fought and died for a cause.

When I chose to stay with Jamal and Bassam instead of being rescued, I was choosing to continue my own fight for that same cause.

Kira wasn't given a choice. This isn't a cause she knowingly signed up for—even if it is one she believes in.

I know you disagree with the plan, but I have to do what I can to help her. I have to finish what I started in Jordan.

And when we have Rafiq in custody, I want to go home with you and finish decorating your Christmas tree. I want to make love with you and tell you what's in my heart.

Please understand why I have to do this.

Love,

Diana

She'd stared at the screen for a long time before she found the courage to hit Save and close the browser. In the hours since she'd typed the words, she hadn't let herself check for a reply. Instead, she spent her time figuring out the gadgets Freya had delivered to her hotel room in the middle of the night.

Now it was seven in the morning as she left the safety of her hotel room. She had trackers, bug-like drones, a Raptor headset that worked as both a radio and a cell phone, and had exchanged the metal rods in her ankle stabilizer with small blades, lockpicks, and other tools.

She placed the suitcase Freya had brought her in the trunk, along with the Historie shopping bag that held the glass ingot. She was about to close the lid when she hesitated.

She reached into the shopping bag and pulled out the bubble-wrapped replica. She peeled away the protective cover, popping plastic in the process.

She held up the teal glass puck to the morning sun. It was opaque, with a dull cortex on the base and sides, just like the real thing.

It would break just like the real thing too.

She stepped away from the open trunk and, with both hands, slammed the replica down, releasing it a few feet above the hard pavement.

It shattered into a dozen pieces.

She found a large, sharp shard, just the right size.

She removed the plastic clip that secured her hair on top of her head and set it on the lip of the trunk, then gathered her hair and placed the shard in the middle of the thick, dark strands, and twisted it into a bun. She secured the mass with the clip.

Now she was ready.

She closed the trunk and climbed into the driver's seat. After removing the boot so she could drive, she set off for the Mayflower Hotel.

*C*hris hated everything about this plan. He understood why Diana wanted to do it, but that didn't make him like the idea.

She'd refused to talk to him about it, knowing he'd try to talk her out of it.

All he wanted was to keep her safe.

He was a SEAL, not a spy. This kind of op had never agreed with him. SEALs were direct. They HALOed or HAHOed in and did the job. Capture or kill. Secure the target. Rescue the hostage. None of this subterfuge bullshit.

He wasn't frigging James Bond, and worse, neither was Diana.

He was on the radio with Freya as he drove with Rand into the city, and said as much.

"She *has* trained for this, Flyte. She was damn good, and I have no doubt she'd be in the CIA now if she hadn't been injured in that car accident."

"But she was, and now she can barely even walk."

"My point is, she's mentally prepared, and she knows the stakes better than anyone." She paused. "Our plan is good, and we *can* protect her. *You* can protect her. We aren't law enforcement. We're not bound by the need for warrants. But also, you and Lieutenant Commander Fallon were issued orders to capture or kill Makram Rafiq before you embarked on the raid in October, correct?"

"Of course."

"Well, then, you'll be doing your duty and carrying out those orders, which, I believe, were never rescinded."

"It doesn't really work that way," Chris said. "For starters, we're on American soil."

"I'm cool with it," Rand said. "The brass won't balk when we bring in Rafiq."

Chris thought of Diana's desire to return home with him when this was over. "They better not balk at extending our leave, then. I've got plans for Christmas."

Chapter Sixty-One

4

*H*er ankle hurt. She wasn't sure if it was the boot, stabilizer, or the joint, but she guessed it was the fact that the metal rods in the stabilizer weren't standard issue with the changes she'd made.

She should have thought of this, but it was too late now. She shifted the weight to the cane and tested the joint to make sure her reaction time would still be there.

Morgan had a similar injury, once upon a time, and she'd talked about how even now, her martial arts reflexes were sometimes slower on that side of her body, even though the pain was a distant memory.

The joint remembered. The joint was slower to respond. Anything that interrupted the muscle memory was an inhibitor, and she couldn't afford that kind of mistake today.

Not now, when she was taking this awful risk.

It would be worth it. The plan was solid.

They'd never see Diana coming.

Timing was crucial. And trust.

It was strange to trust Albrecht, but he had everything to gain by helping them all now. He was going to prison either way, but he had a much better chance of striking a deal that would limit his time inside if he performed his job today.

Betraying them to Rafiq wasn't an option. He'd get a death sentence from both sides if he tried that.

She continued down the block, limping and glad for the wool scarf she'd wrapped around her head and neck. She wore sunglasses against the bright nearly winter sun on the crisp, cold December morning. The wool scarf was so very American, but still reminded her of long hot days wearing a headscarf in the summer sun.

That life was lost to her now, and she'd eventually accept that, but first she had some atoning to do.

She took a deep breath as she timed her steps. It was her fault Kira had been taken. With this act, she'd be doing her part to make up for that.

She reached the intersection, and there, a block away, was the SUV.

She paused, waiting for the flashing white walk light to turn orange. The countdown timer showed five seconds when she stepped into the roadway.

As arranged, the SUV sped up. She braced for impact. Tires squealed, and the bumper lightly kissed her right knee. She launched herself with the booted foot and flew through the air. She landed hard, splaying on the cold asphalt.

She groaned—more real than fake—as she turned on the pavement and pressed a hand to the hip that would have taken the brunt of impact had it been real.

Albrecht jumped from the driver's seat and played his

role of shocked driver. "The light was green! She jumped in front of me!"

She'd played it close enough for about half the witnesses to agree with him. The other half would believe he was at fault.

None of it would matter in the long run. All that mattered now was the public spectacle.

As planned, Chris was on the sidewalk in front of the hotel. Ostensibly the man she was on her way to meet. He came running, dropped to his knees before her. "Diana! Oh my god. Diana. Someone call an ambulance!"

He played his part perfectly.

Academy Award material.

Really, he should have joined Delta Force. Or the CIA.

He knelt beside her, checking her pulse and respiration and even performing rescue breathing as necessary.

First responders came, but the medics who checked her out worked for Raptor. She was loaded in an ambulance and whisked to the nearest hospital, leaving a devastated Chris behind while he and Albrecht were questioned by cops.

The smell of alcohol on Albrecht's breath and shirt would be enough for him to be arrested, and he'd be safely behind bars until this was over.

Inside the ambulance, Freya pulled off the thick scarf and smiled at Tricia Rooks, a Black Raptor operative who'd played medic in this charade. "My chiropractor is going to be pissed when he hears about this."

She and Albrecht had practiced the stunt on Raptor's training track, so she'd landed on that hip a half dozen times today, but during the practice rounds she'd had a foam mat to pad her landing.

"I can't believe you let that traitor hit you with a car," Tricia said.

Freya had only met the woman last night, but already she liked her. "Well, I could hardly let Chris do it. Can't have him getting arrested. And this way, we don't have to babysit Albrecht anymore."

Chapter Sixty-Two

*D*iana refreshed her phone. Finally, the vehicle/pedestrian accident one block from the Mayflower was posted as a traffic delay.

Minutes later, Freya texted her that she was in the ambulance.

Albrecht and Chris were arguing on the street now. Albrecht would send the text to his handler to say he'd tapped Diana with a car as she was on her way to meet Chris at the Mayflower. He'd made sure not to hurt her too badly, but she was on her way to the hospital, where they could grab her.

Freya had assured her that she and Albrecht had practiced the maneuver. The guy was a trained SEAL who'd excelled in the driving courses. Freya had been a SAD operator. This was no big deal except for the trusting Albrecht part, but there Albrecht had major incentive to cooperate. The difference between a few years in prison versus a life sentence.

Albrecht had been stone-cold sober while driving, but he'd been doused in whiskey just before getting behind the wheel to ensure he'd be taken into police custody. He'd agreed to that because he'd known he'd be safer in custody until Rafiq was caught.

When he faced prosecution for treason, Chris and Rand would provide sworn statements detailing how he'd assisted in capturing Rafiq in the end along with statements that they believed he'd been ignorant of Jamal's identity and that it was the young man who'd planted the bomb.

Albrecht had served his purpose. Now, they just needed to capture Rafiq.

Diana watched the entrance to the Mayflower from a coffee shop across the street. She wore a scarf over her head and kept her face averted from the other customers, but no one paid attention to her as she appeared engrossed with her phone.

The car she was waiting to see pulled up to the valet stand, and Diana took a deep breath, tucking her head down even though there was no way Mason could see her as he handed the keys to his vintage car to the valet.

After he was inside the hotel, she rose from her seat and left the coffee shop. She crossed to the valet garage on the side street and entered. The garage next door was the cheaper, non-valet option, and, if needed, she'd claim to be looking for her car and say she lost her ticket.

But there was no one in the entrance area as everyone must be off parking cars on the lower level. She tucked herself into an alcove when she heard an engine and again when she heard the footsteps of the returning valet. He stopped in the office kiosk and deposited the key, then left the garage to return to the valet stand.

She went to the lower level and gave a quick prayer of thanks that Mason's car was in one of the darker corners.

She approached Mason's beloved car with trepidation. They were lucky that it was a classic vehicle that was revered by collectors, because it meant photos of the car—right down to the trunk—could be found all over the internet.

The trunk would be small, but at least vintage cars didn't have car alarms. It was a trade-off. She'd removed the lock-picks from the ankle stabilizer earlier and had them ready. It took her two minutes to pick the lock of the trunk, and she did it with minimal damage to the exterior.

Once she had it open, she studied the small space. She could do this. The battery was at the side, a modification that matched the 1965 Shelbys she'd seen online.

She examined the latch mechanism. It was also as expected. She used pliers to bend the bar so the latch couldn't close around it, then pulled a wool blanket from her bag and laid it in the trunk.

She took a slow, deep breath, then did perhaps the most insane thing she'd ever done in her life. Possibly even more dangerous than refusing to be rescued by Chris in September.

She climbed inside the trunk, pulled down the lid, then threaded a piece of wire around the latch and bent bar to fasten it closed. Once she was settled inside, she whispered into the microphone of the headset, "I'm in."

Chapter Sixty-Three

She thought she might lose her mind as she waited inside the trunk, but in reality, only forty-five minutes passed before the valet came for Mason's car. Still, as miserable as the wait had been, the vehicle moving was worse.

There were so many things that could go wrong. What had she been thinking?

Deep breath. Slow and steady.

As she'd waited, she pushed two bug drones through the access panel in the trunk so she and Raptor and FMV could all listen to any conversations that might take place inside the vehicle.

The tiny drones had cameras as well. Freya had told her they'd been designed by the girlfriend of one of the Raptor operatives who was helping them, and they were better than any drone of its size that FMV had been able to acquire —until now.

Freya was very much enjoying the newfound friendship between Valkyries and Raptors.

There were three places where Mason might be headed—each a possibility for where they could have taken Kira. Their walled estate in Newport News was perhaps the most secure and therefore most likely option.

Freya's money was on the parent company warehouse on the waterfront. It was only a few miles from the third and final option: the construction site for the new flagship store and museum.

All three locations would offer places to hide a prisoner and house a terrorist.

All had heavy security, the warehouse because of the millions of dollars of merchandise it held, and the construction site would have high fences and guards to protect the equipment and structures. Plus the museum alarm system could be armed.

Riding this Trojan horse was the only surefire way to get beyond the perimeter of all three options. Once she was inside, the little drones could do their thing.

The movement of the vehicle told her the car was circling the block to get to the front entrance of the Mayflower. She was wrapped in the blanket and wished she were smaller like Morgan. Not that Diana was tall—she was a very average five-five—but she'd take any advantage she could right now.

The vehicle stopped, and she held her breath as she heard the driver's door open and the valet say, "I'll get your bag, Mr. Gardner."

The moment of truth. Would he go for the trunk? If he did, how hard would they try to open it?

Thankfully, she felt the car shift as a bag was deposited in the back seat.

She was safe. If being crammed in the trunk of a vintage race car was *safe*.

Both the driver's side and passenger's side doors slammed closed.

Dennis Gardner grumbled as he settled in his seat. "He was supposed to grab her, not hit her with a car."

"It was his last fuckup. We'll deal with him after he posts bail. Today, we have to deal with our houseguests."

Houseguests. Plural.

Kira and Rafiq?

Did that mean they were being held at the estate?

The worst part about being in the hospital was not being able to listen in on the bug Diana had planted in Mason Gardner's car. But they needed to keep the ruse that Diana was in the hospital going as long as possible, so Freya didn't dare leave the room.

Her husband was posted as her guard. Cal didn't really look much like Chris—his skin was a lighter shade of brown, and he was slightly taller and had a receding hairline with a short crown of tight dark curls. But still, they could hope that someone not paying attention would only see a muscular Black man with military bearing and assume it was Chris.

For his part, Chris was on the road, following the tracker

planted in Gardner's car and monitoring the one in Diana's boot.

Freya climbed from the hospital bed so she could pace the room. She wore the requisite gown and had removed the uncomfortable walking boot. She paced the room in a pair of slippers provided by the only nurse who knew she wasn't a real patient.

Cal's voice carried through the door. "Dr. Edwards is sleeping."

Freya had a moment to decide if she should step into the bathroom or get back in bed. She grabbed the boot and hurried into the bathroom, where she sat on the shower chair and put the boot back on, tightening the Velcro straps as quietly as possible.

"Ms. Edwards?" The woman's voice accompanied a tap on the door.

Doctor or investigator?

"Yes?"

"I was sent to do a blood draw."

"I'm going to need a minute."

"That's fine. I'll wait."

Seriously? Since when did a nurse or orderly or whoever the woman was wait while hospitalized patients used the bathroom?

Freya considered making dramatic noises in hopes of driving the woman away, but decided to get the interaction over with. Her blood type wouldn't match Diana's, but hopefully no one would notice that right away.

They'd have to sort out the whole medical fraud thing later.

Oops. It's not okay to fake check in to a real hospital under someone else's name?

Freya had taken on oligarchs and once even stopped a coup and a televangelist set on bringing about the end of days, but she wasn't entirely sure how she'd be able to face down the US health insurance system.

It might require faking her own death.

She stepped out of the bathroom to meet the hospital employee. "Is a blood draw really necessary?"

"I don't write the orders. I just follow them." The woman nodded toward the bed. "Get comfortable. You prefer left or right arm?"

She couldn't remember if Diana was left- or right-handed, so she said, "Either."

The band was around her arm and the woman was swabbing the inside of her elbow with alcohol when Freya spotted the syringe full of some kind of liquid. Not a blood draw.

She glanced at the woman's face.

"Honey?" Freya called out. She wasn't worried, but it might go smoother with Cal in the room.

"Do needles make you nervous? This'll be done in a flash. You'll barely feel a thing."

"*Honey,*" she said, louder and with emphasis this time.

The woman picked up the needle. "I promise, you'll barely feel it."

The door slammed open and Cal entered the room, his gun drawn. "Step away from her."

The young woman's eyes widened. "What the hell?"

Freya repeated, "Honey?" This time she said the word sweetly.

Cal nodded. "Trap."

The woman moved so Freya's head and heart were right behind her from where Cal was standing. A shot at the fake nurse could wound or kill Freya too. She held the syringe to Freya's throat.

She was clearly expecting a wounded and untrained archaeologist, not a woman who'd been in the CIA's special forces.

Freya gripped the syringe and the woman's hand and twisted, surging up from the bed as she did so.

The woman's wrist snapped, and now the needle was pressed to her throat. She screeched with pain, but the moment the needle touched her flesh she stilled, eyes wide.

"What's in it?" Freya asked, keeping her voice sweet.

Her nostrils flared and she sucked in a pained breath. "It won't kill me."

"I didn't think it would. You want me alive."

The woman scanned Freya's face. Makeup altered the shape of Freya's features so she bore a passing resemblance to Diana, and she wore a wig that was the same color and cut, but it would never pass a close inspection, which the orderly hadn't done in her rush not to be observed much herself.

"Not you. Edwards."

"Who are you working for?" Freya asked.

Cal took control of the prisoner, not being gentle when he placed handcuffs on the woman's broken wrist. He smiled at Freya. "God, how I love watching you work."

"What took you so long?"

"I was asking a nurse about the blood draw when I remembered the mole."

Freya had seen it too. The dark mole on her left cheekbone had clicked everything into place. The honey trap. "Emily, I presume?"

The woman strained against Cal's grip. "That's not my name."

"No, I don't imagine it is. Now, tell me, are you a freelance spy, or are you working for a particular country?"

Chapter Sixty-Four

*A*s anxious as Chris was driving down I-95, it had to be worse for Diana, who was currently a stowaway in a small, cold trunk with only a thick coat and wool blanket to warm her on the long drive.

For Chris, who'd spent his entire adult life in the US Navy and several years as a SEAL, this op was a test of training unlike anything he'd ever known.

Ops became personal in the moment. When the bullets started flying and things went sideways, he was in it for his team. It wasn't until Diana that the dynamic had flipped, and that was because he'd failed to save her the first time.

Now she was his lover, but more than that, she was his love. His future. His very heart.

He really didn't know how it had happened, but he couldn't deny it had, and she was two miles ahead of him in the trunk of a vintage race car likely heading for a rendezvous with a terrorist.

Beside him, he knew Rand was dealing with his own

issues. He felt responsible for Kira Hanson. They were united in purpose even though they weren't acting on orders from NSWC.

Hell, their XO would throw a fit if he knew what they were doing. But there was no time to bring the brass into the conversation, and they'd just order Chris and Rand to stand down and let the proper channels deal with the situation now that they were on American soil.

No way in hell would Chris trust Diana's life to anyone else.

I'm coming for you, Diana. I have your back.
Trust me.

iana was eternally grateful she hadn't had any actual coffee in the shop that morning. Her bladder would never have survived this if she wasn't practically dehydrated. It was bad enough that her ankle throbbed after being stuck in the small, cold space for so long.

According to her watch, she'd been in the trunk for nearly three hours, forty-five minutes of that before they even hit the road. Newport News was at least another hour and a half away.

In some ways, this wasn't much different from when she'd been a prisoner in Jordan, blindfolded and on the way to Rafiq's compound. She didn't expect to get far inside the Gardners' home or business before they caught her and she was a prisoner. Also, once again, she was leading special forces to a terrorist's lair.

But this time, Chris knew what she was up to. He was following. Listening. She wasn't on her own.

She reminded herself they were all on US soil. Her turf, not Rafiq's. But then, it was also the Gardners' turf, and they were American oligarchs, while she was just an unemployed archaeologist.

She checked the map on her watch and thought about Kira, taken as a pawn in a game she'd never agreed to play.

Ninety minutes at minimum.

Help is on the way, Kira.

She'd have given anything to know help was coming on that last day in Jordan.

⬦

"*I*t's the construction site." Chris didn't know if he should curse or cheer. Each location came with its own problems, but no one had really expected the half-finished museum and retail store would be the winner in the destination lottery.

It wasn't nearly as secure as the estate, and not as confined as the warehouse, and there were fewer places to hide a terrorist or a hostage during working hours.

By the time Mason Gardner parked inside the fenced lot —with concertina wire topping the temporary fencing—it was only midafternoon. Surely workers would still be there?

Or had construction been halted for some reason?

Chris pulled over in a park a half mile from the construction site, forced on the sidelines while Diana made her offensive move to follow the Gardners into the museum.

They listened to father and son bicker as they climbed from the vehicle. "Let me check on her first," Mason said.

"No. After the meeting, we're heading home. You never should have brought her here."

"Would you rather I brought her to the estate, where the staff would recognize her?"

"Kira," Rand whispered.

Chris nodded.

At least they knew she was here.

The voice feed from the car went silent. After a long interval, they heard Diana speak into her headset. "I'm climbing out." She let out a soft groan.

Chris knew it was the first time she'd been able to stretch out after hours in the trunk and vowed to give her a therapeutic massage later tonight.

Just a few more hours, babe, and this nightmare is over.

The next hour would probably be more dangerous than any she'd spent in Jordan.

❦

*D*iana left the headset in the trunk of the car—she didn't want to advertise she had backup—and approached the museum. She discovered new frontiers of fear as she faced the ornate double doors on the work-in-progress museum. Her heart pounded as she pushed open a door. The Gardners hadn't bothered to lock it or rearm the alarm, thank goodness.

But then, they had no reason to expect a Trojan horse. Once she was inside, she released a half dozen drones. Some could fly. Some crawled. They were tiny and programmed to seek out humans. Once they found them, they would hide and record video, which broadcast on a live feed watchable by anyone with the secured link.

The museum interior was further along in construction than she'd expected. Walls and corridors were installed, and they'd begun work on the decorative elements. Half-finished columns from Ancient Greece gave way to the toes of the Sphinx.

She paused to admire the concept. It was a one-to-one scale of the Sphinx paw. Say what you will about the Gardners, but they understood the point of a replica was to inspire awe of the original.

This wasn't a two-story-tall Statue of Liberty, or a half-sized Eiffel Tower.

From there, she moved on. A pyramid mural gave way to a slot canyon. She entered the maze and was deep inside when her stomach dropped. She knew exactly where she was.

This wasn't a generic slot canyon from a generic Middle Eastern desert, this was *the* canyon where she'd been taken that first day.

It was beyond brazen of the Gardners to have duplicated this place when they could have just invented a setting. They'd had this built while she was a prisoner. They must've known she'd seen it.

They hadn't planned on her returning from Jordan alive.

Behind her, she heard the sound of someone racking the slide on a handgun.

"Raise your hands, and turn slowly."

She'd known this would happen. She'd expected it. Planned for it.

She thought about the pain in her ankle. *Use the pain to mask the fear.*

She pressed her weight on her right foot. Pain shot through her leg. She took a deep breath and did as instructed, turning to face two white men, probably in their thirties. One pointed a pistol at her chest. "Rafiq will be pissed if you shoot me."

"Mason will be pissed if I don't."

The second man stepped up and demanded she remove the heavy coat. Once it was on the floor, she rested her hands on her hairclip while he waved a metal detector wand up and down her body. It emitted an electronic buzz at the boot, and he demanded she remove it.

She sat on a fake rock to undo the Velcro straps. When he discovered all the tools and blades hidden in the boot, he demanded she remove the ankle stabilizer too.

After he stripped her of her weapons and gadgets, he forced her to walk barefoot into the next room, an unfinished space where she came face-to-face with both Gardners and a clean-shaven Makram Rafiq.

Chapter Sixty-Five

"Where is Kira?" Diana demanded.

She had to play this game carefully. More than anything, she needed to buy time. She couldn't give Rafiq even a hint of what he wanted until she had eyes on Kira, safe and sound. And she knew exactly what he wanted, so she could draw out the confrontation. She'd figured it out last night as she watched happy customers leave with bulging bags from Historie.

The perfect gift.

But Rafiq was after the gift that kept on giving. The ultimate score.

And he'd never trust the Gardners with that information. They'd cut him out faster than they'd betrayed Diana and Kira. That was why Rafiq had demanded to follow Diana to the US. He knew she'd become a fugitive before she ever returned to Jordan, and he needed to get the information from her firsthand.

"How did she get here?" Dennis asked, glaring at one of

the henchmen. "You said she was in the hospital and the whore would grab her."

Before the man could answer, she said, "I caught a ride with Mason. I want to talk to Kira."

"Who's Kira?" Mason asked.

"I know you're slow, Mason, but you're overplaying it."

Mason took a step toward her. "Cunt. I'll—"

"I also know what Rafiq wants from me. No Kira. No coordinates."

Rafiq cocked his head. "In Jordan, you never let on that you recognized me." His voice was curious. Even respectful.

"I'm not a fool." She smiled and nodded toward Mason. "Not like present company."

Rafiq laughed. "No. That you aren't. You know what I want?"

"Yes. Fahd told me."

He dipped his head in acknowledgment. "And of course, that is what I wanted from the start. Someone my old friend Fahd would trust."

That gave her a jolt. "You knew Fahd?"

He held her gaze, his eyes probing. "Of course. I knew them all."

Her eyes stung with tears as she connected the dots. "You knew…his friend. The one who went missing years ago."

Rafiq dipped his head. Yes. He knew him. And Fahd's friend's fate, which everyone had guessed at, was also clear. Yet another man who'd died to protect the secret Diana now carried.

It wasn't dying for an object. It was dying for a cause.

"You killed him."

A slight shrug. "He could have saved himself. Just like Fahd. I trust you won't be so foolish."

She'd be defiant, but Kira was still missing. "Bring Kira to me, and I'll tell you what you want."

His smile deepened. In addition to his scars, he had dimples. Friendly dimples. "I have a present for you first."

A tingling started in the back of Diana's neck. Never trust a terrorist bearing gifts.

Rafiq clapped his hands. "Bring him."

Him?

The two henchmen left the room, going in the opposite direction from where she'd entered. A moment later, they returned, dragging Jamal between them.

The fifteen-year-old glared at her as he entered the room, his hands and feet shackled together with chains that formed an X.

Her eyes burned as she looked at him. He was a child. A victim of Rafiq. A monster made, not born.

He'd tried to rape her. He'd held her prisoner for six weeks. And yesterday, he'd tried to blow her up with a pipe bomb.

She felt sorry for him and hated him at the same time.

And then there was his brother. There weren't really words to describe how she felt about Bassam, who had at times protected her. But he was never her friend. She knew he would strike like a snake if needed.

Still, in the end, she'd been the viper.

She looked at Jamal, who hated her with all his being. "I'm sorry. I didn't want Bassam to die."

No. She'd wanted *Jamal* to die. He was the one who'd hurt her. Scared her.

Tears spilled down her cheeks as Jamal looked at her with dead eyes.

She didn't regret what she'd done in order to survive.

She'd betrayed Fahd.

Looted a site.

Killed Bassam.

For a cause. The same cause so many others had died for. And if she could just buy more time, they might finally have a victory. Were the drones in this room? Recording everything? Freya had promised the FBI would swoop in the moment they got video of Rafiq.

They were on standby in Newport News. How long would it take for them to get here?

Could they stop what was about to happen to Jamal?

"He tried to kill you," Mason said, incredulous that she would cry at seeing Jamal in chains.

She looked at the younger Gardner, a man whose wealth came from buying artifacts from terrorists. His money paid for attacks on schools that led to the impressment of boys like Jamal into Rafiq's army. "You and your father sent me to Jordan to be abducted and killed."

"I sent you to Jordan to work and study," the elder Gardner said.

"Bullshit. You sent me hoping Fahd would share the secret with me." She waved to the mockup of the slot canyon behind her. "Your canyon replica is the same fucking canyon they took me to the first day I was abducted. The one they wanted me to dig to find artifacts for your Signature Line.

You already had the interactive museum in the works." She swiped at the unwelcome tears. She didn't want them to see her pain, but she couldn't pull herself up.

She and Jamal and Bassam and Kira weren't people to these monsters. They were tools to be used and abused and discarded. One wanted power and destruction, the other two just wanted money.

Money.

Money.

It was galling to see how deeply they'd betray their country for wealth they couldn't possibly spend in this life-time. Not on things they would actually *use*.

A home. A car. A decent set of kitchen knives. These were necessities and luxuries, and both men had more than they'd ever need. But still, they had to have *more*. As if owning all the best kitchen knives in the world could fill the hole where their soul should be.

"We'll give you Kira if you kill Jamal." The offer came from Mason, of course. He was the most soulless of them all. A man who'd never known want or strife. So he sought blood sport.

"Fuck you. I won't stoop to your level."

Rafiq gave Mason a nasty smile. "Yes, child boss man. It's time you got blood on your hands. Instead of paying others to do your dirty work, you kill him."

Mason's face changed as he took in Rafiq's words. First, he was shocked. Then he was…*gleeful.*

He was going to do it.

He was excited by the prospect.

There was no way Diana would walk out of here alive,

but that was especially true if she witnessed the heir apparent murdering Jamal in cold blood.

Rafiq pulled a knife from the sheath at his waist and offered it to Mason.

"No." Diana's voice was firm even as she sobbed. "Don't do this, Mason. There's no going back."

"He tried to kill you," Rafiq said.

She shrugged. "He failed."

"He knew I wanted you alive. He betrayed *me*."

She would tell him to do the deed himself, then, but knew better than to bait a man who lacked humanity. This wasn't a game. Jamal was a person.

As was she.

And Kira.

And still, she watched as Mason Gardner stepped forward with Rafiq's knife in his hand. The boy had been beaten. His face was battered and swollen.

His head lolled to the side, and she watched in horror as Mason grabbed him by the hair and raised his head. With a quick slash of the knife, Jamal's neck opened up, and blood spurted on Mason's face.

Jamal's angry gaze fixed on Diana as life faded from his eyes.

Chapter Sixty-Six

*C*hris and Rand were fully decked out in their combat gear as they moved in on the construction site, Freya whispering instructions in their ears.

"Diana said the layout of the museum is the same as the slot canyon in Jordan. The first rescue attempt."

Chris closed his eyes and remembered the intersecting canyons. He knew the fastest route to the center.

Rand made quick work of the chain-link fence, and they were through in the blink of an eye. They darted from tree to tree, their camouflage gear blending perfectly with the deciduous forest that surrounded the property.

The construction site was littered with temporary structures. Odds were, Kira had been stashed in one of the trailer offices. Chris left Rand to search for Kira, and headed for the museum, where Diana was deep in conversation with the Four of Diamonds.

*D*iana couldn't hold back her anguish and tears. No one mattered to these men. Not the boy who'd been forced into this world with violence and abuse.

She dropped to her knees and touched Jamal's face. She didn't like him. Hell, she'd loathed him from the moment he'd tried to rape her. But she would never forget that he was once a child with a brother and sister. A boy who deserved so much better than the world had given him.

Mason pulled her back from the body, and the henchmen dragged Jamal's corpse out of the room, taking him back to wherever he'd been held before she arrived. She hoped to hell Kira wasn't in the same place.

Her tears vanished as she remembered her goal.

Buy time.

"Where is Kira?" she demanded again.

Mason gave her a nasty smile and raised the bloody knife. He pulled her back to his chest and placed the blade at her throat. "Maybe we should go see her."

Makram Rafiq was no longer the scariest person in the room. Now that he'd scored his first kill, Mason Gardner had a taste for blood.

✦

*T*he world was upside down. Chris stood in a fake slot canyon, not on an official op, staring at the unequivocal face of the fourth most wanted man by the FBI, while retail heir Mason Gardner held a knife to Diana's throat.

And Chris had no shot on Mason.

He was back in the real canyon, with Bassam holding the knife.

Could Diana talk her way out of this one?

"Kill me, and Rafiq won't get his coordinates."

And there was his answer.

Yes. Yes, she could.

Unlike before, when Kramer had been in the tunnel behind him, Chris was on his own. But this time, there was no escape for the men, and no one knew that everything that happened here was being filmed.

"Where is the site, Dr. Edwards?" Rafiq's voice was low and soft. Cajoling.

She fixed him with a glare. "Call off the dog."

Chris smiled. This time, she wasn't negotiating the knife wielder's release. But then Bassam deserved more respect than Mason Gardner.

After a long pause, Rafiq said, "Drop the knife."

"We can't trust her." Mason's voice was petulant.

"She has more loyalty and cunning than you. If you kill her, I will kill you."

Mason flushed. "We've done what you asked. Even brought you here. At great risk to ourselves."

"You did it for money."

"That's why everyone does anything."

"Not me. Not Dr. Edwards."

It was weird to hear a terrorist speak about Diana with more respect than the retail heir did. Another upside-down element.

"So what do you do it for?" Mason asked.

"Me? I am a servant of God. She is a fool who believes understanding history will change men like you. She and I, we're both zealots for our beliefs. The difference between us is I don't give a damn about the history she's peddling except for how I can use artifacts to advance my cause."

As Rafiq talked, Mason slowly relaxed. The knife was no longer tight against Diana's throat.

Chris still wanted to kill the little prick.

The bloodlust was new. He'd killed before, but he'd never seen himself as a killer.

Hypocrisy, probably, but a SEAL had to find a way to cope.

Rafiq shoved Mason aside. "Tell me, Diana. Give me the coordinates."

"No Kira, no coordinates."

"You know why I want them?"

"Yes."

"Do you have them?"

"Yes. Fahd trusted me."

Rafiq grabbed Diana's face, pinching her chin between his thumb and index finger. "Give me the coordinates, Diana, and this will go so much easier for you."

She jerked back, out of his grip. "You don't get it. I chose abduction for a shot at bringing you down. I betrayed everything I believe in because I want to see you captured and killed. And yes, I know where the site is. And I know why you want it. I know that archaeologists all over Syria banded together to protect their country's history and every portable artifact that would've been sold to support your terrorist acts was hidden there. And I will *die* before I give you even a single digit of the coordinates. Because we are *nothing* alike.

"*I* was entrusted when you weren't. Because Fahd *knew* what you are. The archaeologists in your country saw you for the traitor you are, and they hid it from you in a place where you will never, *ever* find it."

Chapter Sixty-Seven

*D*iana knew she'd taunted Rafiq too much, but she didn't care. All she felt was a kind of hate that wasn't measurable or even fathomable.

She pulled the clip from her hair, her movement deliberately casual as she extracted the glass shard from its hiding place. She tossed her head, shaking out her hair as she palmed the weapon.

She wanted to strike out, but it was three against one, and Kira was nowhere to be found. So she waited.

Help would come.

"Very clever of you. You figured it out."

She nodded. "Fahd didn't tell me everything. I didn't know the site was the repository for artifacts. I only figured that out last night, when I started to wonder why you were so desperate to get me alive. The photos I took in Jordan are meaningless without the actual artifacts surfacing on the market. And it's my word against the world if I reveal that I authenticated the artifacts the Gardners just bought from Gillibrand when I was first abducted."

"They're all dead now, Diana. The archaeologists in the pact. Fahd was the last one. He only told you."

She smiled. "And I will take the secret to the grave, just like the rest of them."

Rafiq advanced on her. "You will tell me."

The rage that had been building from the moment she watched the video of Fahd's murder enveloped her. She lunged for Rafiq, but Mason, that little asshole, grabbed her, preventing her from taking down the Four of Diamonds. She twisted and lashed out, and the glass blade opened his cheek. His temple. His chin.

She was going for his eye next when Dennis grabbed her arm.

She kneed Mason in the balls, then turned the blade on Dennis Gardner.

One stroke and he was blinded by a shard from a fake artifact she'd bought from one of his stores. Best forty dollars she'd ever spent.

The man screamed and covered his eye, while Mason writhed on the floor.

She heard a scuffle behind her, and turned, ready to fight Rafiq. Relief jolted through her when she saw him, his face smashed against the floor, and Chris's knee pressed to his back.

Rafiq was nothing but a man. A weak man. And now he was being handcuffed.

Arrested.

No longer a danger to everything that mattered.

Chapter Sixty-Eight

$\mathcal{T}$he FBI had been scrambling to get into position from the moment Raptor tipped them on the location. Once Rafiq had been identified, they had the go-ahead to storm the museum, and they had been moving in from three directions when Rafiq's advance on Diana triggered the final confrontation.

The two henchmen had been in the process of wrapping Jamal's body in a plastic sheet when they were arrested.

Diana had been told that Rand found Kira unconscious in one of the incomplete storage rooms. She'd been taken to a hospital.

Both Gardners were also headed to a hospital, but both would be under guard and once stitched, headed to a federal lockup pending charges. Given their wealth, they were a huge flight risk. It was hard to imagine a judge granting bail, especially not after seeing the video of Mason killing Jamal.

Now Diana had her walking boot back on and was being

questioned as she leaned against the toes of the Sphinx, while Chris was walking the agents through the slot canyon, explaining it was a replica of the one in Jordan where she'd first been held.

The agents questioning him waved Diana and her interviewer over, and she crossed the room to join the tour.

Chris moved to stand next to her, taking her hand in his. She leaned her head on his shoulder.

They hadn't had a moment alone yet. She was desperate to hold him and to be held, but first they had to make certain the Gardeners wouldn't be able to buy their way out of this.

"I never had a chance to explore the canyon beyond crawling through a tunnel," she said in response to an agent's question. "But I studied the maps when I was in the hospital in Germany, so I knew the general layout, and that area"— she pointed toward a small open section—"is where the Bedouin tents were. It's just a much smaller scale than the real thing."

Rand approached, his face tight. "I'm done here and want to head to the hospital."

Diana turned to the agent conducting the interview. "Can we wrap this? I want to go to the hospital to see Kira too."

"We're almost done," the woman said.

They walked through the events one more time, ending in the area where Diana had cut Mason. The blood on her person and the floor was nothing compared to the stain where Jamal had died. Chris's arm went around her shoulders as she stared at the crimson pool.

At last they were released, and she walked with Chris and

Rand to where their vehicle had been moved at the front of the construction site.

Chris looked at the other SEAL and said, "Give us a minute?"

Rand gave a sharp nod, but she could tell he was desperate to get to the hospital.

Chris walked her around the vehicle, giving them a modicum of privacy, and pulled her to his chest. She melted into his arms. His coat was open, and he wrapped it around her, cocooning her in warmth and his scent.

"I'm sorry I wouldn't talk to you last night," she whispered. "I hated doing that to you."

"I was mad, but I understood. And you weren't wrong. I would have tried to talk you out of doing this. And you were right. To do this, I mean. It was the fastest way to find Kira and get inside the perimeter without a warrant." He stroked her back as he squeezed her tight. "You were amazing. I'm in awe of what you managed to do."

"Thank you. And thank you for having my back. Again."

"Always." He placed a finger under her chin and raised her gaze to meet his. "I mean that. Always. I'm in love with you, Diana."

Tears spilled from her eyes once again, but this time it was because she felt hope and alive and a rush of joy that she'd once believed she'd never be able to feel again. "I love you too."

He leaned down and kissed her, and she felt the same pulse of excitement she'd had during their first kiss. Euphoria and bliss. Better than any drug.

When he ended the kiss, she smiled up at him and asked,

"Do you think we'll ever sleep in the same bed *and* have sex?"

He let out a soft laugh. "Why don't we give that a try tonight? After we finish decorating our Christmas tree."

4

<u>Epilogue</u>

*C*hris's fingers closed around Diana's as they rode the elevator to FMV's offices. It had been ten days since Rafiq and the Gardners had been arrested, and Diana no longer lived in fear of being extradited.

They still didn't know who in the Intelligence Community and/or State Department had been paid off by the Gardners, but the investigation had only just begun.

Non-gory still images of Mason and Dennis Gardner with a man who'd once been number four on the FBI's Most Wanted list had been released to journalists, along with descriptions of their collusion to steal artifacts from the Middle East so they could sell replicas to the masses. The story had been covered nearly nonstop for several days, gaining even more steam after Mason was charged with first degree murder.

Overnight, protesters planted themselves in front of every Historie store in the country. Class action lawsuits were being filed by customers who were appalled that their purchases had put money in terrorist coffers.

Rafiq was in FBI custody and faced relentless questioning. As the head of the terrorist network, he knew all the players. Triangular cell structure didn't work when the captive was at the top of the pyramid and knew the names and locations of many of the people who worked beneath him.

But today's field trip to FMV wasn't about Rafiq or the Gardners.

No. This was a small reward to ease some of the horrors Diana had faced.

She hit the Stop button on the elevator and faced Chris, who opened his arms to her. She stepped into his embrace and burrowed her face into his neck. She liked that he didn't question her actions. He just held her.

"I got you," he whispered.

And he did. Every moment for the last ten days, he'd been there for her as she processed everything that had happened and why.

Money, naturally, was at the core of it.

The Gardners had betrayed their country over and over for profit.

Unique artifacts were more valuable to the Signature Line and sold for more than ten times what a foot-tall Venus de Milo statue would sell for.

It was just money.

Chris held her in the stalled elevator and didn't ask when she'd be ready to rise again. Instead, he kissed her neck, then lifted his head. "I love you."

His words were clear and firm and exactly what she needed to hear.

"I love you." She spoke with the same easy conviction. This new foundation was a gift she desperately needed. Guilt, shame, and a thousand other conflicting emotions assailed her. But this thing with Chris was true. Fast, yes. But no less true.

"What are you afraid of in this moment?" he asked.

"What makes you think I'm afraid?"

He cocked his head and gave her a look.

She huffed out a breath. "Fine." She tucked her head against his chest and breathed again. Finally, she lifted her head and met his gaze. "I know Fahd believed in the cause, but now that we're here, I can't help but wonder, what if he —and all the others—died for nothing? What if the tunnel is empty, looted before Rafiq ever learned of it, and so much history has been lost? I see Fahd in my dreams—nightmares—every night. Taking his cuts until he couldn't any longer. He died before he would give up the one site that mattered. What if... What if it...wasn't worth his sacrifice?"

Chris brushed his lips over hers. "Fahd died true to his convictions. It doesn't matter if the tunnel is empty, because the tunnel itself matters. It's two thousand years old, and it took more than a hundred years to carve by hand out of the earth. An aqueduct worthy of the Nabataeans and their waterworks. It doesn't have to be Tut's Tomb to be impor-tant." He smiled and added, "Didn't you say just yesterday that a site isn't about the artifacts, it's about what you learn from them? A lot can be learned from the tunnel. Fahd was protecting that site as much as he was protecting what might be hidden inside it."

She kissed his collarbone. "You are wise."

"This is true."

She laughed. "Ready?"

"For anything."

She hit the button to release the emergency stop, and they rose again.

Ian, his wife Cressida, Freya, Cal, Morgan, Pax, Amira, and Kira waited in the conference room. Rand was skiing in Aspen. He'd still get to watch what they all were about to see, just not live.

They all settled in after hugs and small talk and waited for the clock to tick down to the live stream. Diana felt a flutter in her chest when the feed from the Virginia Laboratory went live. The feeling was strangely like that of the first big drop on a roller-coaster ride.

Exhilarating. Scary.

Another countdown began, this one by the archaeologists embedded with special forces in the field. They gave the signal the mission was a go.

The capstone had been loosened, but still, it took several minutes for it to be moved. Once it was, a drone entered.

Diana squeezed Chris's fingers and watched the feed as the drone descended into the two-thousand-year-old Roman aqueduct that was now a dry tunnel and the repository where a dozen archaeologists had agreed to hide all the portable artifacts they could gather in Syria, once it was clear that the Islamic State was targeting sites to fund terrorism.

In the last week, they'd learned that every archaeologist

who'd signed on to this pact had died in the intervening years. Fahd had told Diana about the tunnel after yet another colleague had died. He'd known he'd be next.

She would have taken it to the grave herself, but she couldn't protect it herself. Fahd had told her she and the Friday Morning Valkyries would know the right thing to do to protect the site. And FMV did know a group who could do just that: the new Monuments officers, officially the Cultural Heritage Monitoring Lab, the Department of Defense's reservist unit that monitored and protected archaeological sites. CHML had the technology to monitor the site from afar, and also affiliation with the Army to protect it physically if they saw signs it had been located.

CHML had managed to get a team into Syria with help from Delta Force operators to confirm what was there. They would monitor and protect the site, fulfilling the role Fahd and the others had all died for.

Now a drone navigated the ancient tunnel, and she saw on the screen artifacts—bowls, tablets, mosaic tiles, tools— that ranged in age from five hundred to eight thousand years old. She was reminded of the stories of the first time Howard Carter got a glimpse inside Tut's Tomb.

As if on cue, Chris kissed her neck and said, "See anything good?"

She turned to him, smiled, and echoed Carter's response. "Yes. Wonderful things."

Author's Note

I began plotting this book more than a year before the US Army reactivated their "Monuments Men" unit, the Cultural Heritage Monitoring Lab, and it was with great excitement that I learned of the work CHML is doing. I'm honored to have recently met two of their members, US Army reservists, who are doing this important work of monitoring sites by satellite and preparing to protect sites in the event of natural disasters. You can learn more about the original World War II unit at the Monuments Men and Women Foundation website.

This book fully merges my Flashpoint and Evidence series. The two have always been connected in small ways, and it was fun to bring the two worlds together in *Trust Me*. On the Flashpoint side, you can read Morgan and Pax's story (and meet Rand) in *Tinderbox*. Freya and Cal are featured in *Firestorm*. In the Evidence series, *Covert Evidence* introduces CIA case officer Ian Boyd to his future wife, Cressida, as they find themselves on the run together in Turkey.

About the Author

USA Today bestselling author Rachel Grant worked for over a decade as a professional archaeologist and mines her experiences for storylines and settings, which are as diverse as excavating a cemetery underneath an historic art museum in San Francisco, survey and excavation of many prehistoric Native American sites in the Pacific Northwest, researching an historic concrete house in Virginia, and mapping a seventeenth century Spanish and Dutch fort on the island of Sint Maarten in the Netherlands Antilles.

She lives in the Pacific Northwest with her husband and children.

For more information:
www.Rachel-Grant.net
contact@rachel-grant.net

Ingram Content Group UK Ltd.
Milton Keynes UK
UKHW010635270723
425883UK00001B/40

9 781944 571658